Ari
in
No
Her first book, *The Female Woman*, was published in 1973, and since then she has been active as a journalist, broadcaster and public speaker. Her second book, *The Other Revolution*, was published in 1978. After the death of Callas, Arianna Stassinopoulos spent over two years travelling around the world talking to people who had been close to her. Granted access to intimate personal letters and revealing taped conversations never before published, she has written a unique and remarkable biography.

'A riveting biography of love and passion in high places' *Daily Express*

'Intelligent and absorbing' *The Sunday Times*

'Spirited, stunningly revealing' *Publishers Weekly*

'Fascinating and compulsively readable' *Washington Post*

'As tempestuous and wrenching as a Balzac novel' *Women's Wear Daily*

Maria Callas —

the woman behind the legend

Arianna Stassinopoulos

Hamlyn Paperbacks

MARIA CALLAS
ISBN 0 600 20402 2

First published in Great Britain 1980
by George Weidenfeld and Nicolson Ltd

Hamlyn Paperbacks edition 1981

Hamlyn Paperbacks are published by
The Hamlyn Publishing Group Ltd,
Astronaut House,
Feltham, Middlesex, England
from
Banda House, Cambridge Grove,
Hammersmith, London W6 0LE.

Reproduced, printed and bound in Great Britain by
Hazell Watson & Viney Ltd, Aylesbury, Bucks

To sing is an expression of your being,
a being which is becoming.

MARIA CALLAS

For Bernard

Illustration Acknowledgements

The author and publisher are grateful for kind permission to reproduce copyright photographs from the following sources: Keystone, London, 1, 18, 25; Dr Lantzounis, 2, 17; Studio d'Arte, Verona, 3; Foto-Semo, Mexico, 4; AGIP, Paris (Robert Cohen), 5, 8; Erio Piccagliani, 6, 13; Metropolitan Opera Archive, 7; Paul Popper, London, 9, 14, 15, 20, 21; Houston Rogers, London, 10; Camera Press, 11, 12, 22; Frank Spooner Pictures, London, 16; Associated Press, London, 19; Rex Features, London, 23, 24; *Paris Match* (Garofalo), 26. Any errors or omissions will gladly be rectified in future editions.

Contents

Preface

WE had arrived at Epidaurus by boat in the pouring rain. Tightly clutching my mother's hand, I walked, along with a big crowd, to the ancient Greek theatre. It was 17 August 1960, just over a month after my tenth birthday, and I was about to hear my very first opera, *Norma*, with Maria Callas. All I knew about her, apart from the fact that she was a 'Great Singer', was what every other Greek between the ages of 5 and 105 knew: that she was the woman in the life of the very, very rich Mr Onassis, for whose familiar thickset figure hundreds of eyes were scanning the theatre's entrance.

Twenty thousand spectators had defiantly taken their seats when an announcement was made that, as the rain gave no sign of stopping, the performance would be cancelled and would take place instead the following Sunday. When I did finally set eyes on Maria Callas a week later, something about her clearly caught the imagination of the ten-year-old. It was that performance, and not the Covent Garden Tosca (her last appearance on the operatic stage) which I saw five years later, that came flooding back into my mind, complete in every detail when, in 1977, a couple of months after her death, I was asked if I would be interested in writing the biography of one of the most remarkable women of our time. Instantly, the memory of that night swept over me together with the unconsciously stored recollection of my excitement, of my disappointment at the cancelled performance, and of the impossible tedium of the year-long week that followed until I actually saw and heard her.

Many times since that night in Epidaurus I have been

transported by the power of her voice and the dramatic truth of her interpretation. I have also been touched by something deeper, by the intensity of the fire I could feel raging inside her, consuming her at the same time that it illuminated everything around her. But it was the memory of Epidaurus that determined me to write her life. Clearly I had been fascinated by her from that first moment, but it was not until some eighteen years later, when I was half-way through this book, that I really understood why. And only then did I also understand why she was the focus of such intense and unceasing excitement wherever she went, why millions who neither knew nor cared anything about music followed her career and her life so avidly, why men and women camped for days outside opera houses to buy tickets for her performances. There was, of course, the glitter of her career and the power of her operatic creations; there was a private life as dramatic as that of many of the heroines she brought to life on the stage; there was Ari and Jackie and Franco Zeffirelli and Winston Churchill and an unending procession of the rich and the famous touching on her life. But these alone still do not explain the unparalleled fascination she generated, nor the hostility she provoked, as intense as the love she aroused.

The life of Maria Callas was both tragedy and fairy-tale. She transformed herself as completely as anyone outside mythology, from a fat, awkward girl into a woman of magnetic beauty and personality. But even while the fairy-tale transformation was taking place, the tragedy had begun to unfold. It was to be played out at many different levels: her unresolvable conflict with her mother, the long, gradual unravelling of her marriage, her deeply emotional relationship with her voice, her terrible dependence on Onassis and the bitterness, agony and humiliation of his leaving her. And underlying all these individual tragedies, there is the struggle that never ceased to rage inside her, the struggle between Callas and Maria, between the legend and the woman, between the image and reality. This struggle that was at the centre of her life is at the centre of this book. I began by writing the biography of Callas and ended by writing the life of

Maria. I began with deep respect and admiration for what she did and what she tried to become. I ended by loving her.

I naturally started by reading all the existing literature on her – the books, the reviews, the profiles and the interviews. Then, for nearly two years, I went round the world talking to friends, colleagues and sometime enemies who had during the fifty-four years of her life been, at some point, part of it. The invaluable advantage of talking to people so soon after her death was the immediacy, the freshness, of their responses before the analysing and assessing had begun. The danger, against which I had to be constantly on guard, was that there were some of her friends, though mercifully very few, who were determined to preserve the mask of La Callas – a Maria consisting entirely of her public image and her public statements, a blameless waxwork free of all untidy contradictions. But the Maria who resisted this shrinking process in life will, I have no doubt, resist it in death.

As Maria's relationship with her mother was at the scarred heart of her life, I knew I had to start with her. It was Christmas 1977, at the time when Meneghini and her mother were fighting over the $12 million Maria had left without a will, and Mrs Callas's lawyers would not let her talk to anyone. I went to Athens, determined not to return to London until I had seen her. One afternoon, a bunch of flowers in my hand, I arrived at her apartment in a primly respectable part of Athens. She cautiously opened the door, took the flowers, thanked me, but would not let me in. Then something happened to remind me that miracles happen on suburban doorsteps quite as often as in sacred books, and perhaps more so. A frail old lady came out of the nextdoor apartment, exchanged a few words with Mrs Callas and promptly collapsed in a faint. We carried her into her flat, rubbed cologne on her forehead and stayed for a while after she had come round. 'You need a drink after that,' said Mrs Callas.

I emerged from her apartment six hours later, only to return the next day, and the next, and the next. The help she gave me and the knowledge I gained from the hours we spent together provided the foundation of understanding on which I began to build the book. What she told me is woven through these pages together with what was said over the following eighteen months by many, many others who fleetingly, or for years, had been close to Maria. Some of them, like her mother, Franco Zeffirelli, and Tito Gobbi, were on my list from the moment I embarked on the book. Others, often people who were by her side at important moments of her life, I was led to gradually as the months unfolded.

The most extraordinary of these meetings was with her godfather, Leonidas Lantzounis, a Greek doctor who had emigrated to America a year before Maria's parents, and there established himself as a successful orthopaedic surgeon. I knew that he had been close to her, but nothing I had discovered so far had given me any indication of the strength of the bond between them. We talked for hours in his New York apartment on the Hudson River, and then he suddenly produced a thick pile of letters spanning twenty-seven years from 1950 to the year she died. Maria, who all her closest friends had assured me hated writing letters, had consistently and in all her vulnerability opened her heart to this man; it was immediately clear from her letters that he provided for her the family love and warmth she always longed for. 'I love you and admire you,' she writes in one of the letters, 'and you are like a blood relative for me. Strange how blood relations are really not strong. My people have given me nothing but unhappiness. You have always been a source of pleasure and happiness.' She often addressed him as dear 'noné', the Greek for godfather, and signed her letters 'your godchild'. Her language is a curious mixture all her own: the grammar and syntax borrow heavily from Greek, French and Italian, and the words, though always in English, are often over-literal translations. The letters I have included in the book are printed as she wrote them – misspellings and all. I owe Dr Lantzounis an immense debt for trusting me with these precious documents that he himself treasures so much.

There were others who were not part of the professional or public side of her life, but who provided much of the intimacy, knowledge and detail that I needed if I were to bring Maria, and not just Callas, to life: Mary Mead travelled with her from hotel to hotel in the desperate, fugitive months that followed Onassis's decision to marry Jackie Kennedy; Peter Diamand was backstage with her after some of her greatest triumphs and a few of her greatest disasters; Nadia Stancioff was by her side all through the filming of *Medea* and with her during that intimate summer on the private island of Tragonisi in the Aegean; François Valéry became her semi-official escort and close friend in the last lonely years. And then there were colleagues such as Jon Vickers, Nicola Rescigno and Sylvia Sass, friends like Vasso Devetzi, Gaby van Zuylen and Christian Bischini, and those linked to her through their work – her agent, her hairdresser, her decorator – who inevitably became part of her everyday life and sometimes her friends. I saw all of them during these two years, often going back to talk to them again and again as my own understanding of her grew and I could more effectively spark from them stories that would illuminate this understanding and memories that needed more digging to bring to the surface. Where our talks were not tape-recorded, if I was in any doubt as to their exact statements as I had written these down, I rechecked with them before the book went to press. Whenever, throughout the book, I record unspoken thoughts or feelings this is not speculation but their own account based on my conversations at first hand or, when the person is dead, as related to me by a close friend or relative.

The most important source of information and understanding was, of course, Maria herself, though rarely through her public statements which often give little or no indication of her real state of being and feeling. In fact, she regularly declared in public the exact opposite of the independently ascertainable truth. She would talk about how happy and content she was when she was in private torment; she would insist on the stability of her marriage and her devotion to her husband a few months before she left him. But we have the letters to her godfather in which she writes as though she is talking to herself, and the occasional intimate letter to a friend. And then there are her talks with John Ardoin, which provide the most direct, the most honest and the most tragic record of her feelings that we have on tape. Only a few minutes of these hours have been published and I am deeply grateful to John for making the complete transcripts available to me.

Every now and then, chance, fate or whoever arranges these things, points the finger at an individual singled out to be not just the greatest in his or her field, but unique, setting new standards by which everyone who follows is automatically judged. Such was Callas. Her genius was that although she was *interpreting*, she made her audience feel that she was *creating* – and with the ink still fresh. However many great artists had imprinted their personality on what Maria was singing, her uniqueness lay in making the audience forget them. She still haunts, and will go on haunting, all the productions of the roles she made her own; there is no higher praise for a Norma, a Violetta or a Tosca today than that 'she is the best since Callas'. By bringing to life operas many had forgotten existed, by going to the heart of the drama in the music and conveying it through her body no less than through her voice, and by inspiring directors such as Visconti and Zeffirelli to create the productions in which her dramatic truth could flourish, Maria revolutionized opera in our time. And by making audiences demand from others these things she had given them, she went further, and revolutionized the art of opera-going too. But over the last two years, as I listened to every commercial recording she made and every pirate recording and rehearsal tape I could lay my hands on, I came to the conclusion that even more important than her revolutionary influence is the fact that she lived and sang, and through breathing drama, power and life into the music, she held – and goes on holding – a mirror to our own most secret passions.

She was, without any doubt, the most controversial, the most disturbing, singer of our century. Even in her prime, her voice was ridiculed as unmusical, ugly, a blasphemy against all ideals of vocal beauty, and even those who know nothing about the musical controversies know about her temperament and tantrums, her abrupt cancellations of long-awaited performances and her lime-lit walk-outs from performances already in progress. What emerged time and again while I was working on the book were valid, often tragic reasons for behaviour that at the time and in subsequent accounts was explained purely in terms of bad temper, impossible demands and vanity. Still more important than these discoveries was the split within Maria that they revealed, a split which she unceasingly yearned to heal.

Through the interviews, the public statements and the private truths, her portrait gradually acquired focus and colour, revealing new clues and new details. It was a bit like watching a Polaroid print develop. Forgetting who had set up and taken the photograph I simply watched, fascinated, as it came to life.

I began by holding her up to the light of close scrutiny. And just as she was in danger of disappearing into a shimmer of ordinariness – of insecurities, of snobbery, of fears, of common humanity – I rediscovered her without illusions in all her *real* rather than her public greatness. By then she had become part of my daily life and had even begun to invade my dreams.

Only when I suspended theoretical interpretation did I begin to know her, and only when I suspended judgement did I begin to feel the full force of the passion that was fuelling her life. It is this passion for life, for her art and for something unknown beyond both, that was compelling her and driving her forever on. And it is this passion that I have tried to communicate in the pages that follow.

Chapter One

PETROS Dimitriadis was sitting on the porch of his home on his name-day surrounded by his seven children and as many guests as the porch would hold. He was humming an old Greek ballad, mostly to himself, under his upturned moustache, through the buzz of talk and gossip. But it wasn't long before his was the only voice to be heard. He had hardly stopped when his audience, which had been gradually swollen by the passers-by, started chanting: 'Give us a song, Petro'... 'Colonel Petro, give us a song'... 'Sing to us, Daddy.' He smiled and looked over the little square which was by now full of people. With the confidence of an old trouper, he let his eye rove round and take in all the newcomers, including the visiting village halls for his concert the following evening. He ceremoniously rested one arm on the ledge of the porch and burst into 'Questa o quella', one of his most beloved Verdi arias. He had never heard *Rigoletto* from beginning to end and had picked up his aria by ear, which is how he had picked up everything he sang.

The audience was spellbound – so absorbed that they didn't even notice the Italian tenor tiptoe away half-way through the aria. They only knew that all was not well with their famous operatic visitor when the following morning the concert was cancelled, the money returned and the tenor found shut up in his room, consumed with envy and self-doubt. Petros Dimitriadis's star had never stood higher than it did that evening. In Stylis where he lived, across the Gulf of Lamia from Thermopylae, his was unanimously regarded as the finest voice. The Italian tenor's withdrawal was only a confirmation and ultimate accolade. Petros needed no excuse to burst into song. He was always singing or humming – even, they said, when he was fighting. An army officer all his life, he was known during the Balkan War as the 'Singing Commander'. Fifty years later his granddaughter Maria would be known as La Divina, the *primadonna assoluta*, the Golden Voice of the century.

Her mother, Evangelia (known in the family as 'Litza'), was Petros's favourite daughter. She had his flair, his showmanship, his strength and quite a lot of his magnetism – but none of his talent. She longed to be an actress, but in a family of army officers in a remote part of Greece before the First World War the mere idea of a theatrical career seemed preposterous. So she followed instead the well-trodden and laudable path of marriage to a graduate in pharmacy from the University of Athens, George Kalógeropoulos. Everybody approved except Petros. 'Don't marry him, Litza,' he insisted. 'You'll never be happy with him.' But a few months after Litza and George met, Petros Dimitriadis died of a stroke brought on by the injuries he had received in the Balkan War. Sixteen days later, in a Greek Orthodox church in Athens, Litza was married to George. They made a strikingly good-looking couple. George with his wide brow, thick auburn hair and manly moustache was what would be called a beautiful man, looking particularly imposing and dignified next to his lustrous-eyed bride in her plain white dress.

They moved to Meligala in the Peloponnese, where George opened a drugstore, the only one in thirteen counties. His customers came from miles away, and soon he had made enough money for the newly-weds to move to what was known as 'the best house' in Meligala. But within six months, Evangelia knew – or rather, decided – that her father had been right. She should never have married George Kalogeropoulos and she was never going to be happy with him. She realized very quickly that his debonair looks were deceptive; he had no thirst for glory, and certainly no drive to match her longing for luxury, action and distinction. She determined, however, at least for the moment, to play the role of a good wife; but even before her first child was born, a year after their marriage, she had given up hoping or trying to make her marriage more than a convention.

Whether George took up womanizing before or after his wife had reached her unstated conclusion that the marriage had been a mistake, is not easy to determine. What is clear is that the more his pharmacy thrived and his status as an affluent and respected citizen increased, the more enthusiastic, in his quiet way, did he become in his pursuit of casual affairs. And Evangelia, following in the time-honoured tradition of Greek womanhood, swallowed her resentment and got what satisfaction she could out of playing the silent but occasionally exploding martyr. At the same time, what with her cook and her maids, she kept herself sufficiently busy with the routine of married life to forget that there was little substance and precious little joy left behind it.

She was eighteen-and-a-half when she left Meligala for Athens to give birth to Jackie, her first daughter, on 4 June 1917. Three years later there came a son, Vasily, who for more reasons than simply the special place assigned to sons in traditional Greek households, stirred in both parents a deeper love than either of them had ever felt before. For a time it even seemed as though Vasily would resurrect the love Evangelia and George had briefly felt for one another, but three years later typhoid fever broke out at Meligala and Vasily was one of the first victims of the epidemic. 'My heart seemed to die with him,' wrote Evangelia years later, 'and I thought I would never live again.'

If Vasily alive had nearly brought his parents together again, Vasily dead made communication between them impossible. Locked in their separate fortresses of grief, they could find no way of building a bridge between them, until George Kalogeropoulos could bear it no longer. Secretly, he conceived a plan of release which showed that there was more daring and imagination in him than his wife ever gave him credit for. Within a few days, he had sold both the pharmacy, his proudest achievement, and their home, and had bought three passages to America.

The day before they were due to sail, he told his wife. She never forgave him; it was 1923, she had no money or qualifications, she had a five-and-a-half-year-old child and was expecting another. So she felt that she had no option but to swallow more poisonous resentment, stifle her pain at leaving her country and her family and follow across the Atlantic a husband she would willingly have drowned in it. Evangelia could not easily have been in a more bitter and heartbroken state than she was during that pregnancy. And on top of everything else, she was continuously seasick. 'All the way across the Atlantic,' she wrote, 'I was wretched.'

They sailed into New York Harbour on 2 August 1923. The country was in mourning for President Harding and the flags were all at half-mast when Evangelia, five months pregnant, together with her husband and daughter arrived in the United States. The first American newspaper that was thrust into the hands of the perplexed Greek couple bore great black headlines which neither of them could read, for they spoke no English. Waiting for them on the quay was Leonidas Lantzounis, who had left Meligala for New York a year earlier. The sight of New York City together with the presence of a friend from home brought out in Evangelia feelings of excitement and adventure that for months had been stifled under layers of grief and despair. George, who had been at school with Leonidas's older brother, was relieved to see someone who could help him through the faltering first steps in a new land.

With Leonidas's help, George found a job in a pharmacy, and while her husband was adjusting to working for someone else, Evangelia threw herself into decorating the apartment they had rented in Astoria on Long Island. Greek carpets, Greek cushions, and Greek icons with a little candle burning beneath them all day in the bedrooms, made the impersonal New York apartment feel much more like home.

At the same time, both parents were getting ready for the arrival of their new son. Neither of them seemed prepared to consider even for one moment the possibility that their new-born child might be a girl. Their yearnings and primitive logic had convinced them that the new baby would be a son who would take the place of Vasily and make their life, so far away from where he had lived and died, complete. All the little clothes Evangelia knitted were blue, and everything they bought for the baby's bedroom was for a baby boy. 'Ever since Vasily's death,' Evangelia said, 'I had prayed for another son to fill the empty place in my heart.'

On 2* December 1923, the expected son failed to arrive. Instead Dr Lantzounis brought to the mother a baby girl weighing twelve-and-a-half pounds. The baby clothes would not have been right even if they had been pink: 'You made clothes for a baby like a doll,' Dr Lantzounis told Evangelia, sitting by her bed, laughing and patting her hand, 'but they are too small for this baby. The nurses can't get them on her. She is like a young lamb, she is so large!'

The first words Maria heard from her mother were 'Take her away.' And her mother's first gesture was to turn her eyes from her daughter and fix them on the snowstorm raging outside the hospital window. As for her mother's thoughts, as she later admitted, they were all loving, tearful thoughts of Vasily. When the nurses asked the mother what name to put on the bead bracelet they give babies in hospitals, there was blank silence. Neither she nor her husband had thought of a girl's name. Plucking a name out of the air, she said 'Sophia'. Her husband interrupted, 'No, Cecilia.' In the end, they managed to agree on Maria. When, three years later, Maria was christened in the Greek Orthodox Cathedral on East 74th Street, she was, like a young princess, given all three names and one more: Cecilia Sophia Anna Maria. Leonidas Lantzounis, the first man to greet her parents on American soil, was her godfather. The man who first put her into her mother's arms became not only her godfather but, right to the end, her loyal supporter and her beloved confidant. About the same time as her christening, Maria

* The first controversy in Maria's life involves the date of her birth. Maria always celebrated her birthday on 2 December, which is indeed when, according to Dr Lantzounis who was present in the hospital, she was born. But her mother, who was no less indisputably present, insists that she was born on 4 December. To complicate matters further, at her school she is registered as born on 3 December, and there is no record of birth either at the New York City Hall or at the Flower Hospital where she was born.

was also given a different surname. Her parents changed their name by court order from Kalogeropoulos to Callas – a symbol of their intention at that time to make America their permanent home. Their Greek friends, though, continued to call them by their original name, so Maria grew up used to both.

It took Evangelia four days before she could look at her daughter again, but it is not easy to resist a four-day-old baby. 'Why don't you love me?' was the question that Evangelia saw in her daughter's big, black eyes; and she finally succumbed and set herself to giving her baby the love she had at first denied it.

There is no baby in the world that does not inspire legends – from knocking the cat out of the window to finishing off all the garden strawberries and being sick for days. When the baby itself grows into a legend, there is no end to the childhood stories that are recollected, repeated, embroidered or invented. There was the doctor who delivered her, taking one look at her and predicting that 'she will break many hearts'; there was Maria herself, three months old and not yet weaned, standing up in her crib and munching zwieback; Maria's baby warblings, of course; and then, at the age of four, Maria crouched under the pianola, pressing the pedals with her hands and, her little mouth half open, listening ecstatically to the first music she ever made.

By the time Maria was four the Callas family had moved from Astoria to Manhattan and were living in Washington Heights on 192nd Street. George Callas had his own drugstore again and was well on his way to fulfilling the dream he had nurtured ever since they had left Greece: to re-establish the business status he had enjoyed in his small community back home. The pianola was one of the first symbols of their new affluence, but it was much more than that. Evangelia, prompted by memories of her father's glorious singing, the dim stirrings of her own ambitions and her daughters' chirpings round the house, was, still only half-consciously, taking steps that would stimulate her children's musical inclinations. Maria's earliest childhood ambition was to be a dentist, but Evangelia was not easily discouraged. A gramophone followed the pianola; the first record that she bought was 'Vissi d'arte' from *Tosca*, and the next, soon after, excerpts from *Martha* and *Aida*. Meanwhile George Callas was busy buying record after record of Greek popular songs. At ritualistically regular intervals fights broke out between the parents over whatever record was on the gramophone, with Evangelia, her big eyes flashing like a jaguar's, shouting to George to take off his lousy Greek records *this instant*, in case her daughters' tastes should be corrupted.

George and Evangelia understood each other now no more than they did the first day they came together. Evangelia's quaint description of her husband was: 'Like a bee to whom every woman was a flower over which he must hover to seek the sweetness.' But he was certainly not permitted to hover in peace. The gramophone became the lightning conductor of the Callas's marriage; the fights over whether it would be 'Ritorna vincitor' or the Greek version of 'Hold me tight, O my love, while I'm dying!' dissolved some of the much deeper and more dangerous tensions in their marriage.

Despite their relative affluence, these first few years in America were not easy. Life was a continuous process of adjustment. Their friends, most of them earlier Greek immigrants, were solid, worthy citizens marked by financial comfort, a certain decent Orthodox godliness and an ardent concern for the God of Opinion. Considered collectively, Mr and Mrs Callas and their friends belonged to what one might call the lower edge of the middle classes. Evangelia was an expert on the minutiae of social position. She never allowed her husband to forget for long that she came from a better family than he, a state of affairs symbolized for her by her family's private cemetery in Stylis.

For a woman of her pretensions, the thought of so quiet a life stretching indefinitely in front of her was quite unbearable. She had been forced to give up her dreams of a career on the stage and she had had to accept that she would never transform her husband into the exciting, important figure she had once dreamed of. She had, in effect, to come to terms with the fact that she would never be distinguished in her own right, nor would she ever be the wife of a distinguished man. But resignation was not part of her character, and her ambitions and drives were promptly and obsessively transferred to her daughters.

Nearly six years separated the two Callas girls, and at that age this gap greatly contributed to the younger sister's idealization of the elder. It was not easy for Maria. She was the younger, the plainer, the fatter, the less charming; and she must have sensed from a time very near the beginning of her life that she was also the less loved. In the competition for mother, Jackie had won outright and, throughout her childhood, Maria remained bitterly envious of Jackie. Yet, at the same time, she adored Jackie, longed to be with Jackie, wanted Jackie's entire devotion.

One July evening when she was just five-and-a-half, waiting with her parents to cross the street to their house, she saw Jackie standing across the road. She pulled away from her mother and ran with open arms towards her sister. A car speeding down the street struck her and dragged her for twenty-five feet before it stopped. George, with Maria unconscious in his arms, and his wife holding the screaming Jackie tight by the arm, arrived at St Elizabeth's Hospital on Fort Washington Avenue to be told that the chances were slim. George was numb with fright and Evangelia nearly hysterical when Dr Korilos, a Greek brain specialist, arrived to reassure them that Maria, although suffering from shock and severe concussion, was not in danger.

She remained in the hospital for twenty-two days, looked after by the nuns. For some time after she went home, she was more irritable and unpredictable than before and more prone to nursery accidents and misadventures. There was always a good deal of skirmishing between Jackie and Maria. Hostilities were conducted in the traditional manner of yelling, hurling abuse, and occasionally, very occasionally, coming to blows, Maria's size compensating to some extent for her age. The one thing which Evangelia would not forgive was 'tale-telling', and her punishment had age-old Greek tradition behind it: she would put pepper in their mouths and on their lips.

Maria's car accident was in July 1929. A few months later the world was shaken by the Wall Street Crash; and for the second time in his life George Callas found himself having to sell his pharmacy and this time there was no question of personal choice involved. Each year, from 1929 to 1933, as the family moved to a less and less expensive apartment and money became for the first time a real problem, there remained for Maria only one fixed point of relative affluence and security: her godfather, Dr Lantzounis, with his presents every Christmas, the traditional candle and silver trinket every Easter and their Sunday lunch outings at Longchamps on 10th Street. Leonidas, or Leo as more and more people were calling him by now, had joined the New York Orthopaedic Hospital shortly after Maria was born and was, by the time the Crash came, already a successful orthopaedic surgeon.

In the Callas home, money was becoming the occasion of incessant complaints, accusations and recriminations between the couple. The main bone of contention was the girls' piano lessons. George Callas, who had to become a travelling salesman of pharmaceutical products to meet his family's basic needs, had already had to make considerable psychological adjustments. He had to accept that he was no longer his own boss with his own business and that there was little prospect of ever having his own business again; he had to adjust to a large drop in his income; and he had to put up with his wife's constant recollections of their comfortable life in Greece. On top of all this he was made to pay out a substantial chunk of his much-diminished income for his daughters' piano lessons four times a week.

To George, this was pure frivolity. It was one thing, he would repeatedly argue, to pay for Jackie's piano and ballet lessons out of their surplus when they could afford such unnecessary luxuries, but a very different thing to take money needed for food and rent and give it to Signorina Santrina for teaching the girls to play the pianola without using the pedals. He could see no justification for this expense and no reason for it other than his wife's empty dreaming of musical and theatrical fame, her way of satisfying by proxy her frustrated ambitions. He told her so. And he told her so again. And again. And every week, as he was counting out the dollar bills for Signorina Santrina, he told her so once more.

Nonetheless, in 1930, at the age of seven, Maria began her musical education. For the next thirty years, gradually and imperceptibly at first but with growing intensity with every year that passed, music and work became the stuff of Maria's waking life and, as far as anyone can tell, of her dreaming life too – more real than anything else, a delight and a torment.

Of course, nothing of enduring importance happens at a single particular moment, but if there was a symbolic point at which Maria's destiny was sealed and when – at least in terms of her mother's commitment to that destiny – there was to be no looking back, then it would have to be one warm May evening when Maria was ten. She was playing the piano and singing 'La Paloma'. Her mother remembers every detail. The windows were open, the lace curtains were fluttering and children were playing in the street. Evangelia looked out of the window and saw the street full of people, standing there listening and applauding – a great crowd of people who would not go away until Maria had stopped singing. Another moment and another warm evening flooded into her mind: the evening all those years ago when, seated by her father's feet on the porch, she had listened spellbound to him singing the Duke's aria.

So when Maria was still talking and dreaming of becoming a dentist, her mother had already made up her mind that she was going to be, not just a singer but a great singer, and not just a great singer but a famous, a world famous, great singer. In Evangelia's mind love, happiness, fame and money were convertible currencies. For the time being this dangerous confusion gave her a blinkered drive and a cloudless certainty that became the vital force behind Maria's life.

Maria was winning singing prizes in school and Sunday school; she was a leading part in school plays and concerts; but only her mother treated these childhood glories as a foretaste of what lay ahead. Everyone else, looking at the

Callas daughters, began by comparing them, and the conclusion was no less conclusive for the six years that separated them. There was a tall slender beautiful girl with chestnut hair and brown eyes, and there was a plump, dark, little girl with enormous pimples and enormous black eyes hidden behind enormous heavy glasses. Maria was regarded as no more than the evening shadow of her older sister, less beautiful, less promising, less 'accomplished'. It seemed clear to anyone, at least on first impressions, that the older sister would have no problem marrying well, she would have a beautiful family and would always be supported, while the younger one would most likely have to fend for herself and would probably remain an old maid – and a young aunt. With every year that went by, Maria was doing all she could to reinforce the impression. All through her early childhood she had been matching herself against her all-too-admirable sister, but she soon gave up, with the same self-protective reaction against what seemed unattainable that made the fox call the unreachable grapes sour.

It must have been fairly early on, even before she entered her teens, when Maria decided that the whole traditional feminine side of life – looks, figure, clothes, the art of being agreeable, of watching the happiness of guests, of making the right, charming kind of small talk – was her sister's domain. For the moment she slammed the door on that side of herself, but was left with the lurking suspicion that behind the door lay a special treasure from which she was barred.

By the time she was eleven, Maria's life had begun to take the shape it would keep until the turning-point of 1937. 'La Paloma' had brought her her first audience, and in a national amateur talent contest on the Mutual Radio network it brought her her first *first* prize – a Bulova watch she proudly wore for years afterwards. Her second public appearance was in a children's show in Chicago. This time she won the second prize, but ample compensation was provided by the fact that it was presented by Jack Benny.

This was the beginning of the long, demanding circus of children's shows, radio programmes and endless contests.

The drive that Maria's mother brought to her daughter's career was only to be equalled by her blindness to Maria's emotional needs. 'There should be a law against that kind of thing,' Maria said bitterly years later. 'A child treated like this grows old before its time. They shouldn't deprive a child of its childhood!' It was not her childhood Maria had been deprived of; it was that special unconditional love that is the greatest gift anyone can give to a child – a treasury of reminiscent gold from which in later life it can draw again and again. All the love and approval Maria was given during this time was strictly conditional. 'Only when I was singing did I feel loved,' she said on one of those very rare occasions when she was prepared to talk about her early life, instead of instantly dismissing the subject.

After she started wearing glasses, at the age of five, she became so convinced of her ugliness that she would avert, or even tightly shut, her eyes, rather than have to face a mirror. She felt, as she herself put it years later, 'detested and detestable'. She saw herself as justifiably rejected, convinced that she was 'an ugly duckling, fat, clumsy and unpopular'.

Starved of love by those around her, she sought to fill the gnawing emptiness inside her with food. It was as though Evangelia, unable to give her younger daughter the love she felt she owed her, was seeking to make good her guilt in the only tangible way she could: by making available to her practically limitless quantities of food. Home-made bread, macaronada (Italian macaroni with mama's own sauce of fried onions and chopped meat), fried potatoes and saganaki (two fried eggs with a soft, mild cheese on top) were Maria's favourites. Indeed for a time no meal, however big, would be complete until she had had her saganaki. Even in the middle of the night she would often wake up and, half asleep, crawl to the kitchen and take whatever candy, cream cake or ice cream was there to bed to eat herself to sleep.

Years later the pattern persisted. We hear the echo of childhood habits in the words of Madame Biki, Maria's dressmaker and friend for twenty-seven years: 'Whenever Maria came to stay with us we would prepare her a tray for the night when she woke up and wanted something to eat.' Except that on the tray there would now be fruit and champagne rather than candy and cream cakes. The vulnerable, unhappy little girl was still very much alive, but by now well under the control of the world-famous Maria Callas.

The memories of her New York childhood are almost exclusively bleak and full of self-pity, but Maria's childhood was by no means all misery. In fact, when she was not pushing and prodding, demanding and expecting, Evangelia could be an enchanting mother. She had a talent for turning a trip to hear a band concert in Central Park into an occasion, and a twice-weekly visit to the library into a religious ritual. Twice a week they took the subway to the library on 42nd Street and 5th Avenue, where Evangelia would, most unsuccessfully, try to encourage them to read the 'great books', especially Tolstoy, Victor Hugo and Dostoyevsky. She had never read any of them herself, but her faith in their greatness could hardly have been increased by the most intimate familiarity. Yet no hymns in praise of Dostoyevsky would drag Maria away from the shelf of opera records. She spent hours listening to them, and for ten cents each she would borrow at least two at a time to take home with her, the Depression having cut short her mother's attempts to build up the family's own opera record collection.

Apart from the library visits, there were two regular outings in the week for the Callas daughters, one of which was more regular than the other. The first was on Sunday morning when Evangelia took her daughters to the Greek Orthodox Church of St Spyridon in Washington Heights. Maria loved the singing in the Church and was fascinated by the ritual, which was as far as her religion went. Her mother's barely went that far; in Evangelia's mind religion had to do with little more than being respectable and ladylike and not having 'sweethearts' outside marriage. The more definite event took place every Tuesday night when Jackie and Maria had their special treat of the week – chop suey at the Chinese restaurant in Washington Heights. While church brought out in Evangelia everything prudish and narrow, the Chinese restaurant brought out her special talent for investing the commonplace with glamour. Through their mother's eyes Jackie and Maria were made to see even the fact that the restaurant had a receptionist as quite magical and out of the ordinary.

In a curious way, though, it was the library on the corner of 5th Avenue and 42nd Street that was the Eden of Maria's childhood. There, away from home and school, she could forget her shortcomings, her miseries and her failures, both real and imaginary, and, in the fantasy of opera, create her own world. Then she would take her treasures home and try to make the world she was creating in her mind displace reality for as long as possible. At home she often listened to the records with her forehead pressed against a window-pane, gazing through her thick glasses and a halo of vapour formed by her breath. What at? Palaces, carriages, jewels and knights in armour? Or was it already red velvet curtains and adoring audiences?

By the time she was twelve, although she was still talking about becoming a dentist, she had discovered that the road to her mother's approval lay through her singing. She knew also that this was the only way she could gain attention, and even popularity, at school. Miss Jennie Sugar, one of Maria's teachers at Public school 189 in Washington Heights, dimly remembered her as 'a pleasant, well-behaved girl' – that is, hardly the pupil who would set the Hudson or the Thames on fire. It was her part in a performance of *The Mikado* at this time that crystallized in Maria's mind the already vague awareness that singing was her only way out of despised obscurity. She soaked up the applause and the compliments of her classmates; popularity, however short-lived, seemed such a satisfying substitute for the love she longed for.

The other thing she learned at school was that to be weak and ignored is to be wretched. This was not, of course, the first time that experiences at school have turned a child into an incipient misanthrope, but Maria's painful time there certainly reinforced her already gloomy attitude to the world. The state of nature, she would have said if she had wanted to turn her feelings into homespun philosophizing, is a state of war, and 'woe to the vanquished' the great law of nature. But now at last she had stumbled upon a way to exchange blow for metaphorical blow with anyone; she would use her voice to put an end to the humiliation of the apparent superiority of everyone else around her. 'I hated school; I hated the world,' was the way she summed up this period thirty years later. The foundation had already been laid for her bleak view of the world and her bitter philosophy of life: 'To live is to suffer, and whoever tells children this is not so is dishonest – cruel. . . . If you live, you struggle. It is the same for all of us. What is different are the weapons you have and the weapons that are used against you. That is the combination of personality and circumstance. That is fate.'

With every day that went by she was becoming increasingly certain that fate had not merely given her a voice as a weapon but had somehow appointed her custodian of it. The first indication that the family had of Maria as a self-appointed authority on all matters to do with the singing voice was one Saturday afternoon when the family, together with a friend, were sitting around the radio listening to a performance of *Lucia di Lammermoor* from the Metropolitan. Lily Pons was Lucia, and she was halfway through the 'Mad Scene' when Maria, menacingly waving her hand in the direction of the radio, and with real anger in her voice, shouted to her across the radio waves that she had strayed off-pitch. The friend riposted that the lady was a great star of the Met, and a mere child like Maria should show more respect. 'I don't care if she is a star,' exploded Maria. 'She sings off-key. Just wait and see, one day I'm going to be a star myself, a bigger star than her.'

This was still more bravado than conviction, but Maria's fighting instinct was beginning to make itself felt. She had by now made up her mind to *be* someone, although it would take another year, her last year in New York, to turn this vague feeling into the determination to become the best singer in the world, the most celebrated and the most envied, and to turn this determination into the absolute singleness of purpose that would guide her life for the next twenty years.

Chapter Two

MARIA'S fighting instinct was beginning to assert itself but it was still her mother who was the force driving her on. Evangelia's head may have been in the clouds about her daughter's prospects, and her heart nowhere in sight, but her feet were solidly on the ground. The conclusion she reached in the last days of 1936 was that, if Maria was to have the teachers and the training she would need for the career Evangelia had been dreaming of, they would have to return to Greece. There, with her family's musical connections and without her husband's constant objections, she could even more thoroughly dedicate herself to the polishing of the treasure she was convinced she had in her hands. However strong the logical arguments in favour of leaving for Greece, the arguments against the move were equally compelling. In the end it was not logic but instinct that resolved Evangelia's dilemma. She had a dream in which her father – the figure who from her childhood had been most irrevocably associated with music – urged her to take her daughter and leave New York for Greece. Jackie was sent ahead, while Evangelia and Maria began packing up their apartment.

George Callas's feelings were ambivalent. He had been living increasingly under the shadow of his wife who was behaving as though she had produced their daughters without his help. Evangelia, in her own unique way, and the three females of the family in combination, had through the years greatly encouraged his own innate tendency to sink into earnest insignificance. So as he was paying for the fares, he was no doubt sighing a deep sigh of relief at the prospect of temporary release, if not from supporting them, at least from being gradually suffocated by them.

On 28 January 1937, packing was interrupted. At Public School 189 on 188th Street and Amsterdam Avenue, it was Graduation Day for the eighth-grade class, Maria's last contact with her school before she set off for what she was looking forward to as her Greek adventure. For Maria the balance sheet of the trip had nothing on the debit side; she was taking few happy memories with her and leaving no good friends behind. Neither in school nor outside it had she discovered anything of the magic of friendship, of that peculiar intimacy which comes to those who have had private languages and private jokes, who have played together in the morning and shared dreams in the twilight, that special hour when everything seems not only possible but achieved. There seems to have been nobody in Maria's childhood, whether child or grown-up, with whom she could share her inner thoughts, her fears and her hopes.

Graduation Day, with its tearful goodbyes and its joyful promises to keep in touch, would ordinarily have been agony for an outsider like Maria, but as the programme included singing it was an opportunity to shine. As part of the operetta based on the music of Gilbert and Sullivan that was the centre-piece of the ceremonies, Maria sang extracts from *HMS Pinafore*. She looked clumsy and uncomfortable, but she sang beautifully and was warmly applauded. Then came the signing of autograph books, the eighth-grade graduates vying with each other to see who could produce the most sparkling wish, the wittiest epigram, the most original phrase. Maria, unable to shine at this particular game, took refuge in a two-line commonplace poem that was revealing of how she felt about herself at the time:

> Being no poet, having no fame,
> Permit me just to sign my name.

And she signed it Mary Anna Callas.

Throughout her life Maria considered herself to be ill-educated, and felt that this was yet another injury inflicted on her by her mother's voracious and impatient ambition.

'I would give anything to know as much as you know,' she told Efi Zaccaria, wife of the famous bass, years later. That graduation ceremony at the beginning of 1937 was the last Maria would ever have to do with formal education.

A few days later, she, her mother and their three canaries were boarding the Italian liner *Saturnia.* Maria spent the first two days being horribly seasick in their cabin listening to Stephanakos, David and Elmina sing, chirp and burble in unison. After the first two days, however, she began to join in with at least as much enthusiasm. And when she wasn't singing in the cabin, she would sing in the tourist lounge. When the Captain of the *Saturnia* happened to walk in one evening and heard her sing Gounod's 'Ave Maria', he asked her to sing at the Church service on Sunday. She refused. Having followed her instincts and refused the Captain's invitation, Maria was, a few moments later, receiving from him another invitation, this time much more to her liking: to sing at a party he was giving for the officers and crew and two Italian contessas from the first class. She accepted eagerly.

On the day of the party she swang back and forth between exhilaration and anxiety. When the time came for her to sit down at the piano to accompany herself, only the exhilaration remained. She took off her glasses, and her black eyes, full of energy and life, completely dominated her face. They distracted attention not only from the adolescent pimples showing under the covering powder, but from the prim blue dress with the schoolgirl white collar, and even from the excess weight spread over the stool. She sang her two favourites, 'La Paloma' and 'Ave Maria', and finished off with the 'Habanera' from *Carmen. 'Et si je t'aime, prends garde à toi,'* sings Carmen, and throws Don José the flower from her hair. Carmen-Maria pulls a carnation from the vase nearest to the piano and tosses it to the Captain.

The Captain was delighted with her voice and thrilled by her sense of drama. He kissed the carnation, and when he was thanking her later he gave her a bouquet – her first one – and a doll, which, almost incredibly, was also her first. Her mother had always prided herself on the absence of such trivialities from her daughters' lives. 'My daughters never looked at dolls,' she wrote later, 'but they read, and at night they would play the piano until eleven o'clock, when I would send them to bed.' Maria packed the doll in her suitcase, took it to Athens and kept it with her all the time she was there, learning to play with dolls at the age of thirteen.

Captain, officers and crew were on the quay to wish Maria good luck when the *Saturnia* docked at Patras near the Gulf of Corinth. The train journey from Patras to Athens was a revelation for Maria. It was a day out of time, an interlude between her hard-pressed life in New York and the absolute regimentation of the twenty years that were to follow. This beautiful March day, Maria's first full day in Greece, was in effect the last day before she shut off everything that did not directly touch on her work. It would be a long time before Maria would once again be open, receptive and unconcerned enough to respond to the world around her with the intensity and sensitivity of that day. She was in fact enchanted with the blue of the sea, the white of the clouds and the mauve of the anemones under the silver-grey olive trees. 'My blood is pure Greek. . . . I feel totally Greek,' she was to say again and again. Her first contact with Greece had awakened powerful feelings, and her spirit seemed to fill and expand, to grow lighter and less anxious. They had lunch on the train with Maria humming to herself as she wolfed the stuffed vine leaves and the over-cooked lamb. Throughout lunch she took her eyes from the window only long enough to aim her fork into her food, and then, until the time came for the next bite, she lost herself once again in the Greece unfolding before her.

Evangelia was in her element. Fully conscious of the approving glances of her fellow passengers, she was wallowing in their admiration. She was wearing a closely-fitted grey suit and a black felt hat with a long brown feather, and she felt more elegant and more assured than she remembered feeling for years. The hat, bought after numerous shopping expeditions for the main purpose of impressing her family, had to have half its brown feather cut off a few days later, after it had nearly put out the eye of an Athenian bus driver, but for the moment the stylish, excessive length of the feather was only attracting some additional attention to the elegant lady in grey and her awkward young companion.

It was night when they arrived in Athens. They were met at the station by Evangelia's three sisters, her three brothers and Jackie. Maria's grandmother, who was ill in bed, was waiting for them at her house beyond the Acropolis where Evangelia and her daughters were to stay for a month before moving to their own house. Uncles and aunts, nieces and nephews, uncles' colleagues and aunts' friends, neighbours and strangers who cared to stop and listen, however briefly, knew by now that the thirteen-year-old Maria, her voice and her career were the reason the family had packed house and arrived in Greece. Tales of prizes Maria had won, vocal feats Maria had accomplished and audiences Maria had conquered were being busily told and retold, and expectations stood precariously high.

Evangelia's aim was to mobilize not only everyone she was related to, but everyone she could lay her hands on, in the cause of her daughter's career. The day after she arrived in Athens, Maria's life became the life of an auditioning machine, producing songs on demand for anyone whom her mother could persuade to sit down and listen. It is little wonder that she contracted such a deep distaste for singing socially on demand that when, during the celebrated first cruise on the *Christina*, Winston Churchill pleaded with her to do him the honour of singing something, she astounded everyone present by coldly replying that she would not.

Evangelia had pinned all her hopes on her family's help. But the family was not impressed. For a start, singing was relegated to a very low rung on the social ladder unless it was obviously successful. So they cautioned prudence, they rebuked immoderate ambition, they scorned quixotic dreams. Good voices and musical talent were no news to them. After all, didn't Aunt Sophia play the guitar beautifully? And how about Aunt Pipitsa on the mandolin? And Uncle Filon and Uncle Efthimios, what voices they had! Uncle Efthimios was, in fact, the encouraging exception: 'Don't push her too fast. She's only a little girl,' he kept telling his sister. 'She's in a new country with a new family. Let her get used to us. Then I'll arrange an audition for her.'

While finding people to listen to her daughter, Evangelia was also busy moving from her mother's home to a furnished house near by. At the beginning of September 1937, Efthimios, through his contacts with the Royal Theatre, arranged an audition for his niece with Maria Trivella, who taught at the National Conservatory in Athens. On the day of the audition Maria was panic-stricken – the same kind of feeling that would grip her almost invariably before she went on stage. 'Before I sing I know nothing, don't remember the part, don't know where I start. It is panic, not knowing one thing before you go on stage.' The morning before the audition, Maria's panic was compounded by her mother's terror. Evangelia's hands were trembling as she helped Maria into her white organdie dress and brushed out the curls on her forehead. Still more anxiety was pumped into the atmosphere and into Maria by the arrival of her grandmother and two of her aunts who, together with Jackie, Uncle Efthimios and, of course, her mother, were to accompany Maria to the audition.

Once she started singing, Maria was free both of her own and her family's fears. 'This is talent!' exclaimed Maria Trivella, and promptly agreed to take Maria as a pupil both for singing and for French. She did much more than that; to help Maria get a scholarship from the Conservatory, she conspired with Evangelia to falsify her age. The authorities, happily accepting that Maria was sixteen and not thirteen, agreed to pay for all her music lessons.

Maria Trivella was not just Maria's first teacher; she was her first surrogate mother. From now on, Evangelia's role as the force driving Maria was secondary. Maria was becoming increasingly self-propelled, though at no time in her life was she to be self-sufficient. There had always to be at her side someone who believed in her, encouraged and sustained her. It had to be someone sufficiently convinced of her gift and greatness to reflect them back to her; and she went on feeding off the faith that she herself had inspired. Maria's professional life could in fact be loosely divided into separate periods, each named after its chief sustaining figure: the Trivella period, the de Hidalgo period, the Serafin period, the Meneghini period, the Visconti period, the Zeffirelli period and the di Stefano period.

The Trivella period was the dream period. The more confident of her talent Maria grew, the more she dreamt of where this talent could lead her. She had never worked so hard. Very often she had her meals in Trivella's studio; when she was at home, her mother would bring them to her room and she would go on working with her plate on her lap. There were no distractions in her life and all her energies were poured, in one uninterrupted flow, into her voice and her singing. She was so utterly taken up by this obsessive attention to her career that at times she seemed totally oblivious to everything else. She never wondered then, and for many years never had to ask herself, what was driving her on. All she knew was that she had a passionate need to set herself apart by being admired and singled out, and in the early years it was this struggle to succeed that dominated her life. It obtruded even on the peace of her few days of rest, and stopped her from feeling pleasure and pride in herself by making her focus all the time on what remained to be conquered.

In those years in Athens she gave an impression of concentrated willpower and, at times, chilly resolution, which was hardly likely to endear her to her fellow-students at the Conservatory. 'Her earnestness was oppressive,' said one of them, looking back on that time. As for Maria, her need to shine and to out-shine meant that she based her relationship with the other students on the same illusion on which she was later to base her professional life. Convinced that when others came forward, she herself went back, she fancied herself locked in combat with the world, continually afraid of seeing her own success overshadowed by the success of others.

It was as if she had joined forces with her mother in pushing aside the needs of the deprived child in her in favour of the nascent primadonna. Yet the needs of the child for love, and for space in which to grow, were not extinguished. Suppressed, they festered and turned instead into bitterness and anger. And the more they were suppressed, the longer the shadow they cast. Resentment and anger accumulated, became a reservoir, almost a quality of her being, lurking in her eyes, circulating in her blood and moving in her breathing.

Later on, at the height of her transformation, she acquired a certain calmness, a certain silence – accessories of the regal dignity which she strove to project right up until the end of her life. As a close friend of hers put it, however: 'When I was near Maria, her appearance may have been of calm and silence, but if I sat near her quietly, without talking, I never felt calm or silence coming from her. Deep down the turmoil was hidden. On the surface everything was quiet; underneath I felt the volcano getting ready to explode at any moment.'

With the little girl in her kept quiet by ever-increasing quantities of food, Maria could, relatively undistracted, dedicate herself to the realization of the artistic greatness she sensed was hers, and the pursuit of the golden chalice of fame and success that she knew would inevitably follow. Madame Trivella was her main teacher and guide during these first two years, but she was not the only one. George Karakandas taught her acting at the Academy and David supplemented her singing lessons at home. George Karakandas was paid; David wasn't. George Karakandas was a well-respected and established teacher; David was totally unknown. But in later years, Maria would say that she owed more to David than she owed to most of her Conservatory teachers. She would spend hours watching fascinated while David, perched in his cage, almost burst his feathered throat singing. She would put her fingers on her throat and watch David's quiver, and every few moments she would break into amazed cries of 'How does he do it?' She felt he had a secret she could snatch from him. So she kept singing with him, trying to control her voice as he controlled his song, until exhausted she had to stop while David went on merrily singing. Maria had lost her race with David, but one morning she took her revenge on the canary breed when, soaring through an aria from *Lucia*, she saw Elmina tumble from her perch to the floor of the cage. Elmina, Maria's first casualty, had fainted, apparently unable to take the excitement of the young girl's vocalizing. After the fainting scene had been repeated twice more while Maria was singing, Madame Evangelia, tired of pouring cognac and water down Elmina's beak, resolved that Maria would never again sing one note until Elmina had first been banished to the most isolated room in the house.

All this vocalizing, the hard work and the sleepless nights were rewarded when, a few days before her fifteenth birthday, Maria made her stage debut singing Santuzza in a student production of *Cavalleria Rusticana.* She had determined that she would win the first prize in opera at the Conservatory and she knew that the decision rested on her performance in *Cavalleria.* Her fighting instinct had been fully aroused. With typical exaggeration, she began telling her mother that if she did not get the first prize, she would give up the stage. She did win, and the applause and the success continued to ring in her ears. They were the first taste of what, magnified and magnified again, was to become a regular occurrence, though never a routine experience.

'I work: therefore I am,' she told Kenneth Harris thirty years later. 'What do you *do* if you do not work?' In Athens just before the war, Maria was not only happiest when she worked, she virtually existed only when she worked. She knew that when she was not working she was least happy, least secure and most prone to start comparing herself with Jackie. Jackie, at twenty-two slim, tall, flattered and admired, had also acquired a highly eligible permanent escort – Milton Embiricos, son of a very rich and well-established shipping family. In the summer of 1939 Jackie and Milton became engaged. Only two months earlier, Mussolini had marched into Albania, and Greece for the first time had a fascist neighbour. But the rumbles of the gathering storm were ignored in Greece as elsewhere; there were no thoughts of war in the family party celebrating the engagement with a trip to Corfu on Milton's yacht *Helene*. Milton put them up at the Grand Hotel and showered all sorts of luxuries on them.

Evangelia was in heaven. Maria was in despair. Jackie was lost to her, about to be taken away and ecstatically happy. And as if this was not enough, Maria, a fat and awkward fifteen-year-old, felt ignored and out of place. She could not wait for that 'special' holiday to come to an end. She looked at her sister's social life as one standing on a cold pavement looks through the window at pleasant firelit intimacies. She felt lonely and frightened by her own loneliness.

At this low point, Elvira de Hidalgo walked into her life; or rather Maria walked into de Hidalgo's. Whichever way it was, for the next five years Maria was to be the most important person in de Hidalgo's life, and de Hidalgo the most important person in Maria's. De Hidalgo, Spanish, lively and well rounded, came straight from the world of Maria's dreams, from the world of the Met, La Scala and Covent Garden. In love with Greece, she had recently joined the teaching staff of Athens's leading conservatory, the Odeon Athenon. It was meant to be for a season; it turned out to be for years. Confusing coincidence with cause is a very tempting error, but there is no doubt that had Elvira de Hidalgo not been trapped in Greece by the outbreak of the Second World War, Maria's career would have been drastically different. It was Evangelia who, her ear always to the musical ground, heard of de Hidalgo's arrival and determined that Maria should audition for her. The result was that Evangelia provided Maria simultaneously with the best teacher and the best mother she would ever have.

The audition was their first encounter. The aria Maria had chosen to sing was from Weber's *Oberon*: 'Ocean! Thou mighty monster.' While Maria was awaiting her turn, de Hidalgo kept looking at that awkward creature in the corner staring at her crushed sandals and biting her nails. 'The very idea of that girl wanting to become a singer,' she thought then, and said later, 'was laughable.' But seconds after Maria started singing, de Hidalgo closed her eyes. What she heard was 'violent cascades of sound, full of drama and emotion'; what she saw was a vision not only of what that voice could become, but of what that singer, that young woman, could become. Maria was admitted to Athens's leading conservatory tuition-free as de Hidalgo's personal student.

Elvira de Hidalgo was to be the first Pygmalion in Maria's life. From the moment Maria arrived for her ten o'clock class, de Hidalgo began the long, hard and often painful process of freeing all sorts of qualities in her pupil, of uncovering all the remarkable capacities which were buried inside Maria, not only the obvious musical gifts but the intelligence, the passion, the willpower and the audacity that were to add up to her uniqueness. As for Maria, with de Hidalgo's guidance she was continually taking herself by surprise. She discovered and began to use musical muscles and dramatic strengths she never knew she had. Until de Hidalgo came into her life, Maria's range was so narrow that many teachers at the Conservatory were convinced that she was not a soprano but a mezzo. Now she started developing her high notes and discovering her low chest notes. It was absorbing, at times exhilarating. 'I was like the athlete,' she said years later, 'who enjoys using and developing his muscles, like the youth who runs and jumps, enjoying and growing at the same time, like the girl who dances, enjoying the dance for its own sake, and learning to dance at the same time.'

Maria arrived at the Conservatory at ten every morning and, apart from a short break for lunch, she worked with de Hidalgo until eight at night. 'It would have been inconceivable to stay at home,' she said, 'I wouldn't know what to do there.' But it was not only that she wouldn't know what to do there. If home is the place where love is, then 'home' had never really been home for Maria. It had been 'there', and her close relationship with de Hidalgo made it easier to be away from 'there' for longer and longer periods.

In Maria's eyes, however, Elvira was more than a mother; with her magical knowledge of whole new worlds of music, with her gifts of singing and with the aura of stage glories around her, she was more like a fairy godmother. The existence of a fairy godmother made it easier for Maria to begin in her mind the process of turning her mother into the wicked stepmother. This childhood tendency of seeing people and things in terms of clear opposites, of 'good' or 'bad', was to stay with Maria long after her childhood. Experience, and her relationship with Onassis, softened the tendency, but it seemed as though nothing could ever eradicate it. People who were 'good', even 'very, very good', like her great mentor Serafin, for example, suddenly became 'bad' and either they later turned 'good' again or, once classified 'bad', remained 'bad' for ever. Elvira de Hidalgo had the distinction of being the only person in Maria's life who remained above such fluctuations of fortune for nearly forty years. Her picture, apart from that of the great nineteenth-century soprano, Malibran, was the only one in Maria's flat when she died.

De Hidalgo's clear sense of the extraordinary destiny ahead of her pupil began to communicate itself to Maria, who was feeling more and more strongly that she had been singled out for a very special purpose. De Hidalgo awakened in her a realization of the greatness and a grandeur of their art. She also gave the ugly duckling her first vision of the swan she was to become. It seemed immeasurably distant from what she now was, but de Hidalgo did more: she bridged the gap between the vision and the reality, not only with her teaching but with her understanding, her encouragement and her love. She taught Maria how to dress, how to walk across a stage and how to walk across a street, how to stand and yet pulsate with movement, and how to move and yet stand tall inside herself. She also introduced Maria to the miraculous possibilities of those two hands and arms that had until then been hanging awkwardly from her shoulders. And Maria began to create miracles with them.

Perhaps the greatest treasure de Hidalgo gave Maria, in the competitive world of opera, was a vast repertoire of tragic, romantic heroines. She gave her Norma, Elvira, Gioconda. In turn Maria would give them as revelations to an unsuspecting musical world. She had learned many of these operas by heart long before she could have sung them properly. Elvira lent her the full scores that she could not afford to buy and Maria, so as to give them back as soon as possible, would learn them off by heart. On top of the bus, walking in the street, eating, dressing, Maria would be rehearsing, her mind full of runs, roulades, trills, cadenzas – the whole panoply of bel canto embellishments.

For de Hidalgo, bel canto was much more than 'beautiful singing'. Many years later, echoing her teacher, Maria defined it as 'a specific training of the voice, the development of a technique for making full use of it as a player of the violin or the flute is trained to make full use of his instrument.' It involved a precision, discipline and sense of authority that came surprisingly easily to the sixteen-year-old Conservatory student. This relentless groundwork was at the heart of the professionalism and perfectionism that marked Maria's whole career. Through the long days and nights of working with de Hidalgo, it was this meticulous technical training of her voice that was the teacher's first priority and that gradually became the pupil's obsession. Long before Maria's heart was filled with broken-hearted queens and tragic priestesses, her mind was full of all the ways she could turn her voice into a perfectly agile instrument, ready to give reality to all the technical feats she was perfecting with her mind. It was part of her instinctive greatness as an artist that, however fascinated she may have been by florid embellishments and athletic feats, she used them but was never used by them.

At times Maria talked of her voice as though it was a Siamese twin, a physical appendage with a life of its own. More often though, she treated her voice almost as a semi-hostile, intractable force outside herself. 'The voice was answering tonight,' she would say, or 'The voice was not obeying tonight.' It was to be a long, continuing struggle.

While Maria was perfecting her roulades, Greece had begun preparing for war. After the fall of France and Italy's entry into the war in the summer of 1940, the tension had been mounting. It was no longer possible to ignore the fact that Greece's involvement in the war was only months, perhaps even days, away. The prime minister, General Metaxas, began speaking publicly of the national danger and quietly, but determinedly, Greece mobilized. On 28 October it began. The Italian minister presented Metaxas with Mussolini's ultimatum: allow

Italian troops to take up strategic positions on Greek territory or war would follow. Metaxas rejected it instantly with no more than a laconic 'No'. Italian troops immediately crossed the border, but were promptly driven back, and the Greek army even found itself occupying about a quarter of Albania.

So when, late in November, Maria made her prosessional stage debut at the National Lyric Theatre, Athens was celebrating and Maria was singing and dancing in a barrel in Suppé's operetta *Boccaccio*. Her part was not the kind triumphs are made of, but if not a triumph it was a solid success. She was applauded, praised, appreciated, for the first time recognized as an established, professional singer. She was finally acting out her mother's fantasies, except that by now they had become her own. She was exultant. And so was Greece; the period that followed the repulsing of the Italian forces was full of elation and what proved to be a short-lived optimism.

As for Maria, she was to have triumphs before which singing in a barrel at the Lyric Theatre of Athens was little more than a practical joke, but then her delight was never directly related to external success. Indeed, the triumphs, won at greater and greater cost, brought her less and less joy. 'I'm never satisfied,' she said thirty years after she had leap-frogged her way out of the Lyric Theatre beaming with happiness. 'I am personally incapable of enjoying what I have done well because I see so magnified the things I could have done better.'

But on that November night in 1940, the first of hundreds of first nights, she allowed herself to wallow in her success. Her whole family was there applauding, yet after the performance it was to de Hidalgo that she ran for reassurance that it had gone well. Yes, it had gone well *very* well, smiled Elvira, and all the sleepless nights and the nerves and the panics were instantly washed away. The more withdrawn she became from her mother and Jackie, the more devotion she felt for de Hidalgo; and the closer she felt to Elvira the more detached and, gradually, the more angry she felt at her own family. All this time she had been driving herself on with huge quantities of food and nervous energy spurred by ambition. Going out, flirting, making friends, formed no part of her life. It was not until much later that she learned about romance and the sudden leapings of the heart – the natural sequel of an unnatural beginning.

Her adolescent urges, however thoroughly suppressed in the daily grind of study and music-making, were making themselves felt. Without being aware of it, she was finding it harder to stifle her resentment towards her mother – resentment for all she had not been, for all the love she had denied her and for all the love she had unconditionally poured on Jackie. Jackie had by now learned to take her mother's special ministrations completely for granted and to be, if not spoilt, outrageously favoured. The result was that Maria seemed to be almost constantly in a state of combustion. She had learned to divert her emotions and wild impulses into her work, but she found it increasingly difficult to do so at home. She felt more isolated than ever, and aloofness became her only shield.

Chapter Three

AT THE beginning of April 1941, the Germans came to the aid of their humiliated Italian allies, and on 6 April they bombed and almost destroyed Salonika in the north. General Metaxas had died a couple of months earlier, but under their new prime minister, Alexander Koryzis, the Greeks were no less determined to fight. Athens steeled herself, awaiting the bombs.

On 6 April at Patissiou 61, Evangelia, Maria, Jackie, her fiancé and Athena the maid were more at one than ever before. Family resentments were for the moment set aside. As soon as dinner was cleared from the table, Maria began singing 'La Paloma'. They all joined in. Suddenly on that first night of the Nazi invasion everything else stopped. Time stopped, everything fell into place, became of a piece. Despite the underlying anxiety about the future there was joy and laughter inside Maria's home. What is more, there was a real, deep peace. Outside there was no doubt that the war was on: the food shops were empty after the housewives' rush to stock up as much as they could, radios everywhere were blaring out warnings, news and information about the dead and the injured, and the cafés were full of men sitting, standing, arguing, swearing and drowning their fears in ouzo and retsina.

Two weeks later, as the Greeks were fighting a series of rearguard actions, withdrawing further and further to the south, the prime minister committed suicide. It was an act that symbolized the growing demoralization of a nation. On 27 April what they most feared took place: the Germans occupied Athens. It was as if the plague had hit the city. The streets became deserted apart from soldiers in Nazi uniforms. Schools, theatres and public offices were closed and there was a six o'clock curfew. Maria, with Jackie and her mother, joined the long lines of women in black headscarves on the sullen pilgrimage from church to church lighting candles for their men, for their families and for Greece. Suddenly the religious ritual became all important. Maria would go into a church, right foot first, crossing herself as she went in and as she came out, and every Friday she would wash all the icons with wine and put fresh cloths on the altar.

Yet Maria was only physically present in all these activities. Her mind remained full of arias, trills and scales, and her heart longed to be back with de Hidalgo. So despite her mother's objections, despite Uncle Efthimios's long, graphic descriptions of what would happen to her one dark night as she was walking home, and despite her own fears of walking alone through the deserted streets, Maria decided that at ten o'clock every morning she would be at de Hidalgo's house. She stayed there the whole day and walked home at whatever time in the evening she stopped practising and studying. She broke the Nazi curfew but not with any great sense of heroism, rather with a matter-of-fact defiance – as if the Nazi soldiers in the streets represented nothing more than an inconvenience and a slight change in her routine.

By the spring of 1941, Crete had fallen to the Germans. The conquest of Greece was total, and the king and his government barely managed to escape to Egypt. Friends had been asking Evangelia for some time now if she was thinking of trying to flee with her daughters back to America, but she never seriously considered it. For a start, Jackie would not hear of leaving her fiancé behind and, war or no war, Maria would not be dragged away from de Hidalgo. At the same time, the last they had heard from George was that he was travelling round the States selling pharmaceuticals and cosmetics, and could not for the moment give them a fixed address; so even if they had been willing to leave, there was really nowhere for them to go.

A few months after the occupation began, life in Athens became a little easier. The Germans extended the curfew to midnight and allowed shops, schools and theatres to reopen. Once more Maria found herself at the Conservatory, but this time not just as a student. While the theatres were closed, the fairy godmother had toiled long and hard on Maria's behalf. The result was that when they reopened she could announce to Maria that she was now, at seventeen, a permanent member of the Athens Opera. Maria's successes in *Boccaccio* and in the student productions of *Un Ballo in Maschera* and *Aida* had made de Hidalgo's efforts much easier, but they did little to lessen the antagonism, the jealousy and the outright hostility that spread rapidly and bitterly throughout the Opera House as soon as the appointment was officially announced.

The chorus of disapproval was, naturally enough, led by the female members of the company, and still more naturally, by the older ones in particular. This hostility, sparked by nothing more than envy and the instinct of self-preservation, was fuelled by one real grievance and one real objection. The objection came from those who genuinely believed that Maria's voice had such physiological flaws that no amount of teaching and practice could produce from it a consistency of sound. The complaints in 1941, about her unruly top or too much metal in her upper register, were in embryo the objections to Maria's voice that persisted throughout her career. In the future they would be elaborated, adorned with musicological jargon and peddled to the multitude by learned critics, but in principle they remained the same objections raised by her Greek colleagues right at the beginning of her career. They could be reduced to one basic observation: Maria's voice was not, and never would be, beautiful in the classical sense. It was muddy in the lower and middle ranges, and sometimes could turn into a squawk in the upper register. It had too much metal in it, too many sharp edges; it could cut as well as ravish. Also Maria would always sacrifice homogeneity of colour, smoothness and other hallmarks of beautiful singing on the altar of emotional truth. So those who rated a singer first, second and third by the conventional beauty of her voice, with expression and dramatic truth coming low on the list, had a genuine objection to Maria's appointment.

Much more important than this objection was the

grievance against Maria herself. According to the rules of conduct that Maria had, largely unconsciously, drawn for herself, she looked on her fellow students and her colleagues as adversaries. Her cynicism about other people's motives was deep, as though she was born into it, instead of, like most people, acquiring it through experience. She was at this time going through what was probably her most egocentric and insecure period, so she could see the rest of the world only in terms of rivalry and domination. And the rest of the world obliged her by behaving as she had assumed it would. So there was little camaraderie, and still less love, between Maria and her colleagues. And Maria as always, in response to what she felt to be withdrawal, denial and rebuffs, threw herself even more obsessively into her work. She adopted an aloofness that hid the pain from the world and to a large extent from herself.

The war continued and Maria became more and more the wholly-absorbed artist at work. First there was the bombing. Athens itself was not bombed, but whenever bombs fell on its port, Piraeus, the sound of the sirens pierced the air in Athens, and everybody was ordered to the shelters. Maria and Jackie ran first to the canary room, picked up a cage each, and followed Madame Evangelia down the one-hundred-and-twenty steps to the cellar. The other tenants, running down the stone steps, some barefoot, others in their pyjamas, would overtake the two girls with their canaries, waving their arms and making loud, reprimanding noises at time-wasting frivolities like canaries. Maria never let her fear of air-raids or of Nazi soldiers on the streets affect her actions, but once in the shelter, the cellar-door firmly closed behind her, she was always violently sick.

Food was the other great problem. Since Greece had always relied on imports for a large proportion of her food, the Allied blockade and enemy indifference caused great hardship, which the Red Cross tried, without much success, to relieve. All food was rationed except for those who could discover and afford the black markets that had sprouted up in odd places. The main black market was up in the mountains, a long, exhausting walk or an almost equally long ride in fragile little cars drawn by temperamental wood-burning locomotives. Sometimes Maria went with her mother and sometimes she went alone, walking home laden with whatever vegetables, chickens or rabbits she had found.

One day in the early summer of 1941, when Maria returned from the mountains, she discovered that the Germans had issued another of their endless series of proclamations, this time against any kind of noise both in public places and in private homes. She exploded, and this became the order she most loved to disobey, with fervour and bravado. On the very evening that the Germans issued their proclamation, she moved her piano up to the door of the balcony and sat there playing and singing at the top of her voice to the great relish of the passers-by who broke into sudden, spontaneous applause. So infectious was the enthusiasm that many of the Italians and some of the Germans in the street joined in.

Throughout the war, Maria's voice proved to be like a magic gift which gained for her friends, food, protection. The first war friend Maria's voice brought her was a young Italian soldier who heard her sing when he was walking past her open window in Patissiou Street. He waited until she came out on the balcony and talked to her, full of emotion at the memories from home that her Italian singing had evoked. They met a few times after that; they would sit on a park bench, Maria singing his favourite arias from Italian opera, and he unable to hold back his tears. He would give her food from his rations, and Maria would go away and hide in doorways, tear the food open and eat it there and then. Her mother was furious that she hardly ever brought anything back, but Maria was too hungry, too lonely and feeling too unloved to share.

Her voice had brought her another war friend: Colonel Mario Bovalti from Verona. At first he started calling at Patissiou 61 and accompanying Maria on the piano; gradually, he began bringing little gifts, sharing his rations with the family and giving Maria a great deal of attention and some much-needed love.

In the autumn of 1941 her voice even saved her life. One night in late August, a Greek Air Force officer, a friend of the family, came to Patissiou 61 with two disguised British officers who had escaped from prison. Evangelia knew that the punishment for sheltering fugitives from German justice was death, and was reluctant to take them in. In the end, however, prodded by her two daughters, she yielded. The two British officers were installed in the canary room, with strict instructions not to cough, not to use a light at night, hardly even to breathe; their only luxury was listening to the nine o'clock news from London. The secret was so carefully guarded that not even Jackie's Milton had been told. If Milton was with them in the evening, Maria's self-imposed duty was to go to the piano promptly at nine o'clock and start singing – anything loud that would muffle the sound of the radio from the canary room. Maria grew really fond of the dark-haired Scotsman and the fair-haired Englishman. They sensed that and also sensed Maria's daring; they therefore went to her whenever they wanted to break any of the rules of shelter, and she would invariably agree to help them get round her mother. One day they even pleaded with her to take them out into the street so they could walk in the sun. Maria, always very practical, said nothing to her mother until she had found some black paint and, with Jackie as her accomplice, had dyed Robert's hair. When Evangelia saw the quartet that came arm-in-arm to ask her permission to leave the house, she laughed too hard to be able to say no.

Six weeks after their Greek friend arrived out of nowhere, bringing the two British officers with him, he came back and with just as few explanations took them away. The day after, Italian soldiers, following a lead they had been given, came to search the house. As they pushed through the door, with their revolvers drawn, Maria, who knew that the letters and photographs the British officers had left behind were still in the flat, ran to the piano, and started singing Tosca – Tosca pleading to save her lover's life, Maria singing to save hers and her mother's and sister's. When Tamino played his magic flute, the wild animals forgot about devouring him and started dancing to the music. When Maria started singing, the Italian soldiers forgot about searching the house, put down their revolvers and sat on the floor in a circle round the piano. They came back the next day, this time knocking instead of pounding on the door and heaping loaves of bread, salami and macaroni on the piano as thanks for the music of yesterday and a plea for more music today.

If her voice was the magic weapon, Tosca seemed to be the magic part. It was Tosca that she sang to distract Milton's attention the first day he heard strange noises coming out of the canary room; it was Tosca that she sang when the Italian officers came to search the house; it was Tosca that she sang the first day she moved her piano to the door of the balcony to disobey the German ban on noise. One evening when she was once again singing Tosca on the balcony a man answered her across the roof-tops singing Mario. The next day when Maria got back from the Conservatory, she ran to the balcony and started singing. The unseen Mario responded again. And again. And again. The duet across the roof-tops continued through July. One July evening when Maria/Tosca ran to the balcony there was a special joy in her voice. That morning the Tosca at the Athens Opera had been taken ill and Maria was asked to take over.

Tosca once again – this time not to deceive the Italian officers or defy the German soldiers, but her first major professional role. Antonis Dellendas, a huge, exuberant tenor and the idol of the Greek operatic world, was her Mario. (The identity of the Mario who sang with her across the roof-tops is still a mystery.)

Tosca gave Maria her first opportunity to display her fierce passion offstage. The elderly soprano she was replacing happened to be, as fate would have it, the leader of those opposed to Maria's permanent appointment to the company. When she heard who was to take her place, too ill to get up and stop Maria herself, she sent her huband to block her way to the stage entrance. One does not need to be a tigress to resent such petty behaviour, but Maria did not merely resent him – she jumped at him and scratched his face with both hands.

There is no doubt that Maria's violent explosions were in the future to be magnified and even caricatured by a press that recognized very early that Callas the Tigress sold many more copies than Callas the Opera Singer, but there is just as little doubt that the potential for violence lurked just beneath the surface in Maria, and the world watched hypnotized as she displayed it in public. The aggrieved soprano's husband, however, did not merely watch, and there was nothing hypnotized about him as, specks of blood on his face, he jumped back and landed his fist on Maria's face. So when Tosca made her entrance on the stage, one of her eyes, under her wide-brimmed hat, was slightly blacker than the other.

But the critics were ecstatic and the audience, as one of them put it, 'electrified'. They were swept along by the passion of this seventeen-year-old Tosca, a woman consumed in turn with jealousy, hate and pain. Maria was famous. And during a war, fame of that kind is not just an ethereal commodity; it has a very practical value, readily convertible into edible offerings. So far Maria's diet, the black market notwithstanding, had consisted mainly of bread and other starches, and as she was allergic to them, she had broken out in boils. By the end of 1941, with the help of better food and an admiring dermatologist, she was completely cured.

For Maria's mother fame *was* an ethereal – almost a spiritual – commodity. 'It was fame I wanted for my daughter,' she said in an interview in New York twenty years later. 'Money came second.' That in her mind justified it all; she did not even feel she had to pay lip-service to any other values. Going after money alone could be seen as base, vulgar and mean-spirted, but it had not occurred to her that there was something not so much vulgar as sad about such a relentless pursuit of fame. In her imagination Evangelia saw her daughter rising ever more gloriously in the world and herself at the centre of all Maria's social triumphs. Social triumphs were not the by-product of Maria's singing; on the contrary, for her mother the singing was the key that would unlock the door to those triumphs. She had always dreamt of seeing her children distinguished, at first she hardly knew as what. By now there could be no doubt. Maria was to be – already was – a famous singer, and Jackie the singing and piano-playing wife of a rich Greek shipowner.

When Maria returned to her dressing-room in the first interval of *Tosca*, her mother was waiting for her. She was waiting for her in the second interval too, and had there been a third interval, she would still have been there waiting for Maria. Indeed, wherever and whenever Maria sang throughout the next year the faithful sentinel was invariably on duty. She was known in the company as Maria's 'Shadow'; she described herself as 'a prize-fighter's second', fanning Maria with a towel before she went back on stage, helping her dress and undress and warding off any over-excitable tenors. And Maria, what with her 'Shadow', her absorption in her work and her unappetizing size, was living the self-denying life of a Vestal Virgin, without the compensating conviction that she would be rewarded in a future life.

The next summer she repeated *Tosca*, this time announced in her own right. The reports about her became more lyrical, enthusiastic and wild with every performance, until by the end of the series of performances in August 1942 men and women were walking nearly ten miles from Piraeus to hear her. Others, confronted at a time of rationing and little or no money with the choice of Maria or a meal, chose Maria. After the *Toscas* were over, the Commander of the Italian Army of Occupation asked Maria, together with five other members of the Athens Opera and a pianist, to go to Salonika, in the north of Greece, to sing to the Italian soldiers. Maria's Shadow asked for permission to accompany her daughter. She is only eighteen, she explained, and Salonika is one of the most licentious of Mediterranean ports. The Italians refused and Evangelia instantly withdrew Maria from the company; the Italians succumbed and mother and daughter were fêted in Salonika forgetting for the four days they were there that Greece was occupied and there was a war on.

Even before the success of *Tosca* and the concerts in Salonika, Maria was ready to tackle anything; no role and no difficulties could intimidate her. She was fearless in the face of challenge and felt convinced that she had the ability to sing any role she could get. *Tosca* was followed by the Greek *première* of Eugen d'Albert's *Tiefland*. 'When you are very young and on the threshold of a career you have all the confidence in the world,' she said in 1961. 'There is nothing you feel you couldn't tackle and do splendidly.'

In this frame of mind Maria turned Marta in *Tiefland* into a challenge and an opportunity to create for the first time for Greek audiences the tormented martyr, the archetypal Romantic heroine. Marta is the oppressed mistress of a rich landowner; she falls in love with a shepherd and at the end of the opera flees with him to the hills. Maria was determined that her performance would be a revelation. She pursued Leonidas Zoras, the conductor, everywhere, demanding extra rehearsals. He remembers how they spent many nights not just going through the score note by note but with Maria testing her interpretation of each musical phrase. Every ten minutes, the oil lamp, filled with wartime watered petrol, started exuding black smoke. Maria would get up, blow it out, clean it, light it again and go on singing. Ten minutes later, she would get up and repeat the same ritual. And so on through the night. Leonidas Zoras had never before come across such patience, persistence and endurance.

The opening night of *Tiefland*, on 22 April 1944, brought Maria her first standing ovation and her first international publicity. An opera written by a Glaswegian of French descent who identified himself entirely with Germany, it was originally put on to placate the Germans who were making threatening noises about the partiality of the Greeks for Italian opera. As a result the *première* of *Tiefland* was widely covered in all German-language papers and 'Maria Kalogeropoulos, Greece's foremost and most beloved opera singer' was at the centre of the coverage.

After the Allies had landed in Normandy on 6 June, the end of the war was at last clearly in sight. In that fateful summer of 1944, Maria had a small part in the only modern opera she ever sang, *O Protomastoras (The Master Builder)* by Manolis Kalomiris, and on 14 August she sang Leonora in the Greek *premiére* of Beethoven's *Fidelio* in the amphitheatre of Herodes Atticus. With the end of the war imminent, Maria sang and portrayed the ultimate victory of love over everything, including fear, tyranny and death. Leonora unlocks Florestan's fetters and as the heavenly tune in the oboe begins, she can only utter half phrases in the background, by the joy and the love that are present. The audience was just as overwhelmed. Maria's performances, even the most elaborate and perfected, had and would always have an element of something fermenting, anticipating in a mysterious manner something still to come. At that particular moment, with Athens on edge, expecting some decisive war news, that quality in her performances struck a chord in the audience that drove them wild. Under the cloudless Athenian summer night they cheered, they yelled, they threw their hats in the air. And you could not tell whether it was the Greeks or their enemies who cheered the loudest. She never sang Leonora again.

In October the Germans marched out of Athens and the Greek soldiers who had been in Italy with the Free Greek Army came back to a liberated Greece. For nearly a week Athens was delirious, and the Athenians, intoxicated, without any help even from ouzo or retsina, were singing, dancing and throwing flowers at each other in the streets. Maria and Jackie climbed up to the roof of their house, tore up the 'occupation money' the Germans had issued and tossed the pieces to the street below, singing Greek anti-German songs. In the background the tension between ELAS, the Communist resistance group, and all the other resistance forces, was growing, until at the end of November it boiled over. General Scobie, commander of the British troops, ordered the dissolution of all guerilla forces; ELAS refused to disband and prepared to fight.

In a few days Maria would be twenty-one. Her father wrote a letter enclosing a hundred dollars but no address. It was the first sign of life from him for six years, and the letter arrived at a time when his younger daughter was at her most confused and uncertain. What should her next step be? A few times she tried to get an answer by reading the cards or even the coffee grounds; she would finish her Turkish coffee, turn her cup upside down and then try to remember what all the different lines left by the grounds meant. Her Aunt Pipitsa, who spent hours every day predicting her own and everybody else's fate, had told her once, but, hard as she tried, she could not remember all the elaborate details.

The day after her twenty-first birthday, on 3 December 1944, fighting broke out in Athens. ELAS and its ancillary Communist groups rose against the government, and in the bloody struggle that followed, Athens nearly fell into Communist hands. The Civil War turned out to be much more bitter and violent than anything Greece, let alone Maria, had experienced during the occupation. Thousands were killed, including Evangelia's younger brother, Filon. Jackie was with Milton when it all happened; Maria was alone with her mother in their flat and they lived there in a state of siege for twenty days. It was by far the worst ordeal they had been through and the solidarity born of misfortune brought them a little closer to each other. They had no way of heating the flat, no light and very soon no food except for a big box of dried beans that they found in one of the cartons containing their Red Cross rations. All they could hear day and night was the sound of explosions, sirens, the rattle of machine-guns and the screams of dying men. For the first time in the last seven years, Maria could neither study nor even sing to herself. They were fast running out of beans and fear was beginning to paralyse her will. Suddenly help came in the form of a small boy with a letter from an officer of the British forces that were assisting the Government against the rebels. He was a devotee of Maria's and was asking them to come to the British Embassy in Constitution Square. It meant risking stray bullets and jumpy partisans, but they had no option. They took nothing with them except their icons and they made it to safety the day before Christmas. The day after Christmas Maria and Evangelia, together with all the Embassy personnel, stood outside the Embassy to see Winston Churchill arrive to thank the staff for their fortitude, before setting off in an armoured car for the Ministry of Foreign Affairs and a meeting with the Greek cabinet.

In the New Year Maria and Evangelia were taken to the Park Hotel to join Jackie and Milton, and they stayed there until a truce was negotiated on 13 January. The task of reconstruction could now begin. And it was awesome;

whole towns and villages had been destroyed, tens of thousands had died in the fighting or from starvation, and the currency had collapsed. Back in Patissiou Street, Maria longed to leave Greece, to leave behind her the mother who seemed determined to run her life and career, to leave Jackie and Milton, to leave her resentful colleagues at the Athens Opera, to leave her own memories of sirens and machine-guns. She wanted to start again, but she had no idea where and still less how to begin.

The decision was made for her when the Athens Opera announced that it was not renewing her contract. 'She has played too active a part in the last months of the occupation,' was the explanation. This was a time, immediately after the most bitter Civil War, when appointments and dismissals were dominated by ideology and political affiliations, and anyone with no strong political commitment was decreed to have been 'on the other side'. Maria had sung for Italian soldiers; she had sung to audiences that included Germans and Italians; she had sung in opera staged to please the Germans; she had accepted food from many Italian and even some German admirers. At the same time she had ignored many of the conquerors' rules and defied some of their orders. She was neither a heroine nor a collaborator. Like the average citizen of an occupied country, she walked the tightrope between self-preservation and a cluster of other higher but less urgent human values. The accusations levelled against her have no foundation in anything other than the expectation – just or unjust – that those with great gifts, and therefore greater opportunities for heroism, should be heroic. But whatever the ideological convictions of those running the Athens Opera, it is not hard to see behind the decision to end Maria's contract the accumulated envy of her opera colleagues.

As to where she should now go, de Hidalgo was insistent: it had to be Italy. Throughout Maria's war career de Hidalgo kept reminding her that only Italy could give her the world fame she craved and which her teacher knew would be hers. Maria, whose respect for de Hidalgo bordered on awe, had not once disregarded her advice. In many ways she was still the obedient, grateful disciple, but, at this turning-point in her life, her instinct was pointing her towards America. And Maria's loyalty to her instinct – even, as she once said, when she could not express or understand it – was unconditional. In vain did de Hidalgo plead with her to reconsider. Maria's mind was made up.

Her mother was totally unaware of her decision. Early one morning in April, as Maria was pouring out coffee for both of them, she said without turning to look at her, 'I'm going to America.' So that was that; except for the long interval of hurt silence that followed.

One last concert in July to raise money for the trip, one last soprano lead in Karl Millöcker's *The Beggar Student* in August, and one farewell lunch given by the mayor of Piraeus in September. Maria had asked her mother and Jackie to stay away both from the lunch and the farewells on the quay. 'I am on my own now, mother,' she said, and Evangelia knew it would be pointless to resist. Only Elvira de Hidalgo was on the quay to see the *Stockholm* leave that sunny September day in 1945. She was saying goodbye to the greatest artist she had come across in her teaching career, and she was at the same time closing, though as it turned out not for ever, the 'de Hidalgo' period in Maria's life.

Chapter Four

MARIA was about to land in America with a hundred dollars in her purse, no idea of where to begin looking for her father and one single operatic contact, the Greek bass Nicola Moscona, who had heard and praised her in Athens. Yet far from feeling terrified, she felt exhilarated. For the first time in her life she had stood up both to her mother and her teacher. She had rejected their authority and, by taking the reins in her own hands, she was accepting responsibility for her life and experiencing for the moment the strength and freedom that accompany such acceptance. When she walked down the gangplank on to the pier the exhilaration that she felt made her totally impervious to the fact that her coat was frayed, her pockets nearly empty, and friends and relatives nowhere in sight.

As Maria emerged from Customs, a man of about sixty with thinning hair and a slight moustache approached her and asked her if she knew a Maria Kalogeropoulos. She fell into his arms and wept for several long minutes before she could get enough breath to ask him how he had found out. He told her, hardly able himself to hold back his tears of joy. He had been reading New York's Greek-language newspapers every day, and a few days earlier something had made him look down the list of passengers bound for New York on the *SS Stockholm*; and there he saw the name of his daughter.

Suddenly Maria had a place to live – a small, modest apartment on West 157th Street – and a father to look after her until the engagements began to come in. After four years of occupation, civil war and deprivation, New York was like a fairyland. For the first few days she floated in a state of childlike astonishment and joy; she could hardly believe that the place was real. The first person she went to see was Dr Lantzounis. She found her godfather married to an American girl exactly her age, who had been head of the volunteers at his hospital. 'God was good to me,' he said to Maria; he had in mind not only his wife Sally but success and a growing reputation in his field. Although he did not know or care much about opera, he was full of encouragement and support; more practically, he asked Sally to take Maria shopping for some less old-fashioned clothes. They got on very well together, the two young women wandering round New York.

Maria spent hours walking, sometimes with Sally, sometimes with her father, sometimes alone, and every few streets she would stop to sample here a cheeseburger, there a pizza, and a few streets later, a pancake or two with maple syrup. 'I was hungry as you are hungry when you have not had enough to eat for a long, long time. I ate and ate...' she remembered years later. Her figure expanded accordingly, but she was totally unwilling to do anything about it. Walking around certain parts of New York she found herself surrounded by women who exuded the kind of elegance and style she had seen before only in fashion magazines. Part of her longed to model herself on them, but knowing how far short of the impossible standard she fell, she rejected it altogether, put on even more weight and began to look almost aggressively inelegant.

After four years of relentless work she was suddenly released from the burden of looming engagements and from the grim pleasures of efficiency. She threw herself into decorating her room, keeping house, cooking for her father and even visiting him with freshly-cut sandwiches at the nearby drugstore where he worked. Then, just as the languid, easy-going, caring part of her was beginning to emerge, she pulled back. Decorating and domesticity were beguiling, but she was not going to be beguiled. The absolute singleness of purpose that had been driving her for the past five years asserted itself again, and, while New York was getting ready for Christmas, Maria began the round of agents, studios, directors, fellow singers and impresarios. The response was dismaying.

'I have sung *Tosca, Fidelio, Tiefland, Cavalleria Rusticana*,' she would proudly announce. 'Where?' was the invariable response. And all she could say, by way of reply, was 'In Athens'. It soon became very clear that fame in an Athenian opera house does not travel well – and certainly not as far as New York. The rejections piled up, each one leaving its deposit of bitterness and renewed determination. It was Maria's first real taste of professional adversity. She had not expected it and was not prepared for it. But Maria Callas, as she called herself again now that she was in New York, knew her value, and if they, whoever *they* might be, did not, time, she was convinced, would put them right.

The first set-back, particularly painful because utterly unexpected, came when Nicola Moscona, the famous bass who had been so impressed by her in Athens, refused to see her, pleading endless engagements. But set-backs only strengthened Maria's determination. She persevered and finally did see him with a specific request: an introduction to Toscanini, who at the time was reigning over musical New York. Moscona refused point-blank to bother the great Toscanini with one more young, ambitious, fat soprano. Maria's only comfort was to promise herself that she would never, *ever* speak to him again. (In 1950, in fact, Moscona sang Oroveso to her Norma, and it is hard to imagine that their exchanges were limited to those between the High Priestess and her father.)

One of her hardest trials in New York was her meeting with the great tenor Giovanni Martinelli who had been a stalwart of the Met for over thirty years. He listened to her carefully and his verdict was a blow. 'You have a good voice,' said the great Martinelli, looking down from the top of the operatic Olympus, 'but you need many more lessons.' Here was the star of the Athens opera being treated like a vaguely promising schoolgirl by a man who occupied one of the chief places in her musical Pantheon. Ever since she had arrived in New York, Maria had been keeping up with all that was going on in the world of music, especially, of course, with everything that was happening at the Met. Reading and dreaming about all these glorious opening nights, she had been feeling more and more like an outdistanced runner. Martinelli made her feel that she was not in the race at all.

The hurt must have been very real, but Maria's response to all blows was to refuse to acknowledge even to herself that she had been hit by them. Not showing that she had been hurt was one of her great talents; she would do anything rather than face her pain. Later, layer upon layer of accumulated hurt and resentment blocked the flow of life in her, stunted the responses of her heart and separated her from any kind of happiness or even contentment, but in 1945 such an attitude of resignation was unthinkable. Whatever Moscona, Martinelli and all the others thought and said, Maria's overwhelming sense of purpose remained. At that time in her life, succeeding was the *only* thing. And there was a perverse kind of blessing in being in a hurry, in having some urgent appointment to keep, even if it turned out to lead to another rejection.

Maria began 1946 in a belligerent mood, prepared to meet new adversities and fresh disappointments with the fortitude of the hard-pressed but well-armed soldier. Her fanatical determination was her shield, but her greatest weapon was her unyielding belief in her worth as an artist. At last, towards the end of January, she met two people who shared this belief. Eddie Bagarozy was a New York lawyer who had been dabbling in opera all his life. His wife, Louise Caselotti, was a mezzo-soprano with a greater experience of Hollywood musicals than of opera, but with a very good reputation in New York as a singing teacher and coach. Maria auditioned for them and instantly found herself with two friends and protectors who believed in her talent and liked her company, and whose Riverside Drive apartment was to become within a few days Maria's second home, as much a refuge from her father's home as de Hidalgo's had been from her mother's in Athens.

It was not that Maria was not getting along with her father, but she was tired of his inability to share or even understand her operatic dreams. Opera bored him and all the technical twaddle about it bored him even more. And as there was no telephone in the flat, Maria had to make all her phone calls pleading for auditions from her father's drugstore to the accompaniment of his 'I told you so' head-shakings. It was becoming exasperating. With the arrival of the Bagarozys on the scene, Maria at last had two people with whom she could talk endlessly about the one thing she really cared for. She also had a telephone.

She would arrive at Riverside Drive early in the morning, work most of the day there, alone or with Louise, and often have dinner with her and Eddie. Once again she was feeling the vitality that comes from being the centre of attention. She had experienced this in Greece, and in New York she had begun to suffer from withdrawal symptoms. Although a crowd of two is not exactly a substitute for a capacity audience at the Met, the effect was unmistakable: Maria was feeling alert and full of hope. She was once again in full sail on the high tide.

She was in just such a mood when she received a phone call from the office of the General Manager of the Metropolitan Opera. Edward Johnson had finally agreed to see her. What happened next was to become part of the Callas legend. Edward Johnson heard her and offered her a contract for the leading roles in two productions of the 1946/7 season: Beethoven's *Fidelio* and Puccini's *Madama Butterfly*. The contract was offered on the spot, and, to the stupefaction of the General Manager and other members of the Met staff present, it was turned down. Maria Callas, at the age of twenty-two, was refusing to make her debut at the Met as Leonora and Butterfly. The decision was not as mad as it seemed. She did not want to sing *Fidelio* in English, and very understandably she did not want to parade her 180 pounds in the role of a fragile, fifteen-year-old Japanese girl. It was nonetheless an amazing response, an immediate and intuitive decision. Surely no opera singer who has made the rounds of the New York operatic world, and has been turned away in every single instance, draws a balance sheet of pros and cons, and comes down against an opportunity to make her debut at the Met on the strength of it.

Everybody jumped on her. What did she think she was doing? Had she gone mad? Eddie Bagarozy, who had read enough of his pocket Freud to know about the unconscious taking control of the reason, stayed away from his office the next day and spent a large part of it tip-toeing around Maria asking her if she was suffering from a death wish, if she perhaps did not *want* to succeed, if she had, after all, given up on life – and other equally meaningful questions. There was nothing covert or ambiguous about her mother's letter which was despatched as soon as the news reached her: 'Have I suffered all these years for you so that you can go and throw away such a golden chance?' At a time like this her father's lack of interest in her operatic career was a positive relief.

'I'm sure I'm right,' insisted Maria. 'My voices have told me so.' Maria had taken to referring to her instinct as 'my voices', at first in complete earnest but gradually, and as she began noticing eyebrows being raised, half-jokingly. Whatever name she may have given it, her decision to turn down the Met contract was a victory of instinct and intuition over logic and reason. It also showed the kind of trust in life which at this time pervaded all her decisions.

Maria may have felt and known that she was right but as she began once again knocking on doors that would not open, she would have had to be superhuman not to begin doubting the wisdom of her decision. The process of doubt and self-recrimination began after her audition with Gaetano Merola, impresario of the San Francisco Opera. 'You are young, Maria,' he said avuncularly. 'Go and make your career in Italy and then I'll sign you up.' 'Thank you,' she replied coldly, with the directness that was to become legendary, 'but once I have made my career in Italy I will no longer need you.'

The post-mortem on all the rejections turned out to be a good deal more painful than the rejections themselves. She found herself looking back in regret and self-reproach. She was to say later that she was her own sternest critic. It was no platitude: she *was*, and to a degree that was draining and at times even self-destructive.

It must have been at the end of the winter of 1946 that Maria finally admitted to herself that despite the defiant 'I'm on my own now, mother', she missed and needed her mother. At least it was then that she wrote to her asking her, almost pleading with her, to come to America. The complex bond of need and resistance that tied her to Evangelia was so strong that she was suddenly overcome by the sense that nothing important could really happen to her unless her mother was there. As Evangelia could not find the money for the journey, Maria tried to get the money from her father, but George, who was in any case earning only a modest salary, did not seem prepared to make the kind of sacrifices that would be needed to bring his far from beloved wife to America. Maria, not easily defeated, went to see her godfather, and asked him to lend her some money for her mother's trip, which he readily did.

So on Christmas Eve, via Marseilles, Paris and London, Evangelia arrived on the *Queen Elizabeth* in New York. Her husband and daughter were there to meet her. Maria was delighted and, even more important, relieved. She had found her father a caring and well-meaning, but at times a very exasperating, companion. He could be maddeningly lethargic, lamentably silent and unable to find much interest in life outside his drugstore and his daughter, and even then the interest was limited. There was, it is true, another side to his character and he could sometimes be supportive, enterprising and high-spirited, but most of the time his provincial narrowness had a dampening effect on Maria's enthusiasm. It made her long for the mother's burning ambition; she had forgotten with distance and time how much she had been scorched by it.

That Christmas of 1946, the first Christmas for nine years that the three of them had been together, was a disastrous beginning. George's extra-marital adventures seemed to have resolved themselves into a steady relationship with Alexandra Papajohn, a homely and unassuming woman a few years younger than himself, who many years later was to become his second wife. As for Evangelia, right from the first night, she slept in Maria's bedroom, thus leaving no one in doubt as to the terms on which she had returned to her 'husband's' home. She came back playing the part of the wronged, self-sacrificing mother who had seen her children through everything while her good-for-nothing husband was idling his life away. It was not a part designed to bring about real family feeling, but at first they all tried to keep up a fiction of intense family affection. After a while none of them could respond, unable to create such feeling when it was clear that there was not an ounce of love between the parents. Maria, having discovered that it was not easy to live in a world that did not contain her mother, was now discovering once again that it was even less easy to live in a world that did.

Her mother had been her closest collaborator and at the same time her most resented adversary. Maria thought that she had missed the first, that she needed to lean on her mother's strength and draw on her faith in her. In fact she had missed the enemy just as much as the collaborator. The enemy made it possible to avoid facing the conflicts and divisions within herself by projecting the cause of all her difficulties on to her mother. She had always blamed her mother for pushing her relentlessly on, so the fact that she was her own worst slave-driver was safely ignored. Yet the sense of guilt she felt whenever she reduced the pressure on herself, even to the extent of spending an hour less vocalizing than she thought she should, was sometimes overwhelming, and guilt would invariably drive her to work twice as hard the next day.

Another thing that she held against her mother was her philistine values and inhibitions, which again made it much easier to avoid confronting the fact that she, too, shared many of these values and inhibitions which, with another part of herself, she thoroughly despised.

Evangelia later declared with pride that during her first forty days in New York Maria, through her mother's efforts of course, was transformed from a fat girl into an elegant, slim young woman – a feat which would have barely been possible even if the forty days had been spent in a total fast. Another thing on which Evangelia prided herself was her success in persuading Maria to start going to church again, a practice which she had given up since her arrival in New York. On many a Sunday morning mother and daughter, dressed in sombre black or blue, would set out for the Church of St Spyridon to pay their respects to a being in whom Evangelia had never really believed and to whom Maria prayed for success with a primitive reluctance to leave untried any possible source of assistance.

Towards the end of 1946 she at last had something specific to pray for. Bagarozy, largely fired by his enthusiasm for Maria, had decided, with the help of an Italian agent, Ottavio Scotto, to launch himself into the most ambitious venture of his life: reviving the Chicago Opera and creating a new company for it, the United States Opera Company, with the specific purpose of bringing some of the best European singers to America. Here Eddie's personality and flair came into their own. He did not have enough money to hire a rehearsal hall but he managed to assemble in New York some of the best talent available in European opera houses, including Max Lorenz, one of the greatest Wagnerian tenors of the day, Hilde and Anny Konetzni from the Vienna Opera, and Tullio Serafin's son-in-law, Nicola Rossi-Lemeni. The curtain-raiser was to be Puccini's *Turandot*, and the conductor, Sergio Failoni, in the absence of a rehearsal hall, had to rehearse the entire company, chorus and all, in the Bagarozys' three-room apartment on Riverside Drive, with Baby, the Bagarozys' dog, providing some interesting accompaniments at unexpected moments.

Eddie Bagarozy had that rare, intangible gift that would have made him a marvellous leader of a mountaineering expedition. In his presence people became at once more adventurous and more determined – more adventurous because there was an audacity in his own nature that immediately communicated itself to others, and more determined because behind the ebullience there was a deep commitment to whatever he undertook and a still deeper commitment to whatever he initiated. While the opera company was rehearsing enthusiastically in New York, the Chicago papers were full of excitement about this great operatic event. Soon the excitement had spread throughout the American musical world. Eddie had managed to get both the *cognoscenti* and the press excited. To the *cognoscenti* he offered *Turandot*, Puccini's last opera, not heard in America for two decades. To the press which loves nothing more than a sensation with a touch of enigma, he had been giving for the previous three months dribs and drabs of information about the 'mystery' Greek soprano who was to be unveiled in the title role. To add a further air of exoticism, she was announced as 'Marie Calas'.

As the rehearsals continued, Bagarozy became more and more convinced that his 'mystery' Greek soprano was to be a sensational overnight discovery. As for Maria, fortified by the scent of success, she fully expected *Turandot* to be a brilliant harvest after the fallow year that was just coming to an end. Suddenly all the resistances and rejections of the last eighteen months were increasing her present sense of exhilaration. *Turandot* had become the stuff of her waking life, more real than anything else. When she was not rehearsing, she was being fitted with her mock-Chinese costumes. And when she was doing neither, she was singing *Turandot* in her head and revolving in her mind the character of the Chinese Princess who puts to death her suitors who fail to pass the test of her three riddles.

Everyone who was present during those rehearsals remembers Maria's Turandot to this day: at the age of twenty-three she had managed to capture both the imperious coldness and cruelty of the oriental princess and the fire and sensuality that are burning underneath. On the surface, Maria's potential for eroticism seemed so faint and tenuous that Louise had argued vigorously against her husband's choice of *Turandot* as the vehicle for revealing Maria to an astonished world. But Eddie, who had from the beginning been fascinated – too fascinated for Louise's liking – by Maria's complex personality, had sensed that the womanliness and the passion were all there underneath the ice of Princess Turandot and the drabness of the awkward twenty-three-year-old Maria.

But the American public was not meant to be astonished – at least not yet. Without warning, the American Chorus-Singers' Union came up with a demand for a deposit, to guarantee payment to the members of the chorus, that Bagarozy simply could not meet. He tried to raise the money. The opening date that had been announced and advertised everywhere for 6 January was postponed for a week, for two weeks, then until 27 January. The enterprise that had started with such an impetuous rush suddenly began to lose momentum. The Union hierarchy were impervious to Bagarozy's charms and the 'angels' began to lose faith. The demoralization spread even faster than the excitement Bagarozy had managed to generate, until he had no option left but to declare bankruptcy both for the enterprise and for himself. The Chicago Opera House organized a benefit concert to raise funds for the artists' return journey and Eddie began selling everything he had – his car, his wife's jewels, his house on Long Island – to pay some of his debts.

Maria was adrift once again. Objectively she was back where she started; psychologically it was much worse. Success, victory, recognition were snatched away from her literally at the last moment. Even her mock-Chinese costumes were taken away from her. But her instinct for survival, her deep, almost mystic, patience, carried her through. Also, being near Eddie made the collapse much easier to take. Sunk beneath demands from creditors, bailiffs, singers and musicians, he could still convince those around him that he was the keeper of some prodigious treasury.

On 6 February 1947 she returned to New York with Nicola Rossi-Lemeni. The first morning back in New York found her at her usual hour at the Bagarozys' apartment going over parts with Louise; the United States Opera Company and Puccini's *Turandot* belonged to the past. Maria was looking ahead to the future, waiting for the lightning to strike. And it did. Giovanni Zenatello, the famous tenor who was now Artistic Director of the Verona Festival, was in New York looking for a soprano for the title role of Ponchielli's *Gioconda.* He was oscillating between Zinka Milanov and Herva Nelli, but Rossi-Lemeni, who had already signed a contract to sing at his Festival the following year, convinced him that he should not make up his mind until he had heard Maria. Maria arrived for her audition at Zenatello's apartment on Central Park West with Louise.

With Louise at the piano she sang the aria 'Suicidio' from *La Gioconda.* She had hardly begun singing when

Zenatello, unable to contain his excitement at what he was hearing, rushed to the piano, turned the pages of the score to the passionate duet between Enzo and Gioconda, and despite his seventy years, he began singing it with Maria with a passion and intensity he had forgotten he possessed. The offer to sing Gioconda at the next Verona Festival was almost an anticlimax after what Zenatello described as 'not so much an audition as a revelation'.

Maria started getting ready for her journey to Verona with the excitement of a young girl preparing for her wedding. Both Evangelia, who worshipped 'the done thing', and Maria, who to a very large extent shared her mother's creed, wanted Maria to arrive in Verona with a complete trousseau of dresses, shoes and handbags, so that she would conquer Europe off-stage as well as on. But the combined funds made available to them by father and godfather only produced two suits and one dress – all in the straitjacketed style that mother and daughter regarded as appropriately restrained elegance and which for many years was the hallmark of Maria's taste. The mini-trousseau ready, Evangelia set herself the task of drawing a list of 'thirteen points' of advice for her daughter, which included the reminder that life was full of disappointments and ended with God's commandment: 'Honour thy father and thy mother.'

All was ready except for one thing: the signing of the contract between Maria Callas and Edward Richard Bagarozy. He was to become Maria's 'sole and exclusive personal agent for a period of ten years', for which 'the said Personal Representative' was to be paid 'the sum equivalent to ten per cent of all gross fees earned by her in Opera, Concerts, Radio, Recordings and Television, said fee becoming due and payable upon receipt of money earned by Artist'. In return for this, Bagarozy agreed 'to use his best efforts to further and promote the Artist's career'. Maria should have been bound to the Bagarozys by sentiment and gratitude, but something in her would not let her sign the contract. Finally on 13 June 1947, the day of her departure, unable to think up a convincing, logical reason why she should not sign it and not prepared on this occasion to follow her famous instinct, she signed –

an action that would later trigger one of the most unpleasant episodes in her life.

As she was kissing Eddie and her mother goodbye on the quay, Maria seemed strangely withdrawn from them. A consciousness of obligation very rarely engenders affection, and Maria was longing, more than anything, for a completely fresh, uncluttered start. On 27 June 1947, the SS *Rossia* dropped anchor in the Bay of Naples, with Maria Callas and Nicola Rossi-Lemeni, two of the main forthcoming attractions at the Verona Arena, on board. Eighteen months later than de Hidalgo would have wished, Maria had arrived in Italy. Geographically it made little sense to go from Greece to Italy via the United States, but many times during her life Maria was to prove that what seemed like diversions turned out to speed her on her way. The longest way round was often the quickest way home.

Chapter Five

THE railway station is not far from the Hotel Accademia but for Maria it could not have been too close. The journey from Naples to Verona had been almost as exhausting as the thirteen days on the *Rossia.* The train was so crowded that Nicola, Maria and Louise Caselotti, who was travelling with them, had to take turns sitting on the one seat they had for the three of them. The heat was stifling, so much so that when she was not sitting down, Maria spent most of the time standing next to an open window, catching the breeze. But a few hours resting at the hotel were more than enough to revive her excitement about *Gioconda,* Verona and the future.

The excitement, however, was mixed with anxiety and fear as Maria was getting into one of her two suits to meet – or rather face – Gaetano Pomari, a representative of the Verona Arena, and Giuseppe Gambato, a representative of the city. They were to collect her from the hotel to take her to dinner; Nicola Rossi-Lemeni and an opera-loving Verona industrialist, Giovanni Battista Meneghini, were going to join them. When they arrived at the Pedavena Restaurant Meneghini was already there, surrounded by a few more city dignitaries. All Maria's insecurities came instantly to the surface, and she spent most of the dinner in silence, by turns dutiful and withdrawn. Yet she was clearly being treated with the respect that was the artist's due, especially as the story of the Director of the Festival, bursting into song with his new Gioconda during her audition in New York, had made the rounds of Verona, growing more dramatic with each re-telling.

Meneghini's interest in the artist was intensified by his fascination with the woman. 'Battista is our local Romeo,' said Signor Pomari to tease him. Verona's current Romeo was a short, wiry man in his early fifties, head of the family building business, an acknowledged bon viveur and a dedicated ladies' man. In provincial Verona, it did not take much to acquire an aura whether of culture or of worldly glamour; but, after war-time Athens and lower-middle class New York, Maria felt and behaved as though she had landed on a dream island of high culture and sophistication. 'I knew he was *it* fives minutes after I first met him,' said Maria some years later, looking back on that first meeting. Perhaps; but what is certain is that she felt warmer, less afraid, more secure and more alive as a result of his presence at the table. Men as lovers had played no role at all in her life, and even her day-dreams were not of handsome princes, but of first nights, singing feats and operatic triumphs. There is nothing to suggest that up until that time any man had inspired her with the slightest erotic excitement, and there is no indication that Battista Meneghini did either.

Yet she liked him. She liked his stability, she liked the way everyone deferred to him and, above all, she liked the way he liked her. She was the exclusive focus of his attention. Whether because of the reports about the mysterious powers of her voice, an intuitive sense of her greatness, or perhaps a bit of both, Meneghini was behaving that night as though he was in the presence of genius – for Maria always a lovable trait. At the same time, unlike many others, he seemed not only aware that the carrier of the genius was a woman, but positively pleased that this was the case. Meneghini had been assigned by the Festival to be the official escort of the visiting primadonna, and before the dinner was over he was determined to see a great deal of her in the course of his 'duties'. And he did – starting the following morning with a day trip to Venice. Maria, who had not been flattered by many men, found herself for the first time consistently and continually flattered by a man who seemed to understand the art of making himself first agreeable and then gradually indispensable to her.

They began exploring Verona and the surrounding countryside. Maria was discovering Italy and at the same time the pleasures of being courted and admired for herself and not just for her voice. And she was enjoying the second discovery even more than the first. In the middle of July she started rehearsing with Tullio Serafin, who had just arrived in the city – and the second gentleman of Verona quickly overshadowed the first. The joys of intimacy took second place to the passion for music, work, success, and the revelation of working with Serafin. 'It was maybe the main lucky thing that happened to me,' said Maria later. 'He taught me that in everything there must be an expression, there must be a justification, he taught me exactly the depth of music . . . I really, really drank all I could from this man.'

Serafin loved Verona and Verona loved Serafin. His bond with the city went back to 1913 when he had conducted the first performance at the Verona Arena. Since then he had become one of the most famous conductors in the world, his engagements taking him from the Rome Opera to the Met and from the Met to La Scala. During these thirty-four years he had worked with the greatest singers of the day and had moulded the career and direction of Rosa Ponselle, who sang her first Norma at the Met in 1925 after eighteen months of working with the maestro. His influence on Maria's musical outlook and direction was to be even greater. De Hidalgo had pointed her towards the bel canto repertory; Serafin led her to it and provided her with all the opportunities to master it on stage. 'As soon as I heard her sing', he said, 'I recognized an exceptional voice. A few notes were still uncertainly placed but I immediately knew that here was a future great singer.' And that knowledge, which was unmistakably communicated to Maria, fortified her, gave her confidence and made the rehearsal period leading up to the opening night less of a torment and more of a delight than any other intensive working period had been.

As the summer progressed, so did her interest in Meneghini. Apart from everything else, he was turning out to be a very serviceable critic. If Serafin was from the beginning her mentor, guide and inspiration, Meneghini was no less sympathetic as a critic; and though astute, he presented no threat to her. Sure of his devotion, she did not have to be on her guard; she could let herself go and accept his, in any case, constructive criticisms without bridling.

Maria could not remember ever having been happier, but not far below the surface, she was, as she wrote to her mother, 'trembling like a leaf' at the prospect of her first night at the huge Arena, singing in front of an audience of 25,000 Italians, each one of whom regarded himself as an operatic expert. During the dress rehearsal, growing anxiety and over-realistic acting led her to fall on the rocky stage of the Arena and sprain an ankle. She spent a painful and anxious night in her hotel room, with Meneghini sitting the whole night at her bedside nursing her back to health and confidence. Ten years later, just before Onassis came into her life and her marriage came to an end, Maria remembered that time with gratitude and the kind of exaggeration that she often used to hide her growing doubts: 'This was just one little episode that revealed my husband's character. I would give my life for him immediately and joyfully. From that moment on I understood that I could never find a more generous man . . . if Battista had wanted, I would have abandoned my career without regret, because in a woman's life love is more important than artistic triumphs.'

That may have been so after the artistic triumphs had been achieved, but on 3 August 1947, as Maria was waiting in the wings to step on stage for her Italian debut, there was no room for anything except the prospect of the artistic triumph ahead. It was not to be. Maria hobbled around with a bandaged leg, self-conscious and suddenly unsure of the enormous stage. The reviewers praised 'the vibrant quality and easy production of her high notes' and 'the timbre of a most moving and individual quality', but this was hardly the praise from which artistic triumphs are made. There was not even the offer of a return visit to Verona. Yet Maria, drawing heavily on Serafin's trust and Meneghini's devotion, sang the remaining five *Giocondas* and then stayed in Verona confidently waiting for the next big opportunity.

Maria, who had said no even when she could not afford it, could now, thanks to Meneghini, be selective without hardship. So the first offer – an invitation to sing *Gioconda* in Vigevano, near Milan – was turned down. The prospect of an interview at La Scala was looming up and Maria trusted the future enough to say no to this run-of-the-mill production in an unimportant town. But the immediate future turned out to be bleaker than Maria and her protector had expected. Mario Labroca, Assistant Director of La Scala, heard Maria sing and muttered something about vocal defects and something else about the possibility of her taking part in La Scala's forthcoming production of *Un Ballo in Maschera*, but a week went by and no more mutterings were heard.

The first week of enforced leisure was largely spent wandering round Verona indulging in an activity the pleasures and agonies of which she was just discovering – shopping. While Maria was discovering shopping, Meneghini was discovering that shopping with his future wife would reduce anyone to blasphemy or tears. She was an undecided and exasperating shopper, and even when someone else was paying she found herself brought to a standstill by the difference between the price she thought something should cost and the invariably higher price it did cost. Later, when she had more money than she could possibly have spent in her lifetime, her greatest joy was to go to Woolworth's or Macy's and devote a whole morning or even a whole day to buying bric-á-brac – a lemon squeezer, a potato peeler, a new kind of coffee grinder. On one occasion in 1962, Maria, lunching at Claridges with Edith Gorlinsky, her agent's wife, spread out the entire loot of her morning's Woolworth's expedition on the table and, pushing the china and crystal to one side, proudly displayed the knick-knacks.

The novelty and pleasure of Verona, shopping and Meneghini's company could not sustain her for more than a week. With Meneghini in tow, she was off to Milan to begin once again the round of agents. For the next two months, and despite Serafin's lobbying on her behalf, it was as if Verona had never happened. Maria was beginning to realize, more fully than ever before, just how extraordinary a musical creature she was. 'Immediately after my debut in Italy,' Maria said later, 'I was not loved that much. . . . No agent would give me a job. . . . I was something new to listen to and they disliked anything that took them away from tradition.' She was described by the Italian critic Teodoro Celli as 'a star wandering into a planetary system not its own'. She would have been much more at home in the nineteenth century than she was in the twentieth. In the century of Pasta and Malibran, the century of unbridled romanticism, the voice became an instrument in the service of emotional drama; and this was the forgotten tradition to which Maria belonged. From the outset she recognized the totality of voice and emotion, the one the perfect dramatic embodiment of the other. She could fan anger into a conflagration, just as she could distil melancholy into an essence that could break one's heart. And, without in any way detracting from the drama, she brought 'finish' back to the music: each phrase, each word, was meticulously weighed; words were used positively as part of the musical sculpture she brought to life; and, although she raised vocal display to new levels of expression for our time, she never allowed it to become just meaningless embroidery. Technique was subordinated to expression and vocal beauty to dramatic truth. 'It is not enough to have a beautiful voice,' Maria explained later. 'What does that mean? When you interpret a role, you have to have a thousand colours to portray happiness, joy, sorrow, fear. How can you do this with only a beautiful voice? Even if you sing harshly sometimes, as I have frequently done, it is a necessity of expression. You have to do it, even if people will not understand. But in the long run they will, because you must persuade them of what you are doing.'

In the end they did understand, although a considerable minority remained unconvinced and bitterly opposed to her. In the autumn of 1947, however, it was those who did not understand who were in charge of the casting, and they clearly could not cope with the 'peculiarities' of the Callas voice. What they were after were beautiful, ravishing voices – Tebaldi voices. Well known as the favourite of Toscanini, Tebaldi had made her debut at La Scala the year before and was visiting Verona surrounded by the aura of that success. The famous rivalry between

Callas and Tebaldi was partly real, partly dreamt up by the press, and largely symbolic of how musically and dramatically irreconcilable these two singers were. The differences between them were reduced by the Tebaldi partisans to 'beautiful' and 'ugly' and by the Callas faithful to 'dull' and 'exciting'. Their orbits first crossed at the Verona Festival. Maria was the mystery visiting soprano; Tebaldi, singing Marguérite in Gounod's *Faust*, was the female star attraction. Although they were obviously aware of each other's existence during the Festival, they did not meet face to face until the following year.

The time when Maria's star would climb higher than Tebaldi's was not far away. Meanwhile however, while Tebaldi was being fêted at one opera house after the other, Maria was sitting in Milan waiting for the telephone to ring and growing more and more depressed. It was Serafin who enabled her to make her next, vital move. An official of La Fenice was despatched from Venice to Milan to sign up Maria for the production of *Tristan und Isolde* that the maestro would be conducting in Venice. It was in fact a package deal: Isolde in December, Turandot in January, and 50,000 lire per performance. Maria signed the contract without reading it, and only after she had signed, did she turn her attention to the fact that she had agreed to sing a part she did not know. She revealed this to Serafin when he arrived in Milan the next day, and fully expected Serafin to be appalled. Instead he was amused. 'One month of study and hard work is all you need,' he assured her. This solid demonstration of his faith in her was enough to wash away the bitter taste of the previous two months.

Suddenly the surrounding world ceased to exist and there was nothing but the role. A triumph was round the corner. It was to be her first triumph outside Athens, and Athens already seemed a lifetime away. The opening night was just before Christmas and her unqualified success made this Christmas – her first in Italy, her first with Meneghini – the happiest of her life. In the New Year, Isolde was followed by Turandot, and the Turandot that she was to have sung in America turned out in Venice to be a marvellous confirmation of the promise Isolde had held out. Her acute sense of what is emotionally right was here enhanced by a no less sure sense of what is dramatically right. That was the majority opinion, but not the unanimous one. Louise Caselotti, who had come to Venice to hear Maria and to look for some work for herself, was, as she put it, 'alarmed' when she heard Maria's Turandot. 'The soaring high notes we admired when we were preparing the part for Chicago had lost their freedom and hovered badly. Her low register was also weak. I knew that she was on the wrong track and told her so.' Even if Madame Caselotti genuinely believed that Maria was on the wrong track, there is little doubt that it was a wrong track she would have given a lot to be on herself.

Maria, despite her public statements to the contrary, would never be indifferent to praise or blame. She resented insincere praise and showed it, but she resented criticism just as much. And criticism from friends was registered as disloyalty, almost betrayal. In many ways she needed betrayal to feed her image of Maria against the world. She was therefore on the look-out for it all the time. Louise Caselotti and her husband were the first casualties. On this occasion, at least, Maria was to some extent right; Louise's frustrated ambitions made it impossible for her to rejoice in Maria's success. But there was also a part of Maria that, as soon as she started getting ready to leave America, wanted a break with the Bagarozys; a break with them would be one more symbolic break with the past, with all its uncertainty, fears and pain. Each new phase in Maria's life was signalled by the breaking of old friendships even more than by the making of new ones. She had almost a bonding instinct towards whoever was dominant in any given period of her life, as if she had time only for her art and one other person, and her other friends would fade into the background. For the moment, Meneghini had replaced everyone else, always by her side through these first uncertain Italian days.

Venice was the watershed. The offers began pouring in. It is true that the musical citadels – La Scala, the Met, Covent Garden – had not yet fallen, but 1948 was a good, even a great year. Maria's itinerary in the course of that year was a complete tour of the great Italian cities: Venice, Udine, Trieste, Genoa, Rome, Turin, Rovigo, Florence. In Trieste Maria sang her first Verdi heroine: Leonora in *Forza del Destino.* Torn between passion and filial love, Leonora gave Maria plenty of opportunities for dramatic expression. And like the great tragedian that she instinctively was, she exploited them all. From Trieste she went to Genoa to sing Isolde once again, this time with her friend Nicola Rossi-Lemeni as King Mark. She sang Isolde five more times in Rome in 1950 and then, as soon as she could choose, she dropped it completely from her repertoire.

After Genoa, Maria spent the whole of June working with Serafin on the creation of one of her greatest roles – Norma. She worked on it with passion right up to the opening night in Florence on 30 November. Serafin and she were becoming inseparable. Not only was he spending all his spare time working with her on Norma but he conducted her in *Turandot* in Rome at the famous Baths of Caracalla and then returned with her to Verona. Her Turandot at the Arena of Verona erased from the minds of the Veronese any qualifications that her Gioconda of the previous summer may have left. But it was *Norma* that was dominating Maria's being, and compared to this absorption the nine *Turandots* and the five *Aidas* that she sang in between were little more than distractions.

Throughout this intense period Meneghini, far from being a distraction, was an inexhaustible source of strength. He was always there to listen to her fears about her work, her worries about her reputation, her complaints about her colleagues; he was there to fortify, protect and encourage her. It was as if Maria was a skinless woman, so nothing was to touch her save his soothing and healing hand. As for Maria, she obviously cared for him, but what that meant was clear neither to herself nor to those around her. Whether it was clear to Meneghini is difficult to say; what seems certain is that, whatever his doubts may have been about the strength of her feelings, he did not behave like someone who felt in any way short-changed in their relationship. There was, however, a chorus of relatives and old family friends, led by Madame Meneghini, who were shouting from the roof-tops that their 'boy' was not only being short-changed but used, abused and cruelly exploited by this wily 'woman of the stage', as Mamma Meneghini insisted on calling Maria.

In July 1948, back in Verona to sing Turandot, Maria found that the Meneghini family's objections to her had penetrated Veronese 'high society'. And there are few things that match the hard, calculating snobbery of provincial high society. Maria found the atmosphere oppresive and even painful. A rising operatic star, praised and admired by everyone, would be expected to find the spectacle of an elderly, strait-laced lady clinging onto her middle-aged son amusing, sad, pathetic – anything but painful. Yet Maria found it impossible to remain detached. The woman who was a revolutionary in her art longed for the conventional in her private life. And the Meneghini family was refusing to accept her into their world. 'They said', she remembered with bitterness years later, 'that I had only come to Verona to marry a rich man.'

In fact Meneghini, despite his family's opposition, would have married her at any time during the year they had known each other. His life was becoming increasingly absorbed in hers, and on the strength of the previous year, simply in terms of hours devoted to her work, he was no longer a manufacturer of bricks but Maria Callas's personal manager. Yet Maria was hesitating. 'I have met a man who is madly in love with me,' she wrote to her mother, soon after she had met Meneghini. 'He wants to marry me. I don't know what to tell him. He is fifty-three; what do you think? He's very rich and he loves me.' Evangelia was far from enthusiastic at the prospect of Maria marrying a man thirty years older than herself and she said so in no uncertain terms. But her mother's opinion in the matter was, in truth, of very little concern to Maria. She no longer felt that her mother's approval of her decisions was essential to her happiness. She went on informing her of what was happening in short letters with long periods of silence in between, but both the letter-writing and the soliciting of her opinion were becoming increasingly mechanical activities. She wrote to her godfather who wrote back telling her to follow instinct, not arithmetic. He, after all, had married a girl little more than half his age and they were blissfully happy together.

Maria's indecision about saying yes to Meneghini was just one instance of her contradictory impulse to drive people away, while suffering panic whenever anyone threatened to desert her. Still, Meneghini was in no great hurry, and Norma and the even more imminent Aida left no spare energy for personal dilemmas. Aida, first in Turin and then in Rovigo, though far too static to be a natural part for Maria, was received warmly and praised lavishly. Renata Tebaldi, whom Maria had briefly met when she was singing Isolde in Venice, was in the audience in Rovigo; at the end of the performance, Tebaldi's loud and distinct 'Brava!' stood out from the cheers of the audience. And it was Tebaldi's salute that gave Maria her greatest joy and satisfaction.

That was on 19 October 1948; and now, with a great sigh of relief, she could look forward to a stretch of forty clear days until 30 November, Florence and her first Norma – the role of the Druid priestess which more than any other became closely associated with her name. November 1948 was spent entirely on Norma. Even Meneghini, who was by now used to her, could not help observing that there was something almost fierce about her absorption in the Druid priestess.

Maria sang Norma ninety times in eight countries – more often than any other part in her repertoire of forty-seven roles. 'Maybe Norma is something like my own character,' she said in 1961, when she was totally absorbed, no longer by Norma and singing, but by Onassis. 'The grumbling woman who is too proud to show her real feelings and proves at the end exactly what she is. She is a woman who cannot be nasty or unjust in a situation for which she herself is fundamentally to blame. With Norma I work as if I had never sung it before. It is the most difficult role in my repertoire; the more you do it the less you want to.' But in 1948, Maria did not simply want, she *longed* to do Norma. It is hard to describe the intensity of feeling that was pressed into these forty days.

'It will never be as good as it is now in my mind unsung,' she said one morning to Serafin, as they were about to start rehearsing. And it is true that very rarely – and more often at rehearsals than at performances – did she have the satisfaction of achieving in reality what she had created in her mind.

Bellini knew that Italians went to the opera house for the song and the singer, and for little else, but in *Norma*, the greatest of his operas, he gave them much more than the simple pleasures of luxurious sounds and sustained high notes. Each aria contributes to the development of the action, and the way the arias blend with the recitatives contributes to the unique power of *Norma* among Bellini's operas. Maria spent a large part of the forty days working on the recitatives. 'Find the rhythm and proportion,' Serafin told her, 'by singing them over to yourself as if you are talking.' Maria had an uncanny architectural sense which told her just which word in a musical sentence to emphasize and just what syllable within that word to bring out. 'It is a deep mystery,' said Nicola Rescigno, who was for a time Maria's favourite conductor, 'why a girl from the Bronx, born into a non-musical family and raised in an atmosphere devoid of operatic tradition, should have been blessed with the ability to sing the perfect recitative.'

The technical demands of Norma went far beyond the recitative. They included complete mastery of trills, scales and all the bel canto ornamentation; great breath control to sustain Bellini's long, aching melodies; and the kind of stamina that would make it possible to remain on stage for three quarters of the opera, with flights of lyricism one moment followed by dramatic outbursts the next. Maria was determined to meet all these demands. And she did – at first with relative ease then gradually with more effort and pain, until, at her penultimate performance as Norma at the Paris Opera in 1965, she was too exhausted even to change into her last-act costume: the red-and-gold cloak for the final act had to be put on over the costume she was already wearing.

Yet in 1948, as Maria was preparing to sing the role, she knew that her technical command, despite the endless hours she had devoted to it, was only the foundation on which her Norma was to be built. Step by step, she has described how she created each new role: 'You read a role and in the beginning you're enthused, you're exalted... then you take the music and you learn it as though you were in the conservatoire. In other words, exactly as it's written, nothing more and nothing less, which is what I call strait-jacketing. Having broken this down completely, then you can take wings...' Norma, far beyond being a great technical challenge for her, was a supreme challenge of heart and mind. Wagner described it as 'all heart, closely, intimately linked to the words'. Mother, warrior, lover, leader, Norma is a Druid priestess who against her holy oath gives way to her passion for a Roman pro-consul, Pollione, has two children by him, and in the process of discovering his betrayal and love for Adalgisa, a virgin of the Temple, experiences and gives expression to the full range of human emotions – rage, hatred, jealousy, fear, despair, tenderness and finally a self-sacrificial exultation that leads her to offer herself as victim on the pyre in Adalgisa's place. 'She seems very strong, very ferocious at times. Actually she is not, even though she roars like a lion,' said Maria comparing Norma yet again to herself.

At the Teatro Comunale in Florence on 30 November 1948, there were no such character comparisons. The comparisons were instead with Ponselle and with Pasta and the effect was, as Stendhal wrote of Pasta, 'an instantaneous hypnotic effect upon the soul of the spectator'. It was a performance that brought out all the lyricism in Bellini's music, and made it possible to understand why his contemporaries compared him to Chopin. Maria was elated by the response of the audience and the critics, but for her, the achievement had been far short of her ideal: 'I can't wait to sing Norma again,' she told Meneghini at the end of her second and last performance in Florence. The next day Maria left for Venice, and Titta – the name to which Giovanni Battista Meneghini now answered – for Verona.

Once in Venice, exhausted but too excited to notice, she threw herself into her second Wagnerian role:

Brünnhilde. *Walküre,* with Maria Callas as Brünnhilde, and Bellini's *I Puritani*, with Margherita Carosio, one of Italy's leading sopranos, as Elvira, were the two major new productions of the 1948/9 Venice season, and Serafin was conducting both. Maria spent most of the time, when they were not formally rehearsing, working either by herself or with Serafin at the maestro's suite at the Hotel Regina. One evening, tired of practising the Ho-jo-to-hos of Brünnhilde, she started sight-reading and playing about with the music of Elvira. Serafin's wife came back from talking on the telephone in the next room and stood motionless in the doorway listening to Maria sight-read one of Elvira's arias. The phone call had been from a desperate Serafin who exactly ten days before the opening night of *I Puritani* had lost his Elvira. Margherita Carosio had succumbed to a particularly nasty form of influenza that had spread through Venice, and she had had to cancel all her performances. So far the arduous search for an alternative had proved entirely fruitless. With her husband's anxious voice still ringing in her ears, Madame Serafin could hardly believe it when she walked into the living room to hear Maria singing Elvira. She said nothing except: 'Tullio is on his way here. Will you do me a favour? When he comes in will you please sing that for him?' When Serafin arrived, Maria did precisely that. He made no response. After all, the next day, 8 January, was Maria's opening night as Brünnhilde.

The following morning at ten, Maria was still in bed when she was called on the telephone: 'Please put on your robe and come down,' demanded the maestro.

'I haven't even washed yet', protested Maria. 'It will take me about half an hour.'

'No, no, no, come down as you are.' And of course she went. At that time she could deny Serafin nothing.

'Sing,' he said.

'What?'

'Sing what you sang to me yesterday.'

There was another man there, whom Maria, the sleep not entirely gone from her eyes, recognized as the Musical Director of the Opera House. Maria leafed through the score and, as instructed, sight-read the aria. Then she stood there perplexed and slightly embarrassed, watching the two men whispering to each other. Finally Serafin acknowledged her presence.

'Well, Maria,' he said. 'You are going to do this role in a week.'

'I'm going to do *what* in a week?' she exclaimed, unable to believe what she was hearing.

'You are going to sing *Puritani* in a week. I undertake that you will have time to study.'

'I can't,' she said. 'I have three more *Walküres*. I can't do it. It's ridiculous. . . . I really can't.'

'I guarantee that you can,' were Serafin's last words on the subject, uttered with the full authority of experience and reputation.

Maria was instantly convinced: 'Maestro, my best I *can* do. More than my best I cannot promise.' She remembered years later that inside herself she was thinking: 'Well, if they are crazy enough to think I can do it. . . . I am still young, and when you are growing you have to gamble.'

She did gamble. The aria she sang was all she knew of the part, and even this she had only sight-read. She did not even know the opera's plot, and it would be hard to find two parts in opera more different than Elvira and Brünnhilde. She sang the mighty, dramatic declamations of Brünnhilde on Wednesday and Friday and spent all the time in between on Elvira's trills, runs and roulades. Sunday morning was the dress rehearsal of *I Puritani*, Sunday evening was the final performance of *Walküre*. Maria sang one of the highest coloratura parts and a couple of hours later she was singing, admittedly not in the original German but in Italian, one of the most formidable dramatic roles in all opera.

Two days later, on 19 January 1949, at the opening night of *I Puritani*, the unbelievers had no option but to believe. It is true that Maria had memorized the music but not quite all the words, yet nobody seemed to mind or even to notice that the prompter kept feeding her lines. When the time came to sing the aria *'Son vergin vezzosa'* (I am a charming virgin), she misheard him and sang instead *'Son vergin viziosa'* (I am a vicious virgin). But to complain about this and a few other small mishaps would have been like complaining that there was not enough salt and lemon to go with the loaves and fishes for the five thousand. Maria's achievement was indeed seen as a miracle – a miracle that everybody except Serafin had ruled out as impossible until it happened. 'What she did in Venice,' Zeffirelli said after her death, 'was really incredible. You need to be familiar with opera to realize the size of her achievement that night. It was as if someone asked Birgit Nilsson, who is famous for her great Wagnerian voice, to substitute overnight for Beverly Sills, who is one of the top coloratura sopranos of our time.'

Maria became the talk of Italy, her feat described in hushed tones as unique and unprecedented. In fact, three quarters of a century earlier, the great Lilli Lehmann had performed a similar feat, but this had either been forgotten or relegated to history where it could not detract from the sensation caused by Maria's triumph. The gamble had not merely succeeded: it marked the turning-point in Maria's career. A singer among singers was being transformed into the singer of the century. From now on the only thing that would break the monotony of Maria's rise to fame would be the difference between the lesser and greater triumphs and the larger and smaller scandals with which her career and her life were increasingly punctuated. The ecstatic notices were for Maria much more valuable than mere praise; they were the certificate of acceptance for which she longed.

There was, however, no vein of complacency in her and no resting on yesterday's laurels. A couple of days after her last Elvira in Venice, she was once again donning Brünnhilde's armour – this time in Palermo. A week later she was in Naples wearing the icy mask of Turandot. She sang four *Turandots,* and then immediately left for Rome where on 26 February she sang her third and last Wagnerian role: Kundry in *Parsifal.* Kundry was not a major part in Callas's repertoire. In fact on 25 November 1950 Maria was to sing her for the last time in a radio broadcast, again in Rome. That performance was recorded, and we can feel from the recording the special drama that Maria brought even to a role that never really became her own. Both Kundry the seductress and Kundry the woebegone come alive as they did on that first night in Rome. Zeffirelli, who was in Rome designing *As You Like It*, remembers going to the wardrobe where his costumes were being made the day after the *Parsifal* dress rehearsal: 'There was no way to get a seamstress to think about my work. They were all fully occupied, around masses of chiffon of all colours, and they were all talking about this phenomenal new singer they had heard the night before. I took a sudden hatred for this woman, depriving me of a day's work, but, nevertheless, that night I went to hear her sing Kundry . . . like thousands of other people, I was immediately taken by the extraordinary quality of this warm personality and the sound of that voice. I remember my ears were absolutely buzzing – the power of this woman and the presence. . . . There was something unique happening.'

Spring arrived and with it a contract from the Teatro Colón in Buenos Aires, but that was not until May. In the meantime, Italy, fascinated by the reports of Maria's feat in Venice, longed to hear her display of virtuosity and versatility. So Radio Italiana invited her to sing a programme of Verdi, Wagner and Bellini arias. That was in Turin on 7 March. A few months later, in November 1949, Maria made her first commercial recording, a selection of Wagner and Bellini arias, that Cetra put out on three twelve-inch records.

She had a month to prepare herself for her South American trip, and the realization that for the first time in two years she was to put a few thousand miles between herself and Battista forced her to focus on the subject of their marriage. She decided to leave Italy for Argentina as Maria Meneghini Callas. Meneghini was granted a dispensation from the Church to marry outside the Catholic faith, and Maria, elated and excited, looked forward to marriage and to future triumphs with Titta at her side. On 21 April 1949, in the Chiesa dei Filippini in Verona, Titta and Maria became husband and wife. It was a very simple, almost sparse, wedding with no one there to represent either the Meneghini or the Callas families: just the priest, the sacristan and two of Meneghini's friends for witnesses.

Immediately afterwards they left for Genoa. It was an apt symbol of the nature of the Meneghini marriage that the day after her wedding, Maria Meneghini Callas was boarding the SS *Argentina* alone. Her honeymoon was spent with *Turandot, Norma* and *Aida,* the three operas she was to perform in Buenos Aires.

Just before she left Genoa, she had sent a telegram to New York: *'Siamo sposati e felici.'* This was how Maria had chosen to announce her marriage to her parents – after the event and in Italian. It was not exactly difficult to translate the message but, as Evangelia was to complain later, what was wrong with 'We are married and happy' or the Greek equivalent? 'After all', she said, 'Maria did not stop being Greek when she married Meneghini, nor did she forget her English.' But Maria loved symbolic gestures and this period – the Italian period – of her life was studded with actual and symbolic breaks with her past.

Evangelia said nothing about her feelings to her daughter. Instead she sent white bridal flowers and a letter: 'Remember, Maria, you first belong to your public, not to your husband.' Maria replied that both she and her husband were perfectly aware of that. The idea that Maria first belonged to herself had never entered her mother's or her husband's head; and at that time it would have seemed totally alien to Maria too. It was ten years later that she got a glimpse of what she had left out of her life, and cried out: 'I want to live.'

Chapter Six

ON 20 May, Maria opened at the Teatro Colón in Buenos Aires with *Turandot,* and one of the most highly prized items for collectors of Callas tapes is a three-minute fragment from this performance, with Maria soaring effortlessly over the heavy orchestration. 'In the role of Turandot', wrote the music critic of *La Nacion,* 'Maria Callas showed all her vocal gifts as well as her magnetic presence.'

Already, in 1949, Maria began shedding operas from her repertoire. After Buenos Aires, she never sang Turandot on stage again. She had already appeared in the part twenty-four times in seven cities. 'I sang Turandot all over Italy', she explained once, 'hoping to God that I wouldn't wreck my voice, because you know . . . it's ruined quite a few voices.'

Serafin, who conducted all Maria's performances in Buenos Aires, also conducted her farewell concert on 9 July – on the 133rd anniversary of the Argentine Declaration of Independence. Despite his presence by her side, Maria was feeling very lonely; she was irritable most of the time and could not wait to get home. She was in constant touch with Battista. He wrote and sent telegrams; she telephoned – after all, the Argentinians were paying. Meneghini wanted to know everything. He had asked the management to send him every review, and in his letters he pulled all unflattering comments to pieces. For although her Norma was unanimously praised, there were plenty of unflattering remarks about her Turandot and her Aida. Each unflattering remark increased Maria's longing to be back in her first real home. Meneghini, like a devoted Italian housewife, had been furnishing and decorating the penthouse he had bought for them. Zeffirelli, who later visited Maria in her home, described its style as 'poor man's Zsa Zsa Gabor': everything gilded, imitation rococo curtains, three different kinds of flowered wallpaper and a pink marble bathroom fitted with golden crystal, golden mirrors and shocking pink curtains.

This was Maria's new environment, and she loved it. She slipped into the role of Signora Meneghini as though all her life had been a preparation for it; she picked up the Veronese accent immediately, and when they were at home she spent hours in the kitchen cooking pasta for Battista. Their home overlooked the Arena of Verona, and from its balcony Maria would watch the Arena at all hours. She watched reheasals, she watched performances; she watched the sun rising and the moon hovering over the deserted amphitheatre. She had travelled a long way since her Gioconda at the Arena only two years before, but pleasant though it was to let her mind wander over what had been achieved, Maria's focus was on the distance still to be travelled. On 18 September, in the church of San Pietro in Perugia, Maria tackled her first oratorio; she sang Herod's daughter in *San Giovanni Battista,* a little-known work by Alessandro Stradella. The music bored her, and she was relieved when the night had come and gone. 'I need never sing an oratorio again,' she told her Titta, before she threw herself into her third Verdi role.

Nabucco at the Teatro San Carlo in Naples was the last main project of 1949. Gino Bechi was singing Nabucco, and Maria was determined to steal the opening night's honours from him. Bechi was Italy's most popular baritone and he was, after all, singing the title role; but Maria did not intend to waste the opportunity of opening her 1949/50 season at the San Carlo by being no more than the first among the supporting cast. Nor did she; that first performance has been preserved in a small archive of primitive recordings – the earliest recording of a complete role sung by Maria – and there is no doubt that on that December night in Naples, she immersed herself totally in her fiery, fearless Abigaille.

'The thunderbolt of my revenge is already suspended

over you,' sings – or rather shouts – Abigaille, the warrior-daughter of the Babylonian ruler, determined to destroy her unfaithful lover and reign over Babylon. Maria sustained the ferocious intensity throughout, unleashing with every word all the fury that Verdi intended, and more besides. Her rousing fierceness was particularly appropriate for the occasion. On the first night the audience at the San Carlo, with the war still in their minds, responded to the stirring chorus 'Va, pensiero' with much of the same intensity and abandon that its patriotic overtones had stirred in the original audience in 1842 and for that matter in the vast throng that sang it at Verdi's funeral. Those who had previously only heard Maria sing arias out of context sat up sharply: Callas on the operatic stage was a different Callas, thriving on the dramatic life she quickened in the other characters as well as in herself.

The New Year began with *Norma* in Venice. Throughout 1950, Maria's fame was growing with every appearance, but while she was travelling from Venice to Brescia and Aida, from Brescia to Rome and Isolde, and from Rome to Catania and Norma, her eyes were fixed on Milan. There had still been no sign and no word, or even whisper, from La Scala. Suddenly, the silence was dramatically broken. Maria was asked to take over the part of Aida which the ailing Tebaldi had had to renounce. So her debut at La Scala was to be as a replacement. Aida was by no means Maria's favourite role, and she would much rather have made her debut at La Scala in a production created for her, but at last, however unsatisfactory the circumstances, there was to be a debut. The first performance of *Aida* was to be on 12 April. The Meneghinis arrived in Milan at the end of March, and Maria had to face her first covey of reporters.

'How are you feeling, Madame Callas, now you are about to sing at La Scala? Are you excited?'

'La Scala, magnificent theatre. . . . Yes, I am thrilled, of course I am thrilled. Great theatre. But I am near-sighted, you see. For me all theatres are alike. Am I excited? La Scala is La Scala, but I am near-sighted: *ecco tutto.*'

The message was quite clear. La Scala had obtained her

services as a replacement but if they were looking for gratitude or reverence, they had better look elsewhere. There was something almost pinched in all of Maria's answers that day. It was clear that she resented being a substitute. It did not come naturally to her, nor did it bring out the best in her. Battista tried in vain to make helpful interjections.

'What about the public, Madame Callas?'

'The public? What about the public? If I sing well they applaud, if they don't like me they whistle. It's the same everywhere.'

'What about your voice, Madame Callas? They say your voice is uneven.'

'Well let them say what they want. I sing the way I sing.'

'And life, what about your life?'

'My life! What a life – moving in and out of hotels, living out of trunks. . . . Some envy me for my trips around the world. Some trips – from one stage to another. . . .'

So the image of the new Aida with which the first-night audience at La Scala had been fed through the press was hardly that of a positive, endearing human being. This time it was not the fault of the reporters either. With her consciously indifferent public responses Maria may have fooled the press, La Scala's management and the readers, but she could not fool herself. She was suffering from her usual first-night nerves – only multiplied a hundredfold. After all, this was La Scala and the audience for the *prima* of *Aida* was unlike any other she had faced before. It was studded with ministers, foreign dignitaries and the bejewelled wives of the Italian Establishment; and in the presidential box was the President of the Republic himself.

Maria longed for a triumph; she expected at least a sensation. Meneghini expected a definite offer for Maria's permanent engagement at La Scala. What they got instead was a polite reception, lukewarm reviews and a Delphic remoteness from Antonio Ghiringhelli, the notoriously aloof manager of La Scala. Ghiringhelli took an instant dislike to Maria. He sensed right from the start that here was an artist he could neither control nor easily.

categorize; and the power she exuded unnerved him. He was much happier in the company of the chorus and the corps de ballet in whose ranks he found the partners for his unending casual affairs. Among the easily overwhelmed chorus girls and ballerinas, it was much easier to maintain his cherished detachment. 'Going to bed with me', was his standard line, 'gives you no hope for a better part. Understand that? *No hope.* But if you don't go to bed with me, you have the *certainty* of no better part.'

This was the man on whom Maria's career depended for the moment, and he seemed determined to thwart it. So Maria sang the remaining two *Aidas* for which she had been contracted and left for Naples. She knew she would be back, and next time on her own terms. Ghiringhelli could delay her conquest of La Scala but he could not prevent it. She sang four more *Aidas* in Naples and as soon as the last one was over she returned to Verona. There were only ten days left before she had to cross the Atlantic for her first Mexican visit. Meneghini, who was, however nominally, head of the family business, stayed behind.

On 13 May 1950, Maria arrived in New York for the second time in her life. Her father was once again there to meet her. From the airport they went straight to the hospital where Evangelia was being treated for an eye infection. Maria had stopped in New York on her way to Mexico to see her parents and her godfather and, more specifically, to show her new, famous, rich self to her mother. This objective could not be accomplished in a few hours between planes and still less in the confines of a hospital. So Maria invited her mother to join her in Mexico as soon as she was well enough. With her round-trip ticket in her pocket, Evangelia was out of hospital faster than any doctor had dared predict. She arrived in Mexico at the beginning of June. She was met at the airport by Maria and a couple of dignitaries from the Opera House; she was ushered into her room at the Hotel Prince – connected with Maria's – by the manager, who had already ensured that the room was full of flowers; and she was instantly showered with invitations to dinners, embassy parties, Government receptions. She was the Queen Mother, and it was clear that everybody adored the

Queen. It was equally clear that Evangelia, although she had had no practice in this role, took to it with the greatest of ease. This was mostly because of her personality, but it must have been made easier by the fact that she had been reheasing the role in her mind ever since Maria held a street audience spellbound with 'La Paloma' back in 1933.

Norma, Aida, Tosca and Leonora in *Il Trovatore* (a new addition to Maria's repertoire) were all widely acclaimed by critics who competed with one another in their use of superlatives and by a public who again and again became almost hysterical in their enthusiasm. As all four performances were recorded, we can actually experience the enthusiasm for ourselves instead of just sensing it through the reports. As John Ardoin observed, 'Callas was born with an instinct to enjoy the upper hand in a dramatic situation.' And at the Palacio de Belles Artes on 2 May, she reached the heights of her performance in *Norma* at the moment of triumph over her faithless lover – when she knows and he knows that she holds not only his fate but the fate of their children in her grasp: *'Si, sorr'essi alzai la punta'* – 'Yes, I raised the dagger over them.'

Kurt Baum was Pollione, and the tension between Maria and him was electric. In *Norma* it remained off-stage, but in *Aida,* where he was singing Radames, it came down to the footlights. Throughout the first act of *Aida* on the first night, Baum kept holding on to the high notes in a manner which infuriated Maria and positively enraged Nicola Moscona, who was singing Ramfis and who took Baum's vocal fencing as a personal affront. Once upon a time in New York Moscona had refused all Maria's pleas for help and Maria had sworn never to speak to him again. Now, at the first interval of *Aida,* Maria and Moscona joined forces in her dressing-room and worked out their plan of retaliation. Instead of Verdi's ending for Aida in the 'Triumphal Scene', Maria would soar upwards an octave and sustain a full-voiced E flat *in alt* virtually all the way through the end of the orchestral finale. The two strategists, like all good strategists throughout history, ensured the co-operation of the two main neutral powers, Amneris and Amonasro, by consulting them in advance. Giulietta Simionato and Robert Weede gave their full consent to the interpolation of the lethal E flat. The jolt that Baum got when he heard the E flat go on and on and on was not exactly lethal, but it led to a full-scale declaration that he would *never* sing with Callas again. As for the audience, they loved it. It had, of course, nothing to do with high art and little to do with great singing, but it had all the excitement of watching someone let go of the trapeze. And opera audiences love a good circus act at least as much as circus audiences do.

The third act had plenty of fresh circus elements in it: Baum over-held just about every note he could over-hold; he forgot to ask *'Chi ci ascolta?'* ('Who hears us?'), so that Aida's father had rather anticlimatically to volunteer the critical information; and after Amneris's re-entry, following Patti's principle that a singer has only a limited number of high notes and when one has been sung it is lost for ever, he simply decided not to sing his lines, thus preserving every ounce of voice for his final dramatic outburst.

'When one is a young performer', Maria once said, 'one is more of an athlete than an artist.' And in Mexico, the artist gave way to the athlete in her, the musician to the show-woman. *Aida* was followed by *Tosca,* and even without Kurt Baum to prompt garish over-singing, something in the Mexican air or the Mexican audiences elicited from Maria the crudest and most vulgarly over-sung performance she ever gave. Maria's Tosca was later to transcend all the limitations of the role and the opera, but that June night in Mexico, it confirmed everything that *Tosca* detractors, including Maria herself, had ever said about the work. The cast of *Aida,* with Kurt Baum and Maria setting the tone, clearly did not take Patti's advice about using up the future. Whatever the artistic merits, the audiences were ecstatic, and Evangelia was bursting with pride.

The public side of Evangelia's stay in Mexico was in all respects a dream come true. Her daughter had reached the pinnacle she had dreamt of, she was there to share the triumphs with her, and everyone was ready to give to the mother her full share of the glory. But that was merely a stage set façade, the public posturing disguising a private nightmare that both mother and daughter were doing their best to ignore. There was no real relationship between them. As Evangelia put it later: 'Maria was formally, sometimes ostentatiously kind, as she might be to a distant relative, a cousin perhaps whom she had known for years and was fond of only at arm's length.' It was as if Maria had put on the whole show to demonstrate that yes, the mother had achieved all her dreams, but no, she had no special claim on the daughter. Evangelia's only source of intimacy with Maria was washing her underwear, black with the dye of Aida's make-up, and rubbing her with alcohol when she got back to the hotel and collapsed into bed after some of the more exhausting performances.

Except for one night. It had been the first night of *Aida* and Maria had already been in bed, with the lights off, for an hour when Evangelia, unable to sleep, heard her sobbing. She went up to her. 'Are you worried that it wasn't a huge success? It was. You know it was,' she whispered to her.

'I don't care about Aida,' sobbed Maria even more loudly than before.

'Then what is it? What is it?'

'I want children . . . I want twins . . . I want many children round me . . . And I want you to bring them up . . .'

She went on sobbing in her mother's arms, until she fell into a deep, deep sleep. In the morning she had to make herself believe it had never happened. When Maria walked to the table where her mother and Simionato were having a late breakfast, her mother leaned towards her to give her a good-morning kiss. Maria pushed her aside: 'Don't, mother, I'm no longer a child!' she exploded. What she dismissed as childish was that tender, vulnerable past that would in fact always be with her; but she shrank in horror from any intimation of what lay beneath the carapace of dedicated professionalism and an efficient marriage. And the price she had to pay for giving way to it the night before was the necessity of suppressing it even more rigorously the morning after.

Such behaviour was not easily accounted for. It certainly outraged Simionato. 'If *I* were your mother,

Maria,' she said, 'I'd give you a good slap.' No doubt Evangelia longed to do just that, but she did not. Later on she was to give Maria quite a few metaphorical slaps, and to say quite a few bitter things, giving vent to her mounting frustrations. For the time being Evangelia and Maria were far too busy being fêted everywhere, and the frustrations were simply allowed to accumulate. Maria even spent a whole morning between *Tosca* and *Trovatore* choosing a fur coat for her mother for the final 'appearance' on the Mexican social scene and for the cold New York winter ahead of her. It turned out to be a parting-for-ever gift, and perhaps it was because at some level Maria already knew as much that she spent so much energy and time choosing the coat and so much money buying it.

The first night of *Trovatore* was on 20 June 1950. It was the first new major role Maria had prepared on her own. Before she left Italy, she had asked Serafin for advice, but he had refused to help her prepare a performance that was to be conducted by someone else. So Maria threw herself into the role on her own, and the performance was the most passionate and full-blooded Loenora she ever sang. A few months later, when she sang it again in Naples, this time under Serafin, her portrayal had become much more lyrical and much less full-blooded. Kurt Baum, who had already forgotten his vow that he would never sing with her again, was Manrico. His presence gave rise once again to some crude but electrifying competitive singing. During the celebrated trio in the first act (with Leonard Warren as the Count di Luna), Maria and Kurt Baum sailed to an unwritten D-flat, each determined to out-sustain the other, and neither prepared to release the note first; it was Baum who was the loser. Leonard Warren only sang one more performance of *Trovatore* and then had to leave Mexico, suffering from the high altitude – and no doubt also from the antics of his two colleagues. For the third and last *Trovatore* Ivan Petroff took the place of Warren, Maria and Kurt Baum outdid themselves in vehemence and overpowering declamations, and the added D-flat was held not for seven measures, as in the previous two performances, but for nine.

This was Maria's last appearance in Mexico for the 1950 season. The following morning she left for Madrid and Meneghini. Her mother was at the airport to say goodbye. In the car on the way to the airport, Maria gave her mother the $700 that her godfather had lent her, and money for her hospital bills. Evangelia was going to stay in Mexico for a few more days, 'catching her breath', as she put it. She was not over-eager to return to New York and a marriage that only seemed emptier as time went on. She spent her last three days in Mexico surrounded by the flowers the hotel manager went on sending up every day, but sunk deep in a sea of foreboding. She never saw her daughter again.

Maria, in Madrid with Titta by her side, felt relieved that Mexico and her mother were behind her. She was exhausted, but in the full pride of this glittering year and, looking ahead from sunny Madrid, all things seemed possible – even an Italian sequel to her Mexican popular triumph. Three months of rest in her new house in Verona lay ahead of her. In a letter to her godfather at the time, she summed up how she felt both about life and her closeness to him:

> Dear Leo, it's true that our lives are very similar. You are married to a younger woman, I to an older man – both happily married. We both have become famous, you a doctor, I a singer – both worked hard and really earned their happiness and success. Am I right?

Maria had earned her happiness and success, but not the ability to relax and recharge herself. Only when she had severe headaches, some of them too painful for her to do anything but rest, would she stay in bed, and even then there would always be a score next to her. Occasionally she might be persuaded by Titta to stay in bed for a little while after the pain itself ceased to issue commands but in general doing nothing was extremely hard for Maria. Even the three weeks of rest were crowded with shopping, adding more gilded swans to her bedroom, or more golden mirrors to the bathroom, and having dinner or drinks with members of the Veronese establishment.

The growth of her reputation could be measured in social terms: invitations were becoming more numerous and more persistent. The first stage of Maria's transformation had been completed, and fashionable Italian hostesses – extremely sensitive barometers of success – began issuing their invitations as if to let Maria know that she was ready to 'go out into the world'. Yet Maria felt unready. She was still awkward at social gatherings and she was so preoccupied with how she looked and how she was dressed that she felt quite drained afterwards. Stepping outside their provincial, tightly knit Veronese circle seemed even more threatening. But fashionable hostesses were very persuasive, and Maria half wanted to be persuaded. After all, social success was an important element of the dream-image she had built for herself, even though ideally she would have liked the social success without all the hard work that other people called 'having a good time'.

'You learn according to the rules and then you forget them,' Maria had said about her singing, repeating Serafin's advice. On stage she put this into practice more brilliantly than any singer in this century, but in life she was never confident enough, never sufficiently at ease, to forget the rules and the form and just be. So her life became yet another performance – one in which she was least assured and least happy. Three months' socializing, on top of practising and worrying about the performances coming up, began to tell on Maria's nerves. She became intensely irritable, annoyed by trifles, exaggerating their importance and unable to shake off her excessive concern with them; and when she was not irritable she would sulk. Sulks were for Maria a rarely used weapon, but they were a weapon that occasionally took complete control of her.

Meneghini so totally identified with his wife's moods that he ended up prolonging and intensifying them. If she made a point against someone or about something which she half knew was unjustifiable and which she fully expected to have contradicted, he took it so seriously that she began to think there must, after all, be something in it. If she railed against someone in a momentary outburst Meneghini's support turned a passing irritation into a real, solid grievance. The more hostile the world, the more convincing was his role of Husband-Protector; and he was very good at painting dragon-like pictures of 'the enemy', so that he would always be there, ready to provide the fortifications to keep the enemy out. During these three months in Verona the two of them spent more time alone together than they had spent in a long while. It is true that Maria's affections were equally divided between her Titta and her piano, but still they were together, and Meneghini found Chopin and Rachmaninoff no more threatening than Verdi and Bellini.

In the meantime Maria had begun working at home on her first role in comic opera – Fiorilla in Rossini's *Il Turco in Italia.* As the young wife of Don Geronio she was busy wandering round her home extolling the joys of infidelity and flirting with the visiting Sultan. For Maria, who had so far brought to life only woebegone operatic creatures, *Il Turco* was a real challenge. 'It particularly appealed to me,' she explained six years later in an article she wrote for *Oggi,* 'because it allowed me to stray from the subject – by this time frequent – of great tragedies in music, and to breathe the fresh air of a very funny Neapolitan adventure.'

She had been offered the part by Maestro Luccia but there was another man who had chosen her and who was the prime mover of the whole enterprise. This man, Luchino Visconti, was to become, after de Hidalgo and Serafin, the third great influence in the making of Maria Callas. She was instantly fascinated by him, a fascination that went much beyond the aura of aristocratic elegance that surrounded him and the fame as perhaps Italy's foremost film director that preceded him. Maria sensed Visconti's dramatic genius and his mere presence at the rehearsals – even when he was not offering any specific suggestions – had a powerful effect on her. 'I was so surprised', she remembered later, 'to see a man of his distinction sit in attentively at almost all the rehearsals, which lasted a minimum of three or four hours – and we rehearsed twice a day.'

The fascination was mutual. Visconti had first seen Maria the previous year during the Rome Opera performance of *Parsifal.* So when the 'Anfiparnaso' group, a group of left-wing artists and intellectuals to which he belonged, decided to revive *Il Turco in Italia,* Visconti immediately suggested Maria. The flighty young wife of an old Neapolitan, madly in love with the faithless Turk Selim, is a long way from Kundry in *Parsifal.* Visconti's imagination bridged the gap. In Rome that October, in and around the Teatro Eliseo on the Via Nazionale, an incongruous friendship began to develop. Over meals, the roles were reversed. It was Maria who sat, enthralled and listening, and Visconti and his 'Anfiparnaso' friends who were doing the talking. Politics, art, revolution, new music, new morals – it opened up for Maria worlds at least as fantastic as a world in which Turkish Sultans descended on Naples. In themselves, intellectual speculation and aesthetic theorizing had no appeal for her, but, filtered through Visconti's personality, they acquired a kind of fascination by association.

'Maria Callas was the surprise of the evening,' wrote the Rome correspondent of *Opera* after the opening night on 19 October. 'She sang a light soprano role with the utmost ease, making it extremely difficult to believe that she can be the perfect interpreter of both Turandot and Isolde.' The cast included Cesare Valletti, Mariano Stabile (Toscanini's great Falstaff) and Sesto Bruscantini, but there was no doubt as to who was the star of the evening: 'The solo voices were splendid, but it required Maria Callas's superb musical flair to keep the others together in the concerted numbers.'

There were only four performances of *Il Turco,* the last one on 29 October. The next time Maria sang Fiorilla on stage was five years later at La Scala in a production created for her by Zeffirelli. In between came the Visconti period of her life. She did not in fact work with him again until 1954, the year that marked their dazzling season at La Scala, yet we can begin dating the Visconti period from the autumn of 1950. It was as if Maria's close contact with Visconti over the rehearsal weeks added, or rather revealed, a whole new dimension of her dramatic personality. His initial influence remained alive, working underground, until the time they came together again for Spontini's *La Vestale* four years later.

By now Italian audiences were so used to Maria's ability to sing anything, and to follow it by singing anything else, that it was no longer stirring news when just over three weeks after she had sung her last Fiorilla, she was back in Rome singing Kundry in a radio broadcast of *Parsifal* with Boris Christoff as Gurnemanz. In between the two, she had been working on a major new role, Elisabeth de Valois in Verdi's *Don Carlo*. Throughout her life, Maria, too driven to pace herself, had to have rest forced on her when her body revolted against overwork, nerves and anxiety. This time, too exhausted to fight the germs, she collapsed with jaundice. She had to leave in the middle of the *Don Carlo* rehearsals and there was no hope of returning. The doctor had ordered not just rest, but complete rest, so all performances of *Don Carlo*, both in Naples and in Rome, had to be cancelled, the only time such an event did not find its way into the headlines as another 'Callas Cancellation'.

Maria's recovery was filled with letters from Athens. Her mother, finding life with her husband increasingly unbearable, had suddenly decided to leave New York and join Jackie in Greece. Filled with bitterness, she poured some of it into her letters to Maria. At first the complaints were directed exclusively at Maria's father, but gradually, when Maria failed to respond, they became reminders of all Evangelia had done for her daughter. The reminders of the past were accompanied by pointed reminders of the stark present – of Evangelia's financial burdens and of a daughter's duty to do something about them, especially since the daughter was married to a millionaire. Evangelia's attacks on her son-in-law became less and less veiled. Ostensibly they were all about his lack of generosity and concern for Maria's family, but behind this litany of grievances was Evangelia's pain at seeing her place at Maria's side filled by Meneghini.

If anyone in the world had a special claim on Maria, a special claim to her glory, it was no longer the mother who had first nurtured her talents, but the husband. Evangelia sensed Maria's withdrawal, and she panicked. The more she panicked, the more strident and reproachful her letters became, and the more Maria withdrew. Every sentence in her mother's letters was an accusation, and every accusation a further invitation to withdrawal. Maria stopped replying. Instead she sent a letter to her godfather:

> ...I beg you not to repeat this Leon – but my mother wrote a letter cursing etc. as is her usual way (she thinks) of obtaining things, saying also that she didn't bring me into this world for nothing – she said she gave birth to me so I should maintain her. That phrase I'm sorry but it's hard to digest. It's hard to explain by writing, Leon, when I see you I'll explain. Only believe me I did and I will do my best for them but I will not permit them to exaggerate. I have a future to think of and also I would like a child of my own.
>
> Please, love me and believe in me – we are so much alike....

She did feel a special affinity with her godfather and commented on it in many of her letters. Besides, she felt enormous gratitude and love for him; he was the only person in her life to whom she could write consistently and intimately, without screen or reservation:

> Nobody else but you dear Leon helped me and gave me courage then, and I'll not forget it. Neither will I forget when I had to fulfill my contract to Verona and I didn't have the money to leave. If it were not for you, dearest.... Not only that but I only had $70 with me – and not one winter clothing. It's hard to believe but it's true.... Please write to me both of you for I sincerely love you both.
>
> I kiss you and Sally so very much.
>
> Please write –
>
> Maria

At the same time, Maria sent a letter to her father inviting him to join her and Meneghini in Mexico in July for her South American season. On the principle that 'my enemy's enemies are my friends', Maria was aligning herself with her father, and taking one more step towards totally closing her heart to her mother. From this point until she died, Maria saw her mother through a distorting haze, as a shadowy, almost menacing figure. Throughout her life she remained in the grip of this unconscious adolescent rebellion – haunted by her mother, but right up to the end frozen in her belligerence.

Meanwhile, Italy was celebrating the fiftieth anniversary of Verdi's death, with festivals springing up all over the country. Maria's Verdi year began at the Teatro Comunale in Florence on 15 January 1951 with her first *Traviata.* She had started working on it in May 1949 when she and Serafin were going by ship to Buenos Aires for seven weeks of performances there. At the time there were no plans for her to sing Violetta, and indeed for over a year before she did sing it she kept declining offers to do so, feeling not yet ready for the part. When she finally accepted the Teatro Comunale's offer, Serafin and she started working together again.

They worked long and hard, but for the first time the magic of their collaboration seemed tarnished. Perhaps because she was no longer prepared to play the respectful student to the celebrated maestro, perhaps because she was still recovering from her illness, perhaps because, however subconsciously, the role of the guru was now filled by Visconti, Maria was constantly irritable with Serafin and ready to flare up. On one occasion she did. It was their first quarrel, the prelude of worse to come, though when the first night arrived there was no trace of animosity. However fierce he could be at rehearsals, once the curtain went up on the first performance, Serafin was always there, ready in every way to support the singers. 'When I am in the pit I am there to serve you because I have to serve my performance,' he would say. and Maria paid lavish tribute to this side of the maestro shortly after his death in 1968: 'We would look down and feel we had a friend there, in the pit. He was helping you all the way. He would mouth all the words. If you were not well he would speed up the tempo, and if you were in top form he would slow it down to let you breathe, to give you room. He was breathing with you, loving it with you. It was elastic, growing, living.'

When the final curtain came down on *Traviata* on the first night and Maria and Serafin acknowledged the applause hand in hand, whatever had passed between them during the rehearsals seemed to belong to the past. 'Here was a great accomplishment', said Serafin later, summing up Maria's first Violetta, 'and it surprised many.'

She left Florence for Naples. There were only a few days before, on 27 January 1951, the fiftieth anniversary of Verdi's death, she was due to sing her first *Trovatore* in Italy. She spent them rehearsing and working with Serafin on her Leonora, perfecting with his guidance what she had achieved a year earlier in Mexico with her instinctive musicianship alone. The reviews of that first night, however, did not suggest that there was anything great or even exceptional about Maria, or indeed any other member of the cast even though it included the celebrated Giacomo Lauri-Volpi in the title role. In fact Lauri-Volpi was so incensed at what he described as 'this dreadful indifference' to vocal art that he wrote an open letter to the Naples press in protest with special vehemence reserved for the failure of the critics to acknowledge the greatness of Callas.

Maria, who in any case was never fond of the melancholy Leonora, was downcast by the lack of enthusiasm and relieved to leave Naples for Palermo where she was to open the spring season in *Norma*. She had barely arrived in Palermo when she received an urgent call from La Scala. It was Ghiringhelli himself: could she come to Milan to take over Aida from the indisposed Tebaldi? No, she could not, was the unequivocal reply. Singing once at La Scala as a replacement was enough. She would sing there again in her own right or not at all. She knew that Ghiringhelli could not afford to withhold a proper invitation for much longer. Nor did he. But he did hold out much longer than it would have seemed possible. When Menotti told Ghiringhelli that his choice for Magda in *The Consul* was Maria Callas, Ghiringhelli exclaimed: 'Oh my god! No, never, never, never! I promised you that any singer you chose would be acceptable to me, but I will not have Maria Callas in the theatre unless she comes as a guest artist.' Menotti went to see Maria and begged her to accept. She refused absolutely; and, as he was going out of the door, she stopped him: 'Mr Menotti, I want you to remember one thing, however, that I *will* sing at La Scala, and that Ghiringhelli will *pay* for this for the rest of his life.'

On 26 May Maria opened at the Maggio Musicale in Florence in *I Vespri Siciliani.* This was to be the opera that brought Ghiringhelli from Milan, contract in hand, offering her the honour of opening the 1951/52 season at La Scala; it was one of her greatest Italian triumphs and the only opera she was ever to direct nearly twenty-two years later. *I Vespri,* based on the massacre of the French by Sicilians at Palermo in 1282, was one of Verdi's less frequently performed operas. The production was revived by the Florence May Festival as part of the festivities for the composer's fiftieth anniversary, with Boris Christoff as Procida and the Austrian-born conductor Erich Kleiber making his Italian operatic debut. Lord Harewood, then editor of *Opera,* was there for one of the rehearsals and he described Maria's first entrance on the stage: '... The French have been boasting for some time of the privileges which belong by rights to an army of occupation, when a female figure – the Sicilian Duchess Elena – is seen slowly crossing the square. Doubtless the music and the production helped to spotlight Elena but, though she has not yet sung and was not even wearing her costume, one was straight away impressed by the natural dignity of her carriage, the air of quiet, innate authority which went with her every movement.' He was equally impressed by what he heard: '... there was an assurance and a tragic bravura about her singing which was frequently thrilling.'

The performance was recorded, and right from the start we can feel the total success with which Maria creates theatre through her voice. The chorus of praise was unremitting and Maria fed ravenously off it, but the applause, the praise and the adulation were nothing compared to the off-stage triumph: La Scala was at her feet, and the terms of her contract included three leading roles, thirty appearances during the initial season and

300,000 lire, practically $500, a performance. This was the laying-on of hands, and Maria was in ecstasy. Whatever glories a singer may have gained outside Italy and however distinguished some of the other Italian opera houses, La Scala offered the ultimate endorsement.

Maria's last performance in *Vespri Siciliani* was on 5 June. Four days later, still in Florence but at the more intimate Teatro della Pergola, Maria was opening in her first world *première*: Haydn's *Orfeo ed Euridice,* written for London in 1791, had waited 160 years for Maria and its first performance. The classical style of Haydn was a long way from Verdi's Sicily, and Euridice had little to do with Elena, but Maria managed the eighteenth-century style as though it was all she had ever sung. Her versatility had by now become legendary among the *cognoscenti* all over the world, and it was highlighted in America by her first recordings. As her fame spread across the Atlantic, the *New York Times* carried a review of Maria in *Orfeo* under the title 'New Yorker excels'.

Athens, New York and Verona were all claiming her for their own. The Scala contract had been signed and Covent Garden was trying to get her to sing *Norma* in 1952. Sander Gorlinsky, who was ultimately to become her exclusive agent, arrived in Verona to make the arrangements. He found Meneghini in one of his 'catch me if you can' moods and left empty-handed. 'I nearly gave up,' he remembers. 'But I decided to go back to Verona and make another effort. When I arrived at the apartment she was in bed and Mr Meneghini mercifully out. "I'd love to do it," she said, and signed the contract there and then, at a fee of £250 a night.'

Full of confidence and expectations, Maria left with Meneghini for Mexico. Her father was already there, waiting for them. George Callas's two-week stay in Mexico was an overwhelming experience. Not only was Maria the heroine of the Mexican public, she was also given almost every accolade by the press and every possible honour and hospitality by the official custodians of high culture and the no less official practitioners of high living. All George Callas's sober reservations about having his daughter on the stage evaporated in the general intoxication. He and Meneghini, about the same age and similar in their sombre make-up, were getting on beautifully together. Their shared pride in Maria was powerful enough to overcome the father's lack of Italian and the husband's tortured English. Maria had little time to spend with her father in between performances and rehearsals, but she enjoyed having him by her side, and knowing that he was there in the darkened auditorium, proudly watching and applauding her. The more her resentment towards her mother increased, the more love and warmth she felt for a father who had never made any demands or burdened her with his expectations.

After three performances of *Aida* opposite Mario del Monaco, who went on heroically over-singing his way through the opera up to and including the dying fall of the final scene, Maria sang her first Mexican *Traviata* with Cesare Valletti. At her husband's insistence, she was paid in Mexico in gold dollars, which Meneghini, like a pirate, put in a little bag bought especially for the purpose.

The Mexican visit was an unqualified triumph, but Maria left for her next stop, São Paulo in Brazil, exhausted, her legs massively swollen and her nerves strained to breaking-point. There was, of course, the wear and tear of travelling and performing, innumerable petty annoyances and vexations on – and off – stage, and lately an unusual loss of sleep. But that was not all. More exhausting than the irritations and the work of the present were the replays of her past – past mistakes, past performances, past judgements – that were going on inside her head. Even more exhausting were her fears for the future. La Scala had surrended, but that was fully as much a source of anxiety for Maria as a source of exultation. The higher she climbed, the greater the reputation she had to maintain, the greater became the burden of the past and future that she had to carry. The past was no more, the future was yet to come – but Maria went on sacrificing the joy of the present to that unborn future and that dead past. It is small wonder she was exhausted.

She had to cancel all her scheduled performances of *Aida* and only appeared in *Traviata,* alternating as Violetta with Renata Tebaldi. The cancellation of *Aida* brought the first personally critical comments from the South American press, which also carried some very unflattering things that Maria was supposed to have said about Tebaldi's Violetta. Had she said them? Had they been distorted? From now on, in the reporting of Maria's sayings and doings in the press, these were to become staple questions. However much Callas lovers might have wished it otherwise, the only correct answer would almost invariably have to be: yes, the press did distort what she said and did, but yes, she *had* said it or done it.

Maria arrived in Rio de Janeiro from São Paulo to be greeted with a press full of Tebaldi's Violetta. She had opened in Rio a week earlier and had been wildly acclaimed. So was Maria when she opened in *Norma* at the Teatro Municipal on 12 September. Parallel triumphs simply increased the tension. Of course tension between primadonnas was nothing new in operatic history, but there was a new element here, not easy to define but unmistakably present: it was the extent of the public's identification and involvement. Maria's comments, blown up by the press, made battle inevitable. Lines were drawn and positions openly taken. The musical world – and by no means the musical world alone – was beginning to be divided into Tebaldists and Callasites.

The stage of open hostilities was now just round the corner, and the opportunity was provided by a benefit concert at the Teatro Municipal in Rio on 14 September. Both Renata and Maria were there to take part in it, Maria to sing 'Sempre Libera' from *Traviata,* Renata to sing 'Ave Maria' from *Otello.* Maria sang, took her curtain-calls and withdrew. Renata, carried away by the tumultuous applause she received, gave not one but two encores. There had been no previous agreement regarding encores, so Renata justified them as a response to the audience's enthusiasm. Maria knew better. Harsh, angry words were exchanged backstage and diplomatic relations were broken off. But it was not easy to break off relations when they had to go on living with, or at least near, the object of their discontent. Maria and Renata had plenty of opportunities, both professional and social, to test their tempers. Sometimes they managed to keep them, but more often they failed. A few days before Maria was due to sing *Tosca* they rather spectacularly failed when an after-dinner discussion threatened to turn into a fish-wives' brawl.

Maria still, despite all her success, saw herself as snatching victory from hostile elements, and found her imagination increasingly peopled by enemies. At this time Renata was heading the parade, but soon she would be supplanted in Maria's Enemies List by someone else. At the end of the opening night of *Tosca* in Rio, Meneghini burst into her dressing-room with rumours that an anti-Callas plan was afoot at the Opera House. Admittedly he was rather given to arriving in her dressing-room with news of this kind, but on this occasion he was followed a few moments later by a messenger from the Director of the Opera House asking her to come to his office. She went, determined to raise hell and ready with all the complaints that she had about inadequate rehearsal facilities and the rumours that were circulating. Before she could open her mouth she was formally informed by Barreto Pinto, the Director, that due to what he described as the extremely unfavourable reactions of the audience to her *Tosca,* her contract was terminated. Whether it was through luck, her instinct for survival, or a sudden aptitude for diplomacy, Maria remained perfectly cool until Pinto had finished. Then in a very business-like manner, she reminded him of his contractual obligations. She insisted on being paid for the second *Tosca* that he would not allow her to sing and on singing the two remaining *Traviatas.* Pinto was furious but he had no option but to concede.

Maria's replacement in *Tosca* was, as fate would have it, none other than Tebaldi. Maria was convinced that fate and coincidence had nothing to do with it; she openly accused Renata of having been behind Pinto's decision to sack her. She was hurt, and made her accusation on suspicion rather than on evidence. The evidence, as far as it goes, tends to exonerate Tebaldi, but by that stage Maria was too distraught to be much concerned with evidence or even truth. *Traviata* was a huge success, but there was already open war between Pinto and Maria. He was so totally in the grip of his petty, unaccountable hatred of her that when she walked into his office to receive her fee before leaving, he jeered at her: 'So you want money on top of glory, eh?' At this point the anger that had been coiled within Maria for the past few weeks could no longer be contained. Beside herself with fury, she seized the ink stand from Pinto's desk and was about to fling it at him, when a secretary rushed forward and snatched it from her hand. There was no blood shed and no one was hurt, but by the time word of the incident had gone the rounds of the international opera houses, Maria might as well have stabbed Pinto with Tosca's dagger.

All these explosions, conflicts and increasingly public personal dramas were enacted throughout the truamatic South American trip with the assistance of a chorus of one: Battista Meneghini. Occasionally when Maria exploded he pacified her, when she sulked he rallied her, but more often he inflamed her anger and resentment. Titta's intentions were unimpeachable, but there was plenty of malice underneath his rather bland exterior. It had to find an outlet, and his wife's real or imagined enemies were the channels nearest to hand. His total identification with Maria's professional interests at least saved her from being on the receiving end of his ill-nature – so long as she continued to put her career first. Meneghini was a born manager, and for the time being what Maria wanted was to be efficiently managed. And that she was. No opportunity to advance her career was lost.

On their way back to Italy, Battista had arranged for them to stop at Idlewild Airport so they could talk with Dario Soria, head of Cetra Records in New York, about the possibilities of a long-term contract. Maria was still on trial in America, but from reports that had reached him and from the few recordings that he had heard, Soria already knew that Cetra needed Maria more than Maria needed Cetra. During their airport talk, with Maria at her most professional, confident and business-like, he was more convinced than ever. The contract with Cetra, stipulating the recording of three complete operas in 1952, was soon signed.

Maria returned to Italy, but South America, and especially Rio, was still very much with her. The trip had brought one of those psychologically charged sequences of events which are of emotional intensity far beyond their intrinsic importance. She longed to command her mind to stop going back to Rio, but how do you command the mind to be still? The memories rankled, sometimes for hours, sometimes for days, and there were moments of acute anguish as 1951 neared its end and Maria was about to enter her year of marvels – a year in which she was to float on a tide of unparalleled success.

Chapter Seven

MARIA's twenty-eighth birthday found her at the Grand Hotel in Milan, where Verdi lived for years and where he died. On the Via San Raffaele, a few minutes' walk from La Scala, the Grand Hotel became Maria's home in Milan. The official opening of La Scala was on 7 December, a few days after Maria's birthday; and Ghiringhelli was determined that La Scala's production of *I Vespri Siciliani* would ensure that the Florence production of the summer before was instantly forgotten. The opera had not been heard at La Scala since 1908, and everything had been done to ensure that the Milanese felt it had been worth reviving. Victor de Sabata, La Scala's artistic director, was conducting, an excellent cast had been assembled, headed by Maria and Boris Christoff, and for once they all had ample rehearsal time. At rehearsals Maria was the wholly absorbed artist, and if sometimes she was as much absorbed in her own artistry as in the composer's music, the *Vespers* fared none the worse for it. Everyone was impressed by her professionalism, overwhelmed by her dedication and stunned by her range. 'My God,' recalled a member of the chorus, 'she came on stage sounding like our deepest contralto, Cloe Elmo. Before the evening was over, she took a high E-flat, and it was twice as strong as Toti Dal Monte's!'

Maria herself resolutely refused to be overwhelmed by the occasion; but it was not easy. She was surrounded by people for whom grand opera was a religion, Milan its Holy City and an opening night at La Scala the most sacred festival in the calendar. Many of the faithful were swollen with proprietorial pride, even though for most of them their only connection with La Scala was that they lived in the same city. Opera was their life, and legend had it that if ever a luckless singer failed to strike a top note, the gallery would join in by chanting the whole aria as it should have been sung. By 1951, they may not have been able to sing the aria correctly, but they were perfectly capable of whistling the sinning singer off-stage, especially if he or she was a foreigner. Music-making was a family business and meddling with it was rarely welcomed. Stendhal had summed up this attitude over a century earlier: 'No truly honest observer, venturing into Italy from abroad, could dare for one instant to deny the hopeless absurdity of presuming to train singers or compose elsewhere than under the shadow of Vesuvius.' Very little had changed by Maria's time.

The glittering first-night audience was cautiously expectant. Maria's fame had preceded her, but it was a chrysalid fame. The Scala audience knew it was up to them to turn it into an internationally radiant butterfly. At the end of the first night, Maria knew that La Scala had surrendered – but not quite, not with the completeness that would make the surrender reverberate round the world. The surrender may not have been total but the applause that burst out at the end of the bolero that opens the last act was an indication of the enthusiasm that Maria had stirred among the Milanese. The critical reaction summed up in *Corriere della Sera* clearly echoed that enthusiasm: 'The miraculous throat of Maria Meneghini Callas . . . the prodigious extension of her tones, their phosphorescent beauty and her technical agility which is more than rare, it is unique.'

I Vespri was followed by *I Puritani* and the Teatro Comunale in Florence, and by more critical superlatives. But more moving and important for Maria than reading adulatory words in cold print the morning after was the live adulation of her audiences on the night. At the end of *Puritani* they shouted, stamped and clamoured for her in curtain-call after curtain-call. And the orchestra, despite the legendary indifference of all orchestras to singers of all kinds, stood in the pit applauding with at least as much passion as the audience. Soon these demonstrations became the talk of the Italian musical world: 'Not since Toscanini ...', whispered the lay connoisseurs. And the critics confirmed it: 'Not since Toscanini.'

Almost anything she wanted seemed within her grasp now. Two weeks into 1952, she sang *Norma* at La Scala. The production was cobwebbed and the scenery dated from 1931, but Maria, according to *Musical America,* 'electrified the audience by her very presence even before singing a note'. She sang eight *Normas* and in between, whether at the Grand Hotel or at the Opera House, in her dressing-room or her bedroom, she worked on her only Mozart heroine: Constanze in *Die Entführung aus dem Serail.* It was a part that made tremendous demands on Maria's stamina, range and agility. In the first aria alone, she was required to touch over twenty high Cs and eleven high Ds. It took a great deal out of Maria and she felt that it gave her very little back.

She more than conquered all the technical difficulties and received unanimous admiration and clamorous ovations, but she never sang another Mozart opera. 'Most of Mozart's music is dull,' she said once at a public Round Table at the Juilliard School of Music in New York. And at one of her master-classes there, the same instinctive reaction was wrapped in the language of musical diplomacy. 'Mozart,' she told a student soprano, 'is often done on the tips of the toes, with too much fragility. It should be sung with the same frankness you sing *Trovatore* with.' Maria, who more than any other singer this century had dared portray in all their darkness man's most primitive emotions, found the emotions of Mozart's music too contained, and she even found it hard to respond to the deeper harmony that is at the soul of Mozart's music.

Maria sang 'Martern aller Arten', the most famous coloratura aria in the opera, twice again in concert – once in San Remo in 1954, and once in 1957 as a showpiece for the gala inaugural concert of the Dallas Civic Opera. She may have called Mozart's music dull, but the passion with which she invested the aria belies the claim. The 1957 concert itself was not recorded but its rehearsal was, and it is a fascinating document of Callas's generosity at rehearsals. She begins at half-voice but the emotion in the music soon engulfs her and she sings the entire programme unerringly with the full intensity of a performance.

She was equally unsparing of herself when it came to her schedule. On 26 April, only a fortnight after the last *Entführung* and with *Norma* in between, she opened the Florence festival with another long-forgotten opera, Rossini's *Armida.* Maria loved Rossini but Armida, which Rossini wrote for Colbran who became his wife, is an almost impossible part, full of perilous roulades, hazardous trills, runs and leaps – and, as sung by Maria, full of dazzling fireworks. Despite the fact that it has five important tenor roles *Armida* is undeniably a one-woman show, and, on this occasion, it was greeted universally as a one-woman triumph, especially by those who knew that Maria had learned the part in five days. At the dress rehearsal, the performance officially attended by the critics, Maria's spectacular memory for once let her down and she emerged from the elaborate litter in which Armida makes her first appearance totally unable to remember her first line. Completely unflustered, she asked for her words and made her entrance again. On the first night she was in absolute control throughout, and during her twelve-minute final scene, she pushed her voice to new limits spanning almost three octaves. It all came to a climax with one of the most elaborate of all Rossini's arias, delivered by Maria in a torrent of sound. 'It is possible,' wrote Andrew Porter in *Opera*, 'to feel that the phrases beneath the florid passages are far too much overlaid with ornament; but it was impossible to regret it when Maria Callas was singing them.'

From Milan to Florence, from Florence to Rome and two performances of *I Puritani*, then from Rome to Verona. There were two weeks left before Maria was due to arrive in Mexico for the beginning of her third tour, and, instead of their being a time of much-needed rest, they were consumed almost entirely by two major additions to her repertoire: Gilda in Verdi's *Rigoletto* and Lucia in Donizetti's *Lucia di Lammermoor.* The slave-driver inside Maria was driving her on more relentlessly than ever. Of course it made sense to have these new roles ready to try in Mexico before exposing them to the more critical Italian audiences, and of course it was wonderful that from the beginning of January to the beginning of May in this New Year, she had sung one *Vespri,* five *Puritanis,* nine *Normas,* three *Trovatores,* four *Entführung* and three *Armidas,* but the price she was paying, although never taken into account, was in fact very considerable. The part of her that needed space to breathe and to grow was being stifled, its need for attention and love ignored or denied. Maria Callas – already, according to many, the most exciting singer on the operatic stage – was shuttling from city to city, from role to role and from triumph to triumph.

From Italy to Mexico. Partnered by Giuseppe de Stefano, she was getting ready to open her Mexican season in *I Puritani.* There was a story behind this choice of opening opera which Antonio Caraza-Campos, the General Director of the Opera Nacional, did not tire of repeating to his guests on the first night. During Maria's first Mexican season, Campos went to see her with a score of *Aida* which had belonged to the nineteenth-century soprano, Angela Peralta, indicating that she had sung a top E-flat at the end of the Triumph Scene; he asked Maria to do the same. 'If you want to hear my E-flat,' she replied, at her most imperious, 'sign me up for *Puritani.*'

Caraza Campos took the point: Maria Callas had stopped auditioning. On 29 May, he and thousands of others heard her high E-flat in *I Puritani* – and much else besides. It was a chaotic performance. Guido Picco's conducting was so haphazard that he seemed half-asleep, and the male singers, with the exception of di Stefano, ranged from bearable to atrocious. The opening night was broadcast and one can hear Maria, time after time, saving the performance from the the total shambles which it nearly became. But she was seething with anger. She, the most professional of professionals, could not bear amateurism and her acute perfectionism made it even harder to bear having the overall effect of a performance diminished or even destroyed by the lack of total commitment on the part of anyone else involved in the production. The devotion to her work that she radiated had an effect on everyone around her. It is true that some, certainly those for whom their work had become routine, were exasperated, but it soon became legendary that when Callas was singing everyone in the theatre performed better: the leading tenor sang better, the conductor conducted better, the usherettes ushered the audience better, the cashier sold tickets better....

Maria's obsession with her work was interpreted by many as vainglorious. In fact, from the very beginning of her career, Maria knew that, however brilliant she could herself be, the real success of a performance depended on the effect of the ensemble. And beyond that, the most intense moments in Maria's life up to that point, the moments when past, future and vainglory disappeared, were the moments of blissful absorption in the role she was singing. Then she stopped being Maria Callas and merged with the emotions of the woman she was portraying – emotions larger than those of any one individual. There was nothing easy or effortless about Maria's greatness, and however much work and energy she devoted to each new role, she always regarded it as 'work in progress', never complete, never final. Lucia was her first new role in Mexico this season. After the 'Mad Scene', she received sixteen curtain-calls and a twenty-minute ovation. The whole audience and the normally blasé musicians in the pit rose together and applauded with an enthusiasm and a persistence new even to the full-blooded Mexicans. Yet Maria's summing up of her Mexico Lucia sixteen years later was: 'Very sure, the first Mexico performance. Absolutely sure, beautiful top notes and all that, but it was not yet the role.' Her attitude to her performances was and would always remain that of the severest of headmistresses.

After the creative euphoria of *Lucia* came a week of acute depression. She was worn out and racked with worry about the *Rigoletto* ahead of her. She had had neither the time nor the energy to rehearse properly, and she said as much to Caraza Campos as soon as she arrived in Mexico. He reminded her that she had signed a contract to sing Gilda at the highest fee ever paid to an artist in Mexico and there was nothing he could now do about it. Goaded by Meneghini, Maria felt bitter and hard done by, yet, at the same time, she was full of self-accusation – not so much because of the punishing schedule she had imposed on herself, as because she feared that both her own performance and the entire under-rehearsed production could turn out to be artistic and critical disasters.

As it turned out, there were many moments when the production verged on disaster and some when it actually *was* a disaster, but Maria's performance, her transformation of Gilda from an innocent young girl into a strong, passionate woman, made the audience see the character in an altogether new light.

There was one more *Rigoletto,* the final *Lucia* and two *Toscas* to be sung before Maria could return home. The press went on eulogizing her Tosca and rhapsodizing over her Lucia but it was the dissenting voices that were ringing in Maria's ears. *Rigoletto* had been an anti-climax and, as one of the critics put it: 'Miss Callas's Gilda did not improve the situation.'

Back in Verona, with the daily pressure of performances and rehearsals removed, Maria for the first time in months had some spare energy, which she promptly turned against herself. The Mexican season was suddenly transformed into a failure in her eyes. The endless curtain-calls, the tempestuous applause, the rave reviews, all were forgotten, and what remained was the 'humiliation' of *Rigoletto.* She swore she would never sing it on stage again – nor did she. With this decision a real opportunity was lost. She could have made the musical world reappraise Gilda as she had made them look with new eyes on Lucia, Tosca, Norma, Armida. Instead she dropped *Rigoletto* from her active repertoire and only sang it again when she recorded it with Gobbi and di Stefano.

Maria's reaction to the Mexican season was typical: a speck of failure was put under the microscope and grew until it had completely obliterated all the surrounding successes, all the peaks of triumph. It was in that physically exhausted, emotionally-wrought state that Maria received a letter from Greece. Her mother had decided to put an end to the increasingly uneasy alliance with her husband. She had gone back to New York to start divorce proceedings and returned to Greece with a temporary judgement for a weekly alimony. But the judgement went the way of many other similar judgements, and nothing was forthcoming. Evangelia, who had always been deft with her hands, began making operatic dolls and selling them first to friends and then, as the word spread, to others. So while Maria was singing Tosca, Violetta, Aida and Lucia, Evangelia was creating images of the characters her daughter was portraying. At the same time her family were continuing to meet many of her financial needs and Jackie's perennial fiancé was also on hand to bridge any gaps. For him this was partly a way of assuaging his guilty conscience for giving in to his family's wishes not to marry Jackie. They were implacably opposed to their son and heir marrying socially so much 'beneath' their own family, and their son and heir was not grown-up enough to stand up to them – at least not yet, as he kept repeating to Jackie.

Evangelia was concerned about Jackie who went on giving piano lessons and even a modest recital now and then; also she was obviously concerned about her own financial future. Most important of all, though, she desperately wanted to re-establish contact with Maria, whose life from such a distance seemed to her mother entirely dream-like. Her letters went unanswered, her desperation grew, and in that desperation she went to consult a medium she knew. It is not quite clear what the medium said. What is clear is that what Evangelia did was the most hopelessly misjudged action she could have taken. She wrote asking for – demanding – a regular weekly allowance and Maria's total backing for the launching of Jackie's career.

The letter was waiting for Maria when she arrived home from Mexico. It is, of course, one of the hazards of letter-writing that you cannot anticipate the state of mind of the recipient at the moment your letter is opened. Maria was in an explosive state of mind; her mother's hectoring letter lit the fuse. At a time when Maria was aiming for the stars, when she sensed limitless possibility, all the things that she fought against in herself – frustration, failure, futility – were projected on to Evangelia. Her mother had by now become in Maria's eyes her mirror image, her lifelong burden, her baseline for judging the distance she had herself travelled from Patissiou Street.

Every word in the letter fed Maria's resentment. The normal human fear of being taken advantage of was magnified in Maria's case into full-scale horror. At the mere suggestion of this, real or imagined, she would simultaneously cringe and attack. Her reply to her mother was ruthlessly direct: Jackie's career was no business of hers and Evangelia was young enough and healthy enough to get a job and support herself.

The war of the letters had begun. It was a contest in bitterness: joyless memories on Maria's side, self-sacrificing memories on her mother's. It was as if Maria was bringing her whole accumulated past up for an airing before, unable to let go of it, she would push it back down again. She was more tied to the past then she ever knew.

On 19 July 1952, the past – this time the not-too-distant past – re-created itself. Five years after her Italian debut as Gioconda in the Arena of Verona, Maria was back in the Arena, once again in the same theatre and the same role. The differences, however, were significant. She was ecstatically welcomed by the huge audience as if she was victoriously returning home. The ecstacy apart, she was now being paid 600,000 lire for each of her six performances. Two days after the opening night, on 21 July, Maria took a step that was to prove more important for her career than it seemed at the time. At her apartment in Verona she signed an exclusive recording contract with EMI. Walter Legg, EMI's director, was present and he breathed a deep sigh of relief and incredulity. The negotiations had begun well over a year before in Maria's dressing-room at the Rome Opera. Walter Legge had just heard Maria for the first time in *Norma* and had rushed back to offer her an exclusive contract. Meneghini and Maria seemed delighted, and they continued to seem delighted as the negotiations dragged on over meals in Verona, in Rome, at Biffi Scala in Milan. At every meeting Maria, like a goddess, expected burnt offerings both from Walter Legge and from Dario Soria (who had by then left Cetra for EMI): 'My arms still ache', recalled

Walter Legge years later, 'at the recollection of the pots of flowering shrubs and trees that Dario Soria and I lugged to the Verona apartment.' Finally terms were agreed and Walter Legge gave them a contract with his signature and asked Maria for hers on his own copy. But it was not to be – at least not yet. Meneghini explained that they had a superstition that prevented them from signing a contract until two weeks after it had been mutually agreed. Instead they gave their *parole d'onore* that the signed copy would be mailed a fortnight later.

It was not. In fact, it was not mailed at all until Walter Legge had flown to Verona and agreed to raise the terms. Meneghini knew when the cards were stacked on his side and he had no qualms about waiting to use them to his full advantage. For him the financial dealings of Maria's career were not a purgatory leading to the heaven of aesthetic experience. Driving a hard bargain was for Meneghini heaven itself, and wherever possible he asked for the payment in cash – even from the Met. Once, in revenge, Rudolf Bing gave him Maria's fee in $5 notes. Given half a chance there is little doubt that Meneghini would have kept rolls of notes stuffed inside his socks.

Still, the enemy was finally conquered, the hard bargain was struck and the EMI contract signed. Walter Legge was destined to be a crucial influence on Maria's recording career and, by extension, a key influence on her career as a whole. He was a fellow-perfectionist and greatly admired the perfectionist in Maria. 'It is easier to admire her than to love her,' he said once; but it must have been love of some kind that bound them together through all Maria's recording triumphs. We can see that love – the love of perfection – in action ten years after their first recording together, when they spent three hours repeating over and over again the last dozen bars of the Jewel Song in *Faust* because neither of them was satisfied.

A few days after the EMI contract was at last signed, Walter Legge and his wife, Elisabeth Schwarzkopf, went to the Arena to see Maria in *Traviata.* Backstage after the performance, the great German soprano offered Maria one of the most moving tributes she ever received: her decision never to sing *Traviata* again.

'What is the sense', Schwarzkopf replied when asked to explain her decision in public, 'in doing a part that another contemporary artist can do to perfection?' In September, Maria went to Turin to record *Traviata* for Cetra. *Traviata* and *Gioconda* were the only two operas Maria ever recorded for Cetra. From then on her recording career was in the hands of Walter Legge and EMI in Europe, and Dario Soria and Angel Records, EMI's transatlantic label, in America.

The Cetra recordings over, Maria and Meneghini left in late October for London with a sense of anticipation which London, now and in the future, was to fulfil and justify. Maria, with her primitively powerful sense of fate, felt at the time as if God was answering her prayers, God was watching over her interests, God was guiding her footsteps. She arrived at the Savoy, which was to be, right to the end, her home in London, with husband and secretary in tow. Enormous bouquets and baskets of flowers were already waiting for her. She had conquered even before she had sung, and on stage she was unmistakably a woman through whom life's vital current passed. *Norma* had been chosen as the vehicle of her debut at Covent Garden. Maria was the only reason for the revival of an opera that had not been heard at Covent Garden since Rosa Ponselle sang it in 1930. And singing next to her in the small role of Clotilde was Joan Sutherland who, fifteen years later, was to sing Norma at Coventy Garden herself. The applause began at rehearsal, with the orchestra and David Webster, Covent Garden's General Administrator, clapping Maria's first London 'Casta Diva'.

The first night, 8 November 1952, was a double revelation. The first was Maria to the audience. The second, and in many ways more important, was the audience to itself. There were hundreds present at Covent Garden on 8 November for whom Maria's Norma was a self-revelation. She evoked emotions and responses they had never suspected were available to them; she provoked a depth and intensity of feeling that went beyond anything they had previously experienced; she made an entire audience feel more vital, more responsive, more alive. It is little wonder that so many deified her.

Opera was suddenly alive again at Covent Garden, no longer an art form better fitted for museums than for the stage, but an art with a glittering present and a future that promised to be even more exciting. There were, of course, as there always would be at Maria's performances, the detractors, headed on this occasion by Ernest Newman who found her 'slightly sub-normal'. And there were, as there always would be, those who complained of harsh nasal tones. But the audience responded in a way that made it clear they knew – or at least sensed – that a new era had arrived in opera.

The fact that with Maria Callas a dramatic new turning-point had been reached may have been overlooked in Italy where the operatic tradition was an unbroken one. In London, however, and even elsewhere in Europe, the life of opera had always been a chain of islands in a sea of indifference. And now there had emerged from this sea a new-found land, recognizable from afar, even by the most indifferent, as a treasure island.

Andrew Porter summed up her Norma: 'Maria Meneghini Callas is the Norma of our day, as Ponselle and Grisi were of theirs.' Philip Hope-Wallace summed up her presence: 'Tall and splendid, like one of Millais' pictures of mid-Victorian divas.' David Webster summed up the response of the Opera House: Maria Callas became his child and Covent Garden was offered to her as a home in which as time went by she grew and flourished, and in which, as if to show her gratitude, she did much of her finest work. It was a celebration all round. Maria brought international splendour to a still provincial Covent Garden. Covent Garden hailed her as *the* new Norma, *the* new operatic superstar, *the* new beginning.

'But does she have to be so big?' That was one of the questions asked directly or covertly in the press commentaries that surrounded her visit. That was also the question that began to work its way more and more pressingly into Maria's mind. When she first appeared in *Aida* at the Arena of Verona, one of the critics had written that 'it was impossible to tell the difference between the legs of the Elephants on the stage and those of Aida sung by Maria Callas'. 'I cried bitter tears for many days when I read the article,' said Maria shortly before she died, the memory still painful and alive. 'It was cruel, horrible.' At the time she was not prepared to do anything about it, but by the end of her *Norma* performance in London, Maria, the actress, was feeling seriously hampered by her traditionally operatic size. Also her headaches, fainting spells and attacks of car sickness had all intensified and she was attributing them to the excess weight she was carrying rather than to anything else.

So gradually Maria came to a decision which was to lead to a fairy-tale transformation that would reverberate round the world. It was still over a month before the time for New Year resolutions when Maria resolved to become in reality the sylph-like creature of her imagination. And unlike millions upon millions of New Year resolutions this one was to stick. There is no doubt that one of the reasons was that, apart from Meneghini, Maria told nobody. An even more securely locked secret, from which even Meneghini was excluded, was Maria's choice of model for this transformation. It cannot have been easy to look at herself in the mirror and then choose the almost invisible Audrey Hepburn as the model of what she wanted to become but then Maria loved challenges – especially self-imposed ones.

In the meantime 7 December, St Ambrose's feast day and La Scala's traditional opening night, was not far away. The blaze of advance publicity, the press coverage, the boxes decorated with clusters of carnations, even the gift of a piece of fabric for an evening-shirt presented to box-subscribers by an enterprising haberdasher's firm – they all proclaimed that this was a big night, an event, a unique occasion. Maria was opening the season as Lady Macbeth and the performance was being televised – the first opera ever to be televised in Italy. It was her first Lady Macbeth, and ten days later, on 17 December, she sang the part for the last time. From then on she was always *nearly* singing the part. She nearly sang it under Toscanini's direction a year earlier in Busseto, near Verdi's birthplace: she nearly sang it in San Francisco; she nearly sang it at the Met; and she nearly sang it at Covent Garden. Those who actually heard her as Lady Macbeth at La Scala experienced exactly what Verdi had put in the music and had even expressly asked for: 'I would like a voice harsh, choked, dark. There are places that must not even be sung, but acted and declaimed with a veiled, black voice.'

Nicola Benois had designed the production and Carl Ebert, who had made a success of *Macbeth* in Berlin in the early 1930s, and again, a little later, at Glyndebourne, was the director. But Maria, as Serafin had impressed on her from the beginning, sought the direction in the music. 'When you want to find a gesture, when you want to find how to act on stage,' she said once, 'all you have to do is listen to the music. The composer has already seen to that. If you take the trouble to really listen with your soul and your ears – and I say soul and ears because the mind must work, but not too much – you will find every gesture there.'

Verdi wanted Lady Macbeth to be 'ugly and evil'. Maria agreed that 'the role, and therefore the voice, should have an atmosphere of darkness'. In fact her voice created, all by itself, drama, scenery and action; and her huge penetrating eyes added to the potency and atmosphere with which she filled the music. The sleep-walking scene electrified the audience and earned Maria seven curtain-calls. Yet there were many who could not cope with what one critic described as her 'almost inhuman vocal qualities'. 'Callas was not in her best voice and at one point was even whistled at,' reported Peter Hoffer in *Music and Musicians.* She had indeed been whistled at but mainly by those for whom a singer who made her voice deliberately harsh and dark as the character in the music demanded was 'not in her best voice'. Still, the thunderous ovation at the end, and the overwhelmingly glowing comments the day after, drowned the voice of the detractors.

The day after Christmas, Maria was back at La Scala singing *La Gioconda.* Ebe Stignani was Laura and Antonino Votto the conductor. He had worked closely with Maria on her two Cetra recordings and was an unequivocal admirer: 'She was the last great artist,' he recalled some years later. 'Just think – this woman was nearly blind, and often sang standing a good hundred and fifty feet from the podium. But her sensitivity! Even if she could not see, she sensed the music and always came in exactly with my down-beat. When we rehearsed she was so precise, already note-perfect. But she had a habit that annoyed her colleagues: even in rehearsal she always sang full voice and it obliged them to do as well. Most singers are stupid and try to save themselves, but a rehearsal is a kind of hurdle. If on a track you must run a mile, you don't practise by running half a mile. For over thirty years I was Arturo Toscanini's assistant, and from the very first rehearsal he demanded every nuance from the orchestra, just as if it were a full performance. And Callas did this too. I remember we had a dress rehearsal in Cologne of *La Sonnambula* at ten in the morning and she sang her entire role full voice; that night we did the *première*! She was not just a singer, but a complete artist. It's foolish to discuss her as a voice. She must be viewed totally – as a complex of music, drama, movement. There is no one like her today. She was an aesthetic phenomenon.'

America was beginning to share the same opinion. Maria had not yet sung there but the Callas legend had preceded her across the Atlantic. Her recording of *Gioconda,* with Votto conducting, had thrilled and baffled opera lovers. The woman who had won fame as Lucia, who had sung Isolde and Armida, could now finally be heard on records singing Gioconda. And the world loves nothing better than stories of superhuman feats that stretch the limits of what is possible: stories of a Lindbergh making the first solo transatlantic flight; of a Blondin who crossed Niagara Falls on a tightrope; of a Mozart writing the overture to *Don Giovanni* the night before the first performance; of a Callas who can sing Brünnhilde on one night and Elvira the next, who is rumoured to be a fabulous Lucia and can be heard to be a marvellous Gioconda.

So the stories of Maria's superhuman feats were going the rounds in America even before the Americans had had a chance to hear her sing in person. Meanwhile, back in Milan, Maria was making quite sure that when they did hear her in the flesh there would be much less flesh to see.

She had begun to think ahead to her first *Medea*: 'My first instinct was to say that the face is too fat and I can't stand it, because I needed the chin for expression in certain very hard phrases, cruel phrases or tense phrases. And I felt – as the woman of the theatre that I was and am – that I needed these necklines and the chinlines to be very thin and very pronounced.' So her resolve to transform her appearance dramatically became stronger than ever. It was strengthened further by the growing admiration from everyone around her, especially – and this mattered to her more than anything – within her own profession. More and more singers, conductors, designers, directors, whether they had worked with her or not, were taking sides. For the moment the admirers were much more outspoken that the detractors. After Maria's *Lucia di Lammermoor* in Florence on 25 January 1953, Giacomo Lauri-Volpi, who was her Edgardo on the first night, actually went into print describing her performance as 'an immense triumph'. 'This young artist,' he said, 'with her ability to rouse the multitudes, may yet lead the lyric theatre to a new golden age of singing.'

Immediately after her four performances of *Lucia* at the Teatro Comunale in Florence, Maria went on to record *Lucia* with Giuseppe di Stefano as Edgardo, Tito Gobbi as Enrico, and Serafin conducting. It was the first recording by the Callas, Gobbi, de Stefano trio. And it was a little spool of tape containing the last three minutes of the second act that persuaded Karajan to conduct *Lucia* at La Scala. He had listened to it reluctantly, at Walter Legge's insistence, but no sooner had the tape come to an end than he was on the phone to La Scala asking for the score of *Lucia* to be sent to his hotel – already determined that he would not only conduct but stage it.

Sandwiched between her *Lucias* in Catania and Rome was Maria's first *Medea* in Florence. She had once again proved that she was vocally unique. She could move with equal success from the florid tightrope walking of Donizetti and Bellini to the soaring, dramatic intensity of Puccini and Verdi, with the fiendish part of Cherubini's *Medea* in between. But Maria longed to be a dramatic, not just a vocal, phenomenon. She had an instinctive sense of drama which is what made the final rehearsals of *Medea* all the more frustrating for her. The lean and hungry look that she longed for was still not there: 'I darkened the colour and all that. It doesn't work . . . and then I was tired of playing a game like – for instance – playing a beautiful young woman, and I was a heavy, uncomfortable woman finding it difficult to move around. . . .' She had studied all her life to put things right musically, but vocal achievements were never for Maria an end in themselves. Her vocal mastery of Medea became an instrument for infusing the tragic princess with the grandeur that would bring her to life. Through her interpretation the contained classicism of *Medea* became torrential emotionalism and a little-known opera a huge box-office success. As Robert Mann put it in *Musical America*: 'The oblivion that has shrouded this opera for a hundred and fifty years is explained by the fact that singers of Miss Callas's artistry and intelligence are so very rare.'

It was the first performance of Cherubini's opera in his native land for nearly forty-five years. For the large Festival audience the evening was an unprecedented experience; but Maria knew – and the knowledge was a torment – that dramatically her Florence Medea was not yet the magnetic demi-woman, demi-goddess she saw in her mind's eye. 'The way I saw Medea,' said Maria a few months before her final *Medea* in 1961, 'was the way I feel it: fiery, apparently calm, but very intense. The happy time with Jason is past; now she is devoured by misery and fury.' Those who were expecting classical tradition and cultured civility came up instead against Maria's raw primitivism – the beast and the goddess in the same body, at war with one another. Norma agonized over taking her children's lives but could not bring herself to do it. Medea not only did it but glories in the murder. And the audience heard and felt the portrayal of unvarnished hatred, flaming jealousy, even raw evil. It was as if that night at the Teatro Comunale in Florence the veil that civilization had fastened over all these emotions was lifted, and in the darkness of the opera house the audience could allow itself to experience emotions which many had convinced themselves were safely under control or even non-existent. Now that Maria was expressing all the feelings they hardly dared feel, suppressed emotions could find a safe outlet and they could do their hating, envying and agonizing through her. The fact that the audience was perhaps the most fashionable of the *Maggio Musicale* in the city the very name of which is a symbol of civilization, added a poignancy – and a certain irony – to the occasion.

Among the fashionable and the knowledgeable in the audience was the Metropolitan Opera's General Manager, Rudolf Bing. Backstage after the performance he made it clear to her and to Meneghini that the Met was eager to welcome her as soon as her commitments allowed. It was not to be as soon as that. Meneghini, who after all had to do something to justify his existence, was once again playing hard to get. On this particular occasion he made financial demands on Bing which he half knew Bing could not, or at least would not, meet. Throughout the endless business talks, Meneghini, with snatches of English and torrents of Italian at his command, was at his most ill-natured. In many ways, of course, ill-nature was about the only thing that saved Battista from total insipidity. In the beginning, as the wealthy *bon vivant* of provincial Verona, he had a certain raffish sparkle about him, but the more international and glamorous his wife's career became the more his own sparkle diminished. And this was not by comparison alone; it was as if in some absolute sense the growing excitement that Maria generated and the grandeur that was increasingly surrounding her brought out all the blandness and pettiness in her husband.

Like so many who feed off reflected glory, Meneghini was becoming more royal than the Queen – always on the lookout for signs of *lèse-Callas*. There was never any lack of ambiguous gestures and equivocal words which Meneghini could decipher as signs of disloyalty. The surest sign in his book was a less-than-total willingness to do anything demanded – which in Meneghinese meant to *pay* anything demanded – to obtain Maria's services. Rudolf Bing had failed to pass the cash test; negotiations were broken off and both Meneghini and, with his help and prompting, Maria, worked themselves up into a solemn rage. Meneghini gave vent to it in a statement to the press:

'My wife will not sing at the Metropolitan as long as Mr Bing runs it. It is their loss.' It was not long before he had to eat his words, but for the time being, instead of New York, Maria went back to London. Once again at the Savoy, she was given the same suite with its beige and white walls, and the special huge mirror over the fireplace. From now on this was unofficially known as 'the Callas suite', and for the older members of the Savoy staff who still remembered Tetrazzini, there was a spasm of nostalgia when the massive bouquets arrived before and after all Maria's first nights. This time there were three: *Aida, Norma* and *Trovatore*. It was her Leonora in *Trovatore* that carried the day. 'In some way I cannot define', wrote Cecil Smith in *Opera*, 'she embodied both Leonora's passionate humanness and the formality with which the score and libretto universalize her emotions. The voice – or rather the use of it – was a source of unending amazement. For once we hear the trills fully executed, the scales and arpeggios totally full-bodied, the portamentos and long-breathing phrases fully supported and exquisitely inflected. The spectacular ovation after "D'amor sull'ali rosee" in the last act was no less than Callas deserved. . . .'

But Maria was not happy: she was not happy with the shabby sets, she was not happy with many of the singers engaged, and she was not happy with the conventional production. She would, of course, have been irritable even if the production had been of the highest artistic standards and the singers perfect. She had, after all, been living and keeping a punishing work schedule on green salads, almost raw meat and electrical massages. And Audrey Hepburn still seemed a very long way away.

She returned to Italy at the beginning of July and spent the summer between the Arena of Verona and recording sessions in Milan. After *Cavalleria Rusticana* with Serafin conducting, she began recording *Tosca* – a recording that was to make history. The combination of four ruthless perfectionists – Walter Legge, Victor de Sabata, Tito Gobbi and Maria – meant that for eleven days at La Scala, where the recording was being made, perfection was relentlessly pursued and miles of tape used. Indeed, miles were discarded: Tito Gobbi had to sing his first act music thirty times, working on the colour and the inflection even in individual syllables, before it would pass, and Maria worked on one phrase, '*E avanti a lui tremava tutta Roma*', for half an hour before they were satisfied.

'Callas paints the Tosca which previously she had only sketched,' was John Ardoin's summing-up of the recording. 'Though she is supreme in realizing the role's full-blooded emotions with realism and taste, it is the small brush-strokes of detail which make the portrait so finished. . . . It is the 1952 Mexico performance polished and made compelling.' On this occasion Maria is in superb company. She had first worked with de Sabata nine months earlier when they opened the La Scala season with *Vespri Siciliani.* The beginning of their relationship was quite tempestuous, right up to and including the dress rehearsal attended by critics and invited guests. There was a slight discrepancy between Callas and the orchestra. De Sabata instantly stopped and shouted 'Callas – watch me!' 'No, maestro,' smiled Maria, wagging her finger. '*You* watch me – your sight is better than mine.' They had both tested their strength, and had both decided that war between them would be too exhausting, so a peace followed, which during the recording grew into a friendship based on total professional respect.

After the recordings were over, Maria had more than a month of rest ahead of her before the resumption of the autumn hostilities. It was spent at home in Verona. Each of these respites had a distinct effect on the Meneghini home: it was filled with more and more gilded objects, the latest gadgets, and every kind of expensive knick-knack. As her home became heavier and more cluttered, the hostess herself was getting lighter by the day. The effect was not yet as dramatic as it was going to be, but Madame Biki, the new influence in Maria's life, was doing her best to accentuate it. Biki, who as well as being one of Milan's leading fashion designers was also Puccini's grand-daughter, was introduced to Maria at a dinner party given by Wally Toscanini. Wally, who was Toscanini's daughter, had become very close to Maria and kept doing her best to wean her father away from his total commitment to Tebaldi. It was Wally who had arranged the audition with her father that led to the plans for the *Macbeth* that in the end never happened. Now she was responsible for another – and much more fruitful – introduction. Biki took charge of Maria's wardrobe and her sartorial influence on Maria was unchallenged, at least for the moment.

La Wally, the opera after whose heroine Toscanini had named his daughter, had been chosen by La Scala to open their 1953/54 season to celebrate the sixtieth anniversary of Alfredo Catalani's death. Renata Tebaldi was Wally and even before opening night the press, the *claqueurs* and the Scala regulars were eagerly anticipating trouble ahead. Ghiringhelli had once again divided the season with Solomon-like fairness: *Lucia, Don Carlo, Alceste* and *Medea* for Maria; *La Wally, Otello, Tosca* and *Eugene Onegin* for Renata. The only thing he could do nothing diplomatic about was the crucial question of who should have the honour of opening the season. The previous season it had been Maria. This season, on the basis of Ghiringhelli's symmetrical justice, it had to be Renata.

Emilio Radius, music critic of *L'Europeo*, suggested with a toucing naïvety that the two rivals should bury the hatchet and have a great public handshake for the greater glory of opera. It is not clear whether Mr Radius's suggestion influenced Maria's decision or not, but there she was on opening night fervently and prominently applauding from her box. 'Happily,' commented *Musica e Dischi*, 'rivalry goes hand in hand with chivalry.' In the proscenium box was Toscanini himself, applauding no less fervently. A couple of nights later when Maria opened in *Medea*, Tebaldi failed to return the compliment. She was not there at all. Nor was Toscanini, who to the end remained one of Tebaldi's staunchest supporters.

Medea was a replacement for Scarlatti's *Mitridate Eupatore*. After Maria's Medea in Florence, the public response was so overwhelming that Ghiringhelli felt he had almost no option but to include *Medea* in the forthcoming season; Maria's Medea demanded to be heard. For Margherita Wallmann, who was directing the production, the last-minute switch was a nightmare. As if all her problems with sets, costumes and staging were not enough, ten days before opening night Victor de Sabata fell ill. Despair crept over La Scala. Suddenly Ghiringhelli saw a saviour in the shape of Leonard Bernstein, who was just coming to the end of a long concert tour in Italy. At the age of thirty-five, Bernstein had written musicals and one symphony, he had conducted the New York Philharmonic, he had taught at Brandeis University, but he had never worked in a major opera house before, he had never even heard of Cherubini's *Medea*, he was exhausted from his Italian tour, he was suffering from acute bronchitis – and he had ten days before opening night. But he fell in love with Cherubini's score at a glance, and to the absolute delight of everybody at La Scala, he said yes. His two main worries after he had said yes were the decomposing first edition score with which La Scala had provided him and his impending meeting with Maria – especially in view of the fact that he wanted to cut out one of her major arias. The decomposing pages went on giving off dust throughout the rehearsal, making tears stream down his face. But Maria found the Bernstein amalgam of sharp wit, good manners and sense of drama irresistible. As for Bernstein, working with Maria was to make up for all the coughing, the sneezing and the tears. 'Then came the famous meeting with Maria. To my absolute amazement she understood immediately the dramatic reasons for the transposition of scenes and numbers, and the cutting out of her aria in the second act. We got along famously – just perfect. She understood everything *I* wanted and I understood everything *she* wanted.'

On opening night, Maria, at her most powerful and most magnetic, had the audience enraptured. Or as Bernstein put it: 'The place was out of its mind. Callas? She was pure electricity.' In the last act, when she is ready to murder her children, she was seen, as the curtains parted, lying head downwards diagonally on the high staircase of the temple, a great blood-red cloak and her glowing auburn hair spread out around her. Totally immobile, gazing into the stormy night sky, she sang her first line: *'Numi, venite a me, inferni Dei!'* (Deities, come to me, infernal gods!) At the first rehearsal, she broke down in tears. 'I can't sing from such a position. It's impossible,' she said to Margherita Wallmann between her tears. But she did, and the tornadoes of applause at the end continued to ring in her ears for hours afterwards.

'This place will sink,' cries Medea. 'You do not mark the centre. Grass, earth, stones, speak to me.' So much of the music Maria chose to sing – and she was increasingly in a position to sing only what she chose – appealed to the primordial emotions, passions and sensibilities latent in modern man. 'Maria identified with Medea,' said Margherita Wallman. 'She was still a very young woman, married to a much older man. I am sure that certain sexual frustrations found an outlet in her work – unfulfilled passions were released in her singing and acting.' This quasi-Freudian interpretation is far too narrow to encompass the phenomenon of Maria. It was not only her own unfulfilled passions that were released by her singing and acting, but the unfulfilled, packed-down emotions of the modern public. Maria went beyond even that. She played out in stark colours throughout her life the conflict going on, in a much less clear and defined way, in each one of us: the conflict between our rational, respectable, conventional, 'normal' self and the deeper, primordial self, home both of the darkness we harbour and of all life-giving forces. The divorce between the two was in her case painful and dramatic. Medea and the respectable housewife represented the two extremes – the uncontainable primitive emotions and the strait-jacketed, meticulous, obsessive order with which she was surrounding herself. It was as if these emotions were to be tidied away in life as were her dresses, with matching gloves and shoes and a label indicating where and when they had been worn. Onassis helped reconcile these extremes for a while. When that was over, all that was conventionally respectable, even prudish, in her came to the surface to stay, increasingly dominating her public pronouncements. 'In those days there was restraint,' she said in 1971 to a student soprano singing 'D'amour l'ardente flamme' from *The Damnation of Faust* at the Juilliard School in New York. 'I wish it were like that now. Now, it's all exposed.' Was this the same Maria Callas who had sung Medea, Norma and Lady Macbeth?

Maria closed the year with *Medea* and it was with *Medea* that she opened 1954, always to sold-out houses. In between there were a few Christmas days at her home in Verona. 'If these were better times for music,' wrote Emilio Radius, 'Maria Callas would be the most famous woman in Europe.' She was soon to be exactly that and more, and the fame had less and less to do with music. Meanwhile she was steadily losing weight and her confidence in herself was rising with every pound she shed. What with her growing success and her constantly improving appearance, Maria was acquiring that honourable kind of self-confidence which alone enables a human being to take the risk of loving others. The security was far from deeply rooted. Even so, it meant that Maria could allow herself to become more relaxed with those around her, more aware of them and more caring towards them.

If headlines could build security the ones that greeted the first night of *Lucia* at La Scala on 18 January 1954 would have made her secure for ever:

LA SCALA IN DELIRIUM
FOUR MINUTES OF APPLAUSE FOR THE MAD SCENE
A RAIN OF RED CARNATIONS

The rain of red carnations had begun even before the audience went wild at the most famous mad scene in all opera. Maria picked up the red carnations one by one in a graceful allusion to the coming scene in which, as the *Opera News* reported, 'she outdid many a stage Ophelia'. The plot of Donizetti's *Lucia,* in which the heroine is forced to marry a man she does not love, was taken directly from Walter Scott's novel. Maria was fascinated by it; Karajan, who conducted and directed the Scala production, was no less fascinated by it, even going to the trouble of touring the Walter Scott country to get the feel of its architecture, its light and its iron-work. The moody, dim lighting Karajan achieved in his production was all-important for the effect of Gianni Ratto's impressionistic designs. Maria hated the bare, stylized sets, but adored working with

Karajan. Her visual realization of Lucia was largely her own and there were touches of striking originality in it. At the beginning of the Mad Scene, she emerged at the top of the staircase with her hair dishevelled, wearing a long white robe over her nightdress with immense sleeves opening in a hundred pleats and with a glazed stare in her eyes. She was not holding a dagger and her reasons for this break with tradition provided eloquent testimony to the integrity of her dramatic sense: 'I dislike violence and I find it artistically inefficient. Where it is necessary to include the shedding of blood, the suggestion of the action is more moving than the exhibition of it. I always eliminated the knife when singing Lucia. I thought it was a useless and old-fashioned business, that the action could get in the way of the art, and realism interfere with the truth.' Is this not the perfect epitaph for a thousand modern productions, as untruthful as they are 'realistic'?

Sandro Sequi, the Italian stage director who watched and studied many Callas performances during her prime, talked about 'the Callas secret': 'This alternation of tension and relaxation, I believe, was the key to Callas's magnetism, why her singing and acting were so compelling. Think of the movement of her arms in the Mad Scene of *Lucia*. They were like the wings of a great eagle, a marvellous bird. When they went up – and she often moved them very slowly – they seemed heavy, not airy like a dancer's arms, but weighted. Then, she reached the climax of a musical phrase, her arms relaxed and flowed into the next gesture, until she reached a new musical peak, and then again calm. There was a continuous line to her singing and movements, which were really very simple. Everything about her struck me as natural and instinctive, never intellectual. She was extremely stylized and classic, yet at the same time human – but a humanity on a higher plane of existence, almost sublime.'

Thousands thought Maria sublime, but just as many were busy enumerating the faults of her voice. Picking at the flaws in Maria's singing, as one of her more ardent Milanese admirers put it, was like pointing out that in Leonardo's *Last Supper* the knives need polishing. Nevertheless the nit-picking was going on, the downright condemnation of her voice as ugly, even unmusical. And the criticism seemed to be growing in direct proportion to the adulation.

There was another battle that Maria was winning, and her victory was reflected in the downward trend of a chart kept at home by the Meneghinis:

Gioconda	92
Aida	87
Norma	80
Medea	78
Lucia	75
Alceste	65
Don Carlo	64

Twenty-eight kilos (sixty-two pounds) lost between the *Gioconda* of December 1952 and the *Don Carlo* of 1954 – the last production in the Scala season. But the figures tell less than half the story; the result was a mythical transformation. 'She became another woman,' said Giulini who was conducting *Alceste*, 'and another world of expression opened to her. Potentials held in the shadows emerged. In every sense, she had been transformed.' She could now even be lifted above three bearers' heads and borne aloft into the temple as the curtain closed on the second act of *Alceste*.

Gluck's *Alceste* had never been performed at La Scala before. Too classical for the Italian temperament, it was nevertheless a wonderful vehicle for Maria, and a wealth of talent headed by Giulini and Margherita Wallmann was lavished on the production. They both loved working with Maria. 'For me', said Giulini, 'she was *il melodramma* – total rapport between work, music and action. It is no fabricated legend. In my entire experience of the theatre, I know of no artist like Callas.' As for Margherita Wallmann, she was fascinated by Maria even before she met her. She had caught a glimpse of her one night in a restaurant; at one moment, Maria removed her glasses: '. . . Her huge, dark eyes, they haunted me, for I felt I had seen them before. One day I realized where. They are exactly like those of the famous statue of the charioteer of

Auriga at Delphi.' There is no doubt that Greek subjects stirred deep emotions in Maria. The classic gestures of Greek tragedy were no mere details in her performance; they came from the depths of her being. But, as always, there were many who disliked Maria in *Alceste* and Klemperer was one of them. Once when Walter Legge took her to a concert of his, Klemperer told her as much: 'Your Lucia is marvellous,' he said. 'Your Aida . . . your Norma . . . but your Alceste, forgive me for saying so, is not good. . . . We must do something together.'

'It would be an honour.'

'What would you like to do?'

'Alceste, of course, Maestro.'

The maestro's reservations notwithstanding, Alceste, the Queen of Pharae, was a fitting vehicle for the new Maria. With no high Renaissance bulk about her, she was in everything linear, elegant, dignified, graceful. In everything, that is, on-stage. Off-stage, even with her new figure, the new Biki wardrobe and Toy the new poodle in tow, Maria was the oddest mixture of grandeur and clumsiness – a combination of the inspired and the commonplace. As François Valéry, one of her closest friends in the last years, put it, 'she could be extraordinarily beautiful and at times almost ugly.' Yet from the moment she stepped on the stage, through some almost mystic transformation, Maria became the character she was to play. Giulini summed up this transformation as he saw it happen during *Alceste*: 'Off-stage Maria is really a very simple woman of humble background. Alceste, however, is a great Queen, a figure of classic nobility. Yet Callas transmitted all Alceste's royal stature. To my mind it is useless to search for an explanation. It is a kind of genius.'

Six days after her second appearance as the Queen of Pharae, Maria made her first appearance as Elisabeth, Queen of Spain, in Verdi's *Don Carlo*. She looked stunning in costumes made of black, silver and white, designed by Nicola Benois and inspired by Velazquez. She had at last reached her target weight and it was an ironic tribute to her transformation that the rave reviews were reserved for her physical appearance and her regal bearing, her singing being much less enthusiastically received. Riccardo Malipiero, writing in *Opera*, felt that '. . . Perhaps Callas' voice is not quite suited to Verdi's music. . . . This wonderful singer, so confident in difficult passages and powerful in dramatic passages, lacks the sweetness and softness necessary in moments of abandon. . . .' Others felt that she would have been better as the fiery Eboli. In fact Ebe Stignani as Eboli got the greatest honours of the night. Nicola Rossi-Lemeni, who had instigated Maria's first engagement at the Arena of Verona, was Philip II. He had remained a friend with whom Maria could relax and be at her most natural – and her most vulnerable. 'Despite Maria's power,' he remembers, 'she often doubted herself and grew anxious, fearing failure. She could never rest because of the great obligations she felt to her work. She frequently asked practical advice about her acting. And if I suggested a gesture or pose she liked, she'd say: "Now, you gave me something I should have thought of myself."'

Somehow Maria never stopped feeling frustration at the fact that she could not do everything, think of everything, achieve perfection in everything. The frustration stayed with her all her life and it grew as the difficulties with her voice increased. Right to the end, when she could no longer sing the high soprano roles and opera houses round the world were offering her any mezzo-soprano part she cared to choose, Maria refused to contemplate any of them, except for Carmen – and she would only sing that on record. It is as if singing mezzo-soprano roles, accepting that she was human and therefore subject to all the laws of waning powers, was equivalent in Maria's eyes to conceding defeat. In many ways she never forgave herself for not being superhuman.

While she was still singing *Don Carlo* at La Scala, she began recording *Norma*. Now she had her chance to help those who had helped her on the way up. It was now her turn to influence the casting and select her conductors – so Nicola Rossi-Lemeni found himself as Oroveso and, although Serafin had no official connection with La Scala, it was he who conducted most of the Callas operas recorded with the orchestra and chorus of La Scala. *Norma* was being recorded at the Cinema Metropol in Milan and

Maria's arrivals and departures were watched eagerly by the local Milanesi. Autographs, hand-shakings, even spontaneous bursts of applause in the street – all the elements of mass celebrity were building up. Visibility bred celebrity, which bred more visibility, which bred more celebrity; all the signs were that Maria was now on that particular carousel for good. Her celebrity was spreading even where she had not yet become visible. Requests for interviews from America were becoming more numerous, and Maria's next goal was to repeat, even exceed, in America the triumph she had won in Europe. During an interview for the American magazine *High Fidelity* in one of the breaks from recording *Norma*, she articulated her artistic philosophy: 'Every year I want to be better than the year before. Otherwise I'd retire. I don't need the money. I work for art.'

As with many of Maria's public pronouncements there was very little of Maria in them, and an awful lot of La Callas. It was more than true by now that she didn't need the money, but the fact that she didn't need it didn't mean that she didn't want it both for itself and as a symbol of others wanting and needing her; nor did it mean that she stopped worrying about it. There was, however, a truly prophetic element in the statement. She did want every year to do better than the year before; and, even though she would never bring herself to speak the word, she did indeed retire when she stopped getting better each year.

Recordings dominated the rest of the spring and summer. The long-playing record had stopped being a curiosity; a huge and growing market had been opened up and Maria's records were in such demand internationally that EMI would not consider doing a recording at La Scala without her. Walter Legge had put together the winning combination of Callas–Gobbi–di Stefano, more often than not under Serafin's baton, and this inspired partnership was to produce some of the greatest post-war recordings. In the spring and summer of 1954 the performances became an adjunct to the recordings. EMI wanted to record Verdi's *La Forza del Destino*; Maria sang it at Ravenna. EMI wanted to record Boito's *Mefistofele*; Maria sang it in the Arena of Verona, though in the end only one aria was recorded as part of a recital disc.

It was almost time for the launching of her American career. The Met had a ceiling of $1,000 an evening for any singer, but for Lawrence Kelly and Carol Fox, two young concert organizers who were hoping to revive Chicago's famous Opera, the ceiling was dictated by what would persuade Maria to appear in Chicago. They agreed to everything: Maria's choice of repertory – *Norma, Traviata* and *Lucia*; Maria's casting suggestions, which meant that Gobbi, di Stefano and Rossi-Lemeni were all included; Maria's, or rather Meneghini's, financial terms – $12,000 for six performances (double the Met ceiling) and return travel and other expenses for two.

The news of Maria's impending debut at the Chicago Lyric had been trumpeted across the States long before the Meneghinis landed at Chicago at the end of October to a barrage of photographers and reporters. Maria's life had become, especially in the popular papers, history and biography, legend and stereotype, expressing all the values of the American Dream. She was living out so many cultural and fairy-tale archetypes the papers had a hard time choosing which to lead on: rags to riches; ugly duckling to beautiful swan; the infant prodigy returning as adult star; the little American from Washington Heights coming back home. The presence of George Callas, the Father, by his daughter's side meant that 'the return of the native' aspect of the legend had no difficulty in winning the day. Maria was given a heroine's welcome even before the sensation caused by *Norma* on the opening night. And after the performance, at the Angel Ball organized for the benefit of the Illinois Opera Guild, she did little more than shake hands and listen to unending congratulations.

Maria had launched the Lyric Opera of Chicago into international orbit. As for herself, the morning after was only a continuation of the triumph of the night before. 'For my money,' wrote Claudia Cassidy in the *Chicago Tribune*, 'she was not only up to specifications, she surpassed them. . . . She sang the "Casta Diva" in a kind of mystic dream like a goddess of the moon briefly descended.' Maria rang Claudia Cassidy after her review. She knew that Cassidy had first heard her singing *La*

Gioconda at Verona, and what she wanted to say to her on the phone was not 'Thank you for the review', but 'Have I improved?' Well, as Claudia Cassidy put it, that was one word for it.

Then came Maria's *Traviata* – an exquisite courtesan dressed by Biki, a fragile creature of feverish excitement, temptations and fears, the girl who fled from artificiality into heartbreak. As Claudia Cassidy put it after Maria's death: 'It's all in Verdi's music, but how many hear it?' It was after she had seen her Violetta that Claudia Cassidy went to the Ambassador where Maria was staying to talk to her. On her way there she stopped at Elizabeth Arden's to buy a lipstick the exact colour of the great bow appliquéd on Violetta's ball gown. Maria snatched it as greedily as a child. 'I love presents,' she said. 'And it's the colour of the bow on my dress. How wonderful!'

Maria was always a greedy child when it came to presents. Like a child she was much less interested in their value than in the fact that they were presents, and like a child she had no compunction about asking for them. 'When you come back to Paris will you bring me my favourite truffles?' she would ask a Greek friend, Christian Bischini, when she had moved to Paris and he was still living in Milan. Or 'Sander,' she would ask Gorlinsky, her agent, later on, 'will you send me those quilts that I liked so much when you go to Germany?' But the bringing of presents by no means guaranteed her favour. Lipstick or no lipstick she liked Claudia Cassidy. She respected her knowledge, her professionalism and of course the fact that she so totally responded to what Maria was trying to achieve on stage.

'Question: Which is Mad, the Callas Lucia or Her Frenzied Public?' – so read the headlines on Claudia Cassidy's review of Callas's last creation in Chicago. 'Near pandemonium broke out. There was an avalanche of applause, a roar of cheers growing steadily louder and a standing ovation, and the aisles were full of men pushing as close to the stage as possible. I am sure they wished for bouquets to throw, a carriage to pull through the streets. Myself, I wished they had had both.' There were twenty-two curtain-calls at the last performance of *Lucia* and still the cheering audience would not let her go. Maria was feeling more vindicated than triumphant. 'There is justice,' she said at the time. 'I have had it. There is God. I have been touched by God's finger.'

She had indeed. But behind the glory, the adulation, the dream come true, a cloud was darkening the sky. So far, it could hardly be seen with eyes dazzled by the blaze of her triumph; it was, after all, nothing more than a tiresome law-suit brought by the disgruntled Bagarozy. The suit, based on the 1947 contract that granted Bagarozy power as the artist's sole representative, claimed a percentage of Maria's fees and the expenses he was supposed to have incurred on her behalf – a total of $300,000. Nicola Rossi-Lemeni, who had signed the same agreement, paid a few thousand dollars and reached a settlement, but Meneghini had no intention of giving up anything, and Maria immediately issued a denial of Bagarozy's claim, declaring that the 1947 contract was obtained under duress and that Bagarozy had done absolutely nothing to promote her career.

The draining effect of the Bagarozy lawsuit would, over three years of expensive and highly publicized legal manoeuvres, grow inexorably greater, and like many of the other clouds over her life, it could so easily have been avoided. Yet it is at midday that the sun begins to set and the same is true of a career, a life. It is at the moment when it is directly overhead that it is beginning its descent. In the end the growing darkness would extinguish even the light shed by a popular acclaim never equalled, before or since, in all the history of opera. But that was still far off, and before that moment arrived the popular acclaim was to become even more deafening.

Chapter Eight

'WHAT have you done with all that weight? How did you make yourself so beautiful?' It was Maria's first day back at La Scala. Blonde, slim, still riding high after the Chicago triumph, she walked into the theatre and was greeted by an amazed Toscanini. The transformation was so spectacular that even Toscanini, whose sight had been notoriously poor, had noticed. The maestro had been lured back to inaugurate La Piccola Scala with *Falstaff,* though in the end it all became too much for him, and he never did. Visconti had been tempted by Maria. It was one of the most striking ways in which she helped revolutionize opera. She drew to the opera houses, and fired with her own vision, first Visconti and then Zeffirelli; together they created the total theatre, the perfect fusion of music, singing and drama of which so many had dreamt, and ushered into opera houses, where conductors were kings, the reign of the producers. And she did this at the same time as she put the singer back in the centre as the chief vehicle for the composer's dramatic intentions. From one perspective we can see every major reform of opera, whether through Gluck, Wagner or Verdi, as directed towards raising the dramatic interest to equal the musical interest. With Maria the dramatic interest not only equalled the musical interest, it often far exceeded it, for she breathed richness into empty melodies, and gave dramatic life to operas which musically hardly deserved to be staged. Virtually single-handedly, she revitalized and expanded the bel canto repertory and made us listen seriously to Bellini, Donizetti, and even Spontini, by bringing to their music and her work a total dramatic commitment.

Spontini's *La Vestale,* with which her collaboration with Visconti was launched, demonstrated this point. Maria had asked for its revival after it had suffered twenty-five years of neglect. Her reasons could hardly have been musical. *La Vestale,* with its pedestrian score and stilted plot. is a kind of poor man's *Norma*: Giulia, like Norma, is a priestess who betrays her calling for love of a Roman soldier; she allows the sacred flame to go out in the temple and is condemned to death for it. When she asked for *La Vestale,* Maria also determined that Visconti should produce it so that together they could transcend dramatically the opera's musical limitations. It was she who sought him out, and she who cleared the way into La Scala for him. He had against him the entire Milanese establishment — those who did not mind his homosexuality objected to his communism and vice versa. But Maria was the reigning queen and Maria wanted Visconti. She wanted to draw into the world of opera men whose hearts were in drama. A few years later she did it again, when she approached Alexis Minotis, the Greek theatre director, and pleaded with him to direct her Medea. 'But I don't know anything about opera,' he protested. 'I don't even like it.' 'So much the better,' she snapped. 'I don't want opera directors. I want *directors*.'

In Visconti, she had that and much more. Opera and drama were in his blood. Born in Milan, at the same moment that the curtain was rising on a performance of *Traviata,* he felt that he had been 'practically raised at La Scala'. He grew up in a home saturated with art, and his family's box at the opera, fourth on the left in the first tier, decorated in red damask, was where as a very young boy he learnt to love opera. In 1897, his grandfather, Guido Visconti, Duke of Modrone, headed a group of Milanese opera lovers who saved La Scala when the commune of Milan had unexpectedly withdrawn its financial support. He then proceeded to perform an even greater service to the house by appointing Toscanini as its artistic director. And now, in 1954, fifty-seven years later, Toscanini and the Duke's grandson had both been lured back.

To Maria, Visconti was a magician. He summoned up imperial, neo-classical Rome with enormous pillars flanking La Scala's stage and with colours cold like white, moon-struck marble. And he summoned up for Maria her Vestal Virgin, complete with every gesture, movement and expression. They met at a point of intensity where there are no barriers. She was fascinated. More, she was in love. Visconti had entered her bloodstream, and Maria, thoroughly oblivious of all her conventional instincts, of her husband and of all those around her, had no compunction about showing it. At first her imagination was aroused by his stage genius, by the energy he radiated as he chain-smoked his way through rehearsals. But gradually the woman in her took over from the artist, and whether at rehearsals, backstage at La Scala or at the Biffi Scala, she scanned the horizon for his large, imposing figure with the elegant leonine head. Visconti was just as fascinated, but sexually he was much more interested – even though the interest was never reciprocated – in Franco Corelli, the young tenor making his first Scala appearance. 'Beauty. Something beautiful' was the way he summed up Maria. 'Intensity, expression, everything. She was a monstrous phenomenon. Almost a sickness – the kind of actress that has passed for all time.' Visconti for Maria was more than a monstrous artistic phenomenon; he was a man.

In the photographs of their rehearsals of *Vestale* Maria appears softer, younger and more beautiful than ever before. In the photographs of the performances she looks almost ethereal. All this newly-awakened femininity needed an outlet, and Meneghini had stopped being a romantic focus for Maria a few days, not to say hours, after they had met. There were, of course, times at the beginning and occasionally even later in their marriage when there was a real glow to the relationship, but these moments were rare. It is true that Meneghini could become luminous at certain temperatures, but very quickly he subsided into his everyday self: an efficient, unimaginative manager with more than his share of vanity and self-importance. Walter Legge described an instance that typified their relationship when the following year, after the first night of *Lucia* in Berlin, he returned to his hotel at three in the morning to be informed by the anxious concierge that Maria Callas and her husband were waiting for him, and insisted on seeing him no matter how late he came. 'There they were, both sitting up in their beds,' recalled Walter Legge, 'woollen undervests visible beneath their nightwear, reading Italian illustrateds, while they waited for an inquest upon the performance. Had she done herself justice? Was her applause louder and longer than anyone else ever had in Berlin? Reassured, they turned on their sides and switched off the lights.'

Towards the end of 1954, other forces and other needs had been awakened in Maria, and it was this awakening that had led to the obsession with Luchino. She was slim and attractive, and for the first time felt confident in her appeal to men, not just as a singer but as a woman. 'Maria began to fall in love with me,' said Visconti a few years later. 'Like so many Greeks she has a possessive streak and there were many terrible jealous scenes. She hated Corelli because he was handsome. It made her nervous – she was wary of beautiful people. She was always watching to see I didn't give him more attention than I gave her.' The jealous scenes did not stop backstage at La Scala. They were carried on at Biffi Scala, the restaurant nearest to the Opera House. Maria would burst in, looking for Visconti if she had failed to find him around La Scala. She would peer through her glasses – often specially put on for the occasion – and if she failed to see him, she would just storm off, ignoring everyone present. If he was there, she had a way of sensing, almost smelling, where he was, and even without her glasses on, darting towards him. There was something spectacular, even sublime, about the way she was prepared to make herself ridiculous. Her passion may have been sparked off originally by high art, but the way it was expressed was pure adolescence.

The total absence of sophisticated feminine tricks – coyness, aloofness and a diplomatic disguising of feelings – is refreshing, but at the same time hard to believe. Yet it is true. Maria at the age of thirty had a violent teenage crush on her teacher, for that was the role Visconti came increasingly to adopt in the course of the production. 'I could forgive her anything,' said Visconti, referring to the jealous outbursts, 'she did all I asked so scrupulously, so precisely, so beautifully. What I demanded she rendered, never adding anything of her own. Sometimes during a rehearsal I'd say, "Come on, Maria, do a little by yourself, do something you like." But then she'd ask, "What should I do? How am I to place this hand? I don't know where to put it!" The simple fact was that because of this crazy infatuation, she wanted to have me command her every step.' Maria had surrendered: the virago in her had gone into hiding and the lost little girl who wanted to be guided, protected and told what to do promptly emerged. 'For me,' explained Visconti, 'she was a wonderful instrument which could be played as I wished and which responded in an inspired way.' And, added the headmaster graciously, 'If put on the right course, she always exceeded your hopes.'

Rumours about the production of *Vestale* had been circulating for some time before the first night, and the temperature was high with expectations. Visconti was making a sensational debut as an opera director... Toscanini was going to be in the first-night audience... the production's budget was an unprecedented eighty million lire... a raised stage had been built over the existing one... the performance was being broadcast... Maria Callas was more beautiful than ever....

On the night itself the spectacle, with the massive three-dimensional sets and the feathered head-gear, was overwhelming. But what distinguished this first Callas–Visconti collaboration, and explains the influence it had on subsequent productions, was that the audience could at last believe in the action on the stage. The highlight of the evening, however, was not part of Visconti's contribution. It was pure Callas. During one of the curtain-calls after Act II, Maria was greeted by a torrent of carnations torn from the garlands that were decorating the opera house. She picked up one of them, bowed to Toscanini who was sitting in a stage box and gave the flower to the old maestro. The house went wild. Maria's exact and instinctive sense of timing, both in character and during her curtain-calls, was unique. Whether through the brilliant attack of her voice, the power to make it sound unexpectedly steely and harsh or the way she would suddenly colour a phrase or shape a gesture to make a precise dramatic statement, she could create intense and unrepeatable moments. The day after the first night of *Vestale,* the front pages were full of the Toscanini carnation incident. And of course full of Maria: 'She looked superb,' wrote Peter Hoffer in *Music and Musicians.* Her appearance was increasingly vying with her singing for first place in the critics' praise.

Her first opera in 1955 was meant to be *Il Trovatore* with Mario del Monaco as Manrico, but five days before opening night on 8 January, del Monaco, at the height of his popularity at the time, succeeded in persuading Ghiringhelli to replace *Trovatore* with Giordano's *Andrea Chénier*, which he had sung three weeks earlier with great success at the Met. Maria, who at the time felt strong enough to undertake anything and who in any case loved launching herself into new roles, agreed to learn the part of Maddalena di Coigny in five days. It was like old times again – as if she could not resist creating new challenges for herself.

She had always thrived on taking risks, but this time she fell off the tightrope. The punishing schedule of the previous six months and the concentrated rehearsals for *Chénier* showed in her voice on the first night, and by now, after her accumulated successes, there were plenty of people eager to magnify any flaw. They waited for her greatest moment in the opera, her big aria 'La mamma morta'; and they did not wait in vain. Maria let a climactic high B get out of control and wobble widely. The result was pandemonium. Loud booing broke out and the hoots and whistles drowned the applause. The composer's widow went backstage to congratulate Maria on her interpretation; the critic Emilio Radius wrote that her performance 'would have left the good Giordano open-mouthed with admiration'; but this solace, like the applause of the night, was tainted for Maria by the echoes of the booing that went on long after the booing itself had stopped. She felt bitter, furious with the hooting and whistling that, as it did not take her long to discover, were led by the Tebaldi faction in the top gallery; but she felt even more furious with herself for having given in to del

Monaco's demand for the last-minute change.

Her conviction that the world was against her had another layer added to it, especially as the rumour was also going round that it was she who was to blame for the substitution. 'They want my blood,' she said, referring to Tebaldi's partisans, and the statement reveals more about her own state of mind at the time than about her enemies' intentions. Everybody was getting a touch of her bitterness these days but it was Renata who became her main target. 'If the time comes,' said Maria in an outburst she would come to regret, 'when my dear friend Renata Tebaldi sings Norma or Lucia one night, then Violetta, La Gioconda or Medea the next – then and only then will we be rivals. Otherwise it is like comparing champagne with cognac. No – with Coca-Cola.' The reporter may well have sharpened what Maria actually said but the public nonetheless believed that the printed words came straight from Maria's mouth, and the Tebaldi–Callas rivalry escalated to open warfare. When Maria opened in Rome a few days later in *Medea,* the local Tebaldiani were there in force, noisily determined to prevent the audience from giving their exclusive attention to Maria.

It was clear that the drama that January night in Rome would not be confined to the stage. By the time the singers took their bows, the conflict had spread to both sides of the curtain. Boris Christoff, who throughout the preparation of the production had been infuriated by Maria's insistence on what he regarded as endless, excessive rehearsals, decided to take his revenge, in classic operatic manner, when Maria was about to take her solo bow. He stepped in front of her, determined to bar her way with his own massive body if necessary. Maria had no option but to concede. Such behaviour was for her only further evidence that she was living in a hostile world, where even her fellow singers had turned against her.

She returned to Milan exhausted. A painful boil at the back of her neck was a constant, tangible reminder of just how run down she was both physically and emotionally. Her doctor ordered complete rest; it was not the first time, nor would it be the last. The opening night of *La Sonnambula* had to be put off for two weeks, to the great delight of Leonard Bernstein who was conducting and who managed to get eighteen orchestral rehearsals for a score that was often done with one. Visconti had found in Bernstein a fellow perfectionist and they spent hours together going over details of the production, including hours sitting in the costume warehouses of La Scala picking feathers for the caps of the chorus.

Maria, no less infatuated with Visconti now than she had been three months earlier, was keeping herself informed of all his movements – even from her sick-bed in the Grand Hotel. Visconti remembered the first time he and Bernstein went to see her. 'When the moment came to leave, we said, "Ciao, Maria. Get well!" and headed for the door. "You stay here!" she commanded me. "I don't want you going off with Lenny again!"' And when, a couple of days later, Maria was going to leave the Grand Hotel and start rehearsing *Sonnambula,* she was no less demanding and no less possessive of her Luchino. During *Vestale* all her jealousy had been directed towards Franco Corelli; now it was Bernstein who became the target. The very things that she had found attractive before – his looks, his forcefulness, his rambling, leisurely voice – suddenly became a threat. She watched their every step together, she even spied on them when they left the theatre to go for a walk or a cup of coffee.

Once at work, however, the love-struck impetuous teenager was transformed into an obedient, almost deferential, disciple, ready to carry out Luchino's every wish. Only once did she protest. *La Sonnambula* takes place in a Swiss village, yet Visconti insisted that Maria should wear her own real jewels at reheasals. 'But Luchino,' she said, 'I am a village girl!' 'No you are *not* a village girl. You are Maria Callas *playing* a village girl, and don't you forget that.'

'You must believe what you see, but truth must be filtered through art' – that was Visconti's artistic philosophy and Maria helped him give it life. He left nothing to chance. With the help of Piero Tosi, the designer, he turned Maria's Amina into a visual incarnation of the renowned nineteenth-century ballerina Maria Taglioni, who had inspired Visconti's conception of the part. Maria looked graceful, fragile – she even looked small. Luchino coaxed the little ballerina steps from her and even taught her how to stand in a ballerina's fifth position. 'A sylphide tripping on a moonbeam' is how Piero Tosi remembers her.

Amina walks in her sleep, and one night she actually walks into a stranger's bed. Elvino, her fiancé, who knows nothing of her sleep-walking, is outraged, and is only finally convinced of her fidelity when he sees her walking in her sleep over a fragile bridge. Piero Tosi recalls that in the dress rehearsal Maria, 'with the lake and the mountains behind her, looked like a shadow, a spectre, floating upwards. When she came to the broken plank of the bridge – where she must simulate falling and all the chorus gasps in horror – I watched her closely. Though she seemed to fall, I saw that she actually remained absolutely still. Yet she caused the sensation of a fall – the fall of a ghost. I was fascinated. I had to know how she did it and so, at the *première*, I stood in the wings near her as she ascended the bridge. Slowly, she began to fill her lungs with air, and this gave an illusion of flight, of floating upward.... Then, when she had to fall, she quickly exhaled all her breath. What can you say? She was a theatrical wizard and knew all the tricks.'

Yet the theatrical wizard was far from confident in her wizardry. She needed constant encouragement. For nearly seven years, Meneghini had been her chief and constant support. He was always in the wings whispering: 'Go on Maria. There's no one like you. You're the greatest in the world.' Now, for the first time since 1947 and the Arena of Verona, his place in the wings had been taken by another. It was to Visconti that Maria turned for encouragement and reassurance. He had to lead her to the stage before each act and prod her to go on. Then she would beg him: 'Please take me to this point', and again 'to this point...' And they would go two feet, and then two more feet, nearer the opera stage. Paradoxically it was during the last act, when her theatrical wizardry was most admired, that she was least secure and needed Visconti all the more to tell her if her tone had been pure, if her phrasing had been good, if she had made any mistakes.

She could not take Visconti on stage with her, so she devised a substitute, which Visconti described with relish: 'I always kept a handkerchief in my pocket with a drop of a particular English perfume on it, and Maria loved the scent. She told me always to place the handkerchief on the divan on which she had to lie down during the inn scene. "That way I'll be able to walk directly to it with my eyes closed." And so that's how we accomplished this effect. Luckily no musician in the orchestra ever decided to wear the same perfume or one night she might have walked right off the the stage and into the pit.'

At the end of the opera, when Amina awakes and is reunited with her fiancé, all the lights both on stage and in the auditorium were turned up full, including La Scala's great central chandelier. The last bars of her final bravura aria 'Ah! non giunge' were drowned in the pandemonium, the bravos and the applause that broke out.

It was another Callas–Visconti triumph. Maria was riding the full swell of this great year and the presence of Visconti by her side made her relish it all the more. As for Meneghini, he did not allow himself to be disturbed by his wife's blatant infatuation, or at least he did not show any signs of being disturbed. So long as there was no chance of the infatuation being consummated, the manager's prudence controlled the Italian husband's indignation. As it happened, he had much less opportunity than usual to act the part of Maria's shadow, as most of his time was spent on the Via Michelangelo Buonarroti where a four-storey house was being turned into a home fit for the Queen of La Scala. If Verona had been Maria's first real home, Milan was about to see her first real palace. The intervening years and Visconti's influence had gone some way towards obliterating the gilded Veronese vulgarity of her first home. The arrogance of style with which Visconti had inspired her was bound to spill over to her surroundings. Still, she had not stopped being Madame Meneghini, so the house on Via Buonarroti reflected Maria in transition. Three quarters Meneghini, a quarter Visconti: all glass and red marble with elaborate antiques, indifferent Renaissance paintings and every kind of bric-à-brac. When he was not supervising Via Buonarroti,

Meneghini was busy negotiating with Lawrence Kelly, who had flown over from Chicago in a final attempt to get a contract out of Maria for the second season of the Chicago Lyric Opera. Meneghini was playing his favourite game of increasing his demands, and as soon as these were granted going away to think up some more conditions that had to be met before actually signing the agreement, and when these were met, remembering a few more points that had not been discussed. . . .

Kelly knew that Maria was not simply crucial for the Chicago season – without her there might not be any Chicago season. So he gave way on every point raised by Meneghini and on every additional point raised by Maria whenever he managed to track her down eating at Biffi Scala. One of the more bizarre clauses in the contract that Maria finally signed was the assumption by the management of the Chicago Lyric of full responsibility during the season for protecting her against legal proceedings by Bagarozy. And one of the more bizarre suggestions Maria made in the course of the interminable discussions involved Renata Tebaldi. 'You should sign up Renata Tebaldi,' she said to Lawrence Kelly. 'Then your audience will have the opportunity to compare us, and your season will be even more successful.' It is impossible to say whether the suggestion stemmed from childish hubris or from unconscious self-destructiveness; what is certain is that Maria was in a provocative mood.

Tebaldi returned to La Scala on 26 April 1955 in Verdi's *La Forza del Destino.* This was the last time she sang at La Scala until 7 December 1959. It was a decision quietly made but tenaciously kept. Renata had decided that La Scala was not big enough for two queens – and she was not going to play lady-in-waiting to Maria.

Six days before Renata opened at La Scala for what was therefore to be her last performance for over four years, La Scala saw Maria for the first time in a comic role – Fiorilla in *Il Turco in Italia.* The same opera that five years before had signalled the beginning of the Visconti stage of her life was now the first opera produced for her by Zeffirelli. At first Maria, fiercely loyal to Visconti, was very suspicious of this young producer who was rumoured to be the great future hope of La Scala and, as Maria saw it, a threat to the supremacy of her beloved Luchino. But she loved his designs for *Il Turco,* and it soon became clear during the rehearsals that here was a director whom she could unequivocally trust and in whose capable hands she could do what, paradoxically, she most loved doing – surrender. It became clear equally quickly that Zeffirelli knew exactly how to bring out the best in Maria. 'Off-stage,' he remembers, 'Maria was not a very funny lady. She was always taking herself so damn seriously. To make Fiorilla come alive I had to invent clever by-play for her. Well, Maria was greedy for jewellery. She had a diamond necklace and an emerald collar and after every *première* her husband added a new souvenir to her collection. So I covered the Turk – Nicola Rossi-Lemeni – with many jewels. I told Maria that as soon as Fiorilla sees him she must be frightened but fascinated by this fool with his splendid ornaments. Whenever the Turk offered her his hand, Maria would take it and examine his rings. She was adorable doing it, really very funny. At one point she even danced a little tarantella and at another took off her shoe to hit her rival Zaida.'

Maria was enjoying herself and La Scala's audience loved the transformation of their foremost tragedienne into an accomplished, effervescent comedienne. At the end of the first night, her dressing-room was full of fans, photographers and fashionable opera-lovers, but when Zeffirelli walked in, Maria left everyone and approached him. 'Your father liked it?' was her first question. Zeffirelli assured her that he had loved it and was coming to see her, but it was taking him some time to cross the stage as he was crippled. Then Maria did something she did all too rarely throughout her life: she followed what her heart told her instead of what the role of the reigning primadonna dictated. She gripped Zeffirelli by the hand and walked out in search of his father. When they found the old man she kissed him and before he could congratulate her, she thanked him for coming to see the performance. Zeffirelli never forgot this, one of the precious moments that, much more than their professional respect for each other, went to cement their deep friendship.

The last performance of *Il Turco* was on 4 May 1955. Maria had exactly thirty-three days before the opening night of what was to be a great Callas–Visconti–Giulini triumph: *La Traviata.* It was Visconti's favourite opera, but the production was built entirely round Maria. 'I staged it for her, only for her, not for myself. I did it to serve Callas, for one *must* serve a Callas.' Visconti began his daring innovations by moving the action about forty years forward to *fin-de-siècle* Paris. The reason? Maria would look wonderful in costumes of the time, in gowns with a tight bodice, a bustle and long train. She did more than that. She looked a dream within the dream of the *belle époque* that Visconti and Lila de Nobili, the designer, masterfully conjured up.

Maria's waist seemed to be getting smaller and smaller. After she had seen Audrey Hepburn in *Roman Holiday,* she was determined to become, or at least to look, even slimmer, so she kept tightening her already tight corset and calling the wardrobe mistress to have the seams of Violettas's dresses pulled in. Maria's transition from fat, awkward opera singer to slender, elegant singing actress was not and never would be complete in her mind. It had occurred with a speed that bewildered her, and part of her remained forever locked in the plump, clumsy adolescent she had once been. She knew she had been fat and might be fat again, a fear felt all the more strongly on the days when she gave in to old temptations and consumed an entire box of *marrons glacés* at a sitting. But worse than that fear was the pervasive and persistent conviction that she was in fact ugly, that the beautiful woman the world responded to was a mask, a disguise, almost a trick. She remained convinced to the end of her life that it was the package of clothes, hair-dos, jewellery, figure and furs that was admired and extolled and never Maria herself. That is why her preoccupation with her appearance was almost obsessional and why so much precious energy was absorbed by the presentation to the world's hostile eyes of little, insignificant, unworthy Maria. Her beauty was a weapon, not a charm, and every warrior's first duty, after all, is to keep his weapons in top condition.

Yet Maria never looked more bruised or more frail than

in the last two acts of this *Traviata.* She sang 'Dite alla giovine', her renunciation of her lover in response to his father's plea, with her face inclined to the floor and her voice a mere whisper that somehow filled the theatre. Those who worked closely with Maria could not fail to sense the deep vulnerability in the woman as well as in the artist. Jon Vickers, who sang Jason to her Medea three years later, always referred to her as 'little Maria'. 'But she won't let the little Maria show through,' he said once. The world had to be content with seeing the little Maria in little Amina, little Giulia, little Violetta. . . .

The Visconti production of *La Traviata* and Maria's portrayal of Violetta were to make operatic history, influencing many directors, designers and singers. 'An opera,' Maria said once, 'begins long before the curtain goes up and ends long after it has come down. It starts in my imagination, it becomes my life, and it stays part of my life long after I've left the opera house. The audience sees only an excerpt.' On 28 May 1955, the curtain rose on the excerpt that the audience was allowed to see. Carlo Maria Giulini described what he felt when, from the conductor's podium, his eyes shifted to the stage, and to Violetta's party: 'My heart skipped a beat. I was overwhelmed by the beauty of what stood before me. The most emotional, exquisite décor I have seen in my entire life. Every detail made me feel I was materially entering another world, a world of incredible immediacy. The illusion of art vanished. I had the same sensation every time I conducted this production – over twenty times in two seasons. For me, reality was on stage. What stood behind me, the audience, auditorium, La Scala itself, seemed artifice. Only that which transpired on stage was truth, life itself.'

Giulini, Visconti and Maria spent hours, days, weeks together going over every detail. At no point did they lose track of their central concept: love was a thing Violetta had never known, even something she shied away from. Her unstated fear was that if she gave in to love she would lose her cold capacity to play with life. Maria's transformation from a woman who lives for sheer selfish pleasure to a woman discovering for the first time her infinite capacity to give was so moving because it had been so deeply felt by Visconti, Giulini and Maria alike.

Words, music and action were in complete harmony. Maria had discovered in the music new movements and gestures, and through her understanding of Violetta's being she had found further colours in her voice, a deeper stillness and new, even sickly tones for the last act. 'I had striven for years,' she explained to Derek Prouse a few years later, 'to create a sickly quality in the voice of Violetta; after all, she *is* a sick woman. It's all a question of breath, and you need a very clear throat to sustain this tired way of talking or singing. And what did they say? "Callas is tired. The voice is tired." But that is precisely the impression I was trying to create. How could Violetta be in her condition and sing in big, high, round tones? It would be ridiculous.' And this sense of dramatic truth informed her every movement, even when she was not singing. Peter Diamand, who was then Director of the Holland Festival and was later to fill the same role for the Edinburgh Festival, remembers a moment in her performance that vividly illustrates this: 'I saw the production three times, and each time in the second act when Alfredo's father comes in and makes a bitter remark about his son being ruined under her spell, Maria would walk across the stage with so strong an air of having been offended that every time I became convinced that something had happened to upset her and that she really was walking out of the production.'

The critics argued extravagantly about this *Traviata*, but it was largely Visconti who came under fire for, as one critic put it, 'disfiguring and defiling Verdi's opera'. The main targets for the critics' anger were two of Visconti's touches which many later came to see as inspired: Maria kicking her shoes in the air before tackling 'Sempre libera' at the end of the first act, and Maria dying on her feet with her hat and coat on, her great eyes staring blankly into space, at the end of the last act. In time Visconti's *Traviata* became one of the most talked-about operatic legends, but for some time after opening night, on 28 May, it existed in a kind of critical outer darkness. The custodians of Verdi's sacred flame pronounced Visconti's treatment irreverent, even vulgar. Maria had her detractors too but they were drowned in the general adulation for her performance, summed up by the critic of *24 Ore*: 'This aristocrat of the dramatic and vocal art was able to return to the opera its aura of fervour, its atmosphere of throbbing anguish of which the director was determined to rob the performance.'

Maria's backstage detractors were much harder to handle. Through the long weeks of rehearsals, Giuseppe di Stefano, who was Violetta's lover, Alfredo, had been storing resentment against her. For him singing was singing and all the time she and Visconti were spending over gestures, movements and expressions amounted to nothing but tedious horse-play. When Visconti began coaxing him and Maria into the intimate love-play he had conceived for Violetta and Alfredo, di Stefano could take no more. He started turning up late and sometimes not turning up at all. 'It's a lack of respect for me, lack of regard, and *also* for you!' fumed Maria. Visconti was much more philosophical. 'I don't give a damn if the fool comes late,' he told her. 'We'll act out his scenes together; worse for him if he doesn't learn anything.' But the tension between di Stefano and Maria was rising and no one needed much vision to predict that at some point it would have to break. That point came on the first night.

At Giulini's suggestion, Maria took a solo curtain-call. Di Stefano boiled over, and before anyone realized what was going on, he had thrown aside Alfredo's clothes, walked out of the production and was soon fleeing Milan. There were three more performances left, and Giacinto Prandelli took over the role of Alfredo. Di Stefano, however, was by no means the only one resenting Maria's blazing success, the adulation showered upon her and the unchallenged way in which, especially after Tebaldi's departure, she reigned at La Scala and held court at the Biffi Scala. The ranks of the resentful were further swollen by Maria's attitude which assumed that the world was a resentful, hostile place. It was as if she was seeking – however unconsciously – confirmation of her instinctive mistrust of everyone. Such confirmation was not hard to find, especially on 5 June, the third performance of *La Traviata,* when Maria's 'Sempre libera' was interrupted by heckling and whistling designed to throw her off course. 'Sempre libera' came to an ominous halt and it took Maria several moments to regain her composure and complete the aria. She demanded a solo curtain-call, and came out determined to defy her enemies, only to find herself overwhelmed instead by the passionate welcome of her friends.

But the resentment Maria aroused was by no means the creation of her own mind. *La Scala* magazine devoted an entire editorial to it soon after the eruption of hostilities during *Traviata.* 'No doubt Callas has many enemies. First of all, her colleagues who are convinced that to be a native Italian and endowed by nature with a lovely voice is all that is needed. They are only concerned with the emission of notes and with singing in the manner of fifty years ago, without ever letting their eyes stray from the conductor's baton. These people, who are organically incapable of sacrifice and effort, who owe nothing to study and all to nature and accident, accuse Maria Callas of aggressiveness because, as the result of much sacrifice and effort, she is vocally and physically able to sing and interpret everything. Shall we say that the clamorous recognition and her own striking personality will rise above the attacks? Is this a consolation for Callas? One thing is certain: the price to pay for separation from the herd is high.'

Contrary to this most popular misconception, shared by Maria herself, separation is by no means a necessary price for greatness, but Maria did feel separated from colleagues and the world around her and often, despite the echoes of clamorous applause in her ears and the presence of Meneghini by her side, she felt very alone. So it was with a child's joy that she welcomed her old teacher, Elvira de Hidalgo, to Milan. Elvira had been teaching at the conservatory of Ankara in Turkey for the previous few years and arrived in Milan at the beginning of August to spend a holiday with her brother Luis who was living there, and with Maria. Pupil and teacher had kept in constant touch through all these years and now at last Elvira could hear the transformed Maria sing, accompany her on shopping expeditions down Via Monte Napoleone, advise her on the final touches for her new house. Maria was at the time recording *Madama Butterfly,* with Karajan conducting and Nicolai Gedda as Pinkerton. For the recording of *Rigoletto* that followed, the magical trio of Callas, Gobbi and di Stefano were once again together; and once again Serafin was conducting. Maria had a selectively short memory and, now that di Stefano had charmed his way back into her life, his operatic walk-out seemed to belong to a very distant past.

It was a hectic summer but not too hectic for numerous fittings at Madame Biki's. The latest Dior originals were added to the latest Biki creations, with the result that Maria's autumn 1955 collection was her most glamorous and eye-catching so far. But it was still a rather straitjacketed elegance, with plenty of severe suits and tailored dresses. On 24 September Maria, wearing one of Biki's creations, arrived in Berlin. La Scala had re-assembled the principals of the original 1954 *Lucia* for two performances as part of the Berlin Festival. Karajan was conducting and it was confidently expected that the 1954 Callas–Karajan triumph in Milan would be repeated in Berlin. In fact what happened far surpassed expectations. Hundreds spent the night before the first performance outside the Opera House, both performances having been immediately sold out and, as the first night was broadcast, the enthusiasm, the ovations and even the stamping of feet are forever preserved on tape.

It was a triumphant ending to an evening that had begun on a note of panic. Meneghini's plane from Milan had been delayed and, minutes before the curtain rose, Maria was still nervously pacing up and down her dressing-room, full of superstitious anxiety at the thought that Meneghini would not be there in time for the start. 'I can't sing, I can't sing if he is not here. . . ,' she had been mumbling, more to herself than to anyone else. The Opera House officials were themselves pacing nervously up and down getting more anxious by the minute. Scouts had been posted everywhere to give the signal as soon as Meneghini's form darkened the door. A couple of minutes after the curtain was due to rise Meneghini appeared – never before had so many people longed to see him so much. He was at once escorted to his box, Maria caught a glimpse of him from behind the curtain, and the performance could begin. *Avanti maestro!* At the end of the performance there was a reception at the Italian Embassy. Efi Zaccaria remembers Maria hovering round the platters of Italian delicacies, frequently darting but rarely settling.

Back in Milan at the beginning of October, Maria could look at 1955 as her greatest year so far. Yet some of the greatest triumphs of the year were still ahead of her. They took place in Chicago, where she opened the season in *I Puritani* on 31 October. Renata Tebaldi followed on 1 November with *Aida.* They shared the star dressing-room but, even though it was Maria's suggestion to invite Tebaldi, the schedule was carefully arranged so that they never met. Maria followed Renata with *Il Trovatore,* Renata replied with *Bohème,* and Maria came back with *Butterfly.* 'I don't ever want to hear her Butterfly again,' said someone after the opening night, 'I'll end up liking this dreadful opera.'

There was no time off for Maria in Chicago. She had chosen to be on show the whole time; when she was not actually singing, she was attending cocktail parties, lunch parties, dinner parties, meeting the press, smiling for photographers, praising the opera management, praising the town or ostentatiously applauding Tebaldi's Aida and Tebaldi's Mimi. Tebaldi did not reciprocate the applause but the town more than reciprocated what Maria had been giving them. As Roger Dettmer, music critic of the *Chicago American*, put it: 'The town, we all know, has been Callas-crazy for more than a year, and none has been more demented than I. In the proper role and in good voice, I adore the woman; I am a slave in her spell.'

And Maria became a slave to her slaves. Never before had an entire town unanimously treated her as a combination of queen, sorceress and divinity. And never before had she put so much energy into gaining or rather maintaining the public's favour; never before had she made such a consistent effort to be universally 'nice' and universally liked. 'Fame,' she once said, 'is a boomerang.' The approval and adulation that fame brought her had become a subtle trap. As she could not, most of the time, get the approval she needed from herself, she came to rely on the approval of others. So the woman who had cast her spell on so many was in even greater need of them than they were of her. The greater the adulation the tighter the trap, especially since, as she said herself, she was plagued with endless doubt and feelings of unworthiness. 'Even when people look at me with obvious affection, that makes me twice as angry. You think "these people are looking at you in admiration – why should they? I don't deserve it."' The less she felt that she deserved it the more she was determined to present to the world a version of herself that did deserve it. But excessive concern with presentation and effect is bound to boomerang too: 'Misrepresentation, as I have found to my cost,' she said a few years after Chicago, 'can happen only too easily.'

What happened in Chicago on the last night of *Butterfly* cannot easily be defined as misrepresentation. Maria saw it as a tragic ending to a frenzied love affair between herself and Chicago, and there were some irreverent souls who saw it as knockabout farce. The third performance of *Butterfly* on 17 November was an unscheduled one. Lawrence Kelly and Carol Fox pleaded with Maria to give one more last performance, and in a glow of goodwill she agreed. One of the critics had said on the opening night that '. . . anything short of a disaster was bound to be a triumph', and this was ten times as true of the closing night. The applause seemed never-ending and Maria was visibly drained by the end. Then the real drama began. Marshal Stanley Pringle and Deputy Sheriff Dan Smith, looking in their felt hats and off-white raincoats as though they had stepped out of an early Bogart movie, had managed to penetrate the cordon the Lyric's management had thrown round Maria and burst triumphantly into her dressing-room. Maria, still in Cio-Cio-San's kimono, was at first struck speechless with anger and bewilderment. When she found enough voice the words that came out were the words of a goddess proudly and indignantly declaring herself above earthly laws. 'I will not be sued! I have the voice of an angel! No man can sue me.' The Marshal, unflustered and unimpressed, proceeded to carry out what the law required: bodily contact with the subject. He thrust the summons into Maria's kimono and, his business completed, turned to leave. Maria made sure that he did not remain unflustered for long. She was hysterical with fury, and the hysteria and the darkness were both immortalized in a photograph that marked the turning-point in the public image of Maria. Her garish Cio-Cio-San mouth twisted with anger, her huge black eyes distorted with raw hate, Maria in one inhabitants of Chicago is irrelevant. The eyes and the in Chicago at what she experienced as betrayal came out as bitter anger. The precise nature of the abuse she hurled on the process-servers, the Lyric's management and the inhabitants of Chicago is irrelevant. The eyes and the mouth said it all. Dario Soria and Walter Legge were both present and with the help of Meneghini and Lawrence Kelly they smuggled Maria out through a side door. She spent the night raging in the apartment of Lawrence Kelly's brother, reviling everyone in and out of sight. Meneghini, as usual, played enthusiastically his role of bellows to Maria's fire. At dawn, having had no sleep at all, she had a bath and was driven, together with Meneghini, to the airport to catch the first plane out of Chicago. At Montreal she changed planes for Milan. Back home, she still felt just as victimized as on the fateful night itself. 'I couldn't have been betrayed worse,' she wrote to Dario Soria's wife. 'When I write you the details you will freeze in horror.'

The question everybody was trying to answer was how had the process-servers slipped through the cordon. The speculations were unending, and so were the conspiracy theories. Lawrence Kelly remained convinced until he died that Carol Fox had deliberately let the process-servers backstage to solidify her ascendancy in the power struggle between them by alienating Maria from him. It was one of the most exotic and unlikely speculations, especially considering that ultimately the incident bound Lawrence Kelly and Maria closer together than ever before.

Meanwhile, the world press was busy reporting or inventing its own details to accompany the Associated

Press photograph of Maria the Maenad. The relish with which the press made front-page stories out of the photograph, much though it hurt Maria, is not hard to understand. Beyond the obvious fact that sensation sells newspapers, anger and hatred have their own appeal, and a picture of a world-famous woman giving way uncontrollably to such emotions was bound to seize the imagination of millions.

She left Chicago utterly convinced that she had been betrayed by the Lyric's management and swearing that she would never *ever* return to Chicago. Yet planning future revenge could not do away with the pain, nor did it eliminate the poisonous resentment. The end of her year of triumphs found Maria in a desperate state. Her dark view of life and the world was once again confirmed, only this time, coming so soon after so much success and so much glory, it was felt more deeply and more painfully than before.

So when she was greeted on her arrival in Milan with advertisements in the newspapers claiming that 'La Callas' had lost her weight by a steady diet of Pantanella's 'psychological macaroni', she was not in a mood to be amused, especially as the ingenious pasta company had produced a certain Dr Giovanni Cazzaroti – complete with medical certificate – to lend support to its claim. Prodded by Meneghini, and with the reports of the Chicago incident still echoing in her ears, Maria did the one thing even a novice public relations man would have advised her against. She issued a writ against Pastificio Pantanella, and this became the second link in the heavy chain of her legal entanglements. Thus began what the headline writers were soon to call 'the battle of the spaghetti'. It dragged on for nearly four years and turned Maria into the heroine of a ludicrous saga that became all the more newsworthy when it was revealed that the head of Pastificio Pantanella was Prince Marcantonio Pacelli, Pope Pius XII's cousin. It was settled in her favour in August 1959, when the Rome Court of Appeals awarded her damages. By then the press had largely forgotten about the Prince, the Primadonna, and the Macaroni, and Maria had other more pressing things on her mind than a four-year-old lawsuit. The Spaghetti victory turned out to be a rather hollow one, though at the time Maria issued the writ it had seemed a victory that she had to win. Together with the bitter after-taste of Chicago, it blighted the celebrations of her thirty-second birthday. It also intensified her already acute sensitivity to any demonstrations of hostility. Such demonstrations by the 'hissing snakes', as Maria had taken to calling them, had by now become an expected ingredient of a Callas night. And the bigger the night, the more likely the demonstrations.

In 1955, La Scala's gala opening night was even more of an occasion than usual. Maria had automatically once again been given the honour of opening the season, this time with *Norma.* President Gronchi was in the audience, Pierre Balmain had created the elaborate floral decorations, and so spectacular was the jewellery worn that, even with the lights out, it never became totally dark in the auditorium. The noise level of the anti-Callas demonstrators matched the sense of heightened excitement. The hissing was irritating, even hurtful, but it was balanced by the unprecedented ovations that everywhere greeted Maria's curtain-calls. What was much more painful for Maria and much harder to bear was the way in which, since the turning-point of the Chicago photograph, every rumour that was put out about her was unquestioningly accepted and passed on.

At the beginning of January, del Monaco, who was singing Pollione to Maria's Norma, was reported in the Italian press bitterly complaining about her: 'As I was preparing to leave the stage at the end of *Norma* I felt a hefty kick on my calf. I stopped for a moment in surprise to rub my leg and when I could finally walk again Maria had taken all the applause.' Maria kicking a fellow singer on the calf in order to steal a solo bow! Hardly believable, and it certainly would not have been believed before that fateful Chicago photograph made *anything* about Maria believable – and the more outrageous the more convincing.

As for del Monaco's story, what seems to have made him explode against Maria was Meneghini's reaction to the torrential ovation he had received during the first act of that January *Norma.* It was still the time of officially-recognized claques which, apart from the unofficial ones organized by devotees or enemies of a particular singer, were sanctioned by the Opera House to raise the general level of enthusiasm. At the interval, Meneghini went up to Ettore Parmeggiani, who had been a tenor at La Scala and was now the official claque chief, and admonished him for what he considered an excessive and non-partisan display of enthusiasm towards del Monaco. Parmeggiani went straight to del Monaco to enlist his support in proving the allegations false. It was as if some malevolent spirit kept pushing Meneghini to intervene, almost invariably at the wrong time and in the wrong way. On this occasion it was spectacularly the wrong time. 'You and your wife,' stormed del Monaco, 'don't own La Scala, you know! The audience applauds whoever deserves applause.' And throughout the performance, whenever they both both off-stage, he went on yelling at Maria.

By this time Maria aroused stronger feelings than any living singer. The mere mention of her name induced paroxysms, favourable or unfavourable according to taste. Was she a goddess for whom there was no place in our second-rate world or one of the most extravagant megalomaniacs ever to walk upon a stage – or was she, perhaps, both? For many who could not fit her into a musical category, her voice was alien, disturbing; and for those who identified beautiful singing with a smooth, contained line and tone, no amount of vocal colour and dramatic authority would compensate for the unsteadiness in the top notes, the occasional shrillness and the veiled quality of her middle range.

It was hoped that Maria's triumphant return appearance as Violetta, in an extraordinary total of seventeen performances during the season, would silence some of her enemies. In fact at the end of one of these performances they showed rather dramatically that, far from relenting, they were growing more enterprising. In the middle of all the bouquets and the rain of flowers at Maria's feet, a bunch of radishes fell on the stage. The audience saw them before the short-sighted primadonna and they gasped with embarrassment on her behalf. Maria the consummate actress rose to the occasion. She picked the radishes from the stage and clasped them to her bosom as if they were the choicest orchids. The story made headlines in Milan and within hours had crossed the Atlantic.

Once off the stage, Maria let the cool mask drop and the tears flooded her eyes. The acclaimed, adored primadonna, gaily spending millions on her houses, jewellery and wardrobe, endlessly smothered in flowers and adulation, experienced demonstrations of hostility deeply and painfully as a direct assault on herself – especially when Meneghini kept focusing on them and inflating them. 'One indignity upon another,' is how he described such hostility, making it even more likely that Maria would allow it to disturb her out of all proportion to its real significance. But there was little time to brood.

In between singing seventeen *Traviatas,* Maria was rehearsing her second comic role, Rosina in *Il Barbiere di Siviglia.* It was a revival of an old stock production put together with no flair or imagination. If one compares Maria's Rosina with her Fiorilla in *Turco in Italia,* it becomes clear that in comedy she needed light-handed and inventive direction such as Zeffirelli provided in *Turco.* If in tragedy an inspired director was important in drawing out her special sensibilities, in comedy he was essential, especially when the comic heroine has to be fresh, feminine, guileful. There was something earnest in Maria which made her gauche and heavy when she was trying to be light and delicate, and when she tried to portray wily womanhood, her dramatic instincts let her down and she ended up being vulgar. She did not trust herself and to compensate she both oversang and overacted. She, who normally achieved the maximum effect with the minimum of movement and gesture, used, according to Luigi Alva who was making his debut as Count Almaviva, 'too much pepper, exaggerating gestures. This coupled with her horrible costumes made everything she did seem ridiculous.' Also *Il Barbiere* is not a primadonna vehicle, and Maria tried to turn it into one. 'She was aggressive, a viper, acting as though Rosina had the whole situation wrapped up in her hands,' said Nicola Rossi-Lemeni, who was Don Basilio. 'But no single artist can shift the emphasis from Figaro and all the other colourful characters so beautifully balanced by Rossini.'

The opening night was a fiasco. It was a fiasco of production, direction, design and characterization. As Giulini put it: 'It was an artistic mistake, utterly routine, thrown together, with nothing given deep study or preparation . . . I conducted every performance with my head down, so I wouldn't see what was happening on stage.' It was everybody's fiasco but it was treated as Maria's. At La Scala, especially La Scala of the fifties, just as in the Circus Maximus, blood had to be shed; and the bluer the blood, the more celebrated the victim, the greater the thrill. The victimization was hardly subtle: there was hissing and whistling, talking while Maria was singing, and even some ostentatious walking out.

It was a night to delight the philistines, but also to destroy some of the more pretentious illusions about high opera and high culture. It was a night that made Maria raise the barricades around herself even higher. And it was the night that gave Giulini what he described later as the worst memory of his life in the theatre and led to his giving up conducting at La Scala. 'The audience is jaded, annoyed, bored, so it prays for a scandal. When Maria's Rosina was whistled and hissed, people went home content. This even though Maria was the prize of the theatre, greatly admired, even to the point of idolatry. As such, she became a target. In some ways she provoked such reaction. Her bows, for example, showed a certain insolence, her iron will to vanquish. With *Alceste,* Maria and I earned respect, esteem, probably because the audience was afraid to expose its ignorance about the work. I feel certain, however, that Maria's greatest triumphs at La Scala – even her incomparable Violetta – left something of a bitter taste in her mouth.'

This bitter taste, even after her triumphs, is the key to understanding why she became increasingly weighed down by the anguish her work was causing her. There was the work itself and the impossible demands she kept making on herself; there was the accumulated resentment when colleagues, designers, directors, opera staff did not live up to her own perfectionist standards; there was the drain of always wanting, and expecting, to be first; finally – and this is the key Giulini hinted at – there was the disappointment, the bitter taste left after her achievements and despite all the acclamation. This was partly caused by the intensity with which she felt the hostility, and partly by the merciless way she judged herself even when everyone else was clamorously celebrating her triumphs. 'Only on very rare occasions do I feel I have given a really marvellous performance,' she once said. 'Here is one of the things that nearly drives me out of my mind. I can never tell absolutely when I *have* given a great performance. For this is the paradox. What an audience feels is a great performance does not necessarily mean the same thing to me. It sometimes happens that I think I have not been doing justice to a role. And yet after such an evening, people come crowding in to congratulate me, and all compliments embarrass me. Then at other times, when I feel I have really given of my best, the audience's reaction is not the same. So the mystery remains. It haunts me.'

Also, of course, Maria had reached by now the fulfilment of her dream, and dreams fulfilled rarely satisfy beyond the period of novelty and a sense of completion. Coping with ambition fulfilled had turned out to be much harder than achieving the ambition in the first place. The force pulling her away from the self-imposed torment of her work was growing all the time.

The season at La Scala ended with Giordano's *Fedora* based, as is *Tosca*, on a play by Sardou, and written, again like *Tosca*, as a vehicle for Sarah Bernhardt. The hatchets were out for Maria even before opening night. She was thought by many to be unsuitable for *Fedora*, an opera with so much realism, unlyrical music and heavy orchestration. On opening night the catcalls and whistles made the point less elegantly and more forcefully. And in the reviews that followed, the main theme of the criticisms of the years to come could be clearly heard: Maria's voice was losing its power. Even among her admirers the same criticism was implied: 'Even if she is not the greatest singer she is certainly one of the world's greatest actresses.' Maria on stage, coached by the Russian actress Tatiana Pavlova, *became* the Russian Princess, Fedora Romanov. Franco Corelli still remembers all the hard work that went into the production for four weeks. More to the point, he remembers Maria, the devoted colleague, whose first commitment was to the total effect of the drama. 'No one can imagine what it meant to me, a virtual beginner on the stage, only in my second year at La Scala, to work with Callas. I learnt so much . . . Maria was extremely thoughtful with me and tried to make everything easy. And she did. She herself was so involved in the opera that she involved me too. I felt it a duty to respond, to work deeply, as never before, in a way I did not fully comprehend, but which I strongly sensed.' Maria's generosity towards those of her colleagues who were at the start of an international career shows just how much she was able to give and how much she did give when she was feeling confident and secure.

La Scala's season was over, and the pall of defeat hung in the air. It had not been a bad season in itself, but it was not being judged by itself. It was constantly judged against the triumphs of the year before – *La Sonnambula, La Vestale, Traviata.*

At the beginning of June 1956, Maria was glad to leave Milan for Vienna, where the majestic Staatsoper was celebrating its first season since its reconstruction after the war. As part of the celebrations, La Scala, with Karajan conducting, was presenting Maria in *Lucia.* The visit began with a sudden fright. Maria had barely settled in the Hotel Sacher when she discovered that the miniature oil painting of the Madonna that she always carried with her was missing. After frantic phone calls to Milan, it was found in her bedroom and a friend was despatched to bring it to Vienna in good time for the opening night on 12 June. The little Madonna was a present from Meneghini during her Verona debut in 1947. Maria, who never went on stage without crossing herself three times, was devoted to her Madonna. And she stayed devoted long after Meneghini had faded from her life. It was much more than a child's need for her doll or an empty superstitious attachment. It was a largely unconscious but deeply fearful recognition that her great powers were loans – the gods give them, the gods take them away. Holding the little Madonna in her hands or crossing herself before going on stage was almost an act of propitiation designed to keep the gods on her side. Among Maria's rituals, the only thing that changed was the way she crossed herself. While she was married to Meneghini, she would cross herself Italian style, with fingers outstretched. Soon after Onassis came into her life, she began crossing herself like a good Greek Orthodox, with the fingers bunched together. And she would often stop at a church she was passing, especially in Greece, to light a candle to the Virgin.

The miniature Madonna certainly performed her miracle on the first night. The applause and the bravos at the end lasted for twenty minutes and Theodor Körner, President of the Austrian Republic, applauded with as much fervour as the rest. Meneghini was watching with the air of a provincial manager who was pleased with a full, enthusiastic house but never doubted he would have it. He had a way of licking his lips which reinforced his air of self-satisfaction. At the end of the opera, traffic outside the Staatsoper had to be stopped, and special police had to be brought in to disperse the crowds and make it possible for Maria to leave the opera house. Italian catcalls and out-of-season radishes seemed a long way away. Maria, whom thousands had already discovered through her records, had once again lived up to the legend that surrounded her.

She sang three *Lucias* in Vienna and the third, on 16 June, was her last engagement until a recording session on 3 August. She was worn out after a week that was emotionally, as well as physically exhausting; July was spent on Ischia, off the coast of Italy, waiting for her strength to return. October and her long-awaited debut at the Met were not far away. While she was resting and swimming in Ischia the news reached her that in the week of her opening at the Met, she was going to be on the cover of *Time* magazine – the authentic seal of international stardom. Henry Koener had been commissioned to paint her portrait for the cover. Their first meeting took place in Venice in the middle of August. Maria was a guest of honour at the Seventeenth Annual Motion Picture Festival and Koener first set eyes on her sitting behind dark sun glasses under a tent on the Lido on a sweltering Friday afternoon. She was again lying under the tent, this time chatting to Carla Moncenigo, a younger friend from the Fenice days, when two young men approached them and asked them out that night. Maria was instantly transformed into a flirtatious little girl. 'I can't tell you now. I have to ask my father,' she replied, pointing at Meneghini who was fast asleep beside her.

Back in Milan the following Sunday, she had her first sitting with Henry Koener. Koener arrived at Via Buonarroti and was rather unexpectedly confronted not with the glamorous Queen of Opera but with another Maria: 'She looked forbidding, like a New York career girl; black dress, dark-rimmed glasses.' That was how some saw this second Maria. Others saw her as a forbidding Greek matron severely dressed in black. Either way, it was not the Maria of the press and the legend. The sittings, in between recording sessions, lasted for ten days and were fraught with tension. 'I hated her, yet enjoyed painting her beautiful face, and I paid her back by making her pose even harder.' These do not sound like the ideal conditions for portrait painting, but they seemed to work, and Maria, Koener and *Time* magazine were all satisfied with the result.

Meanwhile, Maria's recording of *Trovatore* under Karajan was followed by her recording of *La Bohème* under Antonino Votto. Maria had learned the part of Mimi specially for this recording, but she never sang it on stage. Antonio Votto was also the conductor for Maria's third recording that year: *Un Ballo In Maschera.* The name of Serafin is conspicuously absent from Maria's recording output in 1956. The maestro, Maria's most important musical mentor apart from Elvira de Hidalgo, had fallen from royal favour. He had dared to accept EMI's offer to record *Traviata* with Antonietta Stella, since under the terms of her contract with Cetra, Maria could not re-record *Traviata* until 1957. Maria, as sensitive as ever to signs of betrayals and hints of exclusion – even imaginary ones – was quick to retaliate. From the Via Michelangelo Buonarroti came the imperious announcement: no more recordings with Serafin. It was a decision that soon became part of the folklore of ingratitude and ruthlessness that was to surround Maria.

The public personality of Maria Meneghini Callas, the compelling demon born of the needs, fears, aggressions and insecurities of Maria Kalogeropoulos, was still in flux. New York, with its sleepless legions of hidden and not-so-hidden persuaders, PR men, pressmen, photographers, gossip columnists and scandalmongers, was soon to change all that.

Chapter Nine

ON 15 October 1956, on the eve of those two world-changing events, the Suez invasion and the Hungarian Revolution, Maria arrived at New York's Idlewild airport. There to meet her, eleven years after he had met her on his own when the *Stockholm* docked in New York, was George Kalogeropoulos, this time accompanied by Francis Robinson of the Met, Dario Soria of EMI, and an attorney in the event of legal complications. Nor was Maria alone. With her were a husband, two secretaries and her poodle, Toy. And this time George did not have to discover that his daughter was arriving in New York by stumbling across her name in a passenger list. Even if Maria had not let him know, he could hardly have failed to notice that the New York press was full of her imminent debut at the Met. George collected every newspaper and magazine that even so much as mentioned his daughter's name, kept them all in neat piles, and seemed to care more for them than for the recordings that Maria sent him. He never learnt to love opera, but he would go to the end of the world to hear his daughter sing. Whether it was Mexico, Italy, Greece or Idlewild airport, Maria's invitation to be present was a royal command.

In thirteen days, she would be opening the Met season in *Norma.* It had all been agreed nearly a year earlier when, just before going on stage at the Chicago Lyric to sing Leonora in *Trovatore,* she finally signed the long-awaited contract engaging her to sing at the Metropolitan Opera. Rudolf Bing had bowed and kissed her hand and then he had bowed and kissed her hand again and again for the benefit of the swarming photographers determined to get the best shot of the ceremony for the late editions of their papers. 'How much have you settled for? $1,000 a night? $1,500? $2,000?' The press knew that Bing's celebrated principle of never exceeding $1,000 a night had been abandoned. What they wanted to know was: by how dramatic a margin? But Bing, the perfect courtier when he chose to be, was not going to kiss and tell. 'Come, come, our artists work for the love of art! Or sometimes for a few flowers. . . . Let's just say that this time she'll be getting a few more flowers.'

Bing continued to be the embodiment of courtesy and support through the days leading up to opening night. 'We gave Miss Callas treatment no other singer has ever received,' he wrote in his memoirs. 'He was helpful and kind without being gushing,' was Maria's summing-up. And she needed all the support he could give her; on the surface every bit the cool, toughened professional for whom one opera house is very much like another, she was in fact anxious and uneasy. Bing himself was struck by her 'girlishness, the innocent dependence on others that was so strong a part of her personality when she did not feel she had to be wary.' 'Is New York anxious to hear me?' she had written to him from Milan. Indeed it was, replied Bing, who remembers Maria's opening night as 'undoubtedly the most exciting of all in my time at the Metropolitan'.

Maria knew she was on trial, and part of her was sick and tired of being on trial, especially as she knew that she would go on being on trial every time she sang. She had reached the zenith of her career in Milan, London, Berlin, Vienna and Chicago, and yet she knew that in the eyes of the world and in her own eyes she was only as good as her next performance. Two days before the first night, *Time* magazine came out with Maria on the cover and a four-page cover story inside. For a long time after she had read it, Maria abandoned herself to grief and rage. *Time,* following its usual practice, had distributed a questionnaire to Maria's friends – and enemies – and had managed to get many to talk; some indeed had embroidered, or even invented, the stories they told. Their greatest coup was persuading Maria's mother to give them an excerpt from

Maria's last letter to her: 'Don't come to us with your troubles. I had to work for my money and you are young enough to work too. If you can't make enough money to live on, you can jump out of the window or drown yourself.' Maria clearly did not mean these words in the literal sense implied by a printed statement, but there is equally no doubt that part of her did habour the deepest, darkest resentment against her mother. As she herself once said: 'I'll never forgive her for taking my childhood away. During all the years I should have been playing and growing up I was singing or making money. Everything I did for them was mostly good and everything they did to me was mostly bad.' And in 1950, she had written to her godfather: 'As for mother, I gave her all I could for this year. After all it's about time each one arranges his own life as I did mine.'

The revelations about Maria's relationship with her mother were the most damaging for her public image, but there was another quarry that *Time* had relentlessly pursued: Maria's relationship with her colleagues. Right at the start of the article, Maria was described as 'a diva more widely hated by her colleagues and more widely loved by her public than any other living singer'. A colleague was quoted anonymously as saying that 'the day will come when Maria will sing by herself'. To back their nameless source they had di Stefano declaring: 'I'm never going to sing opera with her again and that's final.' As Maria's luck would have it, they had caught di Stefano at a time when his friendship with Maria had reached one of its recurring low ebbs. Seven months later, the man who was *never* going to sing opera with Maria again was recording *Manon Lescaut* with her. He had to eat his words, but the words had been printed and had already contributed to the damage the *Time* article had done.

That damage was almost tangible on the first night. *The New York Times* had announced on the day that 'never had so many Americans tried to pay so much money to hear an opera'. In fact many had paid to see Maria, not to hear an opera. Yet when the person they had come to see made her entrance on the stage, the applause was cold, formal, almost hostile – in ominously striking contrast to the applause that greeted Zinka Milanov when she swept down the aisle to take her seat. New York, the perfect haven for *monstres sacrés,* had decided that Maria had overstepped the limit. It was one thing to be eccentric, extravagant, tempestuous and temperamental, and quite another to be mean and ungrateful to your mother.

So musical – and fashionable – New York had paid a lot of money to come and defy Maria to move them, impress them, convince them that she was all that legend insisted she was. And she did. The first act was difficult, nearly impossible. The heat of a New York Indian summer was exhausting, the tension was unbearable, and Maria, visibly nervous, was not in her best voice. In the second act, the miracle happened. The magic that had been only intermittent and fleeting in the first act broke through and took complete command of the audience. Maria Callas the opera singer who was rude to deputy sheriffs and unkind to her mother disappeared under the force and majesty with which Maria invested *Norma.* Gradually, almost imperceptibly, the audience surrendered. Ten years later, when Maria's voice was nearly in shreds, Harold Schonberg summed up the reason: 'Something in the woman hits nearly every member of the audience right in the viscera. While she continues to have that something, people will tear down the doors and yell themselves hoarse and what you or I or anybody else may say will make no difference.' On that long-awaited and much-feared night, the audience did yell themselves hoarse through sixteen curtain-calls. The curtain-calls were a performance in themselves, culminating in a solo bow in defiance of Bing's instructions when Mario del Monaco and Cesare Siepi withdrew and left Maria alone. A minute earlier she had picked a bouquet of flowers from the stage and offered them each a rose with a smile impossible to resist.

And still the performance was not over. The Trianon room at the Ambassador Hotel had been taken over by Angel Records for a large party in Maria's honour. The guests, according to Dorle Soria, Dario Soria's wife, who had organized it, were a cross-section of the musical, social, diplomatic and press worlds – from the Greek and

Italian ambassadors to Marlene Dietrich and Elsa Maxwell, the notorious socialite and gossip columnist. Dietrich, worried about Maria's health during rehearsals, had spent hours boiling down eight pounds of beef to a quart of purest broth. 'It's wonderful,' Maria said gratefully. 'Tell me, what brand of cubes do you use?'

Exactly an hour after midnight, Maria finally arrived with her husband, Dario Soria and a man whose eyes never left her throughout the party. He behaved like the most ardent fan but was in fact a private detective employed by Harry Winston, the jewellers, from whom Maria had borrowed, for the night, jewellery worth more than a million dollars. She looked like a queen, behaved like a queen, was treated like a queen.

The party was given to celebrate Maria's debut at the Met but, looking back, we can see that it marked a different kind of beginning. Maria was, still almost imperceptibly, being absorbed into the world of the Beautiful People; or rather, she was choosing to be absorbed. It was she, after all, who had asked Angel Records to give this party for her. The morning after the Great Night, hostilites were resumed – at first quietly in the rather lukewarm reviews. The emphasis was on Maria's vocal limitations, with all the usual comments about the veiled middle register and the deficiencies of tone. But one of the reviewers, Howard Taubman in *The New York Times,* made a statement that revealed as much truth about Maria's character as about her voice. 'It is a puzzling voice,' he wrote. 'Occasionally it gives the impression of having been formed out of sheer will power rather than natural endowments.'

A few days later came *Tosca.* Dimitri Mitropoulos, the other great musical Greek, was conducting, and George London was Scarpia. When many trusted colleagues were queuing up for their two pcnn'orth of attack on Maria, George London remained totally loyal. 'When I learned that I would sing Scarpia to Callas's Tosca,' he wrote in a magazine article, 'I must admit I had a few forebodings. So much had been printed about this "stormy" star that I was prepared for almost anything. The first rehearsal reassured me. Here was a trouper, a fanatical worker, a stickler for detail. Remembering my first season at the Met and the forlornness one can feel, I crossed the stage before curtain-time and, knocking at Maria Callas's dressing-room, said a quick "*in bocca di lupo*" ["in the mouth of the wolf" – an Italian charm for good luck]. She took my hand in both of hers and seemed deeply moved. She later told me that this insignificant courtesy had meant a great deal to her.' And the general feeling of competitiveness and enmity around her made it all the more special.

Those who went to *Tosca* to hear 'Vissi d'arte' and other famous set pieces left feeling short-changed. Where was the full, generous outpouring of a Tebaldi or a Milanov? Elsa Maxwell, cheerleader-in-chief for Tebaldi – and a close friend – had, in fact, decided to launch a personal vendetta against Maria. She attacked the 'devious diva', as she had termed her, on practically every ground she could think of; she even managed to detect jealousy of George London in the way she stuck the knife into him at the end of the second act. But there were others in the audience besides Elsa Maxwell and the vocal purists, for whom Maria was a great – the greatest – Tosca. Some would even say that she was a much greater Tosca than *Tosca* deserved. Her understanding of the part illuminated even the smallest gesture and movement. And there were many in that first-night audience at the Met who realized that the brilliance of the Callas Tosca would linger in the public's mind long after scores of other much more vocally accomplished performances had been forgotten.

Ten days after that first night, Tebaldi officially joined the Callas opposition. In a letter that *Time* magazine published on 26 November, and that was to reverberate throughout the musical world, Renata angrily replied to the accusations Maria was reported to have levelled against her. 'She's got no backbone. She's not like Callas,' Maria was supposed to have said. 'The signora says that I have no backbone,' Renata snapped back. 'I reply I have one great thing that she has not – a heart.'

Maria was approaching her thirty-third birthday in an atmosphere of excitement, controversy, adulation and animosity. She only had to appear somewhere – even in a department store – for cameras and microphones to materialize in front of her. On 3 December 1956, the night after her birthday, Maria opened at the Met in *Lucia.* The praise of her high dramatic art was qualified once again by the criticisms of her vocal performance and by the venom of Elsa Maxwell: 'I confess the great Callas acting in the Mad Scene left me completely unmoved. . . . I was intrigued by the red wig she wore through the first two acts but in the Mad Scene she came on as a platinum blonde. Why this change of colour? What did it mean to this egocentric extrovert?'

During her second New York *Lucia* there was another explosion. At the end of the second act duet, Enzo Sordello, who was singing Ashton, held on to an unwritten high note long after Maria had abandoned her high D, which made her appear embarrassingly short of breath. '*Basta!*' she cried, giving rise to the legend that the audience heard her and gasped, thinking that she was hurling insults at her colleague. Sordello's contract with the Met was instantly terminated – at Maria's demand, according to the press and Sordello himself. 'Him or me' was the ultimatum she was supposed to have sent to Bing. The front pages featured Sordello tearing up her picture while Bing's denial of Maria's interference was politely ignored. Sordello, said Bing's press statement, was dismissed because of his continuous lack of co-operation and his persistent clashes with conductor Fausto Cleva. The ladies and gentlemen of the press were amused but not convinced, or at least they were not prepared to allow details and qualifications to water down a vintage Callas scandal.

Maria's nine-week stay in New York was coming to an end, but not before an extraordinary reconciliation. A few days before they left for Milan, Maria and Battista were guests of the Greek film tycoon Spyros Skouras at a dinner dance given for the American Hellenic Welfare Fund at the Waldorf Astoria. Among the other guests was that ever-present barometer of the international social weather, Elsa Maxwell. Some time between Maxwell's first attack on her and the night at the Waldorf Astoria, Maria decided that Maxwell had to be conquered. Not an easy thing, Maxwell *cognoscenti* warned her. Elsa was notorious not only for ruthlessly pursuing vendettas in her column, but for proudly owning up to it. 'I look like a bulldog,' she said, 'and I have a dog's persistence.'

Undaunted, Maria asked Spyros Skouras to introduce them, and at that point she donned a mask that had never been and never became part of her personality. 'I esteem you,' she said to Maxwell who printed it verbatim in her next column, 'as a lady of honesty who is devoted to telling the truth.' Here was the great Callas suddenly transformed into an insincere flatterer for the sake of winning Madame Maxwell's favour. Well, at least she achieved this and much more besides: 'When I looked into her amazing eyes, which are brilliant, beautiful and hypnotic, I realized she is an extraordinary person.' It was not so much love as attachment at first sight. Elsa Maxwell attached herself to her with an embarrassing persistence which Maria found increasingly uncomfortable. She always made sure that she was not left alone with Elsa, even for a few minutes, but at the same time, she was childishly delighted at having so unexpectedly replaced Renata as Mamma Maxwell's favourite child.

In her own way, Maria returned Elsa's attachment. The rebel daughter in search of a surrogate mother had finally found one. The fact that, at seventy-three, Maxwell could more easily have been Maria's grandmother made it all the more secure and attractive. What is more, she could open for Maria a new world of yachts, grand soirées, exiled princes and reigning millionaires. Maria, having conquered the world of opera, was now fascinated by new, still unexplored vistas.

Elsa Maxwell had conquered the world of café society before Maria was born and seemed determined, with her flamboyant parties, to reconquer it at least three times a year. Whether in Paris, New York, Venice or Monte Carlo, she spent other people's fortunes on parties designed to defy all predictions and exceed all conventional expectations. 'I have been called a parasite for accepting the largesse of the wealthy,' she wrote in her autobiography, 'but I contributed as much, at least, as I received. I had imagination and they had money, a fair exchange of the commodity possessed by each side in greatest abundance.' By the time Maria was ten, back in the thirties, Maxwell was already identified as the world's number one party-giver. She gave a Come as Your Opposite and a Come as You Are party in which ladies arrived without skirts and gentlemen without trousers; she gave a *fête champêtre* where Serge Lifar, one of Diaghilev's last discoveries, appeared naked, painted gold on a white horse; she gave a treasure hunt party at which guests stole Mistinguett's shoes and a black swan from the Bois de Boulogne; she gave a party at the Ritz in Paris where the Diaghilev ballet danced on a specially constructed stage; and she gave a party for her seventieth birthday at Maxim's at the end of which Albert, the head waiter, informed 'Mademoiselle' that the bill had been 'lost'.

That was three years before the night at the Waldorf Astoria when the 'Mademoiselle' fell in love with Maria. 'I discovered when I was sixteen,' Elsa wrote, 'that I could not permit myself even to be kissed by a man. Maybe egotism or false idealism prevented me from letting any man know me well enough for such intimacy.' Whatever Maxwell's predilections, for the next three years Maria became for her the object of an almost adolescent passion. For Maria, Maxwell was an unconditional champion and the expert guide to a new world.

Before she launched herself fully into the world of international café society, however, Maria found herself exploring the world of lawyers, courtrooms, judgements and settlements. The morning of the day she was leaving for Milan was spent at the New York Supreme Court giving evidence in the Bagarozy lawsuit. Two weeks later she had to return to Chicago, this time for the actual hearing of the case. As if there had not been enough of a circus in the previous few days, Maria arrived at the airport to find that Enzo Sordello, the fighting baritone, had booked seats on the same plane. He approached her all smiles. Maria ignored the offer of a handshake and refused to address a single word to him, but she did speak to the waiting reporters. 'I don't like that man taking advantage of my publicity.' 'What then did you think of your New

York publicity, Madame Callas?' 'I think it's been wonderful. But this is lousy.' Enormous mink hat, short, pithy answers for the eager reporters, Toy, the perfect poodle, in her arms – the paraphernalia of the public personality was complete. And yet the journalists sensed, and the public sensed, that here was an original whose vivid, utterly unique qualities fitted into no public-personality category they knew.

As the new year began, Maria was testing her power and enjoying her social victories at least as much as her musical ones. After a two-week Christmas holiday at her home, she was back in New York. On 11 January 1957 there was a specially glittering ball, again given at the Waldorf Astoria. There was even a glittering theme to it: a regal pageant. Maria put as much energy into her fancy-dress as she would into her costumes for a performance at La Scala or the Met. She arrived dressed as the exotic Egyptian Empress Hatshepshut, covered in emeralds worth three million dollars. 'Everybody' was there – and so, of course, was Elsa Maxwell, not quite impenetrably disguised as Catherine the Great.

Then came Chicago, the city which Maria had forsworn for ever. She had forgotten her oath and her anger in the case of the city as easily as she had in the case of all those tenors and baritones she had once sworn never to sing with again. Still adamant, however, that she would not sing under the Lyric Opera's management, she gave only a concert in Chicago; in a vivid red velvet gown she looked at least as regal as she had looked a few days earlier dressed as the Egyptian Empress. Two days later, back in Milan, she appeared at La Scala in a chinchilla coat and diamond-encrusted glasses. She was not singing, but the occasions when she was the centre of attention without singing were fast multiplying. This time the occasion was the first night of Francis Poulenc's *Dialogues des Carmélites,* and the evening was in honour of Poulenc himself.

The next occasion was her arrival in London. It is true that the purpose of her visit was to sing two performances of *Norma*, on 2 and 6 February, but the interest and fascination had spread far beyond those with a chance, or for that matter a wish, to hear her. The *Daily*

Mail devoted three columns to the preparations for her arrival and the excitement of those involved in the preparations, both at Covent Garden and at the Savoy. Both performances were sold out before the first day of booking had ended, and among those lucky enough to have got tickets, many came to London specially to hear Maria's Norma. Jacques Bourgeois, the French music critic who was a friend of Maria's, arrived from Paris and, having declared to the passport official the purpose of his visit, was greeted with an enthusiastic, 'Isn't she fantastic!'

And she *was* fantastic – fantastic on the first night and even more fantastic on the second. This greatest of Normas gave on 6 February the greatest performance in the role she would ever sing at Covent Garden. After the torrential applause that followed 'Mira o Norma', her second act duet with Ebe Stignani, John Pritchard, who was conducting, had no option but to break Covent Garden's iron-clad rule against encores. '*Brava Divina*' was the cry that could be heard above the applause. Rudolf Bing sent a telegram congratulating her. 'I am still trying to discover,' Maria wrote back, 'what happened in New York. I am only sorry I couldn't give you personally what other theatres have. I hope next year.' Meanwhile, as *Opera* put it, London's hysterical reaction to her was 'no more than the performance deserved'.

Maria's return to La Scala with *Sonnambula* on 2 March was just as triumphant. Once again she seemed unable to do wrong; once again the world was hers; and another triumph was round the corner.

On 14 April Maria opened in Donizetti's *Anna Bolena* with Gianandrea Gavazzeni conducting. It was her nineteenth role at La Scala. Visconti and Nicola Benois had created designs of such beauty and effectiveness – all in black, white and grey – that the audience broke into loud applause as each new set appeared. But as Visconti put it: 'For *Anna Bolena,* you need more than sets and costumes. You need Callas. Each day I went with her to the tailor to watch over every detail of her gowns, which were in all shades and nuances of blue. Her jewels were huge. They had to be to go with everything about her –

her eyes, her head, her features, her stature.' Maria's costumes, all inspired by Holbein's portraits of Anne Boleyn, were practically sculptured on her figure. Whether slowly and regally descending the long, broad staircase of Windsor Castle or hurling herself on the floor in pain and humiliation, Maria was magnificent.

Here was, as the critic John Ardoin put it, 'the culmination of all the wronged, wounded characters she had previously portrayed'. Here also is the answer to those who have all too glibly summed up Maria as a great actress but not a great singer. She was a great actress *and* she had a unique ability to act with her voice. Her greatness may have been that of an actress, but the dramatic use to which she put the natural gift of her voice was her genius. This is why thousands fell in love with her through her recordings long before they had a chance to experience the Callas presence, the Callas gestures and the Callas movements on the stage, and why thousands who never saw her in the flesh go on falling under the Callas spell on no evidence other than what they hear.

Of course Maria's voice, at the end of her career, was not what it had been at the beginning, but at the March *première* at La Scala in 1957, the combination of her still powerful voice and the inspired way she used it to enhance the drama made *Anna Bolena* the perfect demonstration of the unrivalled way in which at her best she fused the two arts. In the final moments of the opera her voice rises securely to its top Cs and is transformed for Anna's final lines to the rawest of chest notes so that 'Vendetta' is hurled out, transfixing the audience. They were cheering and applauding before the final notes of the orchestra had died away, and that night Maria broke the record of solo curtain-calls at La Scala: twenty-four minutes of continuous applause.

A new peak in the mountain range of voice and drama had been scaled, but it was a culmination rather than a taste of things to come. The future could be seen in a photograph in the Italian press a few days later: Elsa Maxwell in the arms of the waiting Maria at Milan airport. She had arrived at Maria's invitation to see her in *Anna Bolena,* and in between performances and rehearsals for *Iphigénie en Tauride,* Maria had found the time to go and meet her at the airport. For her part, Maxwell was preparing a ball in Venice in Maria's honour and was castigating in her column 'the evil web of invective' around Maria, forgetting that not so long ago she had been one of the web's chief spiders.

Maxwell was back for the dress rehearsal of *Iphigénie.* The result was another column devoted to Maria in which, like a knight protecting his beloved, she threatened to track down those spreading poison about her. That last remark was intended for Karajan and the Vienna State Opera: they had announced the cancellation of Maria's scheduled return to Vienna to sing *Traviata.* In the course of the negotiations, Meneghini had suddenly announced that his wife's fee had doubled. Vienna refused to go beyond $1,600 per performance, and Maria's visit was off. 'I'm not interested in money,' Maria had said, 'but it must be more than anyone else gets.' It was a childish demand for a tangible and much needed confirmation that she was the best. For manager Meneghini, getting a higher and still higher fee for his wife was almost a *raison d'être,* but in Vienna his greed had met retribution. Maria found herself under attack for putting extravagant demands before her art and her commitments, and at the same time she was in the exposed position of being defended by that semi-official mouthpiece of the moneyed *beau monde,* Elsa Maxwell.

While the controversy was raging, Maria was absorbed in the creation of her fifth heroine under Visconti's direction. Gluck's *Iphigénie* was to be their last collaboration, something which neither of them suspected at the time. For once Maria strongly disagreed with Visconti's interpretation. He had placed the opera in the middle of the eighteenth century in an elaborate rococo style. 'Why are you doing it like this?' Maria kept asking. 'It's a Greek story and I'm a Greek woman, so I want to look Greek on stage.' And she went on and on through the rehearsals about wanting to look Greek, even after her glorious costumes, in silk brocade and with enormous trains, had been finished. Visconti considered *Iphigénie* his most beautiful production with Maria and, although this was not the general opinion, there were some stirring moments. Maria made her entrance during the storm scene that opens the opera; she walked up the high staircase and then raced down the steep steps with twenty-five yards of cloak flying wildly in the wind. 'Every night,' remembers Visconti, 'she hit her high note on the eighth step, so extraordinarily co-ordinated was her music and movement. She was like a circus horse, conditioned to pull off any theatrical stunt she was taught.'

Iphigénie was Maria's twentieth production at La Scala and on 21 June President Gronchi, in recognition of her artistic achievements, conferred on her the greatly coveted honorary title of Commendatore. A few days later, Elsa Maxwell conferred on her the honour of a three-day Maxwell tour of Paris – tea with the Windsors, cocktails with the Rothschilds, dinner at Maxim's, the races with Aly Khan.

Elsa had met Prince Aly Khan, the Aga Khan's son, in 1947, and ever since she had been acting as a kind of unpaid propagandist for him, praising his hard work as the heir to the Aga's spiritual leadership of the Ismailis when all the other papers were concentrating on his colourful playboy activities, and defending him from Rita Hayworth's charges when she left him a few months after their marriage. Now in Paris, Aly Khan placed himself at Elsa's disposal as official escort on her Parisian roundabout. Having himself won more than one hundred races as a gentleman jockey, he was the perfect companion for the racecourse. Maria remained impervious to Aly's notorious magnetism, and could work up little enthusiasm for horses; but for the moment, she continued to be eager to try whatever excitements Elsa produced next.

There seemed to be no end to them. Maxwell, who had for some reason been given the Légion d'Honneur by the French government, was at least as much at home in Paris as in New York, and Maria was enjoying getting to know Paris and being fêted and admired, towed in the wake of one who knew which places were fashionable and at what hour of the day.

It was a respite from singing but it turned out to be almost as exhausting. And there was a long summer of recordings ahead. Also, after twelve years, she was getting ready to sing in Athens again. But her homeland was not yet ready to rejoice in her return. Apart from the national reluctance to acknowledge greatness in a fellow Greek, Evangelia's allegations about her daughter had created a very unpleasant stir that was still echoing. What was threatening to turn Maria's visit into a farce even before she arrived was the attempt of the opposition parties to make political capital out of it. They accused the Karamanlis government of getting its social priorities disastrously wrong by agreeing to pay an exorbitant fee to an opera singer when the country was in desperate need of funds for its people. So sensitive and tense was the general atmosphere that the government had arranged for Evangelia and Jackie to leave during Maria's visit; when Maria landed in Athens, they were already in America.

She arrived totally drained from the previous year, longing for a haven. When she found herself instead in the middle of the stormiest sea, she panicked. She was not feeling strong enough to confront an audience stonily withholding sympathy and response, nor did she feel in good enough form to seduce them into surrender. At the same time she knew that a cancellation would arouse even more hostility. She oscillated, prevaricated and finally decided. Her first return concert at the theatre of Herodes Atticus would have to be cancelled. Through a combination of Maria's prevarication and the Greek tendency to postpone the bringing of bad news, the cancellation was announced one hour before curtain time. If Maria had expected disapproval, what she encountered was rage.

When finally, five nights later, exactly thirteen years after she had sung *Fidelio* there, Maria made her entrance on the stage of the ancient theatre, she faced an icy wall of hostility. But now she was ready to use that hostility as a challenge, to ride it out and dissolve it with her magic. Her last aria was the Mad Scene from *Hamlet,* and the ecstatic applause that broke at the end obliged her to encore it; the whole occasion acted as a detonator for all the accumulated tensions of the past week. It was even interpreted by those for whom there is a political motive behind every '*Bravo*' as a vote of confidence in the Karamanlis government.

Back in Milan, the pattern that Maria's life had followed for over ten years now – an excess of activity, effort and tension leading to exhaustion, anxiety and collapse – became actually dangerous. She was thinner than she had ever been; her collar bones were visibly protruding whenever she wore an open dress, and her blood pressure was worryingly low. Her doctor advised the cancellation of all her engagements, artistic and social. Maria decided that cancelling her visit to the Edinburgh Festival with La Scala so soon after the Athens cancellation would be disastrous. And cancelling her visit to Venice for Elsa Maxwell's ball would be such a pity – such a glamorous occasion to miss!

Edinburgh was cold and overcast when she arrived. She was opening the operatic season at the Festival with *Sonnambula.* The first night suffered from her run-down state but as Harold Rosenthal, who saw her on the fourth night, put it in *Opera*: 'Dramatically her interpretation is a *tour de force.* By her very nature Miss Callas is an imperious figure more suited to the great tragic roles of the lyric stage, and yet, although Amina is a Giselle-like figure, the soprano was able by her personality to make us believe in the figure she created.'

Dramatic interpretations, tragic roles and Giselle-like figures were all to be drowned in the torrent of publicity that surrounded Maria's 'cancellation' of her fifth *Sonnambula.* 'Another Callas walk-out' was how it was presented in the British press. The facts were very different. Maria had never agreed to sing a fifth performance; indeed, she had clearly told Ghiringhelli that she would only sing four. It was simply assumed that if she was announced she would have no alternative but to stay on and sing it. It was assumed wrongly. Maria had had enough, and she was not going to sing a performance that was not part of her engagement just to save La Scala's face. The Lord Provost of Edinburgh and his wife, warmly wishing her goodbye at her hotel, understood. The music critics understood: 'One was glad for her sake when she departed for the warm south.' But the world's press, that overzealous guardian of artistic morality, neither understood nor forgave her, especially as departure for the warm south meant Venice and the grand ball Elsa Maxwell was giving in Maria's honour. It was clear that whether or not Maria broke an agreement, she certainly chose not to sing but to be present instead at the party in Venice; she was clearly too exhausted to sing but she was equally clearly not too exhausted to spend all night at the ball. In fact the world's press was full of photographs of her looking her most radiant, confident and polished. Maxwell herself, who at times had the sensitivity and discretion of a rhinoceros, boosted her already inflated ego at Maria's expense. 'I have had many presents in my life . . . but I have never had any star give up a performance in an opera house because she felt she was breaking her word to a friend.' Maria, so quick to imagine betrayal, could not see it when it lay plain before her.

For the moment Elsa could do no wrong. Maria desperately needed someone in her life to play the part of the all-good, all-powerful, mother figure, and Maxwell was delighted to oblige. In her vigorously trivial life, the surface of society, titles, money and gala balls constituted the only reality for her. Maria was a notably beautiful addition to her precious list and Maxwell, with her cultural pretensions, knew perfectly well that she could afford to exchange quite a lot of Counts and Maharajahs for the cachet that Maria was adding to her column and her parties. On top of that, the effect of the *coup de foudre* Maria had dealt her that night at the Waldorf Astoria still continued. So she kept delving into her social repertoire and producing all sorts of toys that would keep Maria, at least for a time, fascinated and involved.

In their competition with opera houses round the world for Maria's attention, energy and time, Maxwell and the *beau monde* had one great thing on their side: novelty. Maria had already sung 22 *Sonnambulas* on stage, as well as 52 *Traviatas,* 41 *Lucias* and 73 *Normas*; and she had in the decade since 1947 created another 28 stage roles. She had not been to as many grand balls. Alexander wept vain tears when there were no more worlds to conquer. From the public's and especially the fans' viewpoint, the world of international café society may not be as important or worthwhile as the world of international opera, but for Maria it was at least a new world.

Maria stayed at the ball until the small hours. It was a performance, and Maria performed without sparing herself. She even sang the blues; sitting on the platform, she sang 'Stormy Weather' with Maxwell at the piano. Maxwell's music-making had been one of the ropes on which she had hauled herself to the top. She started as a pianist in a cinema, pounding out tunes twelve hours a day for the silent films. Then, after the First World War, she made a name for herself in Europe by playing the piano at parties and singing numbers from the latest Broadway shows, or some of the rather attractive songs she had written herself. And now in the summer of 1957, she had achieved the summit of her piano-playing career, accompanying Maria Callas. Even more decisively than usual the singer stole the show from the accompanist.

Maria, perhaps more than anyone else at the party, was much looked at, much talked about, much admired. And doing more than his share of looking and admiring was the second most glamorous Greek present: Aristotle Socrates Onassis. 'I have never,' wrote Maxwell in her column, 'given a better dinner and ball in my life. It had a flare of such joy and happiness. Even two princesses who hated each other were found exchanging smiles, while another comtesse who couldn't remain in the same room with Merle Oberon stayed until 5 a.m.' In fact the party went on for seven days – from the Lido to Harry's Bar, from Harry's Bar to Florian's, from Florian's to Onassis's *Christina,* anchored at the mouth of the Grand Canal. His motor boat, with two sailors dressed in white, was placed at Maria's disposal. The courtship had begun with yachts and motor boats but, as yet, no trumpets and fanfares. Still, it did not escape general attention, though it totally escaped Meneghini's, that Maria had been singled out for Onassis's very special treatment. Maria herself felt pleasantly flattered and generally excited by this new life – but for the moment no more.

Back in Milan, the condemnation of Maria that followed the Edinburgh affair had become almost universal. Even close friends, such as Wally Toscanini, were infected. Wally was so furious with Maria that, for months after her return to Milan, she refused to talk to her. Maria insisted on a public statement from Ghiringhelli setting the record straight over her supposed cancellation. Ghiringhelli refused, and Edinburgh was permanently added as far as the press, the public and even some of her friends were concerned to the growing list of highly publicized Callas cancellations, which so far included Vienna and Athens and to which would soon be added San Francisco. Maria was due to open the San Francisco Opera season on 13 September. Her doctor was against it, but then he had been against the Maxwell ball. The difference was that at this moment in her life Maria was prepared to disregard her doctor's orders for a grand party that she hoped would refresh and relax her, but not for another first night that she knew would be another trial bringing more anxiety and tension.

There were not many days left before the much-publicized opening night, when Kurt Adler, the director of the San Francisco Opera, received a telegram from Maria cancelling her appearances for September, but offering to honour her contract for October. Maria was being driven, along a very circuitous road, it is true, away from her achievements towards new experiences in search of herself. But, looking at Maria's behaviour from Kurt Adler's standpoint, it is not at all difficult to understand his reaction. He exploded with rage, cancelled all her appearances, flew Leyla Gencer from Milan to take over Maria's Lucia, engaged Leonie Rysanek to sing Maria's Lady Macbeth and referred her case to the American Guild of Musical Artists. So another 'court hearing' was in prospect for Maria. On the surface it was a question of deciding whether it would, in fact, have been possible for her to honour her commitments, but symbolically Maria was in the dock for a much larger crime. There was an element verging on religious fervour in the worship of Maria's art, which meant that when she did not display the dedication of a high priestess the faithful felt betrayed. So when Kurt Adler saw press photographs of Maria at Elsa Maxwell's ball and then received a telegram cancelling her opening performances, the rage of the professional was exacerbated by the feeling that sacrilege had been committed.

Maria's critics were growing in number and the criticism was always the same: self-indulgence, failing to meet professional obligations, betrayal of art. Up to 1957, Maria had renounced every aspect of her life that did not directly contribute to her work. She was no longer prepared to make this renunciation. From now on Maria was to come before art. If it was a betrayal, then it was for the sake of another loyalty – the loyalty to herself. But the fact that it included, along the way, absorption into the circle of Elsa Maxwell made her new behaviour much harder for her public to accept.

For the time being, Maria's next important commitment was the final hearing of the Bagarozy lawsuit. She arrived in New York on 5 November and twelve days later it was announced that the Callas-Bagarozy case was over. Ironically, after all the summonses, hearings, unpleasant publicity and strain on Maria's nerves, the case was settled out of court. 'I am tired of being a courtroom character,' was Maria's only comment. The terms were not made public, but there is little doubt that they were no better than they would have been had Maria followed Nicola Rossi-Lemeni's example and settled years earlier.

Four days after the announcement of the settlement, Maria was in Dallas inaugurating, with a benefit concert, the Dallas Civic Opera Company that had just been formed by Lawrence Kelly of Chicago and the conductor Nicola Rescigno. She was rested, in excellent voice and looking her most glamorous. At 117 pounds she was slimmer than she had ever been, and the clinging silk dress she appeared in made her look slimmer still. After the interval, she came back in a dramatic black velvet dress and finished the concert with the Tower Scene from *Anna Bolena*.

She returned to Milan and to the rehearsals of *Un Ballo in Maschera.* The minute she set foot in La Scala she knew that the Edinburgh incident had not been forgotten. The tension poisoned the atmosphere and made the rehearsals almost unbearable. Her first *Ballo* at La Scala should have been an occasion for celebration. After all, ten years earlier, she had auditioned for the part of Amelia there, was assured by the artistic director that she would be considered, and then waited anxiously for days for a phone call that never came. Now, Maria, the unchallenged Queen of La Scala, was being given her own production directed by Margherita Wallmann; but it was not easy to celebrate when the queen was in disgrace. Ghiringhelli, the only man capable of clearing Maria over what had happened in Edinburgh, was still refusing to make any public pronouncement. What made the tension even greater was her relationship with di Stefano, who was singing the hero, Riccardo. It was so strained that rehearsing the long, passionate love duet in Act II was, even for an accomplished actress like Maria, an ordeal. But there is nothing like the presence of an audience to diffuse backstage tensions and ignite the performance. The opening night, on 7 December, was broadcast and is preserved as one of her most exiciting Verdi performances. When compared with Maria's 1956 recording of the opera, this live performance has an added dimension of intensity and power. 'On records,' she herself had said, 'one has to reduce everything to a minimum, because everything is so exaggerated in sound.' On the stage there was no need for restraint. Maria was electrifying. And Gianandrea Gavazzeni, who conducted the five performances, described Maria's musical gift: 'I feel she was born with some kind of sixth sense. One of her great gifts was to differentiate styles of expression – Rossini from Bellini, Donizetti from Verdi. Even Verdi from Verdi. She had a strange, burning inner quality. You only need hear a note or two to recognize her voice. She was always different, yet always herself.'

Immediately after the fifth and final performance of *Ballo,* Maria left Milan for Rome to begin rehearsals for the production of *Norma* that was due to open at the Rome Opera House on 2 January 1958. She saw 1957 out by singing 'Casta Diva' on Italian television and she saw the New Year in at the exclusive Rome club, Circolo degli Scacchi. Even more significant for the events that would unfold in the first days of 1958 was the fact that she was *seen* seeing the New Year in *and* drinking champagne *and* staying up late. How late 'late' was soon became a matter of dispute: some said 1.20, some 2, some 3 and some were whispering 4.

What made these details suddenly very important and brought out the censorious nanny in music-lovers was that when Maria woke up the next morning, less than thirty-six hours before curtain-up, her voice had gone. She could hardly whisper, and she soon realized that she simply could not sing. An urgent call was put through to the management of the Opera House. A substitute had to be found. The artistic director rushed round to the Hotel Quirinale. 'Substitute? Impossible,' he snapped. 'This is no ordinary evening. This is a gala opening! The house is sold out, and the public has paid to see and hear Callas.' The President of Italy was going to be there with his wife, and so was a large slice of Italian society. It had been planned months in advance and it was being treated as the artistic event of the year. On top of all that it was being broadcast. There is no way Maria can cancel, insisted the management. There is no way, echoed Meneghini. There is no way, repeated Elsa Maxwell, who had by now joined the anxious vigil in Maria's suite. Maria kept spraying her throat, taking all the prescribed medicines, crossing herself in front of her little Madonna, putting hot compresses on her chest; but the Voice was not going to obey. Only a miracle would bring it back, and the miracle was not happening. There was no doubt in Maria's mind that she could not sing, and yet this supposedly strong, tough, stubborn woman, the tigress of the international press, feebly gave in; the eagle had been brought down by a flock of sparrows. 'I don't want to be bullied by anybody,' she had said once. 'My own convictions and inner feelings tell me what I should do. Maybe those feelings are right or maybe they are wrong, but I stand up, and have the courage to do so.' By allowing herself on this occasion to be bullied, and deciding, against her instincts, to go ahead, Maria was about to create the greatest scandal of her career and the most widely publicized scandal in the history of opera.

'Norma approaches, and the star of Rome veils itself in

terror,' sing the Druid priestesses at the beginning of the opera. Maria made her entrance and from the first phrase she knew that she was not going to get through it. She was in agony, her voice painfully strident and slipping away from her with every note she sang. It is obvious from the tape of the broadcast that there was no room in Maria's mind for any thought of drama or interpretation. All her instincts were directed towards one thing – survival. The audience sat in amazed silence; it might almost have been embarrassment. At the end of the first act some found their voice. There were loud shouts of 'Go back to Milan' and 'You've cost us a million lire!' But underneath the noise of those shouting, the same stunned silence could still be felt.

Back in her dressing-room, Maria, white and trembling with exhaustion, took her decision thirty-six hours too late: she could not go on. Panic broke out among the management. Despite all the warnings, despite the fact that everyone was perfectly aware of Maria's condition, no one in the Opera House had thought of making arrangements for an understudy. Latini, the general manager, was beseeching her to go on; Elsa Maxwell was dabbing her face with cologne; Margherita Wallmann was trying to convince her that the hardest moments of the opera were behind her; Santini, the conductor, was appealing to her artistic pride, other voices were reminding her of what she owed to Italy, pointing out that the President himself was in the audience, even insisting that the evening could still be saved if she merely walked through the part declaiming it without singing. The interval was going on and on; the audience were getting restless; the rumours were getting wilder. Everyone's eyes kept darting to what was once the Royal Box. No, the President was still there. Yes, the President was still waiting. And then suddenly the President had gone. He had been told minutes before the public announcement and had left only to discover that his chauffeur was not waiting outside. The poor man had taken what he felt was a safe risk, found out what time the performance was due to end and had gone to the cinema. He lost his job, but he was by no means the only casualty of the night. All over

Rome, husbands or wives were coming home unexpectedly early, with dire consequences. Or even when they were expected: one straying husband, arriving at the time the opera was supposed to have ended, described in detail to his wife a performance she already knew had been cancelled.

Maria left the Opera House through an underpass that led directly to the Hotel Quirinale. It was just as well. All the street exits including the stage door had been blocked by angry crowds waiting for Maria's exit. When it was clear that their prey had somehow escaped them, they moved on, still shouting and gesticulating, to Maria's hotel. Some of them stayed there until the early hours of the morning, punctuating her sleeplessness with their bitter abuse. Maria, awake throughout, spent the night waiting. Waiting for what? For someone to arrive from the Opera House and explain that it had all been their fault for forcing her to go on? For someone to arrive from heaven and wipe these nightmarish hours out of her life? For the morning newspapers so that she could read what she had already heard, already knew they felt about her? 'This second-rate artist.' began *Il Giorno,* 'Italian by her marriage, Milanese because of the unfounded admiration of certain segments of La Scala's audience, international because of her dangerous friendship with Elsa Maxwell, has for several years followed a path of melodramatic debauchery. This episode shows that Maria Meneghini Callas is also a disagreeable performer who lacks the most elementary sense of discipline and propriety.'

It seemed that there was no news other than of Maria. The papers were savage – *'Scandalo!'*, *'Disgrazia'*, *'Insulta'*. Mercifully the new day brought not only vicious press reports; it also brought phone calls and telegrams from all over the world, from colleagues and friends reassuring Maria of their support and understanding. Visconti's was one of the first telegrams to arrive. Not much later came a phone call from the President's wife herself. Maria had immediately sent a letter to her and her husband explaining and apologizing. And Signora Gronchi called to assure Maria that neither she nor her husband had been offended, and no apology was necessary. But tempers were still running high. At the Biffi Scala in Milan diners actually came to blows when one of them dared to speak up for Maria; and in the Italian Parliament, Deputy Bozzi denounced Maria for her slight against Italy and its Head of State. In these circumstances the Opera House, in the interests of public order as they put it, asked the Prefecture of Rome for an order banning Maria from claiming her right to sing the remaining three performances of *Norma* for which she had been contracted – in effect banning her from entering the precincts of the Opera House. The order was granted and Anita Cerquetti was flown in to take Maria's place. Maria, embittered, exhausted and lonely, had no option but to flee Rome for Milan. She made sure that the flight was a richly operatic performance. Dressed in a severe tailored suit with dramatic make-up and a veil over her face, she appeared, after five days of isolation, in the lobby of the Quirinale, where a huge crowd of photographers was waiting for her.

Later in the year the memory of her humiliation was sufficiently alive for her to sue the Rome Opera House for the sum of 2,700,000 lire in fees for the performances she had been barred from singing as well as for travelling expenses and an unspecified sum in damages. Another legal battle, another battle she would eventually win, another hollow victory paid for with conflict, separation, worry. 'Always a fight – that's been the trouble with my career, I've always had to fight. And I don't like it. I don't like fights and I don't like quarrels. I hate the nervous mental condition they engender. But if I have to fight, I'll fight. Up to now I have generally won, but never with any feeling of elation. They are bleak triumphs, simply because it was necessary to fight in the first place.'

There were to be more triumphs before the dramatic change now approaching in her life, but they were all bleak, won against the background of growing isolation. The world Maria had conquered was crumbling around her. She was losing the joy she had once found in the love and challenge of her work. And she knew it. All those who are still seeking an explanation for the declining number of her performances and new roles after 1958 have the answer, clear and unambiguous, from her own mouth: 'When you are young, you like to stretch your voice, you enjoy singing, you love it. It's not a question of will-power, it has nothing to do with driving ambition. You simply love your work – this beautiful, intangible thing which is called music. If you sing out of pleasure and enjoyment things come beautifully. It's like getting drunk – only from pleasure, the pleasure of doing something well. Just like an acrobat when he feels on form and feels the happiness of the public and is inspired to more and more adventurous feats of daring. The more you enjoy it, the more you feel like doing.'

And the less you enjoy it, the less you feel like doing. It is clear that she was enjoying work less and less, especially after the open hostility she felt from everybody at La Scala. The strained civility of the previous months between Ghiringhelli and herself had collapsed, after the Rome scandal, into undisguised antagonism. 'I love the Scala above all other theatres,' Maria had said. 'I consider it my home.' Now her home was spurning her. It was the most painful blow of all, and it cost Maria more than her disputes with Rome, Vienna, Athens and San Francisco put together.

She had never felt as much pained relief at leaving Milan as she did this time. A concert in Chicago, the hearing before the American Guild of Musical Artists and, if that went well, a season at the Metropolitan, were ahead of her. On her way to Chicago she stopped for six hours in Paris. In her present dejected state the welcome Paris gave her overwhelmed and, for the moment, restored her. It coloured forever her view of the city she was eventually to make her home. A huge crowd of photographers and radio, television and press reporters were at Orly waiting for her. Maria, in a beige mink coat, a velvet hat and with Toy in her arms, was ready to meet the French press for the first time. She was clearly moved – as if they were all there to remind her that she was still glorious, still loved, still supreme.

The questions jostled each other: 'All the journalists have left Paris to be here with you. *N'est-ce pas magnifique?*' 'Are you not moved by the welcome Paris is giving you?'

'What about Rome?' Maria answered patiently, smilingly, while Toy, very cosy in her arms, devoured the orchids she had rested on her lap. 'Rome has at least allowed me to count my friends,' was Maria's half-sweet, half-bitter reply to the Rome question. 'Thank you to all those who have defended me.'

Maria, who had not yet sung in Paris, had Paris at her feet. After a quick change at the Hotel Crillon, she arrived at Maxim's for the dinner given in her honour by EMI's French counterpart. As Maxim's monthly newsletter proudly proclaimed on its cover: *'350 minutes à Paris – 84 au Maxim's'*. The chef had created a special dish for her, *La selle d'agneau à la Callas,* and next to her plate had been placed a little transistor radio on which she could hear her recording of *Trovatore* the French radio was broadcasting. No detail and no courtesy had been overlooked. Even her superstitious belief that thirteen at table was unlucky had been catered for: the other guests had been warned that if one of them had to leave the table for a few minutes, another was to get up from the table at the same time. As *Le Figaro* put it: 'Paris gave Maria the welcome it reserves for sovereigns and honoured prophets.'

The ten minutes of applause in Chicago even before the concert began seemed a pale welcome by comparison, but none of this could dispel her growing concern as the day of the hearing before the American Guild of Musical Artists approached. It turned out to be a great performance. The immediate cause of the hearing was Maria's cancellation of her appearance in San Francisco but, for well over two hours, putting aside the regalia of the Queen of Opera, she defended herself and her entire professional record to the jury of twenty men whose verdict would determine whether she would appear at the Met eight days later. The verdict was equivocal. Maria was not suspended, but she was reprimanded. She could, therefore, go on singing, but it was to be under a swelling cloud of professional disapproval.

She started rehearsing for her first *Traviata* at the Met. It was the revival of the Tyrone Guthrie production, with shabby, unimaginative sets, co-singers who ranged from indifferent to downright bad and grossly inadequate rehearsal time. Maria, who knew just how much her own performance depended on everything and everyone else on stage, was angry and apprehensive. 'I try always to have a decent company around me,' she explained once for the benefit of those who accused her of being too demanding, 'and about that I am touchy. Because if I work up to a certain atmosphere and suddenly my colleague bursts out with a ridiculous phrase or sings without feeling, then this hard work of creation – which may have taken half an hour of performance – is shattered in a split second. One then has to work for another half hour to rebuild it.' But on this occasion she decided to say nothing and show nothing – with the press and the public eagerly looking out for signs of the famous Callas temperament, she could not, and would not, risk another confrontation.

The first night of *Traviata* on 6 February turned out to be one of Maria's greatest personal triumphs. It was not the perfect *Traviata*, but it was clearly the most exciting, the most dramatically true Violetta the New Yorkers had ever seen. Thirty minutes of curtain-calls with Maria called back again and again left no one in any doubt as to whose night this was. 'We pay for these evenings,' was Maria's comment on the hysteria that so often surrounded her first nights. '*I* can ignore it. But my subconscious can't. And that's worse. I confess there are times when part of me is flattered by the high emotional climate, but generally I don't like any moment of it. You start to feel condemned.' It was as if, never able to enjoy the present, she felt subconsciously condemned to live up to the future expectations the hysteria aroused, condemned to go on performing at a level and intensity that would justify the hysteria, condemned to repeat and exceed the feats of the first night on the second and on the third and on the fourth. 'The more fame you have, the more responsibility is yours and the smaller and more defenceless you feel.' So she said and she never ceased to believe it.

She longed for relaxation, for peace, for mental stability – words which crop up again and again through what she said and wrote. In New York, among two *Traviatas*, three *Lucias* and two *Toscas*, she chose as her guide to relaxation and tranquillity Elsa Maxwell. The result was exhaustion and excitement – excitement because of the luxury and glamour that Maxwell and her friends introduced her to; exhaustion because that world, far from being a world of relaxation, demanded a constant, relentless performance. George Bernard Shaw had called Maxwell the eighth wonder of the world. Shavian irony aside, there was nevertheless something to wonder at in the way this seventy-three-year-old woman, whom someone else had likened to a baby whale stranded on a beach, had for years stayed at the centre of the Beautiful People, with the rich fawning on her and the famous dancing attendance.

Busy acquiring a first-class season ticket to Maxwell's world, Maria was at the same time scoring an artistic triumph in *Tosca.* This time her dramatic guide and inspirer was not a producer but a conductor and a fellow Greek, Dimitri Mitropoulos. He had also conducted her first *Tosca* at the Met in 1956, but this time there was a new fire, a new and deeper intensity in their collaboration. 'You must give the public shivers,' Maria said fifteen years later to a student soprano at the Juilliard School. On 28 February 1958, her Tosca did give the New York public shivers. And on 5 March, she did it again – and more so. She gave them shivers not only when they saw the knife gleaming as she was about to kill Scarpia, but even when she knelt to pray: 'She really prayed,' remembered Mitropoulos. 'It wasn't just for the audience.' Maria's father was there for the first night. So, of course, was Elsa Maxwell. 'Why should a woman,' she wrote, 'capable of so noble an expression in the classic arts, be tortured by a destiny that makes her happiness almost impossible? Her mother, I believe without question, has been the cause of this situation.'

Evangelia, now divorced from her husband, had been living in New York for over a year, but Maria, who shared La Maxwell's belief, had coldly refused all attempts by friends and relatives to bring her and her mother together. She had slammed that door on her past and its pain, and *nothing* was going to make her open it again. All her pent-up affection flowed towards her father instead. Two days before the first night of *Tosca* she even appeared with him on Hy Gardner's television chat show. George was dignified, almost respectful, and above all proud. As for Maria, she spoke devotedly of her husband but refused to be drawn on the subject of her mother. Hy Gardner, who also had a column in the *New York Herald Tribune,* had met Maria at a lunch given in her honour by publisher Henry Sell. 'I came to lunch expecting to meet a cold, tempestuous but talented female ogre,' he wrote in his column, 'and found instead a warm, sincere, handsome and down-to-earth human being, a real live doll.'

Perhaps because he clearly responded to Maria, perhaps because Maria was herself feeling more relaxed and secure, the programme was a much greater success than her *Person to Person* interview with Ed Murrow a month earlier. The *Herald Tribune,* commenting on the Ed Murrow programme, had described her as the 'epitome of moderation and easy-going good humor'; in fact, from beginning to end during the fifteen-minute interview, Maria, the fascinating, unpredictable artist, had yielded to the conventional matron, and the result had been frigid propriety. Still, millions of people across the States who had no interest in opera had now seen her on the small screen. So celebrity fed upon and reproduced itself and the cycle quickened. Standing near the pinnacle of world-wide fame, Maria was ambivalent about it, wallowing in the attention and admiration one moment and in the next becoming snappish, resentful and fearful that it would all come to an abrupt halt.

Her stay in New York was coming to an end and she had still not reached an agreement with Rudolf Bing about the next season, about what it would include and in what order. They had discussed a large number of possibilities. At one point, Bing even asked her whether she would consider singing the Queen of the Night. 'It doesn't make sense for you,' she replied, 'to pay such a large fee for such a small part.' 'Sing for a reduced fee,' Bing came back. 'I will if you can prove to me that there will be fewer people in the audience.' They talked a lot, but Maria left New York with nothing settled.

On the way back to Milan, she stopped in Brussels where Malibran is buried. It was a quick visit in between planes, to honour the great nineteenth-century soprano but a cluster of meetings and people had been fitted in as well. With the growth of Maria's reputation, the queue of opera directors, concert organizers and festival managers was growing longer, and Meneghini made sure that they had a long wait. 'We can't talk now,' he would say, taking out his diary, 'but if you come to Milan/London/New York I'll see you there.' And then, 'I'm too busy now, but in two weeks I have half an hour at the airport between planes. We could talk then.' And there he would be the important Mr Meneghini, followed around from city to city, airport to airport and hotel to hotel. Peter Diamand, who wanted to book Maria for the 1959 Holland Festival, had been asked by Meneghini to meet them at the airport in Brussels, where they would talk. They did not. 'I followed them round the city seeing people and unveiling things, and got back to the airport with them, not of course having exchanged a word. Fortunately I had anticipated this and had booked a seat on the plane to Milan. Even more fortunately Meneghini fell instantly asleep and did not wake up until we had reached Milan. So Maria and I enjoyed ourselves making all the arrangements for her participation in the Festival.'

Maria's first public appearance in Italy since the Rome scandal was on 9 April at La Scala. The opera was *Anna Bolena,* and such was the hatred that had been stirred up against her since her 'walk-out' that in the square outside the Opera House an entire company of armed police stood guard, ready to go into action if the anti-Callas protestors got out of hand. Inside, the plain-clothes policemen had been posted in strategic positions along corridors, and in foyers and boxes. But they could not protect Maria against the implacable indifference displayed by the audience throughout the first two scenes.

Then came the third scene and the dramatic turnabout. Piero Tosi was present: 'As two guards came to seize her, Callas violently pushed them aside and hurled herself to the front of the stage, spitting her lines directly at the audience: "*Giudici! ad Anna! . . . Giudici!*" (Judges! For Anna! . . . Judges!). It was not theatre any more, it was reality. Callas was defending herself, all but saying, "If this is my trial, judge me.... But remember I am your Queen!" She dared her accusers and stared them down, dramatically surpassing anything she had ever done, singing with scorching brilliance. When the curtain fell, the audience went mad. Uproar, sheer lunacy. Then Callas swept forward for her bows, inflated with her power, her victory, her magnificence. And every time she came forth, she grew more, more, more. You could not dream what she did. It was a show within a show.'

The final show took place as Maria emerged at the stage door ready to leave the theatre after the performance. She was dressed for confrontation: long, black chiffon dress, all her diamonds and a face stark white with the accumulated tension of the night. She was expecting to meet the hostile crowd that had been waiting at the square when she had walked into the theatre before the performance. Instead the crowd was cheering. Word of her triumph had spread through the square as people were leaving the theatre and instantaneously, as if by a miracle, the crowd's mood was transformed from anger to idolatry. Maria's walk through the long loggia to the Biffi Scala where her car was waiting became the slow procession of a Queen through her cheering subjects. The police who, guns at the ready, had been holding back the angry crowd only a short while earlier, looked on with stupefaction. Some even joined in the cheering. 'After Callas drove away,' recalled Piero Tosi who had run to the stage door after the performance, 'none of us could go home to sleep and we milled around for hours in a kind of shock and ecstasy.'

Maria was herself in ecstasy as she drove home. Nothing delighted her more than turning a predicted defeat into a glorious victory. But what was waiting for her at Via Buonarroti was a cruel sight. The door, the walls, the threshold, the windows, the whole entrance and front of her treasured home, had been smeared with dung and covered with obscene writings. Just as swiftly as her magic had changed the crowd's anger into cheers, the sight of hatred made visible turned her happiness into agony, her conquest into humiliation. 'Is it all worth it?' was the question that once again rose inside her, demanding an answer. She was getting very close to deciding that it was not. What is more, the police seemed singularly unconcerned when Meneghini called to notify them, and there was precious little sympathy from La Scala.

Maria felt herself surrounded by hostility, indifference, envy and resentment. She was suffocating, and as soon as the last performance of *Anna Bolena* was over, she and Meneghini fled Milan for Sirmione, on the shores of Lake Garda, where they had bought a house earlier in the year. Meneghini had overseen everything, from the rebuilding and furnishing of the villa to the lawns, the hedgerows and the flower beds. Maria divided her time in Sirmione between her piano and Imogene in Bellini's *Il Pirata,* her next role at La Scala. The night was her favourite time for working. She would lie in bed, score in hand, with Meneghini asleep beside her and Toy in her arms. This, as she said herself, was her happiest time, even happier than the glamorous first nights with all the anxiety that preceded them and the self-recriminations that followed them.

But another opening night loomed ahead. On 9 May, Maria opened in *Il Pirata.* Ghiringhelli pointedly ignored her throughout the rehearsals and, despite the presence of sympathetic colleagues, Maria found the atmosphere at La Scala cold, artificial and hateful. As she wrote in *Life* magazine: 'If the theatre of which you are a guest adds to the tension of a performance by continual harassment and rudeness, art becomes physically and morally impossible. For my self-defence and dignity, I had no choice but to leave La Scala.' Rumours of her decision had been circulating for months and intensified in the few days before the last performance on 31 May. It was to be her 157th appearance at La Scala and, as it turned out, her last appearance there for over two and a half years.

In the final scene, Imogene, who knows that her pirate-lover must die, in her grief and fear sees in her mind's eye the scaffold on which he is to be executed: *'La . . .vedete . . . il palco funesto'* (There, behold, the fateful scaffold). By coincidence, *'palco'* means both scaffold and theatre-box in Italian. Maria seized the moment and the coincidence and with that dramatic audacity that was uniquely hers, she brought performance and reality together. She walked across the stage and with scorn in her eyes and a gesture of contempt, she spat the line *'il palco funesto'* straight at Ghiringhelli's empty box. The allusion was impossible to miss, and the public, sensing that they were losing her, called her back time after time after time. Now it was Ghiringhelli's turn for revenge. He gave a signal for the heavy safety curtain to be lowered abruptly, cutting off Maria from the audience, the cheers, the applause and the flowers with which her fans had wanted to shower her. 'As I walked for the last time out of the theatre that had been my operatic home for seven years,' remembered Maria, 'they were standing out in the street throwing flowers for me. They had finally found a place where they could say goodbye.' Ghiringhelli retained his celebrated aloofness: 'The primadonnas pass, La Scala remains,' was his laconic comment on Maria's departure.

Breaking with La Scala was an emotional as well as professional uprooting for Maria. Ever since she first sang at Verona, married Meneghini and called herself Maria Meneghini Callas, she had been putting down roots in Italy. Her home in Milan and her country house in Sirmione nourished the roots, and her reign at La Scala was the tap-root on which the life of the tree depended. Leaving La Scala was the first symbolic departure; it was to herald a series of exits at least as dramatic as any she had achieved on the operatic stage.

Chapter Ten

AT THE beginning of June 1958 Maria arrived in London to take part in the Gala celebrating the centenary of Covent Garden. The Savoy felt more like home than Via Buonarroti, London more like home than Milan, Covent Garden a peaceful harbour after the cold, stormy sea of La Scala. The behaviour of the management at Covent Garden could not have been more strikingly different from that of their counterparts at La Scala. Lord Harewood even gave up his private office to her for use as a dressing-room, thereby simultaneously keeping Maria happy and solving the appalling problem of dressing-room precedence for an evening which included, apart from Maria, Margot Fonteyn, Jon Vickers, Joan Sutherland and Blanche Thebom. The judgement of Solomon was that Number One – which by some historical accident is really Number Five at Covent Garden – should go to Dame Margot Fonteyn. So Lord Harewood's office was cleared of all its usual equipment, a dressing table was installed and the room was filled with flowers.

On that night, 10 June 1958, Covent Garden shone with stars; but Maria out-shone them all. She sang the Mad Scene from *Puritani,* and was called back eight times. After the show, about two hundred performers lined up to be presented to the Queen. Maria, in a shimmering black sheath gown singularly inappropriate for curtseying, was among the first. When it was all over, she left the Opera House, relaxed and glowing, for a late supper with Lord and Lady Harewood. She was, as one newspaper put it, the star of the week. A few days after the Gala she was being introduced to millions of television viewers on Granada's programme *Chelsea at Eight*. She sang 'Vissi d'arte' from

Tosca and 'Una voce poco fa' from *Il Barbiere di Siviglia.* 'In the brief space of twelve or fifteen minutes, she showed what greatness is in opera,' wrote one television critic. 'Television was made for things like that – and she was made for television,' said another. 'She sang magnificently. She looked superb,' added a third.

Three days later the star of the week could be heard in a live broadcast of the first night of *Traviata.* The intervals, for those who were present and no doubt for those at home, too, were hot with dispute. She was not in very good voice and the main subject of the disputes was how much these vocal deficiences mattered. According to Peter Heyworth, not very much: 'Callas's understanding of this great part,' he wrote, 'finds its way into the smallest gesture and movement, into the nervous passage of a hand around the face, the terrible fragility of body that in the last act turns every movement into a labour, and the fearful abruptness with which the gaping image of death is all at once *there* in her staring eyes... And then Callas does after all sing. She may not on Friday have done so with beauty of tone, but in almost every other aspect it was a performance of outstanding distinction and musicality, full of detail that again and again illuminated the part as though for the first time.' But according to Philip Hope-Wallace the vocal deficiencies mattered a lot: 'Some of us remained only fifty per cent enraptured. Personally I suffered much.'

The Callas controversy was still raging when Maria left London for Milan and from there for two months' rest in Sirmione. But playing Chopin and Brahms in Sirmione, beautiful and serene though it all was, was not enough for Maria. Her deep, persistent restlessness could not be assuaged by relaxing on the shores of Lake Garda in the company of a husband who was spending most of his time plotting her autumn and winter engagements. All was arranged: two recordings in London (which was to become Maria's recording headquarters after the end of her association with La Scala); a nationwide concert tour of America; *Traviata* and *Medea* at the Dallas Civic Opera. But one very obvious gap remained: the Metropolitan. Rudolf Bing knew that he wanted Maria for a series of twenty-six performances in three operas – *Macbeth, Tosca* and either *Lucia* or *Traviata* – but Maria seemed unable to decide exactly what she wanted from the Metropolitan.

She left for New York on 7 October, with no decision made, and she left New York for Birmingham, Alabama, the first city of her concert tour, with everything still unresolved. The whole tour had been flawlessly organized by the Russian-born American impresario Sol Hurok, perhaps the most colourful and successful showman in a field which has always abounded in them; it was said of Hurok that he was to music what P. T. Barnum was to the circus. The first leg of her tour took her from Birmingham to Atlanta, from Atlanta to Montreal and from Montreal to Toronto. From Toronto she flew to Dallas. The Met season was about to begin, and still no decision had been reached.

On 31 October, the opening night of her Dallas *Traviata,* she received a telegram of congratulations from Bing. 'But why in Dallas?' was the question at the end of the good wishes. One answer was that Dallas had given her everything she could have wished for, and more: a new production of *Traviata* directed by Zeffirelli; a new production of *Medea* directed by Alexis Minotis, the great Greek director whom she had herself wooed into opera for the first time; Jon Vickers, later one of the greatest Tristans and Otellos of our time, for her Jason; Nicola Rescigno, her favourite conductor of the moment; and unconditional enthusiasm and admiration combined with gratitude that she was there to turn a cultural backwater into the centre of operatic news by her presence. This last was the key – the real answer to Bing's question, 'Why in Dallas?' Maria was tired of fighting, tired of being attacked and misrepresented in the New York press, tired of once again having to seduce the blasé Met audience into surrender. It is true that when she received Bing's schedule of her performances she had genuine objections to the way he had alternated Lady Macbeth, full of heavy dramatic demands on the voice, with fragile Violetta; but only a much deeper reluctance can explain her inability to decide what exactly she wanted from the Met and to communicate her wishes clearly through all these frustrating months of futile negotiations.

On both the first and second nights of *Traviata,* the Dallas State Fair Music Hall was filled with over 4,000 adoring Callasites for whom Maria could do and sing no wrong. They loved the Zeffirelli production, which presented Violetta's story in a series of flashbacks, and they certainly did not seem to care – or indeed to notice – that Maria was by no means in her best voice.

At rehearsals, she amazed everyone, from Minotis to the wardrobe mistress, with her dedication, her stamina, her passion for work. Minotis remembers her dropping in on a chorus rehearsal once on her way to a party. Elegantly and elaborately dressed, she watched for a few minutes. 'Then gradually she takes off her fur coat, throws away her hat, her shoes, the belt of her dress and within seconds she *is* Medea. That was Callas. Once she was in the surroundings of her art nothing else existed.'

There was real artistic fusion between Maria and Minotis. Married to the great Greek tragic actress Katina Paxinou, he found in Maria another great actress with the same powerful dramatic instinct. One morning in Dallas, he saw Maria kneeling beating the floor in a frenzy, to summon the gods, the very gesture that he and Paxinou had discovered in their search to recapture the movements and expressions used in the time of Aeschylus, Sophocles and Euripides. 'How did you know?' asked the astonished Minotis. 'I felt it would be the right thing to do for this moment in the drama,' was Maria's answer. Her dramatic instinct went beyond logical explanation.

Maria was totally possessed by this production of *Medea.* She breathed Medea, felt Medea and could hardly sleep because of Medea. 'She would ring at three or four in the morning,' remembers Minotis. "What exactly did you say this afternoon when I come out and climb the steps – from the left or from the right?" She was not asleep. She was rehearsing on her own. What we had worked out together, she would pass through her own filter, to understand, to assimilate, to make part of herself.'

These were Maria's secret moments of glory, of passion, of intoxication, when her instinct for creation and completion – at times even stronger than her instinct

1 *Above:* Thirteen-year-old Maria with her mother

2 *Below:* Maria outside her Athens home, 1939

3 *Above left:* Maria in Verona, 1949, just before she married Meneghini

4 *Above right:* Maria as Violetta in Mexico

5 *Below:* Maria and Meneghini at a reception in Milan, 1950

6 Maria in *Traviata* at La Scala

7 *Above:* The picture that established the image of the tigress: Maria exploding at the U.S. Marshal who had just served her with two summonses at the Chicago Opera House, 1955

8 *Below left:* Posing in her latest Biki creation

9 *Below right:* Maria at home in Milan

10 As Medea at Covent Garden, 1959

11 *Above:* Soon after their first meeting: Maria and Onassis absorbed in each other,

12 while *(below)* Meneghini looks on

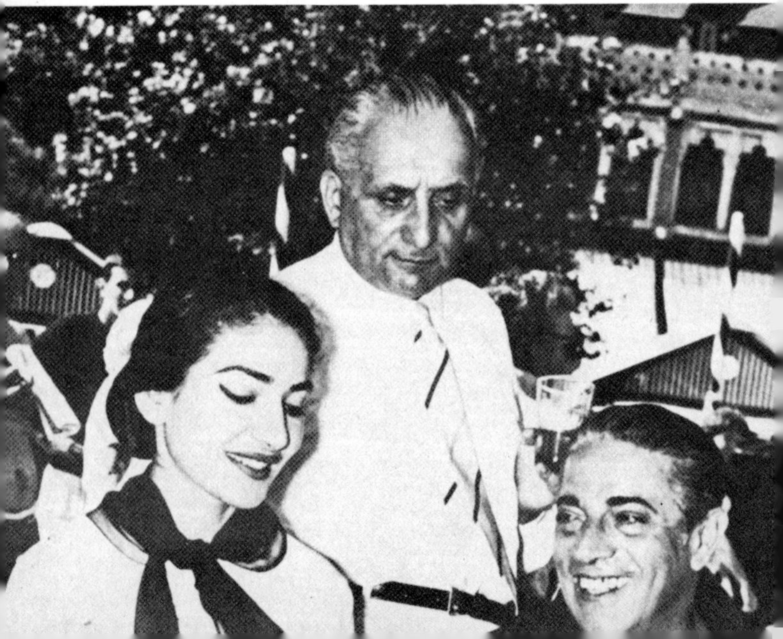

13 Maria as Giulia in *La Vestale*

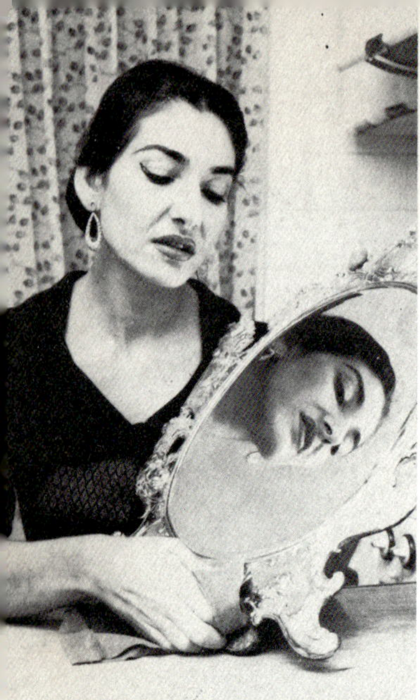

14 & 15 *Above:* Rivals for Onassis: Maria at home, and Tina on the Onassis yacht

16 *Below:* Elsa Maxwell accompanying Maria

17 Maria on holiday on Ibiza

18 A scene from the film of *Medea,* directed by Pasolini

19 *Above:* Cruising in the Bahamas on the *Christina* a few months before Onassis's marriage to Jackie Kennedy

20 *Below:* Onassis and Jackie Kennedy at their wedding on Skorpios, 20 October 1968

21 *Above:* With Princess Grace and Prince Rainier

22 *Below:* Maria with Zeffirelli after the performance of her last opera, *Tosca,* at Covent Garden

23 During Maria's last days in Paris

24 Maria on one of her daily walks in the streets of Paris

25 After Maria's death, her mother at her Athens home

for survival – found its fulfilment. That sacred, consuming passion that she and Minotis shared was communicated to everyone else in the production. Rivalries, potential jealousies, even egos, seemed to have evaporated. Teresa Berganza, very young and very beautiful, was singing the maidservant, Neris. It was Maria who showed her how to act the part, and worked with her on it; and on the first night, when Berganza stopped the show with Neris's aria, Maria waited – almost with pride – until the last waves of applause had subsided before she continued. Jon Vickers was fascinated by her. He remembers their first meeting when they were rehearsing at an old Exposition Building – big, cold, draughty, with tape on the floor marking out the stage. 'She arrived looking very elegant and very grand, and started giving me orders as if to test what mettle I was made of: "Don't do that"; "Don't do the other"; "Don't look at me that way". I stopped, looked straight at her and said: "Madame Callas, Alexis Minotis has already put me through the production. You show me what *you* are going to do." We never had another problem working together. Her dedication was quite extraordinary. At the dress rehearsal, the day before the first night, we worked straight through until two in the morning. "I hope I have something left for tonight," she said as we were saying goodnight. She was a superb colleague, giving you something to work with and wanting you to give it back. She never tried to steal the limelight or upstage anyone. The enormous revolution that took place in opera after the war happened because of two people: Wieland Wagner, who totally changed the approach and emphasis of the physical aspects of stage direction, and Maria Callas, who took her talent almost to the point of masochism to serve her work and find its meaning.'

This was the intense atmosphere backstage in Dallas when on the afternoon of the dress rehearsal a telegram was brought to Maria from Rudolf Bing, demanding an immediate confirmation of the proposed Met schedule by ten o'clock the following morning. Maria, partly because of her total involvement in *Medea,* partly because, as she put it, she was not going to be intimidated by Bing's 'Prussian tactics', ignored both the telegram and the ultimatum. The following morning, only hours before curtain time on the first night of *Medea,* another telegram arrived. Maria was being formally informed that her contract with the Metropolitan was being cancelled forthwith. 'BING FIRES CALLAS' ran the banner headlines. The musical world was astounded, and Maria's hotel was invaded by the international press.

It was an unbroken rule of Maria's to speak to no one on the day of a performance unless it was about something connected with that night's opera. But on 6 November 1958, she did not stop talking right up to the moment she had to go on stage. The whole day had been an electrifying performance. Mary Mead, who lived in Dallas and had become a close friend of Maria's, remembers the day in every detail: 'She started with a phone interview to *Time* and she did not seem to hang up the phone once. How she could still talk, let alone sing, I don't know.' That night Maria *was* Medea, singing out much of the fury she had not talked out during the day. She was not singing just for her adoring Texan public; she was singing for Bing, for New York, for all those celebrating her humiliation. And she was magnificent.

Nor did it end with the performance. Maria Seconda (the name Maria had given to Mary Mead) was giving a supper party for her, and when Maria arrived there at one o'clock in the morning, there was a huge truck in the front yard from a television company, and the phone was still ringing. She left Mary Mead's house at five o'clock in the morning and after a few hours' sleep Dallas's *primadonna assoluta* began talking again: to the American press, to the Italian press, to anyone who would listen – and everybody did. 'I cannot switch my voices. My voice is not like an elevator going up and down. . . . So Mr Bing cancels a twenty-six-performance contract for three *Traviatas.*' 'When I think of those lousy *Traviatas* he made me sing without rehearsals, without even knowing my partners . . . . Is that Art? . . . And other times, all those performances with a different tenor or a different baritone every time . . . . Is that Art?'

Bing had not exactly remained speechless. 'I do not propose,' began his press statement, 'to enter into a public feud with Madame Callas since I am well aware that she has considerably greater competence and experience at that kind of thing than I have.' Sarcasm, formal eloquence and sardonic wit were only a few of the weapons in Rudolf Bing's arsenal. He used them all. Maria had taken on a formidable antagonist – a man who thrived on public fencing, a man who early in his career had perfected the art of dealing with awkward customers at Peter Jones's hairdressing salon, and who towards the end had informed the French press, busy complaining about the performance of a Met singer, that 'Miss Peters may have had a bad night but the Paris Opera has had a bad century.'

'Although Madame Callas's artistic qualifications are a matter of violent controversy between her friends and foes,' continued Bing's statement, 'her reputation for projecting her undisputed histrionic talent into her business affairs is a matter of common knowledge. . . .' He went on in this vein until Maria began to feel grateful for Ghiringhelli's dismissive one-sentence statements to the press in their feuding days at La Scala. 'So, on with the season!' were Bing's final, fighting words.

Maria continued her concert tour of America from Cleveland to Detroit, from Detroit to Washington, from Washington to San Francisco and Los Angeles; concerts punctuated by an Elsa Maxwell dinner in New York in honour of Karajan, a dinner at the Waldorf with Aly Khan and Noël Coward and a dinner in Washington given in her honour by the French Ambassador. Meanwhile the Met controversy smouldered on. It ranged from avowals of total support for Bing's action to demands for his resignation. Whatever the results of the theoretical argument over Bing's decision, back in Milan at the beginning of December, Maria was feeling its practical effects. She was celebrating her thirty-fifth birthday and looking ahead to a winter almost devoid of performances. Almost, but not quite. On 19 December, she was at last due to make her debut in Paris. It was a Charity Gala concert, with the proceeds going to the Légion d'Honneur. The seats were being sold for the highest price ever charged at L'Opéra, and the list of those who were going to be present included Charlie Chaplin, Brigitte Bardot,

Emile de Rothschild, Juliette Greco, Françoise Sagan, the Windsors, Jean Cocteau and Aristotle Onassis. Even the twenty-four usherettes were part of Parisian high society, selling programmes in their ball gowns to raise money for the Legion.

Among the flowers Maria received in her hotel on the morning of the Gala was a huge bunch of red roses; the good wishes were in Greek and the signature, Aristotle Onassis. Among the flowers that arrived at lunch time was a huge bunch of red roses – the good wishes were again in Greek and the signature, Aristotle. And in the evening just as she was about to leave for the opera house an identical bunch arrived with the good wishes in Greek and no signature. 'How romantic he is!' was Maria's only comment to her husband. Later Meneghini remembered – or imagined – that there was a strange tone in her voice as she said that.

The concert was to be followed by a sumptuous supper for 450 guests, and the press was full of the event for days before. *'L'impératrice du bel canto'*, as one French paper called her, was reminded on her arrival that when she had passed through Paris at the beginning of the year, she had told the French that, if she lived among them, she would never be angry again. 'Yes,' repeated Maria at a press conference in her hotel suite, 'only the French have sought to understand me.'

On the night of the performance, an Italian paper took a straw poll among the crowd gathered outside the opera house. 'Why are you here?' the reporter asked. 'To hear Callas,' was one answer. 'We hope there will be a scandal,' was another.

But there was no scandal, only a triumph. Maria sang arias from *Norma, Il Trovatore* and *Il Barbiere,* as well as the whole of Act II of *Tosca,* with Tito Gobbi and Albert Lance. The evening was televised in nine countries, so that Maria's triumph and the delirious ovation she received reverberated beyond the French capital throughout Europe. At the supper afterwards she looked glorious. Wearing a diamond necklace worth more than a million dollars (lent to her by Van Cleef and Arpels), and radiating confidence, she was gracefully accepting congratulations from a long line of enthusiastic admirers. Aristotle Onassis was among the first. Stocky, black-haired and olive-skinned, he looked like a Greek peasant and yet in his dinner jacket he radiated a natural elegance many would have envied.

It was as if everyone present that night had one wish, one desire only, to honour Maria. Her warmth for the French had been more than fully matched by their devotion to her. She may have been barred in the course of one year from Rome, La Scala and the Met, but before the year was out she had discovered another kingdom and taken it by storm.

At least this is how it looked at the beginning of 1959, but it would soon be obvious that another kind of conquest was now consuming her. First, however, she crossed the Atlantic again for two concerts – one in St Louis and one in Philadelphia – organized once more by Sol Hurok. Then, on 27 January 1959, came her first appearance at Carnegie Hall in a concert performance of *Il Pirata* under the auspices of the American Opera Society. The following morning the many reviews included one which gave thanks to Rudolf Bing for having left a gap in Maria's diary that allowed her to accept the invitation to sing in *Pirata.* She had worn a long white gown and her only props were a thirteen-foot red silk stole and, of course, her hands, her eyes, her movements and her magnetism. 'As the other soloists filed out for the seventeen-minute final scene,' wrote Louis Biancolli, 'all the lights but those over the exits and the musicians' desks suddenly went out. Slowly Miss Callas rose, drew close her red stole, and an eerie glow fell on her face. At that ghostly juncture Miss Callas made the most of her strange and haunting timbres. It was something to be left in the dark with the voice of Maria Meneghini Callas.' Suddenly a concert version had become infinitely more dramatic than the average full-scale operatic performance.

The next day, Maria, banned from America's foremost opera house, was honoured by the city in which it stood, and in which she was born. The citation, presented by Robert Wagner, New York's Mayor, was 'to the esteemed daughter of New York, whose glorious voice and superb artistry have contributed to the pleasure of music lovers everywhere'. A few days later, by which time Maria was back in Milan, Leonie Rysanek was making her debut at the Metropolitan as Lady Macbeth in the production designed for Maria – the most expensive the Met had mounted up to that time. Leonard Warren, the Met's great baritone, was Macbeth, but disappointment was hovering over the auditorium even before the curtain went up. The audience could hardly be prevented from making imaginary comparisons. Bing, who had foreseen this, had hired a claqueur to shout into the auditorium 'Bravo Callas!' at the moment of Rysanek's entrance. He had briefed him to station himself at an angle which would minimize the chances of her hearing it. His aim was to neutralize some of the heavily partisan Callas feeling in the audience by triggering the American love for the underdog. Considering the impossible task she had undertaken, Leonie Rysanek did very well, but the sense of loss could still be felt in the auditorium as the first-night audience was filing out.

Back in Milan, the rhythm of Maria's life had completely changed. Her professional diary was empty for the whole of February; in fact there was nothing in it until 16 March and the recording of *Lucia* in London. It was as if somehow she knew she needed, and had therefore given herself, a fallow period to prepare for the much more dramatic changes in store. Meanwhile she was desperately trying to convince herself and the rest of the world that it was business as usual. April 21, her tenth wedding anniversary, provided an excellent opportunity. On the arm of Battista she made her entrance at Maxim's for a celebration dinner punctuated by the arrival of letters, telegrams, gifts, flowers and still more flowers. 'I could not sing without him present,' she said. 'If I am the voice, he is the soul.' They cut their almond anniversary cake, the orchestra played 'Happy Birthday', and all Maxim's joined in the clapping which ushered in the couple's second decade together. From Maxim's, together with a few friends, they went on to the Lido and there, until the early hours of the morning, continued celebrating what the world saw as a great partnership and a happy marriage.

Throughout the previous couple of years, as her doubts were growing more insistent, Maria's public pronouncements seemed designed to keep them at bay and to feed the image of the perfect marriage: 'I dress for my husband. He likes me to look well dressed *always*. He takes a vivid interest in my clothes, his favourite colour being red.' Or 'Marriage is a full-time job. Put as much into it as you would into any career,' she said to a girl at a party. When the girl reminded her that she seemed, in that case, to have made a success of two careers, Maria smiled and, patting her husband's arm, replied: 'But this is the one that matters.' She was even heard saying that 'If he asked me to, I would stop singing.'

Maria's public statements, like those of most public figures, were a combination of truths, half-truths and lies. In the case of her marriage, they reflected very dramatically the conflict that was going on inside her, but which for the moment she was determined to silence with overblown expressions of gratitude and overpainted pictures of perfect harmony. There was in her a terrible yearning for the perfect marriage – a longing for loyalty, for security, for some backdrop of trust beneath the shifty, polite evasions of the world. She thought she could conjure all that up through words and will-power, but the waves of reality were soon to sweep over the sandcastles.

Meanwhile, in her concert tour of Germany, which took up most of May and was a wild success, she used every opportunity to reiterate how much of her career and her glory she owed to her devoted, beloved husband. There was just under a month left before London and *Medea*. Covent Garden had come to a barter agreement with Dallas; they would send over their new, much-praised Zeffirelli production of *Lucia* in return for the Minotis production of *Medea*. The international musical world was applauding this transatlantic arrangement, and rumour had it that Rudolf Bing was watching anxiously. Maria would sing in both *Lucia* and *Medea* even though the Covent Garden *Lucia* had originally been designed for Joan Sutherland. Maria had flown over from Milan for Sutherland's dress rehearsal. Sitting in the Grand Tier, in a sable coat and sable hat, she listened entranced. 'I would have been jealous of anyone singing so well, but not of you,' she told the woman who, seven years before, had sung the tiny part of Norma's confidante, vowing as she did so that one day she, too, would be out there like Maria in the centre of the stage. 'Whatever the press may say, you have a great Lucia,' she told David Webster in his office at Covent Garden. 'Don't even ask me to sing Lucia again. You have your own great British Lucia now and you should be proud of her.' Confronted with real talent, the artist in Maria always recognized and acknowledged it. Zeffirelli remembers bringing her a record of *The Golden Age at the Metropolitan*; she giggled outrageously when she heard Tetrazzini and Galli-Curci, but when Rosa Ponselle began to sing, she kissed the record-sleeve and held it tight to her heart.

Before London and *Medea* there was Venice and another ball – this time given by the Contessa Castelbarco. Maria was the guest of honour; Tina Onassis, in a Jean Dessès dress and a spectacular tiara, was one of the most beautiful women present. Tina's lovely eyes seemed at times to look at the world through lowered lashes, but nevertheless she did notice very early on that her husband's glance was, as if magnetized, pursuing someone around the ballroom. She followed his gaze – and at the end of it found Maria. It did not take Ari long to find himself a seat next to her. Nor did it take Tina long to move next to both of them. They had only met Maria twice before: once at Maxwell's Venice ball and once after the Gala at the Paris Opera. Within a few minutes Ari had invited the Meneghini-Callases aboard the *Christina*. 'We can't,' said Maria, 'I am singing *Medea* at Covent Garden.' 'We'll be there,' replied Onassis promptly, to the amazement of Tina who knew that he detested opera.

And that, of course, did not just mean that they were there to go to the performance and then congratulate Maria backstage. It meant that Onassis invited another thirty-seven friends to join them for the performance and a grand party afterwards. 'Mr and Mrs Aristotle Onassis request the pleasure . . .' read the invitations. In Covent Garden's Crush Bar before curtain-up, visibly excited, Onassis poured champagne and proudly distributed tickets to his friends as though *Medea* had been his very own creation. A few minutes before the overture began, he escorted Lady Churchill to her seat and took his own next to Tina. It was the first time he would see Maria in an entire opera.

Nobody can really know what went on in his mind in the darkened opera house as, sitting next to his wife, he watched the woman who was to replace, and far surpass, her in his love. What is certain is that later that night at the party he gave for her at the Dorchester, only one person existed for him: Maria. It was as if he was there not so much to meet as to divine her every wish. The Dorchester ballroom had been decorated entirely in pink and filled with pink roses and a fashionable crowd that included Randolph Churchill, Margot Fonteyn, Cecil Beaton and John Profumo. Neither Maria nor Meneghini was unaccustomed to luxury, but even they had never encountered such prodigious hospitality. It was a party on a scale far grander than all the other parties, dinners and balls that had been given for her. It was the abundance, the energy, the vigour, almost the grandeur that this short, thick-set, frog-like man radiated that was communicated to everyone around him, from the hotel manager to the most junior waiter. On the night of 18 June, Maria was the only focus for all this energy. What would she like to hear? A tango? The band leader is summoned, £50 put in his hand and a command issued: play nothing but tangos. And all night, Onassis, aroused by the smell of impending conquest, exceeded even himself. It was after three o'clock when Maria left the Dorchester, and in the foyer she was prophetically photographed in a triple embrace with Onassis and her husband on either side of her. The invitation to cruise on the *Christina* had been repeated several times in the course of the night, and Maria had promised to let him have an answer soon.

First, however, there were four more *Medeas* to be sung in London and a concert at the Holland Festival. There were thousands of people to welcome her at Amsterdam airport when she arrived there on the Sunday evening before the performance. Deeply moved by the reception, she drove with Peter Diamand, the Festival's director, to the Amstel Hotel where she was staying, and where, after her triumphant concert on 11 July, a reception was held in her honour that lasted until morning. 'We must talk, the two of us, without Titta,' she told Peter Diamand at the reception. The following day they drove to Keukenhof near Leiden where they had lunch among the tulips. Walking in the lush park afterwards, she asked Peter not to send her fee to the Callas-Meneghini joint account: 'Keep the money until you hear from me. There will be many changes in my life in the next few months. All my instincts tell me so. You'll hear many things. . . . Please stay my friend.' 'Maria, *che melodramma!*' protested Peter Diamand. 'No, not melodrama, Peter – drama,' she said, but she looked radiant as she was saying it.

She had made up her mind: they were going on the *Christina*. Tina Onassis had called twice: 'We so much hope you will come.' Meneghini had put up a good fight. 'I have to be in touch with my mother who is ill,' he said at the end, almost in desperation. 'No problem,' replied Onassis, 'there are forty-two radio telephones on the *Christina.*' It was Meneghini's last card, and he had lost. He could not swim, he hardly spoke English, barely spoke French, and was constantly seasick, but the decision had been taken. In record time, Biki prepared for Maria a magnificent cruising wardrobe: twenty dresses, trouser suits, negligees, bathing suits.

On 22 July, they flew to Monte Carlo. They were met by Ari, Tina and Ari's sister, Artemis. The next day the other guests arrived: Sir Winston and Lady Churchill, their daughter Diana, their canary Toby, Churchill's secretary Anthony Montague Browne, Churchill's doctor, Lord Moran, and the head of Fiat, Umberto Agnelli, with his wife. Prince Rainier was there to see them all off on the *Christina*. The only other time Maria had seen Churchill was in Athens during the Civil War when in a crowd of people she waited outside the British Embassy to watch him arrive in his armoured car.

By the time the Churchills and the other guests appeared, Maria had already been shown the sea palace that was to be her home for the next three weeks; and the sophisticated *femme du monde* was transformed into a wondering girl. She laughed, she chattered, she asked questions, she enjoyed what she heard and what she saw: lapis lazuli balustrades, solid gold fixtures in every bathroom, dolls designed by Dior for the children, an El Greco in Onassis's study, a jewelled Buddha, the oldest known to exist in the West, a swimming-pool decorated with an enlarged reproduction of a mosaic from the Palace of Knossos, marble bathrooms and ornate dressing-rooms for the guest suites . . . Tina had once said that for Ari the *Christina* 'was not a fantastic plaything but a real passion. He is almost like a housewife fussing over it, constantly looking to see that everything is being done well, constantly looking for things to correct and improve.' It had a crew of sixty, and the staff included waiters, valets, seamstresses, masseurs and two chefs – one exclusively for French cuisine, the other for Greek. Both menus were available and the guests could choose. Maria mostly ordered raw meat and green salads, and then, as was her lifelong habit, picked from everybody's else's plates what she wanted. The feeling that she had entered a fairy-tale world began to overwhelm her. She had brought with her a score of Bellini's *La Straniera.* She did not touch it.

The first few days were difficult. Meneghini was grumpier and gloomier than she had ever known him. He was maddeningly lethargic and seemed unable to take an interest in anything except endlessly cataloguing what he saw as the other guests' slights towards him. Maria found his worries, his complaints and his judgements of everyone, and especially their host, exasperating. Onassis was only nine years his junior, but Meneghini seemed determined to behave like an ailing grandfather. Maria was divided between the marital proprieties and her instinctive longing to be close to Onassis.

By the time the *Christina* had reached Piraeus the Greek gods seemed to have decided whose side they were on. The sea became rough, the weather stormy; Meneghini and most of the other guests took to their rooms, leaving Maria and Onassis alone in the deserted games room gazing at the roaring fire in the lapis lazuli fireplace and talking until the early hours of the morning. Something remarkable was happening to Maria: for the first time in her life she stopped being the sole object of her own absorbed attention. The self-absorption, it is true, had been for the glory of her art, but this did not change the fact that it had excluded all others; the attention she had given her husband was no more than an expression of her gratitude that he, too, had recognized that the world revolved round her and her art, and seemed well satisfied that this should be so. Now, suddenly, Maria had been displaced from the centre of her world. She was deeply, passionately, in love. For a few days she went on fighting the feeling, resisting the realization, attributing the glow of happiness when she was near Ari to their common origins, his charm, his fascination for her; but it was only a matter of time – and a short time at that – before she surrendered.

As for Ari, he behaved as though he had thought of nothing in the past month except Maria. And in a sense that was true, except that Ari, as she was to discover, was capable of being monomaniacally obsessive about more than one thing at a time. He was in raptures over *Medea,* even though his dislike of opera was well documented, and he was full of enthusiasm and ideas about Maria's future, even though his ignorance of opera was at least as great as his dislike of it. He spent hours talking with her about the possibility of a Monte Carlo Opera Company built for her and around her. He did, after all, own a controlling interest in virtually all the major business activities in Monte Carlo.

In the long hours they spent together they mostly spoke Greek to each other. They talked much of the future but they talked even more of the past. And mainly *his* past. Maria could not hear enough. He talked of Smyrna, on the coast of Turkey, where he was born seventeen years before her; he described the Greek quarters where he lived; he talked of his father Socrates and his uncle Homer, prosperous merchants of cotton, raisins, tobacco, figs and anything else the Anatolian interior produced. He talked of his mother Penelope, who died of a kidney operation when he was six; of his father's remarriage to her sister, of his grandmother Gethsemane whom he adored; of his time as a choirboy dressed in gold-braided cassock and surplice

('I still have a fine singing voice,' he teased her laughingly); of the time he pinched the attractive English teacher's bottom and was suspended for several days as a result; of his first love and his first 'mistress' when he was thirteen. He talked of the Turkish attack on Smyrna in which tens of thousands of Greeks perished, of his father's arrest and the horror that followed, of his decision to emigrate to Argentina, and the crossing crammed with hundreds of immigrants packed together, of his arrival in Buenos Aires on 21 September 1923. He was sixteen and had sixty dollars in his pocket. When Maria was born three months later, he was working for a Buenos Aires telephone company. The pay was not very good, he told her, but there were plenty of pretty telephone operators.

He would always talk to Maria about the women in his life in a way that made her feel flattered to be the culmination of such a long and varied list of conquests. In his search for the steady partner, which had already begun at the age of sixteen, he used to grade his dates meticulously in ten different categories ranging from receptivity and dress to love of the sea and love of parents. Before he was twenty-four, he was Greek Vice-Consul General in Argentina. He had not yet found the perfect mate, but not very long after that he found the perfect ships with which to begin his unique shipping career – two Canadian vessels, belonging to a company that had suffered huge losses during the Depression.

He loved talking to her of his struggles more than his victories, and he loved hearing of her own struggles. As he was to say later, 'I have always had a great admiration for Madame Callas. More than her artistic talent, even more than her success as a great singer, what always impressed me was the story of her early struggles as a poor girl in her teens when she sailed through unusually rough and merciless waters.' The long, hard roads they had travelled, separate but parallel, until they became what the popular papers never tired of describing as 'the world's two most celebrated Greeks', had finally come together in a love for one another that at times seemed almost predestined. Each liked the fact that the other was also a fighter, and a winner, with whatever cards life had dealt them. In fact Aristo – as his family called him in Smyrna and as Maria loved to call him herself – always played down the prosperity and standing of his family before the Smyrna disaster, so that nothing would be allowed to detract from the romantic picture of the man who had started with nothing.

He ordered the captain to stop the *Christina* at Smyrna, ostensibly to show his guests the place where he was born, but in fact to bring to life for Maria the past he had been telling her about. At the beginning of August the *Christina* anchored at Istanbul, still referred to by the Orthodox Greeks as Constantinople, their Church's most sacred place. The following morning the Patriarch received Onassis and his guests. When they knelt to receive his blessing, Ari and Maria were next to each other. He called them 'the world's greatest singer and the greatest seaman of the modern world, the new Ulysses'; he thanked them for the honours they had brought to Greece; he blessed them. For Maria, this was the moment of complete surrender. She was deeply moved, as if the Byzantine ritual, the solemnity of the old Patriarch, the special blessing for the two of them – as if all these corresponded to the drama being played out inside her. More; it was as if the Patriarch's blessing was a blessing on their union, a formal permission to Maria to acknowledge the emotions that had been awakened in her and give them their proper name. 'But she is already married,' Meneghini was heard whispering bitterly. He could feel Maria's emotion, and although nothing had yet been said, some part of him knew that Maria was already thinking of herself as another man's wife. 'It was an outburst of nationalism,' he would insist later, the bitterness still very much alive. 'It left Maria with the physical mark of exultation. She was no longer the same. How could I defend myself against the new Ulysses?'

Aristo was her first deep experience of loving and being loved – the world and everything in it was illuminated by a different light. Meneghini was right. Maria *was* no longer the same. He had brought love, frivolity, passion and tenderness to the life of a dedicated nun who had begun to lose the taste for her vocation. He had broken that single-minded and in many ways glorious obsession with her work that had excluded so much, and he had opened the way for a host of feelings never experienced and impressions never before sensed. For the first time she was not dominated by the constant tug of engagements, commitments and looming first nights. So she could wake up in the morning without a sense of apprehension, and soak up the sun during the day and Ari's stories during the night as though there were no conflicts and no troubles. Ari came alive at night, especially after midnight, and then he loved telling the stories of Greek myths, as others tell fairy-tales to children, or conjuring up all the sea monsters he had heard sailors talk about. He could summon up the spirit of the places he had been to, the force of the elements, the strangeness that lurked in the sea around them.

Maria was swept along by his headlong impetuosity as by a hurricane, and that day in Istanbul the last resistance crumbled. The same night there was a party for them at the Istanbul Hilton, as there had been parties wherever they had stopped. Meneghini felt too weak and tired to go, he stayed on board. Maria came back in the early hours of the morning and found her husband waiting up for her. There was a moment – but only a moment – of hesitation. How do you tell a husband to whom you owe so much, who has proved so invaluable in the past, who has devoted himself so completely to you, that you are leaving him? In Maria's mind, there was only one way: 'I love Ari.'

'I felt I was going to burst into tears,' Meneghini recalled later, 'at my age too. . . . It was as if a fire was devouring them both.' He did not cry, but the rest of the cruise was a long supplication. The supplication was punctuated by arguments that lasted well into the night and shouting matches at the end of which he would subside into whining passivity. The tension had infected all the other guests, except for Sir Winston, who in his lofty detachment seemed impervious to what was going on. Yet the others could not shake off the feeling that, as he dozed after lunch on the deck of the *Christina* with his hat over his eyes, he was absorbing all the panics and dramas, and smiling benignly. The engines were always slowed down when Churchill was having his afternoon siesta, and the cruising speed was determined so that there would be the least vibration in his suite. But for the first time since he had met Onassis, his host was not constantly hovering over him. The honour of his presence had been overshadowed by the emotional explosions on board. As for the beautiful Tina, she remained a neutral hostess presiding over the conventions which were being grimly observed among the confessions, quarrels, vows and recriminations.

Finally, a long week after she had anchored in Istanbul, the *Christina* sailed into Venice. The crew, who had silently observed it all, had been placing bets as to who was going to leave with whom. Maria and Meneghini left first, aboard one of Onassis's private planes. They landed in Milan and went straight to Sirmione. On Maria's hand there was a bracelet engraved with the initials 'TMWL' (To Maria With Love). It is true that Onassis had given a TTWL bracelet to Tina and was a few years later to give a TJWL bracelet to Jackie Kennedy, but for the moment Maria wore her own with joy and pride, not least in front of her husband.

The next day, 17 August, at nine o'clock in the evening, Onassis turned up at Sirmione. 'I could hardly believe my ears,' remembered Meneghini, 'when I heard his voice singing "Maria, Maria" under our window.' He had come to inform Meneghini that he intended to marry his wife, and that no obstacle would be allowed to stand in his way. Meneghini felt completely powerless, not only in the face of his wife's decision, but more particularly before the confidence and assurance that Onassis radiated. 'This man has billions, you must understand,' he said to one of the many journalists who flocked to Sirmione in the next couple of months. It was the rich man's impotent envy of the super-rich, the stingy millionaire's resentment at the extravagant multi-millionaire who knows not only how to make multi-millions but also how to spend them.

Meneghini warned Maria that this would be the end of her career; he accused her of ingratitude; he pleaded with her. But threats, accusations and pleas were all in vain. At four o'clock in the morning, Maria left for Milan with Onassis. Her life, as she had instinctively sensed a month earlier, walking among the tulips outside Amsterdam, was about to change dramatically. Onassis himself, having removed Maria from the not-so-firm clutches of her husband, now had to decide what he was going to do with his own marriage. Soon after he arrived with Maria in Milan, he flew to Venice, where Tina was waiting for him on the *Christina.*

Meanwhile, on Via Buonarroti, Maria was keeping out of the way of as many people as possible. 'She avoided us all,' said Biki. 'She was almost ashamed at what had happened. She was too direct and honest to enjoy false situations and compromises.' There is no doubt that the Greek matron in Maria greatly disapproved of what the other Maria had done. After all, it was only two years earlier that she had proclaimed to the world that decorum was the essence of her life. Her morality, though never clearly thought out or articulated, was narrow and often intolerant. The role of the mistress did not come easily to her – it was one of the many indications of the depth of her love for Onassis that she was prepared to play it for so many years.

The doubts and the judgements of the matron in Maria added up for the moment only to a small, nagging voice rarely listened to and most of the time silenced by the upsurge of excitement and hope that had flooded through her. 'I had the feeling of being kept in a cage for so long', Maria was to say later, 'that when I met Aristo, so full of life, I became a different woman.' The transformation was less visible but no less dramatic than the weight-shedding that shook the world. Maria had lost so many of her sharp corners and so much of her defensive aggressiveness that when she met Ghiringhelli in the course of making the arrangements for her recording of *Gioconda* at La Scala, the icy superintendent, confronted with all this unexpected softness and charm, thawed like a snowman in the spring sun. In less time than anyone would have thought possible, he had asked Maria to come back to La Scala to sing anything she chose and on her own terms. All that remained was finding the appropriate time to make the reconciliation public. La Scala was delighted. And so was Maria. On 2 September 1959, she arrived at La

Scala to start rehearsing for the recording. 'One really had to protect her physically from the press and the photographers,' remembers Peter Diamand who had accompanied her when she tried to walk across to the Biffi Scala for lunch. 'And then anyone who was with her was torn away and interrogated: "How do you know Madame Callas?", "What did she say to you?", "Who are you?" "I am her Egyptian hairdresser," I said to one Italian reporter who proceeded to print it in his newspaper, under the title *Parla il parrucchiere della Callas,* together with all the details I gave him about how her hair goes all soft and smooth when she's singing Violetta and all crisp and wild when she's Medea.'

On 3 September Maria and Aristo were discovered dining tête-à-tête, with violins softly playing in the background, at the Rendez-vous in Milan. At three o'clock in the morning, with Maria carrying a bouquet of red roses, they were photographed arm-in-arm going into the Hotel Principe e Savoia. The next day Via Buonarroti was under siege; but reporters and photographers alike waited in vain. Two days later, Maria issued a statement: 'I confirm that the break between my husband and myself is complete and final. It has been in the air for quite some time, and the cruise on the *Christina* was only coincidental. The lawyers are working on the case, and will make an announcement. I am now my own manager. I ask for understanding in this painful personal situation.... Between Signor Onassis and myself there exists a profound friendship that dates back some time. I am also in a business connection with him; I have received offers from the Monte Carlo Opera, and there is also a prospect for a film. When I have further things to say, I shall do so at the opportune moment, but I do not intend to call a press conference.' The only excuse for this naïvely insincere statement is that her lawyers had demanded it to increase the chances of divorce by mutual consent.

When Onassis was besieged by reporters on the same day at Harry's Bar in Venice, he was much less discreet. 'Of course, how could I help but he flattered if a woman with the class of Maria Callas fell in love with someone like me? Who wouldn't?' It was, unintentionally, one of his most revealing statements; the little Smyrnan refugee with his tankers and his billions needed women 'with class' to confirm his own worthiness. He needed these shots of flattery like an addict, and with time and his advancing age, he needed bigger and bigger doses for the same effect. The most celebrated singer of the day was a big enough dose until a still bigger dose was needed in the shape of the world-famous widow of an American President. This does not mean that he was not in love with Maria. There is no doubt that he was, but her fame was one of the most important ingredients in the inflammable mixture which, ignited by some spark – perhaps their first meeting, perhaps her Medea – had blazed up into love. 'He just wanted to add lustre to his tankers with the name of a great artist,' said Meneghini in one of his outbursts. 'They love each other like children,' he said at a quieter moment. He found it impossible to reconcile these two observations, yet they were reconciled simply because there was truth in both of them.

While Meneghini, having suddenly moved from the wings to the centre of the stage, could not stop talking, Tina Onassis was maintaining a dignified silence and at the same time showing the flag at the Maxwell annual ball in Venice, being photographed dancing in the arms of the bronzed Count Brando d'Adda. The press could not have enough. As, apart from Meneghini, the leading figures were not very forthcoming, they needed subsidiary characters to keep the drama alive. Evangelia was certainly good for a few column inches. She was tracked down at Jolie Gabor's jewellery shop in New York where she was working. Evangelia and Zsa Zsa's mother had appeared together in a television programme about mothers and famous daughters, and at the end of it Madame Gabor had offered Maria's mother a job. 'Meneghini was a father and mother to Maria,' she said, having suddenly discovered all sorts of previously unnoticed qualities in her son-in-law. 'Now she no longer needs him. But Maria will never be happy; my soul says it. Women like Maria can never know real love.'

Maria hardly expected support from her mother, but she had expected support from her most loyal and least tactful champion so far – Elsa Maxwell. She did not get it. Elsa maintained throughout the dignified silence of a betrayed lover, and when she finally broke it, in her role as a self-appointed watchdog of public ethics, it was to side unequivocally with Tina. While she was often seen with Tina, she deliberately kept out of Maria's way, and when she was asked at her suite in the Hotel Danieli in Venice whether her friend Ari was going to marry her friend Maria, she emitted only an openly disapproving 'I guess not'.

'We are all like personages in a drama,' said Meneghini, always ready with a quote as if he was determined to make up for ten years of public silence in ten days. 'They are Maria, a Medea; myself who can be a tough nut; and Mr Onassis, a multi-millionaire.' The theme, which might have appealed to any opera composer from Donizetti to Kurt Weill, instead inspired *Time* magazine to cast its own under the title *Love and Money*.

Maria Meneghini Callas, a famous diva	Soprano
Giovanni Meneghini, her ageing husband	Bass
Elsa Maxwell, her trusted confidante	Baritone
Evangelia Callas, her estranged mother	Contralto
Aristotle Onassis, a wealthy shipowner	Tenor
Athena Onassis, his beautiful young wife	Mezzo

Meneghini may have been cast as the bass but he had written himself the biggest singing part, covering the entire range of dramatic emotion from joviality to self-pity and resentment. 'I created Callas, and she repaid me with a stab in the back. She was a fat, clumsily-dressed woman, a refugee, a gypsy when I met her. She had not a cent nor any prospect for a career. I had to rent her a room at a hotel and had to put up $70 so she could remain in Italy. And now I hear that I am accused of having exploited her.'

Every now and then self-pity and self-mockery met: 'You'll see, if everything is split and we have to divide our poodle, Maria will get the front and I will end up with the tail!' Meneghini seemed to be walking away with the best lines. At long last the man always behind the first lady had an opportunity to voice the accumulated resentments of all the years. Evangelia, a past master at venting her resentment, was competing for attention: 'I was Maria's first victim. Now it's Meneghini. Onassis will be the third.' 'Maria would marry Onassis,' she added, 'to further her limitless ambition.'

She could not have shown less understanding of her daughter. Ambition was the last thought in Maria's mind on 10 September when, as soon as the recording of *Gioconda* was over, she was at Milan airport, boarding the private plane Onassis had sent for her. She flew to Venice and together with Toy – tail and all – she went aboard the *Christina.* Onassis mounted the bridge and with a large flamboyant gesture set off the siren that indicated the *Christina*'s departure. It was a long, loud, piercing sound. They were off, with only two other guests on board: Onassis's sister, Artemis, and her husband, Theodore Garoufalidis. A few days earlier, Tina had taken her two children and, without letting her husband know, had fled to Paris and her father's home on Avenue Foch. She had had enough. Onassis had followed her on his private plane ('It's never flown so much since he bought it,' the pilot was heard exclaiming), half wanting a reconciliation and half dreading it. Tina knew that she did not want one. She had been hurt and humiliated in public and she was not going to believe his half-hearted protestations.

It is true that Onassis was not happy about the break-up of his marriage to the mother of his children and daughter of Stavros Livanos, one of the oldest and most established Greek shipowners. But for the moment, with Tina in Paris, he was free to have what he *really* wanted: a two-week cruise with Maria. And before setting off, tired of hearing from the Greek shipping community how foolish he had been to treat Livanos's daughter in this manner, he exploded to a reporter: 'My father-in-law hasn't enough to buy Niarchos's art collection, let alone my hobby enterprises.'

There were no explosions aboard the *Christina.* The crew could not remember seeing him so relaxed and at peace before. As for Maria, there are no happier pictures of her than the shots on the deck of the *Christina.* It was as if within days, hours, she had drunk in all that peculiar, languid serenity produced by the ease and abundance of Mediterranean life. Her longing to merge herself with another human being had been at last fully awakened, and the end of her cherished separateness was a celebration.

It was hard for her public to understand. And as the number of her recordings and performances began to fall and continued to do so, it would be harder still. If we compare her last complete year before Onassis to her first complete year with him, we have in figures the magnitude of the change in her life. In 1958, she gave twenty-eight performances of seven operas in six places around the world; in 1960 she gave seven performances of two operas in two places. The figures become even more astonishing. In 1961, she gave five performances, all of them of *Medea* – two in Epidaurus and three at La Scala. In 1962 she gave two performances of *Medea* at La Scala, and in 1963 she sang no opera on stage at all. There were concerts and some recordings, and in 1964 she returned to opera for her last stage performances ever – a magnificent swan song at the time when she could feel Onassis and her dreams of a family life with him slipping away.

'Onassis destroyed her life,' said Biki, who, apart from designing her clothes, remained a close friend. 'She sacrificed her voice, her art, her career for this man,' said (or thought) thousands of music lovers. But it is impossible to look at Maria's life the year before the cruise on the *Christina* without coming to the conclusion that Onassis entered her life precisely at the moment when she was longing for something or someone to give her the motivation to stop living and working as she had been ever since she was a little girl at the Athens Conservatory. With Aristo, there was for the first time a really powerful counter-attraction to her art. Far from being his victim, it was Maria, or rather Maria's need, that had made him part of her life. 'I had become prematurely dull and old. I had got heavy, thinking of nothing but money and position,' Maria said a few years later, looking back. 'Life for me really began at forty, or at least nearly forty.'

A woman who can say, with whatever degree of exaggeration, that life for her had really begun only after she had met a particular man, cannot be considered his victim or even the victim of her own desires. Maria's tragedy was to think that because Ari was the one who awoke so much life, so many slumbering feelings and sensations in her, he was also their only source – as if only he could dispense these newly-discovered treasures. So her fear of losing him was compounded by her fear of losing the aliveness and the joy that he had brought into her life.

On the *Christina,* Maria found herself living entirely in the present, or rather in a state of healing timelessness. Onassis, who could see the effect it was having, wanted to preserve it for her as long as possible. His friends in the Greek Navy did their best to help him. Half an hour before the *Christina* was spotted on the horizon twenty white-clad Greek sailors cleared the people off the jetty at the bay of Glyfada near Athens on 'the harbourmaster's orders'. At the same time, naval patrols were hauling swimmers and skin-divers out of the water. When the *Christina*'s launches reached the jetty, only Onassis's brother-in-law came ashore and announced to a Navy officer in a loud voice that 'Madame Callas left the *Christina* at Brindisi'. But the reporters who sailed out in a fishing boat knew better. There she was on the deck of the gleaming, white yacht, and there he was beside her.

The launches brought the directors of Olympic Airways back to the *Christina,* and Onassis interrupted his holiday for a meeting of the board. For Maria the timelessness continued until the next day when she had to fly from Athens to Bilbao for a concert; she had never given a performance from which she felt so detached, and she had never received a chillier reception. It was as if she had arrived in Bilbao in a daze, had given her concert in a daze and, on her return, had talked to the waiting reporters at Athens airport still in a daze, describing Bilbao as a 'silly little engagement'. The description did not enhance her popularity in Spain but, by the time the Spanish press had gone on the attack she was back with Ari on the *Christina.* She left them both at Monte Carlo and flew straight to London for a concert at the Festival Hall on 23 September. She was in great form and the new softness and lightness were there for all to see and hear. It was her first concert appearance without all that massive jewellery – just a simple necklace and Ari's TMWL bracelet – and the *Daily Mail* described it as 'one of the most dramatic and memorable nights in London's music'.

But professional engagements were now squeezed into the gaps of an increasingly hectic and emotionally demanding private life, and when they could not be squeezed in, they were cancelled or postponed. Her television concert was postponed because she had to be in Milan for a conference over the settlement of joint property. Also, Nicola Rescigno was ill and Maria was increasingly loath to sing with any but her own conductors. In the end, the programme was televised on 3 October with Sir Malcolm Sargent conducting. 'The great Callas,' he said, with arms outstretched towards her as he introduced her to the orchestra.

A few days earlier Meneghini had filed suit for legal separation. The hearing, after a postponement, was finally scheduled to take place in Brescia on 14 November. In between there were Maria's engagements in Kansas City and Dallas. For a short while it seemed as though nothing had changed, except that there were even more reporters than usual who seemed to have one question only: 'Will you marry Mr Onassis?' The penalties incurred by the new super-personality that she had become included a bomb scare at the Midland Theatre in Kansas City which turned out to be a hoax, but only after the entire bejewelled audience – an audience that included ex-President Truman – had vacated the theatre.

To coincide with Maria's arrival in the States, Elsa Maxwell broke, after a fashion, the silence about Maria that until then she had affected in her column. 'That much-heralded diva arrives in America,' the column began. There followed a report of a conversation between herself and Leonard Bernstein.

B: How do you feel about her?
M: I don't feel anything.
B: But you must take some stand.
M: Do you mean morally or musically?
B: Both.

M: Musically, I can only say that she is the greatest artist in the world.

The rest was silence.

The news from Dallas was worse than silence. On 6 November, Maria sang the penultimate *Lucia* of her career in Zeffirelli's new production borrowed from Covent Garden. 'I've only come because of you,' she told Lawrence Kelly. She was nervous and unprepared, but her dramatic sense was as unerring as ever. She had refused to wear the blood-stained dress designed for Joan Sutherland; she was, as always, against any garishness that would seize the audience's attention and distract them from the real drama. Vocally, though, she was in such bad form that she nearly broke down in the Mad Scene. 'It was painful to hear her miss the high E flat so cruelly,' said a lifelong fan who was in the first-night audience. It was infinitely more painful for Maria. 'I had the note. I had the note. What happened? What happened?' she kept repeating to herself all the way to her dressing-room, as though the Mad Scene was still going on. She suddenly stopped, took a deep breath and sang five consecutive E flats. She could sense that she was losing her fight with the Voice. Two nights later, for her second performance of *Lucia,* she left the E flats out. She would go on fighting but there were to be fewer and fewer trapeze acts. They were no longer worth the agony. 'You cannot serve two masters,' she told Zeffirelli. 'All she wanted,' he remembers, 'was to be with Onassis, to be his wife, his woman, his mistress. If he had not pushed her to go on singing, as a kind of showcase for himself, she would have probably stopped altogether.' On 9 November, Maria, having cancelled her appearance in *Il Barbiere di Siviglia,* flew from Dallas to Milan. The court hearing in Brescia was only a few days away.

Very early on the morning of 14 November, a large crowd began to assemble outside the courtroom of this small industrial city. Meneghini arrived first. For the previous couple of months, he had been receiving letters congratulating him on 'finding his peace at last' and 'being well rid of her'. 'Get a nice Italian girl next time,' one correspondent had advised him. Now the Brescia crowd was loudly applauding him. There was complete silence when Maria arrived. Whatever the crowd may have thought of doing or shouting before they saw her, there was something regal and contained in her presence that commanded respect.

They came out six hours later. Judge Cesare Andreotti had made the ritual attempts at reconciliation before getting down to the serious business of dividing the spoils. There was remarkably little rancour as the settlement was being reached. Maria kept Via Buonarroti, most of her jewellery and both ends of the two poodles. Meneghini kept Sirmione and all the real estate they owned; the paintings and all other valuables were equally divided. Meneghini's original writ had spoken of Maria going to night clubs and other places with a man 'whom she described as her lover' and 'behaving in a manner incompatible with elementary decency'. He had applied for the separation to be granted in a judgement against his wife, but by the end of the six-hour hearing he had agreed to separation by mutual consent.

The following morning Maria flew to New York on her way to Dallas and the last engagement fixed by Meneghini. When she got into the plane, she discovered that the seat next to hers had been reserved for the most enormous arrangement of red roses. There was nothing on them but 'TMWL'. It was the kind of gesture which Meneghini would have thought 'disgusting'; that is how he had described Onassis's gesture of putting £50 into the hands of the band leader at the Dorchester to play tangos for Maria all night. 'And she was impressed,' Meneghini had added, puzzled. He had been just as puzzled by her anger on the fated cruise when he had so ludicrously undertipped the water-carriers they used from one of the islands that Onassis had to interfere and add a handsome sum himself. Meneghini had expected Maria to be angry at their host for subtly and publicly humiliating her husband. Instead she had exploded against *him* – against his meanness, against his habitual, calculating mentality. Maria, who had to fight this tendency in herself all her life, suddenly could not bear seeing it in such stark colours in someone else. 'I am always careful,' she said once, 'always afraid that I will die, or live the end of my life, in poverty.' Every now and then, the old money terrors would hit her and, even though she knew that her alarm was baseless, she would castigate herself for her extravagance; at such times any expense, including one as trivial as a television set, seemed reckless. Peter Andry remembers Maria calling him at EMI, shortly after she had let him down at the last moment over a recording of *Traviata,* to ask if he could get her a discount on the new television set she wanted to buy.

Despite all her success and the fulfilment of so many of her dreams, Maria never really trusted life. But being near Aristo, with his boundless trust in life's abundance, made her fears seem absurd and the behaviour they gave rise to, odious. She wanted to escape from them; Meneghini was not even aware that he had them. Maria could see the exaggeration and the extravagance in many of Onassis's gestures, but she enjoyed, even loved, his expansiveness, especially after her husband's penny-pinching.

With the two *Medeas* in Dallas over, the twelve years of Meneghini management were over too. As soon as the break-up of their marriage became public, the offers flooded in from agents wanting to represent her. Meneghini, for his part, was inundated by requests from hopeful sopranos, and even tenors and baritones, to take their careers in hand. 'Just bring me,' he said, 'one who sings like Callas, who has a mind like Callas, a heart and temperament like Callas, an ambition and fierce dedication like Callas, and leave the rest to me.' That can be taken as the last word on the Pygmalion-Meneghini myth which, in his less honest moments, Meneghini himself did a lot to keep alive.

Maria had been legally separated for eleven days when Tina Onassis sued her husband for divorce in the New York State Supreme Court on the ground of adultery. The marriage that had been described as 'the happiest between Cannes and Palm Beach' was coming to an end. On 25 November, Tina called reporters to her Sutton Square home in New York and issued a statement:

> It is almost thirteen years since Mr Onassis and I were married in New York City. Since then he has

become one of the world's richest men, but his great wealth has not brought me happiness with him nor, as the world knows, has it brought him happiness with me. After we parted this summer in Venice, I had hoped that Mr Onassis loved our children enough and respected our privacy sufficiently to meet with me – or, through lawyers, with my lawyers – to straighten out our problems. But that was not to be.

Mr Onassis knows positively that I want none of his wealth and that I am solely concerned with the welfare of our children.

I deeply regret that Mr Onassis leaves me no alternative other than a New York suit for divorce.

For my part I will always wish Mr Onassis well, and I expect that after this action is concluded he will continue to enjoy the kind of life which he apparently desires to live, but in which I have played no real part. I shall have nothing more to say and I hope I shall be left with my children in peace.

Maria was with Onassis on the *Christina* in Monte Carlo when Tina's statement appeared in the newspapers. They were expecting and fearing the worst: the citing of Maria as the adulteress. But Tina had other, older scores to settle, so the lady with whom her husband was supposed to have had an affair 'by land and sea' was cited as Mrs J.R. It did not take the gossip columnists long to discover that Mrs J.R. was Jeanne Rhinelander, an old school friend of Tina's. Back in 1954, when Tina was staying in the South of France she had, on an impulse, driven over to her friend's home in Grasse, only to discover her husband there in what are commonly known as 'compromising circumstances'.

Five years later she rather spectacularly took her revenge, and at the same time prevented the divorce from escalating into an even bigger scandal, as it would have if she had cited Maria. While in Monte Carlo Maria could hardly believe her narrow escape, in Grasse Jeanne Rhinelander was fighting off reporters. It was her turn to issue a statement: 'I am astonished that after so many years of friendship of which everybody knew, here and in the United States, Mrs Onassis should try to use it as an excuse to obtain her freedom.'

It was a difficult time for Maria. His pending divorce was emotionally much more wrenching for Onassis than he cared to admit. That in itself was a source of agitation to her, but it was not the worst of it. While Maria wholeheartedly wanted her divorce, Onassis never really wanted his, despite his protestations to Meneghini about his determination to marry Maria. He spent weeks and months away from Tina but he would ritually call her from whatever part of the world he happened to be in, every day at six p.m. her time. He was not the first man, nor would he be the last, who wanted both his mistress and his wife.

In Monte Carlo, he had suddenly decided to behave discreetly. Maria was nominally booked into the Grand Hotel, and the night Tina's statement appeared he dined alone with Prince Rainier and Princess Grace. The next day his own statement appeared, much shorter and much less revealing than Tina's: 'I have just heard that my wife has begun divorce proceedings. I am not surprised, the situation has been moving rapidly. But I was not warned. Obviously I shall have to do what she wants and make suitable arrangements.' In fact he was hoping for a reconciliation and he began working towards it – phone calls to Tina, phone calls for the children, talks to friends who could intercede. Maria retreated to Milan and, in one of those ironies that filled her life, she spent her thirty-sixth birthday, the first since her separation, in the company of her ex-husband.

Five days later, Renata Tebaldi returned to La Scala in *Tosca* after an absence of nearly five years. It was a triumph. The applause went on for over ten minutes and there was a rain of flowers while the audience rhythmically chanted her name. 'A state of delirium,' was how *La Notte* described it. The following morning, as Maria was reading the ecstatic reviews, she could not help but be uneasily aware that by her own choice she had no fixed operatic engagements of her own in prospect. Her work that had been everything was for the moment nothing.

The feeling of relief at having escaped from what had become a prison was mixed with fear of the emptiness that, with Aristo embroiled in his own divorce, gaped ahead of her; but her reaction to Tebaldi's return was yet another indication of a new mellowness and a new maturity. When asked whether she would be present at the opening night, she replied: 'Now that Renata Tebaldi returns to La Scala, public attention should be focused on this important event without direct or indirect interferences of any kind. I have closed many chapters this year; it is my sincere wish that this chapter too be closed.'

She had indeed come to terms with many things, including Rudolf Bing and the Met. She had initiated the reconciliation herself, even though she had no plans or even the wish in her present state of mind to sing there. She wanted the reconciliation for its own sake, for personal rather than professional reasons. 'The return of a prodigal daughter,' ran Bing's polished public response, 'is no less welcome than the return of a prodigal son.' So there was Bing once again in the role of forgiving father.

Maria needed all the inner peace and outer harmony she could get if she was going to cope with the concentration of unpredictable energy that had entered her life in the form of Aristotle Onassis. The Italian papers were full of reports of his activities, and the innuendoes were unmistakable. 'Mrs Jeanne Rhinelander, who was cited in Mrs Onassis's divorce suit, was seen dining in Monte Carlo last night with Mr Onassis. He had invited her to the night club of the casino. They stayed there until the early hours of the morning ...' He would call to explain. Then he would not call for days. Then he would send flowers. She would call. He had gone. He would suddenly arrive or send for her. The pattern of the next eight years had been set. 'A man can't really change himself,' she had said a year before she met Onassis, 'but a woman can change herself.' We may smile at the old-fashioned statement, but there are plenty of women in Greek villages today who still believe it; and when she fell in love with Onassis, Maria showed that she both believed it and acted on it. Their nine years together, instead of being a series of battles between two giant personalities, turned out to be the willing surrender of one to the other. It is true that she would occasionally rebel, but it was a rebellion deeply rooted in dependence.

In just over three months, Maria had left her Italian husband and manager, and was on the way to abandoning her Italian identity, in search of herself in a Greek lover, her Greek origin and a fashionably rootless cosmopolitanism. But a shift, even more significant, had begun. For years she had lived on will-power, determination, courage, audacity – even aggressiveness. From now on, having chosen to make someone else the centre of her life, she would need qualities she had never before developed: empathy, patience, understanding – qualities that were all so easily turned, self-destructively, into resignation, passivity, even submissiveness.

Chapter Eleven

IT WAS as if she had said to herself: 'First you must become the great Maria Callas. Then you can become a woman.' She set about the second task with as much determination and single-mindedness as she had brought to the first. When, at the beginning of 1960, rumours began to spread, and were soon confirmed, that Maria had no singing plans at all for the months ahead, the general feeling was that she had thrown herself into Onassis's arms so violently that she had lost her balance. The truth was far more complex. In an interview with David Holmes broadcast in 1958, she had expressed bitter resentment at the terrible weight of her career and had declared her intention of retiring within a year. In a subsequent interview she spoke about the growing fear of going on the stage: 'The more I grew in reputation the more frightened I got.' Underneath Maria's prodgious capacity for work, her forceful personality, her unique ability to take risks and her superhuman will-power, lay a quivering bundle of vulnerable feelings. Her strength was, and had always been, rooted in weakness. And now hard work, tensions, fears, condemnations and relentless self-criticism had all become too much. She longed to break free. And some part of her knew that singing was not the whole purpose and meaning of her life. Onassis made her aware of her own sensuality, he made her feel the need for a man in a way she had never felt before, and he was her first real lover. Maria discovered sex at thirty-six and she discovered it through Onassis. That alone would have been a strong bond. 'It was a definite sexual passion,' said Zeffirelli, who had frequently stayed with them on Skorpios. 'She found real, sexual fulfilment with him.'

There was more. In Maria's battle for a greater experience of life and of herself, Onassis opened the door to a wonderland of new adventures, new sensations and new insights – the promise of a whole new beginning for which she had been longing anyway. She may have been longing for it, but she had certainly not predicted the emotional upheaval it would create. All she really understood was work, and suddenly she was not working. She had been deprived, even though of her own free will, of the one thing that had so far given meaning and direction to her life.

At first Onassis had become the centre of her new dream, which had replaced the dreams of glory that had soured into frustration and nightmare; he had himself done everything to earn this position. But then the affair that had begun with such an impetuous rush lost its momentum. After Tina's divorce petition he had suddenly withdrawn – not for the first time in his life when faced with the inescapable necessity of deciding. He kept appearing and disappearing, no longer to be relied on for the support she needed, now more than ever.

Nineteen sixty began with the first major crisis of her voice. Maria had repeatedly, both in public and in private, stressed the effect of her emotional state on her voice. Although true of any singer, it was especially so in her case after her legend had been established and her fears had begun to grow with it. It was as if each fear, each anxiety and upheaval, had an instant, audible effect on her voice. 'Only a happy bird can sing,' she said once. And another time: 'It is not my voice which is sick, it is my nerves.' Her nerves were certainly ragged at the beginning of 1960, her blood pressure was worryingly low, and she was suffering from sinus trouble that made singing extremely painful. She did not want to sing but she wanted to know that she *could* sing. So she would go into her music room, sit at the grand piano, still piled high with music, and try to sing something, anything. Then the pain – a pain that started in her throat and travelled all the way up to her forehead – would force her to stop.

The newspaper reports about how she was defeated and finished had already begun. On top of all that her mother brought out a book, *My Daughter Maria Callas,* which led to a spate of articles implictly, and in some cases very directly, accusing Maria of unkindness and ingratitude. Evangelia, with her amber hair drawn up in a chignon, and dressed, as always, with a prim, lady-like elegance, received the journalists in her seven-dollar-a-week hotel room near New York's Puerto Rican district. At sixty-two she was still handsome, and now looked much more like her daughter than she had before Maria's transformation. The book was her story of Maria's life as told to Lawrence Blochman, and in it, as in her life, she continued to act out the part of the injured and abandoned mother. She had even tried to find an explanation for Maria's explosive temperament by tracing her tantrums to the concussion she had suffered after her car accident when she was five.

Evangelia, who had left her job at the Gabor jewellery shop, was for the moment living on the advance from her book. She had great dreams about its success, but as Maria refused to rise to the bait, or indeed make any comment on the book, it sank as soon as the first flurry of interest was over. 'Where should I find a suitable husband?' Evangelia had said in one of her interviews. 'I do not want to marry a man with no money. I'm poor already, why should I want to make myself poor twice over?' Evangelia's obsession with money and fame, the very obsession on which she had brought up her daughters, showed through unmistakably. Maria, who had slammed the door on her mother and the past so resolutely that she thought it would never open again, began to realize that she could not so decisively edit her life. She always saw herself as the victim of her mother and her childhood, and so would always be haunted by both. Maria's relationship with her mother remained, right to the end, at the troubled centre of her life. Her spectacular weight loss, her relationship with Onassis and the fact that 'she didn't like her mother' were the three facts known about her, even by people who hardly knew she was an opera singer. The last was an emotion with which thousands could identify – among them many of those most indignantly denouncing Maria for her unnatural behaviour.

Her godfather wrote to her, urging a reconciliation with her mother, but Maria's recent wish to heal rifts did not extend to Evangelia, and her longing to be a 'normal' woman, now stronger than ever, did not extend to wanting a normal relationship with her mother.

'I don't want to sing any more,' she said. 'I want to live, just like a normal woman, with children, a home, a dog.' Aristo was, of course, the key-piece in this dream jigsaw of normality and, as the year went on, he was spending more and more time with her – with as little explanation as when he had begun spending less and less time with her. His presence helped soothe her nerves and – even though she was not yet ready to put it to the test – helped her voice more than all the medicines and vitamins the doctors had been prescribing. It was like a new honeymoon, only this time, with Tina adamant about the divorce, it was almost official. The crew of the *Christina* were told to treat Maria in everything as *la patronne,* which they did with pleasure. Aristo never contradicted an order she had given, except once when he ordered that Tina's portrait be put back when Maria had it removed from the games room. The staff had warmed to her, especially after she adopted Onassis's habit of going to the kitchens to taste all the different Greek dishes before meals and make both ecstatic noises and expert comments.

It was just as well she had no singing engagements, as keeping up with the thundering pace of the relationship challenged even Maria's enormous energy. It did not take long for Tina's and Ari's friends to accept that it was Maria who was now going to be at his side, and to welcome her like loyal subjects receiving the new consort. After all these years of obsessive concern with artistic standards – her own and others' – she was suddenly surrounded by people who cared much more for reputation than for talent. For them the important thing was success, and their ambition to be on cruising terms with the successful. Here Onassis was unrivalled; nobody could surpass the guest list of the *Christina*. Greta Garbo, Ava Gardner, Marlene Dietrich, Cary Grant, Winston Churchill, ex-King Peter of Yugoslavia, ex-King Farouk of Egypt, the Begum Aga Khan, the Maharani of Baroda, together with assorted barons, bankers and beautiful people, had all at one time or another sailed on the *Christina*. And they had all sipped their cocktails at the main deck bar, which was not easy to beat for ostentatious vulgarity. It was a blatant reminder of Olympic Whaling, which had been one of Onassis's massive enterprises: the bar-stools were covered with the skin of the scrotum of a mature whale, and whales' teeth provided both the foot rests and the bar-rail, which was in addition engraved with scenes from the *Iliad* and the *Odyssey*.

Maria was fascinated by this buccaneering side of Onassis and from now on she too would live his battles with world oil interests, with Prince Rainier and even with the American and Greek Governments. 'She is the only woman,' confided Onassis to a friend, 'with whom I can discuss business.' She loved the business conundrums on which he thrived and the baroque negotiations off which he fed. It was another way of saying that she loved him, because Onassis never really separated his business from his private life. The centre of the Onassis empire was wherever he happened to be and the Onassis coterie was made up of his favourite mixture of business, the *beau monde* and show business. He had offices all over the world but his own private office he carried in the inside pocket of his jacket – an old notebook fastened with rubber bands. Nobody used friendships and social contacts as effectively as he did to open all sorts of business doors. Helen Vlachos called him 'the top public relations genius in the world, and he concentrates on one client – himself.'

Being part of his life was being part of a whirlwind. Maria spent less time in Via Buonarroti during the first half of 1960 than she had spent even during her busiest working-time. It was clear that Milan would very soon stop being her home. Together, they began looking for a new one. His divorce had still not come through, so there was a lot of talk about marriage at this time; it was something to be relished in prospect but still safely out of reach. Maria, who wanted a real home with big open fires where she could imagine little children running about, began looking at châteaux in France.

At the beginning of March, Ari left for Gibraltar where

he was joined by Winston and Clementine Churchill for a cruise across the Atlantic. They had agreed – or rather Ari had decided – that Maria would stay behind, so as not to embarrass the Churchills who had been close to Tina and very fond of her. Whether he was cruising with the Churchills or going on long business trips to Argentina, America or Saudi Arabia, Maria was often left behind. The life of a sultan's odalisque was a long way from the life of an international superstar, but Maria slipped into it as though she had been trained for the role.

Shortly after the end of the cruise, Ari arrived in Paris to talk with Tina. It was the last attempt at reconciliation, and one of the more desperate arguments he used was that it would give much pleasure to the Churchills. The last attempt failed, but something important was achieved. Tina agreed to drop her New York divorce suit and instead get one of the quick divorces that could be obtained in Alabama. Soon after the meeting, Aristo and Maria went together to see the Château du Jonchet in Eure-et-Loir. A month later he was divorced; but the château had not been bought.

In July, Maria made a hesitant attempt at a come-back to record Verdi and Rossini arias for EMI. The recording took place in London, at the Watford Town Hall, with Antonio Tonini conducting. It was a disappointment; Maria refused to give permission for its release and, what was worse, her self-confidence – so fragile at this stage – was damaged even further. But she left for Ostend, determined to go ahead with the concert she had agreed to give there. On the morning of the performance she woke up to discover that she had hardly any voice left. She called Peter Diamand who had arrived the night before. 'Hallo, Emmanuele,' he said, convinced that the hoarse voice on the other end of the phone belonged to a male Italian friend. 'It's not Emmanuele, it's Maria. Please come to my hotel. I don't know what to do. I can't sing tonight.'

Nor could she. The concert was cancelled, and a few hours later she left Ostend, terrified at the prospect of the two performances of *Norma* she had agreed to give in Epidaurus in August. She had only agreed because of

Onassis; doing what she knew would make him happy had become essential to her own happiness. As soon as making money had lost its challenge, Onassis had turned his eyes to Greece. Ulysses was his favourite hero. He identified with his wanderings and his tribulations, and he longed to be able to identify with his triumphant home-coming. Creating Olympic Airways was the first step, but he wanted to forge more links, to have more tangible proof that he belonged to Greece and that in some ill-defined way Greece belonged to him. To have his established mistress score a triumph at the ancient and revered theatre of Epidaurus, and to be there to share the honours, would be another link with Greece. Maria, apart from wanting to please Ari, was herself beginning to feel the emotional call of her homeland. Greece was one of the bonds that joined them, and she valued everything that kept him close to her.

It was the strength that she drew not only from his presence but from knowing how important it was to him that made her overcome her fears and go ahead with *Norma.* They spent most of the month before leaving for Greece in Monte Carlo. That summer of 1960, that magically happy summer, he put everything aside to be with her; they were constantly together. Onassis, who had never in his life kept regular hours, had found in Maria someone who had no trouble living according to his peculiar clock that often reversed day and night. If he was spending the night doing business – or talking it, which he loved at least as much – Maria would be working on her Norma, unless of course she had joined the men, absorbing everything like a sponge as she had done all those years ago at the Athens Conservatory when she listened in on everybody elese's lessons as well as her own.

Many nights were spent at the Maona, Monte Carlo's latest night-club. Soon the story began to spread that the club had been named for them: MAria, ONAssis. In fact the club's godmother was Tina Onassis, and it was she who had given it its Polynesian name. It was at the Maona with its Hawaiian decor that Ari and Maria were photographed dancing together. 'It is impossible,' wrote the *Daily Express,* 'for them to dance cheek to cheek as

Miss Callas is slightly taller than Mr Onassis. But as she danced she has lowered her head to nibble his ear and he has smiled rapturously.' From the outside it looked as though their marriage was imminent. 'I am fairly certain they will be married before the year is out,' a close business associate was reported as saying. And the marriage looked no less immiment from the inside – so much so that on 10 August, once again at the Maona, Maria made public their intention to marry. The next day Onassis had dismissed the report as a fantasy and Maria's remark as a pleasantry. It was a public humiliation, but Maria, as she had said herself, knew 'how to wait'. Years later, after Jackie Kennedy had become the second Mrs Onassis, Maria would admit bitterly that patience does not always pay. 'I should have insisted that he marry me in 1960. Then he would have done it.'

Instead, the subject of their marriage was to become a regularly renewed disappointment for her. It would come to the surface; it would subside; it would swell again. For the time being, Maria was satisfied. 'What Onassis offered me,' she was to say, later, 'was the feeling of being totally appreciated.' The little girl who had always felt that she was only loved when she was singing was at last loved whether she sang or not. In fact her singing never meant anything to Onassis except as a vehicle of her success. Soon it was to be the vehicle for what was for him a solemn ritual – Maria returning to Greece at his side to appear as Norma in Epidaurus.

On the first night torrential rain made it impossible for the performance to begin. Twenty thousand men, women and children poured out of the stadium into cars, boats and buses as the deluge continued. They were back on 24 August for the new first night and, as soon as Maria appeared, they rose to their feet. Patriotic and artistic fervour combined in one of the greatest ovations Epidaurus and Maria had ever heard. If, as many would argue, her Norma was her masterpiece, then the night of 24 August must be considered the culmination of a career which had in many quarters already been written off. In the ancient theatre which had witnessed the birth of Greek drama, Maria went beyond acting and opera and touched the hearts of thousands who knew nothing of either. From her very first notes, the audience was magnetized by the power she displayed. And yet there was a new tenderness, a real mother's feeling coming through in the way she responded to her children. 'Maria identified with Norma greatly,' said Zeffirelli. 'In a way it was her own story. Maria, after all, is a high priestess – the high priestess of her art. Yet, at the same time, she is the most fallible of women. Very human. As Norma, Maria created the maximum of what opera can be. In a lifetime, one can see many great things in the theatre, but to see Maria Callas in *Norma,* what is there to compare to it?'

By the end of the performance, the crowd at Epidaurus would have replied with one voice: 'Nothing.' She had entered into Norma and exposed in all its nakedness her inner turmoil. She had carried the audience and herself into a realm far beyond everyday life or everyday art. Beneath the star-filled Greek sky, a crown of laurel leaves was placed on her head. And at the end of the applause, which at times had seemed as though it would never stop, it was not excitement or joy that filled the resonant silence that followed – it was awe.

For two men sitting side by side in the front row, the awe was mixed with pride. George Callas and Aristotle Onassis had met in Epidaurus for the first time; the Greek multi-millionaire and the Greek pharmacist had spent hours talking to each other. 'He is *dombros,* your father,' Ari said to Maria – and *dombros,* meaning direct, honest, with no pretence, was a term of high praise in Onassis's vocabulary. It was one of the contradictions in his character that, although he had a craving for the famous and the important, some of his happiest moments were spent drinking ouzo and talking to the simple Greeks, the islanders and the peasants he met wherever he went. He never lost the emotional capacity to relate to them on their own terms – which after all, at a level not far below the surface, were his own terms too. Whenever he was in Greece, whether doing business or relaxing, he began talking the language of the market-place. As for Maria, she loved speaking Greek with him, singing the folk songs of the taverna with him, picking and eating from his plate, or following his example in eating with her fingers *à la grecque*.

In the euphoria of her happiness with Aristo, she forgot all caution, and although she had to sing a second *Norma* four days after her first performance, they stayed up late every night, and explored the countryside together during the day, spending hours in the scorching August sun. The result was that on the day of the performance she developed a high fever and felt so weak that the doctors refused to allow her out of bed. But now the famous Callas will took over. Nothing was going to stop her from honouring her contract; however high her temperature, she was not going to let down Aristo, Greece and the public that had four days earlier crowned her with laurel leaves. She sang and it was another triumph. In her new expansive mood, with Onassis's prompting and to complete the all-round celebrations, she gave her fee of $10,000 for the creation of a Scholarship Fund for Young Musicians.

Then with her confidence regained she arrived in Milan where she recorded *Norma* at La Scala with Serafin once more on the podium. It was like the old days, except that she felt a new woman. And she was looking forward to working again with Visconti in a new production of Donizetti's *Poliuto*, the opera she had chosen for her come-back at La Scala. But the days when she drilled and groomed herself like an Olympic athlete before the rehearsals for a new opera began were over. If she had been an instrumentalist, it might have been possible to combine a full-scale musical career with Ari's life-style; she might, perhaps, have been able to maintain an outstanding artistic position and a complete and sustained relationship – even though she had more than once said that such a relationship is a full-time job. What was not possible was to remain the queen of the operatic world and at the same time become the *ex officio* queen of the *beau monde*. There was little doubt what her true inclinations were; even when she was most deeply involved in the *beau monde*, she always remained in her heart an outsider. Its attraction for her, real though it was in the Maxwell days, would have been quickly exhausted if it were not for

Aristo fuelling it. It was part of his life; it had to be part of hers. But athletes, whether of the voice or the track, cannot stay up all night and practise the next day.

Yet we can hear in her last recording of *Norma* just how much her experiences with Onassis – both the joyful and the painful – had enriched her art. John Ardoin, comparing this with her earlier recordings, stresses the depth of expression in the new one that transcends technical polish: 'This *Norma* is more giving, more many-sided, more complex and drawn in finer lines. "Casta Diva" is quieter, more mesmerizing. . . . Along with this, the fearsome Norma remains intact; indeed she draws a new strength through the gulf of contrast Callas meticulously establishes.' Maria clearly had a greater store of emotions on which to draw. Experience had enhanced the richness and depth of her feelings, but dramatic singing at these new exalted heights demanded a unique, and uniquely cruel, combination of the asceticism of St Francis, the physical stamina of a marathon runner and the experience of life of Madame de Pompadour. For over twenty years, she had demonstrated both the asceticism and the physical stamina; but they were alien to her new life. The day before rehearsals were due to begin, her voice was in poor condition, and she felt tired and apprehensive. Then the thunderbolt struck. Visconti was walking out on *Poliuto* in protest against the Italian government's censoring of his film *Rocco and his Brothers* and the ban on his stage comedy *Araldia,* which was considered obscene. 'I'm finished with any artistic work in Italy,' he announced. At the same time, he sent a telegram to Maria explaining how it hurt him to abandon *Poliuto,* and 'above all because it prevents me from working with you, which is the work that gives me the greatest fulfilment. Although I apologize to you dear Maria, I am sure that you will understand my state of mind and approve of my decision. I embrace you, as always, with all my admiration and immense affection.' Maria wrote back full of sympathy, saying that she had been 'counting the hours' waiting for them to begin working on *Poliuto,* but that she was even more distressed because he was being 'tormented'.

Entirely blameless this time, she was caught in the middle of the censorship war. Herbert Graf stepped in to save *Poliuto* and to direct Maria in her return appearance at La Scala after thirty unceasingly publicized months of absence. The opening night was not only the highlight of the Italian musical season, it was an Aristotle Onassis spectacular. Prince Rainier and Princess Grace, and the Begum Aga Khan were among his guests, the rest being assorted members of his international coterie and Elsa Maxwell, who had been especially flown over from the States. She had nursed her wounded feelings long enough, and seemed at last prepared to accept the unpleasant fact that her beloved Maria now belonged to Onassis. It was almost like old times again, with her next column dedicated to Maria's opening, which she described as something out of the Arabian nights. Sixteen thousand carnations given by Balmain decorated the auditorium, and some among the audience of three thousand had paid, according to Associated Press, £800 for a single ticket. Onassis arrived as the overture was beginning and slipped quietly into his box.

'Maria,' said Nicola Benois who designed the production, 'badly needed a strong hand to guide her, to give her courage – the hand of Luchino.' On that night courage was infinitely more important than artistic guidance. The presence of Ari and his fashionable friends, in addition to the usual Scala audience ready to pounce on her first vocal slip, terrified her. It was not just stage nerves; it was a deep, paralysing anxiety as if something cold, horrible and humiliating was about to happen to her. It was as if all the whistling and booing, the throwing of radishes and walking out, all the manifestations of rejection that she had experienced at one opera house or another, had merged into a single overwhelming spectre and come to haunt her. And echoing through all these in her mind's ear was a prolonged roar of laughter.

She gave a performance almost designed to avoid risks, to avoid that nightmare roar of laughter. The woman whose audacity and determination to achieve the impossible had become legendary made her singing entrance as though she was carefully and hesitantly feeling her way into the part.

The choice of an opera that posed few vocal problems was in itself a clear sign of Maria's longing to be free of nervous tension – even at the expense of selecting for her return to La Scala an opera in which the heroine, Paolina, is less important than the hero, which demanded no great and potentially dangerous dramatic outbursts, and which gave her few chances to show that she could still command an astounding range of dramatic emotion. But the end of the opera was quite miraculous. 'It was,' wrote Andrew Porter, 'an almost physical enactment of the workings of grace, from the first stirrings when this pagan heroine listens to the Christians' hymn, to the supernatural radiance which floods her in the final scene as she resolves to join the Christians in martyrdom.' The audience gave her the triumph she feared would elude her. As always, it was not as bad in action as in prospect. But the agony of the prospect extracted a higher and higher toll from her. Even after the opera was finished, her performance had to continue, for the evening was crowned with a supper given in her honour by Prince Rainier and Princess Grace. After the celebrities and the gossip columnists had gone Maria could give her four remaining performances without that ruthless spotlight on her. Ten days after opening night, at an ordinary matinee, with no sharp-tongued columnists and bejewelled socialites, her performance demonstrated unequivocally that it was not her voice that was the cause of her decline, but her fears. 'No one will believe me,' wrote Andrew Porter in the *Musical Times,* 'when I say I heard the only performance, of the five she gave, in which Maria Callas found her peak form (a matinee on 18 December, for the record). But so it was. She was spellbinding, secure, confident and inspiring confidence.'

But the reviews after the first night read like obituary notices and by the end of the fifth performance Maria was a physical and emotional wreck. The irony was that, as her fears and her life-style made her appearances rarer, their very rarity, together with that life-style, invariably turned each performance into a celebrity occasion which further increased the tension and her fears, until by the time of her *Norma* in Paris in 1964 she had to be calmed with pills and injections before she could go on stage. It is hardly surprising that, as a result, her appearances became even rarer. From now until the end of her life she sang only three operas on stage – *Norma, Medea* and *Tosca* – but she discussed a very large number that never moved beyond the discussion stage. Each year consisted of what she sang and what she was in the process of negotiating to sing, and as the first list shrank, the second grew longer.

At the beginning of 1961 she and Sander Gorlinsky, who had since the end of her marriage become her exclusive agent, were in the process of negotiating with La Scala about the title role in Bellini's *Beatrice di Tenda* for the spring and with the Dallas Civic Opera about a production of *Orfeo* for the autumn. Onassis too was full of projects for her. It was some time since Maria had last announced to the press, 'My relations with Mr Onassis involve business matters', but business matters continued to be discussed. There was, for a start, the question of the Monte Carlo Opera Company, but Onassis's heart was in other projects closer to his own taste and understanding. Ever since Carl Foreman, his guest on the *Christina,* had offered Maria a part opposite Gregory Peck in *The Guns of Navarone,* Onassis had been trying to get her to do a film. He was particularly enthusiastic about turning Hans Habe's German pot-boiler *The Primadonna* into a film – with Maria, of course, in the lead. There is no doubt that he would have felt much more comfortable if Maria had been a film star instead of an opera star. Not being overwhelmed by the great Callas, as most men surrounding her were, meant that he could directly respond to her as a woman. This had made wooing her easier; but the total absence of any feeling for her art was making loving her more difficult. Maria, as an Italian friend of hers put it, had found bread for her teeth. But then so had Onassis. Here was a woman more famous than he was and whose fame was rather more solidly based than his own. Mystified and perplexed by her art he began to degrade and even openly to ridicule it. He had never enjoyed opera except in Epidaurus and on gala nights, and it satisfied no emotional need in him. Singing to bouzouki music, smashing plates and other uninhibited expressions of emotion were always much more to his liking.

When, for Maria's sake, guests on the *Christina* turned the conversation to opera, he would very swiftly steer it into more familiar waters – and not always with his famed charm. Once the discussion turned to Maria's Tosca and someone quoted Puccini's description of himself as 'a mighty hunter of wild fowl, beautiful women, and good libretti'. 'That's the best thing I've heard about him,' said Onassis looking straight at Maria, 'except that he needn't have bothered about the libretti.' Yet despite these philistine outbursts, he had a genuine feeling for music. During the war, he had persuaded Ingse Dedichen, the Norwegian shipping heiress with whom he was living at the time, to teach him to play some Bach on the piano. He could not read music but he practised the same piece for six months until a few years later he could astonish Artur Rubinstein and everybody else present at a Hollywood party by playing it effortlessly and with much feeling. He was always venturing into unexpected areas, amazing everybody with his knowledge, as he amazed Margot Fonteyn when one night he started discussing 'entrechats-six' with her. It was a dancer in Anna Pavlova's company visiting Buenos Aires who had taught him, but he had cared enough to learn. He never cared enough to learn much about opera, at any rate more than had been necessary for courting Maria.

Meanwhile Maria wanted to know about everything that was part of his life – a friend of hers who saw her for lunch in London could hardly believe the change: 'She talks of nothing but politics, tourism and the future of air travel.' Under the stimulus of her love her life expanded, its colours heightened. She adopted his interests, she adopted his friends, and two of them, Panaghis Vergottis and Maggie van Zuylen, were to become two of the people closest to her. She had never before revelled in friendship, nor drawn much strength from it, but loving Onassis had made it easier for her to open herself to others. She, who had always had difficulty with intimacy of any kind, began to discover its joys. Vergottis was just seventy when Maria met him in London at the Dorchester party after *Medea*. His friendship with Ari dated back to the thirties when Vergottis, an established shipowner with a long family shipping tradition behind him, met the young Onassis on his way up. 'One of my dearest friends, if not the best I have,' was the way Onassis described him to Maria.

For Maria, Vergottis soon became a kind of cultural bridge between her new world and her new interests and the world of opera and music that had been her home for over twenty years and her kingdom for nearly ten. In her new world she was largely surrounded by people who would announce with shrill intensity that they *loved* music. Vergottis made a more than welcome change. He was not only interested and knowledgeable on the subject of opera, he was passionate about it. A tall, handsome man, almost invariably dressed in a dark suit and white shirt, he was one of the aristocrats of the shipping business, following developments in the world of art with at least as much avidity as he showed for the shipping world, and carefully restricting his business life to the afternoons – after a good lunch, often at Claridges or the Ritz, and after he had lit his second or third cigar of the day. He had never married, and his life was instead crowded with a succession of colourful mistresses. His home was the Ritz in London, but even after all these years of living there, his suite remained as impersonal as the first day he had moved in, without a single photograph or *objet d'art* that belonged to him; almost the only personal thing he had was a carpet that he loved, and even that was kept in the storeroom of the Ritz. Maria loved to tease him about his obsessive rituals, such as buying his cigars each morning from a cigar shop across from the Ritz, always six at a time, or ordering his dark suits and white shirts, all together, once every ten years, and always in the same style. At the height of their friendship, Maria was for him daughter, confidante and embodiment of his lifelong love of the arts. She was also a Greek, and although Vergottis felt more at home at the Ritz than on Kephalonia, the island of his ancestors in the Ionian sea, he was intensely proud of his nationality.

Maria felt not only admired but loved when she was with him, which made her open her heart to him, especially about Aristo. Very soon Vergottis became the official envoy between Maria and Onassis, intervening whenever hostilities between the two super-powers reached breaking point. Maggie van Zuylen was the other go-between in this at times impossible relationship. It was at her Paris apartment on Avenue Foch that Maria and Ari met again for the first time after his marriage to Jackie, and it was she who often talked Maria into seeing Ari again after, like a hurt child, she had sworn never to do so. The range and intimacy of Maria's friendship with Maggie throws much light on what she was seeking during this part of her life. Maggie's life had been the opposite of Maria's. Born in Alexandria of Syrian parents, she met the Baron van Zuylen during his travels, and so totally swept him off his feet that he went ahead and married her despite his father's violent disapproval. The old Baron, who had destined his son for at least a Grand Duchess, promptly disinherited him and for three years they lived off loans on his name, the Stock Exchange and Maggie's poker, occasionally leaving restaurants by the back door when all else had failed. Then the old Baron met his daughter-in-law and was, in turn, swept off his feet.

Maggie van Zuylen instinctively had what Maria never had and never really acquired. She had that intangible quality which makes a courtesan out of a woman, a sexual worldliness which turns her into a seductress who knows how to create pleasure for a man. For about ten years she remained an endless source of worldly advice for Maria. A regular guest on the *Christina,* she would always be prodding her to organize things for Ari – card games, boat parties, new people, anything to keep her man amused. 'You are always shown to best advantage,' she would tell her, 'against the background of all those guests and activities so that he can get away from all that, into your arms.' Maria tried – tried, tried and went on trying – right down to organizing parties for card-playing which she detested. Unable to master the rudiments of female artifice, she grossly overvalued its importance and admired anyone who had mastered it as thoroughly as Maggie. She felt her to be a ruler over a mysterious territory in which she longed to be at home. She never stopped to wonder why, if all these techniques for 'winning men and keeping them' were so successful, Maggie's husband had kept a mistress for thirteen years, an actress who had become a permanent fixture in his life. 'Never create jealous scenes,' Maggie would tell Maria, especially when there was good cause for creating them. 'Be unfaithful. The greatest, the most effective jealousy scene you can create is a nicely publicized affair on the side. A man can't go on being interested, especially sexually interested, in his wife, if he feels too secure in her.'

Maria did once follow Maggie's advice when she was photographed kissing Pasolini on the lips, just before Onassis was to set off for a Caribbean cruise with Jackie and the Radziwills. Unfortunately Pasolini's inclinations were so well known that the most she could have hoped for from such a photograph was a weary smile on Ari's face. Whatever the effectiveness of her advice, Maggie van Zuylen was an arresting, sparkling personality; she had once been a great beauty, and although twenty-three years older than Maria would always remain much more secure as a woman. Unlike Maria, she was totally at ease wherever she was and whoever she was with – whether with André Malraux, who described her as 'the least cultured and most brilliant woman I ever met' or with Georges Pompidou, of whom she once said that one of his eyes was that of a Jesuit and the other that of a thief.

This ease facinated Maria, for whom everything – her art, her charm, even her social life – had been hard work. For her part, Maggie, who had never worked, had never created anything except evanescent evenings and had never read a book from cover to cover except, once, a life of Marie Antoinette, found Maria's application and success overwhelmingly attractive. It is interesting that Maggie's other great friend was Coco Chanel, another highly successful woman who had worked hard for everything.

Maggie was Maria's first intimate friend, someone with whom she could discuss everything, from her sex life with Ari to the *placement* for a dinner she was giving. But Maggie was strictly *mondaine,* and there were stirrings and longings in Maria that in Maggie's case were buried far too deep to feel. For the time being, the contrasts between them tied them to each other more tightly than any matching qualities could have done. The frustrated artist with her two children and her six grandchildren met the celebrated singer longing to fulfil herself as a woman, and what followed was a fusion based on opposite needs. 'The only things that interest me now,' said Maggie towards the end of her life, 'are having dinner with Maria and Ari and playing gin rummy.'

In the first flush of her more-than-requited love affair with France and the French, Maria had announced that she longed to live in Paris, and ever since that moving reception at Orly in early 1958, more and more people, things and feelings seemed to be drawing her there. Ari and Maggie were, of course, the main attractions. It was not by accident that the apartment she rented was at 44 Avenue Foch, Maggie's at 84 and Ari's at 88. Her work was also increasingly moving her to Paris. Michel Glotz, head of Pathé-Marconi, the French counterpart of EMI, had become a good friend, and Georges Prêtre was to become her favourite conductor. At the end of March 1961, he conducted the recording of 'Great Arias from French Opera' that Maria did at the Salle Wagram. It was an entirely new repertoire for Maria. Delilah's Spring Song, Orpheus's Lament, the Habanera from *Carmen* – they all demonstrate that if only Maria had not stuck to the soprano repertory long after she could no longer sing it, she could have had a new and thriving career as a mezzo: 'I'm seriously afraid,' wrote Roger Dettmer in the *Chicago American,* 'that if she pursues this course her mezzo colleagues one and all will flee to the wings where Maria Callas stands ready, waiting to go on with possibly the supreme Carmen since Calvé, the definitive Delilah our age has lacked, the humanizer of Gluck in this era of classical frigidity, and who knows what other wonders. The queen is reborn, long live the queen.' But all these remained the dreams of reviewers, opera managers, thousands of Maria's fans and, every now and then, of Maria herself.

Meanwhile Georges Prêtre was helping her rebuild her

shaky confidence. Young, exuberant, a judo black belt and devoted to Maria, he became a friend and a source of support both during and in between performances. 'When she is working she is always nervous,' he said just before Maria's last appearance. 'She thinks of nothing but the performance. She can't sleep. She is always screwing herself up to do even better. But on holiday, when we were cruising with Mr Onassis, I don't believe she even thinks of it.' Her engagements were increasingly being fitted in around her cruises. Immediately after her recording in Paris, she left for Monte Carlo and a cruise; and after her next engagement – a concert at St James's Palace with Sir Malcolm Sargent accompanying her at the piano – she left London, no less promptly, for yet another cruise.

What had driven her along from performance to performance and from recording to recording without pause was now a faint echo, a memory with no power to revive the reality. 'You haven't practised once,' said Princess Grace to her in amazement at the end of a three-week cruise. 'Margot Fonteyn wouldn't go for three weeks without working out.' 'I don't need to,' was Maria's reply. 'I can go for a month without.' It would have been more accurate to say: 'I don't want to; I don't want to go on vocalizing and acting and studying roles and doing all the things I've done all my life.' Zeffirelli remembers visiting her in Paris to talk about doing *Tosca*: 'The first thing I noticed were the long nails of her beautiful hands and I realized that they were the nails of someone who had not touched the keyboard of a piano . . . for at least two years . . . and I told her that. I said, "I'm very sorry because, obviously, you haven't been practising your voice." She said, "How do you know?" I said, "Look at your finger nails." And then she realized, looked at them and made a beautiful gesture with her hands, like a little girl, and she said, "Yes, all right, but I've been distracted. . . . I am trying to fulfil my life as a woman."' Despite Aristo's restlessness and his need for action and movement, she found herself on their cruises basking in a mood of timelessness that made ambition and even achievement seem unimportant, almost irrelevant.

All this augered badly for Maria's return visit to Epidaurus in August. But she was, after all, a toughened professional, and within hours of finding herself in the ancient theatre, the old drive and perfectionism were back. The last four days before the opening night of *Medea* on 6 August 1961 were spent rehearsing without stop. With Minotis, who was delighted to be able to transfer his production to the centre of ancient Greek drama, she worked late into the night, perfecting her movements, her poses, the play of her accusing hands, her fierce pacings to and fro before the palace, the violent caressings of the two children she is about to kill. On the night before the performance she even asked for a bed to be made up for her in a room in the Museum of Epidaurus so as not to be away from the theatre. Cherubini's music was written during the French Revolution, but as Peter Heyworth put it, 'Maria Callas is much nearer to ancient Greece than to revolutionary France. While Cherubini trundles out his clichés she storms the heights with Euripides.'

It seemed as though the whole of Greece longed to hear her storm the heights. The dress rehearsal was given for the neighbouring peasants who filled the theatre and applauded with passion the Greek Medea who had sung all over the world and had now come back to sing for them. From very early in the morning on the day of the first performance the road from Athens to Epidaurus, 200 kilometres to the north, had been closed to southbound traffic to make it possible for the hundreds of cars leaving the capital for the ancient theatre to get there before nightfall. Among them were the cars of the Prime Minister and most of the Cabinet. The Prime Minister took his seat for the performance three minutes before Elsa Maxwell took hers. Ghiringhelli was already there, and so were David Webster and Wally Toscanini and Prince Rainier's uncle and numerous other citizens of the *beau monde.*

The orchestra came in, but all eyes were still watching the entrance for the instantly recognizable figure of Aristotle Onassis – the man whose name had already entered the Greek language as a synonym for legendary riches. They watched in vain. Onassis, aboard the

Christina, was heading towards Alexandria. Business, he said later to friends who were describing Maria's triumph to him, had sadly kept him away. Business was one reason; another was that he had had one too many of Maria's first nights, receiving congratulations on her behalf and getting uncomfortably hot in the warmth of her reflected glory. Jackie Kennedy may have been famous – perhaps even more famous than Maria – but she had not achieved anything in her own right, so although he had plenty of problems coping with her, his male vanity had no difficulty coping with her celebrity.

He missed Maria's greatest triumph in Epidaurus, seventeen curtain-calls, twenty thousand spectators in ecstasy and, on the hills round the theatre, standing, sitting on stones or perching in trees, thousands more who had not been able to get tickets for the performance but were going to hear her anyway. Once again in the front row, looking very dapper in his white tuxedo with his trim little moustache, was George Kalogeropoulos; this time, next to him, was his elder daughter. There was an emotional meeting between the two sisters and they all had dinner together after the performance, but the reconciliation went no deeper – nor did it include Evangelia.

Onassis arrived just in time for the second *Medea* on 13 August; and then, having once again donated her fee to the Scholarship Fund for Young Musicians, Maria was off on the *Christina.* But she, who could mesmerize an audience by her mere presence, seemed to lose this power when it came to Ari. Her love and happiness with him were becoming more burdened with apprehension, with a fear of the pain of losing him. She always minded their separations much more than he did and, when she forgot all Maggie's good advice and complained, she was an easy victim to his self-justifying and hectoring tactics. He had begun to take on a new tone of ownership and affectionate mockery, and the affectionate mockery was becoming increasingly less affectionate and more mocking. What were at first only love-bites began to leave scars and to hurt. Maria's tolerant, understanding attitude was largely determined by policy and was, therefore, extremely precarious. When it all got too much for her, she would explode, leave the room where he was or the table where they were eating, and sulk alone with the pain that had caused the explosion. As soon as he sensed her retreating, he would advance and reconquer her, and then it would all be beautiful for a while, until once again he would be off for days on end, sometimes without even telling her.

While Maria had been cruising on the *Christina,* Meneghini had lodged a new demand with the Civic Tribunal in Milan to annul their separation by mutual consent, and institute in its place a separation order that acknowledged Maria's responsibility for the breakdown of their marriage. Meneghini was boiling in his statement to the press: 'She's not behaving like a woman of her position . . . has made nonsense of the Court Order that we should remain faithful to one another. . . . I want to whiten my name and I want to proclaim that it was because of her that our marriage was destroyed . . .' Reading about Maria's glittering new life from his self-imposed exile in Sirmione must have been agonizing and infuriating. The woman whom he had very revealingly called 'my *chef d'oeuvre'* had walked out of his life and was clearly wasting no time looking back. By reacting like the wronged husband in an old-fashioned melodrama, he hoped to remind her of his existence and force her to look back. Nor was he going to stop there. From now until the end of Maria's life Meneghini played the part of the chorus, commenting on what she did or what was done to her and predicting what she was going to do or what was going to be done to her. And he went on acting the part of the chorus even after her death, making it clear that Maria, dead or alive, remained the centre of his life.

In the summer of 1961, Maria must certainly have wished he had found another centre. And she must have wished it even more strongly later on when he produced photographs of her with Onassis – especially one where they were kissing at a night-club – to prove her infidelity. Using a technicality in the Italian divorce laws that made it possible to go on talking of infidelity after a separation, he was trying to prove something that nobody doubted in the first place. Maria, caught in the trap, tried to disprove it, using as her evidence the status of the other people present in the photographs. The unstated but all too clear implication was that sleeping with one another is not something that goes on in such exalted circles. It was one of the fictional public statements to which Maria was prone, as if she was driven to them against her will by the gap between her impulses and her actions on the one hand and her beliefs on the other. And it was her beliefs rather than reality that almost invariably dominated her public statements, which is why they so often sounded stilted, rigid and unreal.

Commenting on Maria's behaviour and predicting her future was not the prerogative only of ex-husbands. It was open season for friends and foes alike. And on the basis of their statements, it was sometimes difficult to tell them apart. In the middle of October, Visconti joined the fray. 'I adore Callas,' he said, 'but I don't think she will sing again, except perhaps once a year. She knows that two years ago she was very great and that her great moment must pass. As a woman she is still young but as a singer she is not so young and the voice changes with age. Besides, now she's involved with private stories, which is not good for her.'

It was quite a blessing at the time that, ever since the break-up of her marriage, Tina had maintained a ladylike silence on the subject of the new woman in her ex-husband's life. She was in any case too busy fulfilling her desire for a real home, with winding staircases and family portraits on the wall. On 23 October, at the Greek Orthodox Church in Paris, she married the Marquess of Blandford and became the chatelaine of Lee Place, her new husband's estaste in Oxfordshire. The Duke of Marlborough, the bridegroom's father, and George Livanos, Tina's brother, were the witnesses and for a change the spotlight was on Tina as the scores of photographers burst into the church to immortalize the Marquess and his Greek Marchioness, still wearing the coronets of flowers they had on for the ceremony. When Ari and Maria flew into London a couple of weeks later, most of the questions were about Tina. 'Our relationship has always been most friendly and, as far as I know, we are still on the best of terms,' was Ari's reply.

Maria was in London to record a selection of Rossini, Donizetti and Bellini arias. It was another in the series of recordings made but never released. Only one aria from *Pirata* was accepted by Maria as good enough for general release. Back in Milan, she was anxiously trying to get into shape for the opening night of *Medea* at La Scala. It was again the Minotis production, although the settings had had to be totally rebuilt and adjusted to the Scala stage, and it was once again Jon Vickers who was her Jason. The opening night on 11 December soon became part of the Callas folklore. She was not in very good voice and during her first act duet with Jason when she pleads with him to come back to her and their children, she sounded really weak, lacking the strength to give it the intensity it needed. Thomas Schippers, who was conducting, recalled what followed. 'From the top of the gallery came an awful hissing sound, like a typhoon, that covered the entire auditorium. Maria continued and finally reached the point in the text where Medea denounces Jason with a word "*Crudel!*" (Cruel man!). The orchestra must follow this word with two forte chords, then wait for her to sing a second "*Crudel!*" before it can continue playing. But after the first "*Crudel!*" Maria completely stopped singing. . . . I watched in disbelief as she glared up into the auditorium and took in every pair of eyes in the theatre, as if to say, "Now look! This has been my stage and will be mine as long as I want it. If you hate me now, I hate you just as much!" I saw this, I felt it. then Maria sang her second "*Crudel!*" directly at the public, squashing it into silence. Never in my life have I seen anyone dare such a thing in the theatre. Never. And there was not a murmur of protest against her after that. I was paralysed. . . . I had no idea when she was going to sing again. She controlled the whole thing.'

When she started again on the words, '*Ho dato tutto a te*' (I gave everything to you) she shook her fist at the gallery. This was precisely the kind of behaviour that the other Maria, the Maria who talked so much about respectability, would have disdained. Here was another rift that ran deeply inside her. There was the great artist who accepted everything – including hate and jealousy and ugliness and pain – as part of life and gave raw expression to them, and there was the other Maria, prim, proper, puritanical, sincerely worshipping 'the done thing' and ardently believing in conventional morality and in what, time and again, she would refer to as normality. The imagination of this other Maria was peopled with mythical 'normal' men and especially 'normal' women, into whose ranks she longed to rise.

There were two more performances of *Medea.* In between, in agonizing pain, she had to have a sinus operation to make it possible for her to sing the third *Medea* on 20 December. While the newspapers, which had noticed the absence of Onassis from her bedside during her convalescence, were forecasting the end of their relationship, Maria was joining Ari in Monte Carlo for Christmas. Such reports were to become a constant feature of the next six years. This time they were wrong in fact but right in spirit. The beginning of 1962 found Maria anxious and introspective. Surfeited with applause and praise, she hoped through Aristo and their love to find something more real; and she had convinced herself that it was to be found in something solid, in a family and children. But talk of marriage, of finding a house together, had become less and less frequent. Maria was discovering, as Tina had discovered before her, that home for Onassis was wherever he was, provided there was a telephone on the spot and a night-club not to far away. The *Christina* was the nearest thing to a conventional home that he ever had. He was to meet his match later when it became clear that Jackie wanted a home – at least a home with him – even less than he did.

For the moment he was offering Maria everything except what she deeply wanted. *La passione dei sensi,* as an Italian friend of theirs described their relationship, was still alive, but it could not alone sustain their life together, and the pleasure she got from the round of parties, balls and night-clubs had begun to suffer from the law of diminishing returns. Ari was a confectioner, and although he was a Confectioner Royal, Maria was finding out that confectionery will not satisfy for long those who seek the bread of life. With her fortieth birthday not all that far away, she could feel her life slipping by; and before it was too late she wanted to live out all the passion and the love that were inside her. 'In operas,' she had said once, 'I've played heroines who die for love – and that's something I can understand.' Both the conventional woman in her who longed to be 'normal' and the passionate woman who could understand dying, wanted marriage. She had had, through her art, glimpses of another reality, another world: '. . . a world I would like to live in all the time. It's a – no, I won't say superior – it's a very nice, good world. No envy, no gossip, no nonsense, everything so pure and serene. But there is great passion, great love there, too.'

The tragic irony was that the man with whom she wanted to turn this world into a permanent reality could not imagine life except in the centre of the world of envy, gossip and nonsense. There was what can only be described as a deep seriousness in Maria. By nature and inclination she was an enemy of the world where all is sacrificed to the amusing. Surrounded by people from the world of the yacht and the private jet, with more than their fair share of joyless affairs and loveless marriages, she often felt lost and lonely. She was attracted to its glamour but frightened by its emptiness, and the novelty and the glamour were already beginning to fade. She never really smoked though she did have an occasional cigarette when others were smoking around her; she was never a drinker though with Onassis she began to have more than a token glass of wine; and she disliked dancing except, as she said once to Princess Grace, 'with my husband or the man I love'. So she hated night-clubs, and yet in 1962 and for that matter in 1963, she spent many more nights in night-clubs than in opera houses and concert halls. And during these years more column inches were written about her night-club appearances than about her appearances in opera houses. Sometimes, the headlines were fully interchangeable. 'Callas walks out', read one of them. The story was that she had walked out when a dancer was announced as *'La Callas du Striptease'*. 'The truth,' said Maria later, 'was that at the end of the number I had asked to be taken home simply because I found it rather boring.' News of Maria's celebrated ferocity had reached even the furthest outposts of the *beau monde*. It was well known that she had claws and could bite. 'Why are people nervous about meeting me?' she asked Derek Prouse when he went to see her in Monte Carlo for the *Sunday Times*. There is in fact no record of any member of the *beau monde* having been mauled by her. 'Ours,' said one of the more perceptive among them, 'was the kind of immunity accorded to exotic tribes.'

Maria rarely felt part of Onassis's world, and it certainly never became her own. When he left her, she left it. In a sense, Onassis never belonged to it either. He was too full of life, too close to the earth, the sea and the elements not to feel the emptiness and even the desperation that so often fuelled the way that he and those around him lived, which is why he is loved talking to fishermen and even idealized their lives. Every now and then, he would go across to Nidri, two miles from Skorpios, to have an ouzo with Nikos. Nikos was known as the 'Gelastos Psaras' (the Laughing Fisherman). He had even fixed on the stern of his fishing boat a wooden plaque of a happy face with an open smile. 'Ah, Niko,' Onassis would tell him, 'there are only two happy people in the world, you and that face.'

At times he displayed an almost monkish loathing of the international socialites flocking to Monte Carlo and was glad to exchange the lot of them for an invitation to spend a weekend with Churchill at Chartwell – which he did finally receive. There is no doubt that he was much happier as Churchill's court jester than the *beau monde*'s king. Both Ari and Maria were romantic snobs, impressed by power, by names that had made history or that were old when history was young, but Maria's snobbery was highly theoretical. 'One' was 'normally' impressed by such people; therefore she must be too. Yet she would not sing for Churchill if she did not feel like it, nor would she take even a few steps out of her way to befriend the powerful and the great. Onassis, on the other hand, would turn his life upside down, and often did, especially when there was a chance of impressing, upsetting or irritating Niarchos. The vanity and rivalry of these two men, both parachutists into the established Greek shipping community, put in the shade any recorded rivalry between warring primadonnas. At times it seemed that they bought their ships, chose their friends, closed their deals and married their wives for the sole purpose of impressing each other.

Maria, who had no trouble identifying with most of Aristo's rivalries and enmities, never really understood this one. It was too personal, too irrational, too paranoid, and it threw a shadow over his life right to the end. A month before he died, knowing he was dying, he made Tryfon Koutalidis, Olympic's lawyer, swear that the fight against Niarchos would go on after his death. Maria, who knew Onassis as only love can know, could see how destructive this obsession was and begged him to put an end to it. Even the children, and especially Alexander, had been infected by it. They had been brought up to think of Niarchos as 'the other side' which, considering that he was married to their aunt Eugenia, their mother's elder sister, made things emotionally rather confusing for them.

At the time of the break-up of their parents' marriage, Alexander Onassis was twelve and Christina nine. They had instantly and instinctively turned against Maria. She was 'the other woman', 'the singer' as Alexander would call her to the end, who stole their father from their mother. They were not going to forgive her, especially as even after Tina had remarried they went on hoping their parents would come together again. In their minds 'the singer' was always the obstacle. Maria, who had no problem conquering a hostile audience, was quite lost when it came to conquering Aristo's children, even though she knew how much this meant to him. The first time she was in London after the beginning of their relationship she went to Harrods and spent a long time choosing cashmere sweaters and scarves for the children. Scornfully, Alexander and Christina left the presents unopened. Maria went on trying, but nothing changed. Christina was merely cold with her, but Alexander went out of his way to upset her, irritate her, if possible provoke an explosion. Zeffirelli remembers one hot August afternoon on the *Christina*: 'We had finished lunch and most people were getting ready to have a siesta. Maria always had an hour's siesta and all guests on the boat were expected either to do the same or to make sure they made no noise. Then suddenly in the middle of this marvellously peaceful afternoon there came a thundering noise and the boat began to rock. Alexander had chosen this moment not only to water-ski round the *Christina* but also to create an artificial storm with his speed-boat.'

It was only one of a series of practical jokes played on Maria by Alexander. Ari thought them all very funny, and not once did he take her side against the children. So although at first Maria complained, gradually she stopped, feeling that more might be achieved if she said nothing. Onassis, in fact, far from reconciling the children and Maria, used their dislike of her to his advantage: for at least as long as it was necessary to go on providing reasons and explanations, he would put forward the emotional upheaval it would cause the children as the main reason for not going ahead with their marriage.

There is no doubt that his children, and especially his son and heir, were extremely important to Onassis, even though he often treated Alexander as an extension of his own outsized ego rather than as his child. There was equally no doubt in anyone who saw them together that the children had closed their hearts to Maria long before, and had determined to dislike and resist everything about her – especially her clumsy attempts to win them over. Of course, if Onassis had really wanted to marry Maria, his children's wishes would have been firmly set aside, which is exactly what happened to them when he decided to marry Jackie, even though at the time the children were of an age to make their wishes much more clearly and unambiguously felt. Christina referred to her stepmother as 'my father's unhappy compulsion', and the kindest thing that Alexander had to say about Jackie was: 'My father needs a wife, but I don't need a mother.' In 1962 he did need a second mother, but he did not want 'the singer' in this role.

Meanwhile, on 27 February, the singer was singing again, at the Festival Hall in London. Included in the programme was 'Ocean! thou mighty monster', from

Oberon. It was the first time Maria had sung in English in public and it was also the first time that the English musical press turned against her. There were the complaints about the atmosphere on the night, with the fancy lighting and so many fancy unmusical people – an atmosphere reminiscent of pop singers and night-clubs and, according to *The Times*, 'unworthy of Miss Callas'. Then there were the comments on her voice, which rankled for days afterwards. 'It has been clear for some time that her voice has been sinking in pitch,' said the *Sunday Telegraph*. 'Her voice is now quite ugly, and even out of tune,' said *The Times*. But the audience was ecstatic. The orchestra stood up and joined in the applause and the social press gushed endlessly: 'Her voice is the magnet that has inexorably attracted a high-society audience from their planes, trains and cars which normally on the Friday before Whitsun would be rushing them out of the capital,' wrote Anne Lambton. Some magnet had certainly attracted them, but it had very little to do with her voice. At the interval there were many more references to the absence of Onassis than to Maria's middle register. After the concert Vergottis gave a supper party for Maria at the Savoy. The table was decorated with flowers shaped into a capital M and the guests around it included a fair proportion of the entries in *Debrett*: a Duke and his Duchess (Bedford), two Marquesses and their Marchionesses (Camden and Tavistock), a Knight and his Lady (Renwick), Dame Margot Fonteyn and assorted Esquires and their wives. 'I had the great joy,' said Maria later of Vergottis, 'of considering him more than my father because I never really had a father or a mother. I was very happy and he knew it, and he considered me his greatest joy. He was very proud to travel around with me and participate in my glory.' In many ways Vergottis was more than a father for Maria; very soon he became a surrogate husband, filling the gaps that Onassis left, frequently travelling with her wherever she was singing, always supportive, always ready to discuss everything with her, whether financial, artistic or personal, and always happy, as Maria put it, 'to participate in my glory'. All these were things that Maria needed but that Onassis was prepared to provide only intermittently and on his own terms.

After a ten-day tour of Germany, she was back in London for a recording of mezzo arias. 'Is Callas becoming a mezzo?' many critics were wondering. Because of the distinct breaks between her three registers, Maria had always sung with three 'voices' and even talked of 'my three voices'. She had worked hard all her life to produce seamless lines of sound in a constant struggle with technique, an unending battle to overcome the natural limitations of her voice. Now, when her upper register was becoming more difficult to control and the shrillness at the top more pronounced, Maria had to rely on her middle voice, which had always been full and mature. She contemplated the mezzo repertoire that could open in front of her. She saw herself as Dido, as Carmen, as the fiery Eboli; she recorded mezzo arias in London; two years later she even recorded the whole of *Carmen.* But imprisoned in her legend, and by now afraid of the hard work such a new careeer would involve, she dared not take the step that might have added years to her artistic life. At that moment she was too full of other hopes and later she would be too beaten.

That spring, while she was in London, Maria heard of her mother's attempted suicide in New York. On the table in Evangelia's hotel room were found a note to Maria, a note to the public and small gifts for her friends. A few days after she had been admitted to Roosevelt Hospital the doctor who had treated her wrote to Maria,

> Your mother, Mrs Evangelia Callas, was brought to The Roosevelt Hospital on Thursday, April 26, 1962. She stated that she had taken an indefinite amount of hypnotics in an attempt to injure herself .... Her hospital course was good, and it was felt that she could be discharged on April 29, 1962. She was seen by a psychiatrist in consultation, Dr William Boyce, who felt that while she is an unstable personality, it is reasonably safe to return her to her present environment.

Evangelia later spoke of her suicide attempt as another effort 'to rouse Maria'. Maria was roused, but even her concern was cold. A year later she was writing to Dr Lantzounis: 'If she is sick (mentally) tell me if it is necessary to put her in some good home – maybe in Europe where things are cheaper. I don't know – but please help me.'

In May Maria was in New York, but her godfather's attempts to persuade her to go and see her mother were all in vain.

On 19 May 1962 her life touched for the first time that of the woman who, six years later, was to take her place at the side, though never really in the heart, of Aristotle Onassis. It was at New York's Madison Square Garden, and the occasion was a star-studded celebration of President Kennedy's forty-fifth birthday. Maria's contribution was to sing the 'Habanera' and the 'Séguedille' from *Carmen.* She was wildly applauded by a packed crowd of 18,000. The next day she left for Milan and one of the greatest ordeals of her career.

She was due to sing two more performances of *Medea,* but at the rehearsals the sinus trouble she was suffering from made singing high or long notes intensely painful. On the first night, nerves and fears meant that she was in agony even before she opened her mouth, and when she did sing her first line *'Io? Medea!'* (I? Medea!), suddenly, and to the horror of everyone present, her voice cracked. The rest of the performance was a superhuman effort. The next morning unfavourable reviews were tinged with a note of sadness for a voice in shreds. The second *Medea* was the last time she ever sang at La Scala, but discussions and negotiations continued on all sorts of fronts and the list of might-have-beens grew with each month that passed: *Les Huguenots* with Sutherland, the Countess in *The Marriage of Figaro*; Monteverdi's *Poppea*; even *Tristan und Isolde.* More realistically a new Visconti production of *Trovatore* for Covent Garden, with Giulini conducting, was discussed again and again.

The mere thought of committing herself to a new production filled Maria with anguish, but it was psychologically important for her to keep the negotiations going and to close no more professional doors. She became the mistress of delaying tactics. 'Madame Callas,' wrote Sander Gorlinsky to David Webster, 'has pointed out to me that until now her fee at Covent Garden has been very low, considerably less than she receives in other opera houses, and this time she really wants a fee in accordance with her reputation and box office draw.' Negotiations over her fee would certainly keep the dialogue going for a little longer; then there could be negotiations over the tenor, the conductor, or rehearsal time. Only the most loyal opera managers – and David Webster was one of them – would play her game, having sensed that behind it lay anxiety rather than primadonna tactics and tantrums.

After the Scala *Medea,* Maria, heartbroken and weary, withdrew to the *Christina.* Ari was her great passion but at moments like that he was more: he was her liberator from the slavery to the voice, to reviewers and to the public's reactions. At the same time Aristo, more than anyone else before or after, could, with a word or even a look, tumble her into a state of self-conscious insecurity. He intensely disliked seeing her with glasses and had several times, and in the presence of others, told her that they made her look plain. And Maria, who never managed to wear her contact lenses without discomfort, kept carrying her glasses in her hand: putting them on to orientate herself and quickly taking them off again. So most of the time the world around her was hidden in a menacing mist – half-seen people and things that, as a result, took on a sinister vagueness. Beauties are traditionally measured by the havoc they cause but Maria never considered herself beautiful. She never liked her body; she was always self-conscious about her legs and she was only really confident about her long, expressive hands. 'She is not very beautiful,' Biki said, 'but she has that indefinable something that you find in certain animals like the hare, the eagle, the racehorse.'

The indefinable quality was something that Maria recognized and sought in others. 'It makes you feel like quicksilver, vibrant, alive,' she said once. 'To me it's a sign of energy and youth, call it what you will. Animals are like that, too – dogs look at you and try to see what is in your mind before you say it. I like to be with quick people, quick thinking, quick talking.' That quickness, that aliveness, was one of the things she most loved about Ari, even though on its negative side was the restlessness that she so much wished was not there. It is quite remarkable how little Maria tried to change him. He, on the other hand, could not resist playing Pygmalion. Having so far failed to persuade her to do a film, he took it on himself to change the way she dressed. His own clothes always suggested that he had several other things on his mind while dressing. Later on they would give rise to one of Jackie's most constant jibes: 'Look at him,' she would say. 'He must have 400 suits. But he wears the same *grey* one in New York, the same *blue* one in Paris, and the same *brown* in London.'

Yet his tastes in women's clothes were very definite and he would telephone Maria at Biki's during one of her fittings to make sure that his instructions were being followed. He loved her in black, and at that time Maria was ordering one black dress after another, even though her own favourite colours were red and turquoise. And always plenty of shawls. 'Not even the best fashion models,' remembers Biki, 'could wear shawls as Maria could. Like the ancient Greeks, she had a long torso and short legs, the exact opposite of a model's figure. But, what do you want, she wore clothes like no one else.' Onassis also made her change the way she did her hair. He sent her to Alexandre in Paris, who disposed of her long mane and created for her instead a short hairstyle – jollier, younger and more sophisticated. Maria was enjoying the transformation. Her readiness to change the outward appearance was part of her readiness to throw the old Callas away in search of a new identity.

On 4 November 1962, Maria broke her five-month silence to take part in a performance televised from the stage of Covent Garden. In her short Alexandre hairstyle, she looked young and radiant. She sang 'Tu che le vanità' from *Don Carlo,* followed by the 'Habanera' and the 'Séguedille' from *Carmen.* During the 'Habanera' her heavy diamond bracelet suddenly fell from her wrist. Without for a second stepping out of role, she went on singing and, with her unique sense of dramatic timing, she stooped at an appropriate moment on the stage, picked up the bracelet, put it on and continued. A potentially embarrassing moment had become part of the performance. Then once again she fell silent – this time for six months.

The year closed with a letter from the Welfare Department in New York informing Maria that her mother had applied for public assistance and that, in accordance with the law, she was 'responsible for her support to the extent of her ability to contribute'. The letter found Maria in a particularly bitter mood. Through her book, her appearance in a night-club and her attempted suicide, Evangelia had succeeded in finally making the breach with her daughter irreparable. Yet at that lowest point in their relationship, the daughter was obliged to begin supporting the mother. Afraid that the papers would find out about her mother being on welfare, Maria wrote urgently to her godfather giving him complete authority to reach a settlement. At the end of January she received a letter from him with the details of the agreement he had reached:

> I wrote to your Mother and to Mr Copeland of the Welfare Department to meet me in my office on Monday, January 28th. I found Mr Copeland to be a gentleman and a reasonable man and in front of him I told your Mother that if I ever hear that she makes a television or night-club appearance or anything that draws publicity I will stop her allowance the same day. Your Mother reassured me that no such thing will happen and Mr Copeland agreed that my request is extremely reasonable. Because your Mother's rent is $130.00 a month I gave her a check for $200.00 and promised her that every 25th to 28th of each month I will send her a check for $200.00. Of course I realize that with such a rent it is not enough, but if she can abstain from publicity for six months to a year I told her, and I am quite sure you will agree, you will increase her allowance.... Maria, your Mother left the office in good spirits and I hope she will keep her promise.

But Evangelia found it very difficult to abstain from publicity. When Maria read an interview her mother had given to the Italian magazine *Gente,* she exploded in a letter to her godfather: 'You have got to help me put *some* sense into her head and make her realize her position and shut her lovely mouth. Anyway that's like cancer. I'll never get rid of her and the consequences.' The letter was permeated by her fears and doubts: 'I have a wonderful friendship with the person you know,' she wrote, as so often in her letters referring to Onassis in the abstract rather than by name, 'but I think I have gone through too much and started working too early in life not to feel tired and with no enthusiasm left for anything.'

The year 1963 had begun in mingled hope and doubt and, whenever her relationship with Ari showed signs of flagging, her doubts re-awakened. Would she be able to keep him? Was she doing the right thing? Was she good enough? Maria, who wanted the perfect relationship at least as much as she had wanted the perfect performance, constantly blamed herself whenever real life with Aristo did not match her dream: if only she had planned things differently, surely there would have been no conflicts. At the beginning of their relationship she had found it much easier to relax and accept life as it unfolded, but now, three years later, she started feeling that, because it was only through effort that she had got everything she ever wanted in her life, it was only through effort that she would keep Onassis. However, this meant being and behaving as she thought Aristo would like her to instead of as she felt – and there are few things more frustrating. She began to feel that she was making for an enchanted land that was receding as she was approaching, and her longing for a future together made it, as time passed, much more difficult for her to enjoy their present. With no professional engagements to distract her, her life had merged with Aristo's: dinners at Maxim's, the races, other people's first nights, waiting for the dawn at Régine's, a medley of new clothes, new people, new sensations. Prince and Princess Radziwill – Stass and Lee – were among the new people. They had come into Ari's life shortly after he divorced Tina, and they were becoming an integral part of it. If Maria's life story were ever turned into opera, the first appearance of Lee Radziwill would be signalled by a hint of prophetic uneasiness in the music. It was Lee who, later in 1963, brought Onassis and her sister Jackie together. For the moment the Radziwills were simply a glamorous addition to the circle.

In a few months she would be forty, and she was driven to impose some order on what was for her a sprawling life given meaning by the fact that he was at its centre. Order meant marriage and children, and she knew that at her age having children was not something she could indefinitely postpone. She wanted to find peace in a domestic idyll; he could only find peace in excitement. 'After you reach a certain point,' Onassis had said, 'money becomes unimportant. What matters is success. The sensible thing would be for me to stop, but I can't. I have to keep aiming higher and higher – just for the thrill.'

While Onassis was aiming higher and higher, which included turning Lee Radziwill into a close friend, Maria had started working on her voice again, preparing for a recording of French arias at the beginning of May and for a concert tour of Europe that started in Berlin on 17 May and ended in Copenhagen on 9 June. Maria played it safe for these concerts both in her programming and in her singing, which at times sounded tentative and almost lifeless, though the old genius inevitably broke through here and there. 'I must find my joy in my music again,' Maria had said, but it turned out to be a nearly impossible undertaking – from now on there would be only glimpses of the old joy obscured by fears and anxiety. Afraid to compete with her own earlier self, she was just as afraid to stop. 'If I don't have my work, what do I do from morning to night? . . . I have no children, I haven't got a family . . . what do I do if I don't have my career? I can't just sit and play cards or gossip – I'm not the type.'

Work had become a necessary second best to children and a family. Even so, Maria, with Ari at her side, had no difficulty in doing virtually nothing for the whole of the summer except cruising on the *Christina* and seeing more of Greece. More of Greece included the rocky island of Skorpios, shaped like the scorpion that gives it its name, and covered with magnificent olive trees. Onassis fell instantly in love with it. 'You can even see Ithaca from it,' he said to Maria. His dream was that one day, through some kind of miracle, and despite its 58,000 people, he could buy Ithaca and become its modern Ulysses. When he saw Skorpios, ten miles to the north, he decided to abandon the chimera of owning Ithaca and buy instead the island nearest to it. He decided to buy it on the spot and to turn it into his paradise kingdom covered in olive groves, cypresses and bougainvillea, with a copy of the Cretan Palace of Knossos at the top of the hill.

Maria was on the *Christina* when she heard that Meneghini's attempt to change the terms of the separation order, and put the entire blame on her, had failed. But this was by no means the last Maria would hear of her ex-husband. From the Hôtel Hermitage where she was now staying when she was not on the *Christina,* she wrote to Dr Lantzounis:

> My husband is still pestering me after having robbed me of more than half my money – by putting *everything* in his name since we were married. Therefore *created* and took advantage of scandal to keep me in court and keep therefore my money. Italy is not America and I was a fool to marry him in Italy and more of a fool to trust him.

Very soon after the decision of the Milan court Meneghini announced to the press that Onassis had left Maria for Princess Radziwill, adding: 'I always knew their friendship would have a sad ending for Maria.' He was the only one drawing conclusions with such certainty, but there were plenty of others speculating about Onassis's friendship with Lee Radziwill. In the *Washington Post* the influential columnist Drew Pearson asked: 'Does the ambitious Greek tycoon hope to become the brother-in-law of the American President?' Even Robert Kennedy, with a political campaign round the corner, got worried. 'Just tell Lee to cool it, will you,' he told Jackie.

On 8 August, Lee broke off her holiday on the *Christina* to fly to her sister's bedside in hospital. Jackie had just given birth prematurely to her third child, a son, Patrick Bouvier Kennedy, who died next day with his father by his side. After the baby's funeral, Lee flew back to Athens, and over dinner described to Ari and Maria just how weak and desolate Jackie was. Onassis instantly offered to put the *Christina* at her disposal. Lee, no less instantly, rang her sister to pass on the invitation: 'Tell Jack that Stass and I will chaperone you,' she said. 'Oh Jackie, it would be such fun. You can't imagine how terrific Ari's yacht is, and he says we can go anywhere you want. It will do you so much good to get away for a while.' Jackie eagerly agreed. The President was much less enthusiastic, and so was Maria. Jack Kennedy could justify his lack of enthusiasm by reminding Jackie that during the Eisenhower administration Onassis had faced criminal charges of conspiring to defraud the American Government by not paying taxes on surplus American ships. The President could point out the possible political embarrassment such a cruise might cause. It was much harder for Maria to explain her own anxiety to herself, based as it was on nothing more solid than her intuitive conviction that the cruise would open a Pandora's box that she would never be able to close.

Without entirely knowing why, she railed bitterly against Ari. He was selfish, indifferent to her wishes, not bothering even to find out what they were. She sulked, she nagged, she implored and finally she gave notice: she was not going on the Jackie cruise. In that case, said Ari, I'm not going either. In fact he had all along intended to offer not to be present on the cruise so as to minimize the chances of political embarrassment for the President. It was a pretty safe diplomatic offer; he knew perfectly well that Jackie and Lee would never accept it. 'I could not accept his generous hospitality and then not let him come along,' explained Jackie. 'It would have been too cruel. I just couldn't have done that.' Nor did she.

At the beginning of October, Jackie arrived in Athens and a couple of days later the *Christina* set sail from Piraeus for Delphi. Onassis told the swarming reporters: 'We'll go where Mrs Kennedy wishes to go. She is in charge here. She's the captain.' Maria read what he said in Paris. The world press was full of the First Lady's Greek Cruise. In addition to the Radziwills, the President had asked Frank Roosevelt, the Under-Secretary of Commerce, and his wife Sue to accompany Jackie. 'Your presence will lend respectability to the whole thing,' he told Roosevelt. The other guests were Princess Irene Galitzine and her husband, Accardi Gurney, a bachelor friend of Lee's, and Onassis's sister Artemis with her husband. 'Onassis is no more conscious of his wealth than Rock Hudson is of his good looks,' Jackie was to say later, looking back on the cruise. Just for her, the *Christina*'s crew of sixty had been augmented by two hairdressers, a masseuse and an orchestra for dancing in the evening; just for her the *Christina* had been stocked with eight varieties of caviar, fresh fruit that had been flown in from Paris, rare vintage wines and buckets of red mullet packed in ice.

The first stop was Lesbos and the second Crete, but the photographers looked in vain for Onassis among the party disembarking from the *Christina.* To avoid too much adverse publicity, Ari had offered to stay on board whenever they were in port. But he knew very well that the next port of call was Smyrna, nor was he surprised when Jackie, Lee and everybody else aboard insisted that they could not go sightseeing around his birthplace without him as their guide. So four years after he had, full of emotion, shown Maria round the landmarks of his childhood, Ari found himself revisiting his past once more, this time with Jackie at his side and the world's press in full pursuit. The picture of a radiant Jackie next to a relaxed Ari was flashed round the world. In the House of Representatives, a Republican Congressman questioned the conduct of the President's wife, while in Paris Maria was asking herself questions about Ari's motives and, much more important, Ari's love. The President called Jackie to plead with her to return to Washington, and Maria called Ari to ask what exactly was going on. But the *Christina* sailed serenely on her way. On the last night of the cruise, Ari showered his guests with parting gifts: Lee got a string of pearls; for Jackie, however, there was an array of gifts crowned by a massive diamond and ruby necklace. There was no longer any doubt as to which of the two sisters he preferred.

'Jackie has stars in her eyes – Greek stars,' said a member of the White House staff when Jackie returned home on 17 October.

Maria's eyes were full of angry fire. It took all of Maggie van Zuylen's ingenuity to mollify her and reconcile her with Ari. Once they were reconciled, Maria could allow herself to feel all the joy of having him back – and to show it. But they were not together for long; Ari was soon off doing his business round the world. On 22 November, just over a month after he had come back from the cruise, he was in Hamburg launching a tanker. It was there that he heard the news of Jack Kennedy's assassination. He flew immediately to Washington, and William Manchester remembers him in the White House the night after the funeral. 'Rose Kennedy dined upstairs with Stass Radziwill; Jackie Kennedy, her sister and Robert Kennedy were served in the sitting room. The rest of the Kennedys ate in the family dining-room with their house guests, MacNamara, Phyllis Dillon, Dave Powers and Aristotle Onassis, the shipowner, who provided comic relief of sorts. They badgered him mercilessly about his yacht, and his Man of Mystery aura. During coffee the Attorney General, Robert Kennedy, came down and drew up a formal document stipulating that Onassis give half his wealth to help the poor in Latin America. It was preposterous (and obviously unenforceable), and the Greek millionaire signed it in Greek.' It was like an Irish wake. A desperate gaiety had seized everybody, including Jackie, who could not stay on her own for a second. In this atmosphere Ari the comedian came to the fore – his repertoire ranging from subtle jesting for the tragic court to crude, red-nosed buffoonery.

He flew back to Paris in time to celebrate Maria's fortieth birthday. The shuttle between the two women had begun.

Chapter Twelve

MARIA was apprehensive. She could feel the most precious thing in her life, her relationship with Aristo, slipping away from her. Back in Paris, Ari was elated. At a time when the world's eyes were on the White House, he had manoeuvred himself into its innermost circle; and Ari the self-dramatist was enjoying the recounting of the tale at least as much as the experience. Maria was not surprised by his elation. She knew well by now that when it came to the famous, Ari was like a dipsomaniac with the bottle, so she simply listened patiently to his detailed account of the Kennedy wake. But she desperately needed something to clutch on to, something to bolster herself with. In her mind's eye the old triumphs trooped by in all their glory, helping her to make her decision. She wrote to David Webster at Covent Garden. Yes, she was ready to do *Tosca*, but she would only do it if it was *now*. It was now that she needed the healing absorption of work. Zeffirelli was already at Covent Garden directing *Rigoletto*. He was the man Maria had phoned before she sent her letter to Webster: 'Franco, I'll do it if you'll help me.'

Zeffirelli had six weeks in which to mount a brand new production as well as carry on with *Rigoletto*. At first everyone at the Opera House thought it was madness, and was violently against giving in to the caprices and last-minute decisions of La Callas, but Webster's and Zeffirelli's enthusiasm soon became infectious. No detail was too small for Zeffirelli. In an Indian shop in London he found the sensational stole – six feet long and six feet wide – that Maria was to wear in the second act, and he spent hours in Covent Garden's paint shop, overseeing costumes being sprayed and backcloths painted. It was there that the critic Clive Barnes found him when he went to interview him: 'Do you always do two productions at once, Franco?' The boyish smile was even more disarming than usual: 'No . . . sometimes it's three.'

The rehearsals were pure joy. Zeffirelli, Maria and Tito Gobbi – perhaps the greatest Scarpia ever – had come together to create a masterpiece out of one of the most popular operas in all music. *Tosca,* which has been described, not altogether unfairly, as 'a shabby little shocker', was transformed in their hands into an unforgettable dramatic experience. So total was the absorption of Gobbi and Maria in their roles that when, during a full dress rehearsal, three days before opening night, Maria's wig brushed against a lighted candle and caught fire, she went on singing, and continued to do so even as smoke poured from behind her head and Tito Gobbi rushed across the stage to put the fire out. At another rehearsal, the blade of the retractable knife that Maria was using to kill Scarpia did not slide back into the handle, but she was so totally enveloped in Tosca that she noticed it only after she had drawn blood, and only just in time to avoid plunging the knife right into him. It was Gobbi's turn now to remain in character; he gasped a horrified 'My God', and continued with the scene.

Maria would ring Tito every morning to discuss with him what new ideas she had had, what changes she felt they could make, what to concentrate on in the morning's rehearsals. Even after she had stopped singing, right up until the time she died, Maria would ring Tito: 'I don't have anything to say,' she would tell him. 'I just need to hear your voice.'

There was a deep, instinctive understanding between the two of them and Zeffirelli, who had determined not to do *Tosca* until he could find the soprano with the dramatic personality to bring his vision of the role to life. He had found her in Maria. 'I wanted her played as an exuberant warm-hearted, rather sloppy, casual woman, a kind of Anna Magnani of her time. . . . Well, Maria carried it off, creating this magnetic, temperamental creature. From her entrance to her exit she held the audience absolutely breathless.' In the first act Tosca rushes to the church to see her lover Mario Cavaradossi who is painting an altar there. She erupts with jealousy when she suspects he has been unfaithful to her, and only when he convinces her that he has not does she begin to calm down. 'Even though she is in church,' said Zeffirelli looking back on Maria's performance, 'she begins to talk about making love with Cavaradossi. She giggles and laughs and hugs and kisses him, then pulls herself together saying, "No, don't touch me in front of the Madonna. . . ." They might have had it right there in the church. Tosca was ready.'

As opening night approached panic began to grip her again. For the first time since Onassis had become the main focus of her life, she was rediscovering the exhilaration she used to find in her work. She was living an existence utterly remote from Aristo and his world, and she was feeling almost grateful that she could still use her art as a shield against being totally submerged by him. But she could not, hard as she tried, keep the panic at bay. She developed a high temperature and all the symptoms of bronchitis. When Tuesday 21 January dawned, her temperature was still over a hundred. She knew by now that all these symptoms began in her head, her nerves and her fears, and she refused to give in to them. She even refused to let David Webster make an announcement before the performance asking for the audience's understanding. As it turned out, it was the last thing she needed. The opening performance was an unqualified triumph.

Maria had first sung Tosca in Athens when she was eighteen. Now she was forty, and the sensuality she brought to the part was new to her and revolutionary for the audience, used to grand Toscas in massive robes with walking-sticks, gloves and large feathered hats. She also plumbed new levels of distress and jealousy that had eluded her even in her memorable *Tosca* recording twelve years earlier. What sounded like a childish tantrum in the 1952 recording became, in 1964, the deep suffering of a woman torn with jealousy: new depths of sensuality, new depths of jealousy, but also new depths of tenderness. Her eighteen months of absence from the operatic stage, full of emotional experience as they were, had brought forth a rich harvest of dramatic truth, and on the first night the audience, fired by that truth, acknowledged her come-back and triumph with a huge standing ovation.

'She has done as much for Italian opera as Verdi,' Zeffirelli has said. That night at Covent Garden, no one would have been inclined to find exaggeration in his statement. If what art brings to us is in itself only one half of the experience, the other half being what we bring to art, then part of Maria's greatness was to *make* the audience bring more to the experience, and give more of themselves to it. She did this as well as bringing more of herself to the part than anyone else before her. Although throughout her career she lost no opportunity to tell the world how little she liked *Tosca*, it was the vehicle for one of her greatest dramatic creations. Not only did she redeem the gruesome plot and bring magic to the audience – which others, after all, had done before her – but she broke away from all convention and revealed depths in the role that few suspected were there. She also managed to achieve the near-impossible feat of transforming 'Vissi d'arte' from a disconnected showpiece into an integral part of the musical drama – a powerful account of what was going on in her soul, mind and body at that moment. Zeffirelli's production, still unsurpassed in London, Paris or New York, strengthened the music's menacing undertones, emphasized its violence and made primitive passions and emotions instantly credible. The second act set, with sinister shadows cast on the long wall from the light of a roaring log-fire, looked like Hell, which is what Zeffirelli had intended. 'The action,' he explained, 'is exactly like what takes place in the arena during a bull-fight. Each of the characters in turn is the bull and the matador.' And the characters remained in character throughout. 'Maria,' remembers Tito Gobbi, who loved her and adored working with her, 'was Tosca every second of the performance. The way she moved and sang, the way she listened to colleagues when *they* sang. She filled dramatic pauses with her presence, her ability to sustain tension. She was genuine, authentic without the old clichés. If something unexpected occurred – one night Maria accidentally fell down – it was absorbed into the drama. No one in the audience knew we hadn't planned it that way. We adjusted, we felt totally free to realize our parts. Better than Callas we will never see.'

The celebrated rape scene that has now become part of the *Tosca* tradition was born in a moment of dramatic inspiration. 'I pursued her, but she knew she couldn't get away and in her frenzy instead of running from me, she finally ran towards me, this poor, frail woman, and began beating me on my big chest with her fists. . . . I burst into sadistic laughter . . . then, with all my force, I grasped her hands and opened them up, then spread her arms, crucifying her. Maria knew at once what I was doing and responded with such suffering. It was a totally spontaneous thing that happened between us.' Maria's palpable suffering and humiliation made it much easier to identify a few minutes later with her vengeful fury. Her cries of '*Muori dannato! Muori! Muori! Muori!*' (Die, damned one! Die! Die! Die!) were so spine-chilling that, as Dulcie Howard put it, 'even if the knife wound had not been fatal, Scarpia could not have gone on living under the barrage of such implacable hatred.'

The reviews of the London *Tosca* seemed to reach new heights of adulation: 'A performance of indescribable brilliance and fascination'; 'No other living singer could come within a mile of her'; 'Her voice has rarely sounded more warm and vibrant'; 'How am I to describe the full magic of that performance?'; '. . . a great artist at the top of her dramatic and musical form'. Last year's obituaries were forgotten and instead everyone was talking of the turn of the tide.

On the morning of her third *Tosca*, the *Guardian* carried a sensational open letter to Maria from Neville Cardus – doyen of English music critics – reviewing her entire career and proposing a dramatic change for the future. 'Really, dear Madame Callas . . . your admirers are your worst enemies. They actually protest overmuch that your voice is "better than ever". For my own part I could almost wish that it had worsened. Then there would be some hope of your liberation from more or less brainless parts in Italian opera. A high shriek is fatal to a singer appearing as Norma, Elvira, Lucia, or any of that kind.

But a high shriek could be a histrionic asset if you are acting with body, eyes, temperament as well as voice, Kundry in *Parsifal* or Elektra or Salome in Strauss's operas. . . . Opera for you now is the ranging world of Wagner, Strauss, Berg and other composers who could give your intelligence something to get its teeth into and kindle the Callas imagination, flammable now surely from hot kindling of personal experience. . . . There is still time left to you to fulfil this destiny. . . .'

Time there was: what was lacking was the commitment and the passion needed to embark on a new career. 'What will-power must have gone into your career,' an interviewer exclaimed once. Maria corrected him: 'Not will-power. Love . . .' And now love was driving her elsewhere. For another eighteen months, Maria would draw on her reserves of will-power, the echoes of the love she had put into her work and the deep faith that Michel Glotz and Georges Prêtre had in her; the result would at times look like a new beginning based on a new maturity. In the spring of 1964, at the EMI studios in Paris, the future looked very different. With the triumphant *Toscas* behind her, she wanted to do more, to prove to herself and the world that her vocal problems belonged to the past, that they had somehow been 'solved'. With Nicola Rescigno conducting, she began recording Rossini, Donizetti and Verdi arias, but some were only released years later, while others have never been issued at all.

In the middle of the recording, she received a telegram from New York informing her that her father was critically ill at Lenox Hill Hospital and that before he was admitted, he had got married to Alexandra Papajohn, who for years had effectively been his wife. Maria's concern at her father's critical condition was overshadowed by her outrage at his remarriage and at the way she had found out about it. She sent a telegram to her godfather:

RECEIVED CABLE FROM PAPAJOHNS ABOUT FATHER BEING OPERATED AGAIN AND CRITICALLY ILL PLEASE FIND OUT AS I AM RECORDING AND CANNOT MOVE WAS SHOCKED AT HIS MARRIAGE PLUS TRIP TO NEW YORK BOTH ABSOLUTE SECRETS TILL YOUR LETTER MOST

DISGUSTED AND UNHAPPY SORRY TO BOTHER YOU BUT AM IN FULL WORKING SEASON LOVE MARIA.

The news added to Maria's nervousness and anxiety during the recording sessions and, as always, it showed in her voice. At one particularly rough session, she was so nervous that Michel Glotz called a break to calm everyone. During the break he played a tape of 'Ritorna vincitor' from *Aida,* which Régine Crespin had recorded for EMI the previous day. Nicola Rescigno recalls the transformation that then took place. 'This is not Verdi or *Aida,*' she said. 'It's like a funeral march. Come on, Nicola, let's do it.' And just like that, with all Maria's fire and passion, they did it in a single take.

The incident holds a key to Maria's gradual withdrawal. Her passion, her mind, her experience and her genius – they were all still there, but most of the time Maria herself was not there with them. 'Maria,' said Zeffirelli once, 'found in her art an outlet for all her problems.' As her problems with Onassis were growing, she needed the outlet all the more. She needed it, but she did not want it. Zeffirelli, who at the beginning of May arrived in Paris to start rehearsing with her for a new production of *Norma*, knew that. 'Artistically she had travelled the full road, so, at a certain point, she tried to do the same in her personal life. She was simply reaching up.' Neville Cardus had urged her to fulfil what he saw as her destiny, but Maria knew that her artist's destiny was not the only one, and she was reaching up for that other destiny that included her art and so much more besides.

There is no doubt that if Maria had had her wish she would by this time have been nursing a baby, with Aristo at her side. But what she was doing instead was rehearsing *Norma* for her first full opera in Paris and the last new production she would ever do. During the rehearsals she received demands for $4,338.37 for her father's hospital bills. Before an opening, her housekeeper Bruna had orders to hide from her any letters or telegrams that might disturb her, but, on this occasion, the letter got to her. 'Tell my father not to give my address to people,' she wrote to her godfather. But what came out much more strongly in her letter was her bitterness at the thought that another – a 'stranger', as she put it – was now closer to her father than she was: 'So dear Leo, make it quite plain to him. He chose others. He can keep them. I'm out for good. . . . I hate to offend the Papajohns but as friends all is well. As my stepmother etc, I do not care to have any relation of any sort. I'm too old for such nonsense. . . . I hope the newspapers don't catch on. Then I'll really curse the moment I had any parents at all.' And there was a P.S.: 'Please keep me informed and don't let him die where I might be criticized.'

When she was under pressure, Maria could not think of anyone except herself. Every event, even the most dramatic, was seen through calculating eyes. And the time leading up to the opening night of *Norma* was full of tension. She gave everything of herself to the part. Zeffirelli remembers how he begged her to be prudent, to avoid unreasonable vocal challenges. 'I can't, Franco,' she kept saying. 'I won't do what Anna Moffo does in *Traviata*. I won't skim through my music. I have to take chances even if it means a disaster and the end of my career.'

She knew that she could, if she wanted to, avoid the danger of the high notes altogether; she also knew, as Zeffirelli kept telling her, that most people would not have known the difference, and those who did, if they really understood what Callas was, would not have cared in the least. But when Maria left out a high note, as she did in Kansas City in her Lucia, she could not help feeling that she had cheated, and her pride, her conscience, would simply not accept it. She may not have followed Zeffirelli's vocal advice but being around him was exhilarating for her. 'During *Norma*,' remembers Zeffirelli, 'I felt her great beauty constantly. I tried to feed this great beauty back to her in every way I could. I admired her, complimented her. Everything I did was to make her look better, to reflect to the public what I saw in her, what she was for me.'

At this time, when Onassis was bringing out all her insecurities and feelings of unworthiness, she needed more than ever Zeffirelli's reassurance. Everything in Zeffirelli's *Norma* was designed to enhance the beauty and the new, deep softness that Maria brought to it. It was an exquisitely romantic production, all four acts taking place in a great forest in which the foliage changed with each season. Maria was swathed in silk and chiffon, and in the second act she seemed to float – a vision of a thousand shades of cream, pink, apricot and lilac. The reviews varied widely depending upon which of the eight performances the critic saw, and which act he was focusing on. 'Sublime from the second act onwards,' wrote Claude Samuel about her first *Norma*; 'The best first act since 1952,' wrote Harold Rosenthal about her fifth; but it was the fourth *Norma*, on 6 June, that was soon to become part of the Callas legend. The excitement that had surrounded her first full-scale appearance at L'Opéra reached, that night, its climax. Onassis, who had missed the first night, arrived for the fourth with Princess Grace and the Begum Aga Khan. Their presence, together with that of Charlie Chaplin and most of his large family, Rudolf Bing, Yves St Laurent, members of the French government and numerous socialites, turned a fourth night into the big *Norma* night with all the trappings of a gala. From the first notes the faithful in the audience knew that a battle between Maria and the Voice was being fought in front of them. Every phrase was rife with danger. The gala trappings, the all-pervading sense of being judged, Aristo's presence – they had all brought out the tremulous Maria lurking inside the grandeur and aloofness of the great Norma.

Her most passionate admirers and her most implacable detractors seemed to have made L'Opéra, that Saturday night, their meeting place. Up to the beginning of the last act, although Maria had missed a few of her high notes, there had been no opportunity for a real showdown. It came during the final scene when Maria broke on a critical high C. Most people present had never heard a professional singer break in public. While the bulk of the audience was suffering with her, there was uproar from the anti-Callas faction: whistling, booing and shouts of 'Take her back to her dressing-room'. Maria raised her hand and motioned the orchestra to start again. It was an extraordinary risk. And she won. The note was perfectly placed and the audience went mad. But it was by no means the end of it. This cracked high C unleashed such passions that they overflowed into the corridors of L'Opéra after the performance. Someone shouted 'It's a disgrace!'. 'You know nothing of art!' yelled a Callasite in reply. A respectable old lady was seen pulling the glasses off another of the enemy faction. Yves St Laurent actually kicked the shins of yet another. Eventually, the Republican Guard had to be called in to break up fist-fights. While Maria was being embraced and congratulated by Princess Grace, the Chaplins, Rudolf Bing and, of course, Aristo, the fighting continued. And it was still going on when she left the Opera House in Onassis's Rolls Royce with a few hundred admirers covering first her, and then the car, in flowers.

Rudolf Bing remembered later that when he went backstage to her dressing-room he did not know whether or not to refer to the episode of the note that broke. 'It's like a woman wearing a very low-cut dress, you're not sure whether it's more rude to look or not to look. I decided not to mention it and she never mentioned it either.' She never mentioned it but she was haunted by it. 'It hurts to feel hated,' she said later. And she did feel hated – hated and humiliated and even more sure than before that what she was hankering after was not going to be found through her work. 'Oh, why can't I sing Norma in a forest all alone, me and the moon, instead of having to go through this,' she said to Zeffirelli when they were alone in her dressing-room.

Having Aristo next to her at such a time was like a balm. She needed his strength and his love and she needed him there as a focus for *her* love. He, on his part, loved her more now than after her greatest triumphs. Her vulnerability brought out in him the urge to protect her, to shelter her from pain. He talked to her of Skorpios, of its olive groves and its sparkling sea, of leaving Paris the moment she was free. He promised, like a god who has such things to give, to make her happy.

They left Paris as soon as the last *Norma* was over. At the beginning of July she had to come back for her long-awaited recording of *Carmen* with Georges Prêtre conducting and Nicolai Gedda as Don José. She looked tanned, radiant and had a few extra Greek-fed pounds on her. The Salle Wagram, where the recording was being made, windowless and desperately hot, felt like a prison compared to the Mediterranean she had just left and to which she longed to return. As far as she was concerned, *Carmen* could not be finished fast enough. The sessions seemed interminable and, as if the elements conspired to make it even more so, torrential rain with thunder on the last Saturday of the recording made it necessary to repeat the celebrated quintet in the second act about twelve times. A private plane was standing by, ready to whisk her away the minute it was all over.

It was a blissful summer. They spent hours making plans for Skorpios and spinning dreams. He wanted a full moon for every moonlit night; she wanted eternal summer; he wanted to grow tobacco plants like the ones they had in Smyrna, tall, ungainly plants that flowered and scented only at night and closed up their hoods and withered during the day – they reminded him of himself, he said; she, more realistically, wanted the island always in bloom. They spoke Greek all the time, and by now Maria's Greek was almost as perfectly idiomatic as his. Many friends noticed just how devoted they seemed, and how eager he was to have her share his every thought and include her in all his plans for the future; so much so that rumours began to float about that they had already been secretly married in Las Vegas. They had not been married but they were definitely having a honeymoon.

One of the plans discussed during that happy summer was that of turning Maria into a shipowner. Vergottis, who spent part of the summer with them on the *Christina*, was full of enthusiasm for the idea and he promised to find the perfect ship for her. In September he called them to announce that he had found it: it was a tanker of 27,000 tons, it was called *Artemision II* and it cost $3.9 million. Over dinner on the *Christina* the three of them decided to go ahead and make an offer. Just over a month later, on 31 October, the ship had been bought by Overseas Bulk Carriers, the company set up by Vergottis to operate it. Maria bought a twenty-five per cent holding in the company, Vergottis another twenty-five per cent and Onassis fifty, the plan being that he would later give Maria twenty-six per cent of his share, thus establishing her as the majority shareholder. All these details would, in time, become the mouldy fodder of the English courts, but on the night of 31 October they were part of the discussion among the three of them during a celebration dinner at Maxim's to congratulate Maria on becoming a shipowner. 'Greek men sharpen their wits over things,' she said later, 'I admired their conversation which is not the usual gossip and dress conversation. . . . They loved discussing business and I kept pestering them in a nice way, an affectionate way.' She kept pestering them, wanting to find out more, to absorb more, to understand better Ari's world.

In just over a month she would be forty-one and she was ready to take on anything – including living two lives to the full. Professional life at her high competitive level is too demanding for most human beings, and fashionable life, if taken seriously, can be tougher still. In 1965 she tried to live both at once, squandering her energy as though she was running out of time – which in a sense she was.

On the day after her forty-first birthday, she began her recording of *Tosca,* which was to be followed in the new year with eight performances of *Tosca* for L'Opéra. A few days before opening night on 19 February, France Musique broadcast an hour-long interview with Maria. At times she sounded like a Chinese sage: 'Those who have fear cannot reach great heights', or 'If you are not sure of something, do not risk'. This last statement was curiously prophetic. Up to this time her entire life had been a stark contradiction of it; but from the end of 1965, it became more true with every year that passed that Maria would not take risks unless she could be sure of succeeding.

She opened in *Tosca* in a state of euphoria fully justified by the ecstatic reception she received. The entire Zeffirelli production, which had been brought over from London, was a triumph, and Maria even agreed to sing an additional, ninth, performance on 13 March.

The next day she flew to New York for two performances of *Tosca*, which, as one critic put it, 'became personal triumphs of the wildest, most rewarding, insistent kind.' From Paris, she had written to her godfather: 'I hope the lawyers of the doctors don't sue me upon my arrival. I would hate that.' But there was no danger; Leo Lantzounis had made arrangements for the bills to be paid in instalments from the money Maria was sending him for her parents. Her father had recovered by now, but the days when he was present at Maria's first nights, sharing her triumphs, were past. 'I wish you were my father,' Maria had written to Leo. And it was Leo and his wife who were there on 19 March, when Maria opened in *Tosca*. Fausto Cleva was conducting, Franco Corelli was Cavaradossi and Tito Gobbi once again Scarpia. The Met was sold out weeks ahead and standing-room went on sale the Sunday before. On Thursday evening there was already a long line of standees armed with sleeping-bags, blankets, pillows and a banner which they hung on the front of the opera house: 'Welcome Home, Callas.'

Seven years had passed since Maria's last appearance at the Met on 5 March 1958 – also as Tosca. The artistic conditions under which she had to work were, if anything, worse: she was expected to sing in one of the oldest and ugliest productions of *Tosca* with scenery that was actually shaking; she was not given a single stage rehearsal and there was only one piano rehearsal in a studio with no light and no props. Yet not once did Maria complain, even though on top of everything she had not been consulted on the choice of conductor. Opera officials watched her in amazement. Many, still tied to the apron strings of the romantic myth, were worried that the cooling of her personality might have put out the fire of her voice. 'She's mellowed so much,' said one, 'I bet she's lost the fire of her performance.' But the flame was as incandescent as ever. A huge house was there to bear witness to the fact and a huge crowd was outside waiting – some hoping for a miracle that would get them a seat, some watching the celebrities arrive. Suddenly, a few moments before curtain up, the crowd began to applaud. All eyes turned in the same direction: Mrs John F. Kennedy, still very much an American heroine, had arrived.

The atmosphere was electric from the outset. At the

sound of Tosca's first 'Mario', still off-stage, the audience gasped. Her entrance was greeted with a roar of applause which went on for an astounding four minutes. The conductor had no option but to stop the orchestra and wait for it, if not to die out, at least to quieten. Maria froze, and not for a second, while the applause was going on, did she step out of character. It was at the end of the performance during the sixteen curtain-calls that she displayed that special Callas genius for acknowledging applause. The performance was scheduled to end at 10.40. It finished at 11.40, the extra hour having been taken up by the audience cheering, breaking into the middle of scenes and applauding, applauding, applauding.

From *The New York Times*, the *Washington Post*, *Opera News*, the *Saturday Review*, *The New Yorker*, *Time* and a score of other papers, there sounded the same celebratory note.

> 'Miss Callas entered, and all things came to a halt....'
>
> 'A gasp went through the audience.'
>
> 'Her conception of the role was electrical.'
>
> 'Miss Callas is a unique creature – already, in fact, a legend....'
>
> 'Her face mirrored even fleeting expressions implicit in the music....'
>
> 'She was an electrifying figure on the stage, youthful, graceful, sensitive, beautiful to contemplate – and she lived the role as no other singer within my memory ...'
>
> 'If she did not care to sing a note, she would still rank among the genuine dramatic interpreters of our time.'
>
> 'Hands. Just to watch Miss Callas's hands at work almost recreated the opera. They caressed, stretched out in love and hatred, fluttered helplessly like a caged bird.... At times she even sang through her hands.'
>
> 'The stage presence shown by Callas in her performance would have raised the hackles on a deaf man.'
>
> 'Her performance raised all kinds of hope that even the minor, trivial, technical problems of her recent years may be behind her. In any case, in fair days and foul, the

> Callas singing has been the voice of pure and palpable passion.'
>
> 'Here we have a woman who, like her or not, is the most important person singing in opera today. Her greatness is in her fierce and all-pervasive power to realize every dramatic nuance of a character and to recreate that realization through the overwhelming use of her body and voice.'
>
> 'Anyone, admirer or not, must admit that she has earned the right to stand at the top of a pyramid, with a total production – scenery, direction, conductor and cast – designed upwards in a consistent structure.'

But standing at the top of a pyramid felt much more like a burden than a privilege to Maria. It was as if with each celebratory adjective and with each adulatory word she read, the load she carried was becoming heavier. 'After all,' she said in an interview with David Holmes, 'what is the legend? The public made me.' The legend had become an adversary who fed off her. The more she identified with it, the greater the responsibility she felt towards it, the greater the fear that she might betray it. News of her New York triumph had very quickly reached Paris and everybody was expecting her to return exhilarated; instead she arrived exhausted. There were five performances of *Norma* at the Paris Opera looming up and then *Tosca* at Covent Garden. But first there was a special edition of 'The Great Interpreters', a television programme in which she sang arias from *Manon, La Sonnambula* and *Gianni Schicchi,* and after which she received hundreds of letters thanking her for 'meeting the people' in this fashion and urging her to do more of it.

The first night of *Norma* at L'Opéra was on 14 May. In the last few days the fear had been mounting. On the night itself, full of injections and medicines, Maria felt that she could not even walk to the stage. In a talk with John Ardoin – her most moving outpouring on tape – she talked with pain of the gulf between the legend on the stage and Maria in her dressing-room. 'Can you go and tell them, John,' she said, or rather cried out, 'that I am a human being and I have my fears. . . . when they only see you sparkling under the lights, the limelights . . . how can people know you? How can newspapermen know you?'

She did go on. An announcement was made asking for the audience's understanding. It turned out to be unnecessary for the first performance, but very necessary for the second. By the third, Fiorenza Cossotto had replaced Maria's old friend Giulietta Simionato as Adalgisa. The understanding Maria had asked from the audience had so far been automatically extended to her by all her colleagues, who sensed the agony she was going through. Cossotto was the exception. Zeffirelli remembers with anger what happened: 'In the duet, Norma and Adalgisa must sing in close harmony holding hands. When Maria would signal to end a phrase, Cossotto would ignore her sign and hold on to the final note for a few extra seconds. So ungenerous. Maria was hurt by this. I went backstage and swore to her I would never work with her again. And I never have.' But this did not help during the next three performances that Maria had to sing with her. Fiorenza Cossotto was determined to outsing the great Callas. It was hardly an achievement, as even Maria's most ardent fans would acknowledge that Cossotto, with her thoroughbred voice, could securely grasp high notes that Maria only snatched at.

The night of Maria's last *Norma,* 29 May, was another gala night, with the Shah of Iran in the audience. Maria's doctor had tried to persuade her not to go on, so shattered were her nerves, but she found the prospect of facing the uproar of yet 'Another Callas Cancellation' even harder than the prospect of her performance. She went ahead. By the third act, it was clear to those close to her that she could not finish. To top it all, Cossotto treated their big duet like a duel. It was painful to watch Maria desperately trying to keep up with her rival singing at full voice. She practically sleep-walked through the end of the third act, and as soon as the curtain came down, she collapsed and was carried unconscious to her dressing-room.

The curtain fell never to rise again. An hour later, supported by two men, Maria left L'Opéra for ever. 'Forgive me – I shall return to win your forgiveness,' she whispered to the waiting crowd. Her eyes were moist, her face white; she was crushed, and the crowd had sensed it. After her Rome 'walk-out', there had been an uproar against her, but now, apart from the few Cossotto supporters bursting into cheers for their favourite and catcalls for Maria, it was as if the audience was stretching out to give her of their strength and their love.

At the zenith of her power, ten years earlier, she had been asked how she felt about the endless controversy surrounding her. 'When my enemies stop hissing,' she had said with that mock aggressiveness behind which she hid her fears, 'I shall know I'm slipping.' They had not entirely stopped hissing, but their hisses were only a faint, hesitant echo of the past. As Maria's nightmare was beginning, the bulk of the audience was shouting 'Bravo'. In the pain of her breakdown, everything seemed meaningless. She knew she could not go on singing without destroying herself, and she also knew, with that clarity that pain often brings, that the hectic gaiety of Onassis's world was not where happiness, let alone meaning, could be found.

'What are we in search of? Have you ever thought of that, John? What are we in search of today?' she asked John Ardoin. The life inside her was crying out for some clue to existence. She could find no such clue but at least for the moment there was her love for Aristo and his love for her from which she could draw hope. She would use this love to ward off despair, but in the process her love itself became desperate.

Meanwhile four *Toscas* in London loomed threateningly ahead of her. Maria could not bear either to contemplate or to cancel them. Georges Prêtre talked to her on the phone before he left for London; she told him nothing of her fears. Her suite at the Savoy was waiting for her and her plane ticket had been bought. The Friday before the Monday she was due to arrive in London, she was seen and photographed at the Rothschild Ball in Paris. The Wednesday after she was due to arrive – forty-eight hours before she was due to sing – the London papers were full of 'the mystery of missing Maria Callas'. In the evening, she rang David Webster at home. She was ill; her blood pressure was dangerously low and her doctors would not allow her to travel, let alone sing four performances. Panic broke out: people had been queueing around Covent Garden for five nights to get tickets; all performances were sold out; Georges Prêtre and Tito Gobbi were waiting for her to start rehearsing; and the last performance was a Royal Gala in the presence of the Queen. David Webster talked to the doctors, then he talked to Maria in Paris, then he talked to Maria again and again, and finally he got on a plane and arrived on her doorstep. He pleaded with her to sing at least once, at the Royal Gala; and Maria, who genuinely cared for Webster, gave in.

Marie Collier took over the first three performances and Maria herself arrived at the Savoy on 3 July. The following night, on the eve of the performance, in a room next to hers, a Canadian businessman did not sleep. Maria spent the whole night singing Tosca – beautifully, according to her neighbour. But she knew that singing Tosca beautifully alone in her room was no guarantee that she would sing it beautifully on the night itself. She had said as much herself a few years earlier. 'I say to my friends, if I had a performance tonight look how beautifully I'd sing. But probably if I did have the performance then I would say just the opposite. "Oh how horrible I feel and I don't feel like singing. Why do I have to sing?"'

There was something cold about that gala night on 5 July. It was as if Maria could feel the disappointment and disapproval of her absent friends, those who had queued uncomplainingly for days and heard Marie Collier instead of their idol. And the gala audience, with its inevitable complement of those who were there to be seen rather than to hear, did nothing to dispel the chill in Maria's heart, despite the enthusiastic applause that greeted her curtain-calls at the end. Part of her surely knew, as she left Covent Garden for the Savoy, that this was the last time; she would never sing another opera.

That summer on Skorpios she was aching for a new beginning, with no more struggle and no more torment. 'Love is a single thing,' she was to say three years later. 'You love, you worship and you honour, they go together.

You can't love in a different manner. They say, oh well, I'm attracted and all that. No. You love, then you worship, then you honour.' It could have been a line from any one of her heroines who loved totally, heedlessly, obsessively. It nearly *was* Lucia's: 'My hopes, my life, I pledged to this one heart.'

But that summer was their worst time together so far. Onassis, a master of the art of pleasing women, was no less a master of the art of crushing them. And there was something in Maria's way of treating him like a sultan or a god that brought out the despot in him. Underneath the easy sophistication of the café society *habitué* (and not far below the surface) Onassis had retained all the primitive male impulses of the old-fashioned Greek. Ingse Dedichen, the woman he nearly married during the war, remembers the first time he beat her up, leaving her 'like a boxer who had just lost a fight'. 'Every Greek,' he told her afterwards, 'and there are no exceptions, beats his wife. It's good for them. It keeps them in line.' There is no evidence that he ever beat Maria, but all the suppressed violence in him came out in the way he treated her, especially in front of his children. He would walk ahead with them, leaving her behind, and he belittled her constantly: 'What are you? Nothing. You just have a whistle in your throat that no longer works.'

At the beginning of their relationship it had been just the occasional jibe, but in the summer of 1965 it suddenly became unremitting and, for many of Maria's friends, unbearable to watch. Zeffirelli was one of them. One day on Skorpios he took Onassis aside: 'Listen, Aristo,' he said to him. 'I don't know the details of your private relationship, but it is very distressing to people who love Maria to see her treated like this.' It had, of course, no effect and Zeffirelli found himself resisting their invitations more and more, simply because he felt powerless to protect her either from Onassis or from herself. Maggie van Zuylen, on the other hand, tried to make Maria see everything as part of life. 'Of course he loves you. That's why he yells and abuses you and puts you down. If he didn't love you he would just ignore you and be totally indifferent to you.' And there were times in their relationship when Maria so desperately needed to clutch at something that even these straws of Maggie's were better than nothing.

Throughout this summer, they were hardly ever alone. Ari was constantly surrounded by a retinue of aids and managers – all of them men, all of them in a hurry, and most of them intent on putting up a barrier of male mystery impenetrable to mere women, even if they happened to be celebrated opera stars. There was quite a lot of the boy hero in Onassis. And as the feelings he shared with Maria, especially over the last year, had become deeper and more intimate, the boy hero had become frightened. Maria was so much more real than Tina or his various mistresses that he feared she might draw him into a true and complete relationship from which he could not run away. So he turned against her and at the same time he clung to his wandering masculinity even more fiercely than before, almost challenging her to make him give it up. Maria could see that she loved a man suffering from almost pathological restlessness and, despite his joviality, from chronic dissatisfaction; she could see that while she wanted a family, he wanted the world. She could even see that under the tide of his will, her own will was draining away. But perhaps the test of great passion is not that it is blind but that it survives even when those in its grip can see clearly. She had given her power over to him, and he, now feeling the stronger of the two, was dictating the terms of their relationship.

After her last *Tosca,* there was nothing that really mattered in her life except Aristo. There was, of course, as there would be right to the end, much talk about many projects that Maria was considering with her mind though rarely with her heart. For the time being, the film of *Tosca* was the project most likely to materialize. Zeffirelli was going to direct it, and he had great dreams for Maria: 'She will immediately impose herself as what the French call a *monstre sacré*, she will be the new Greta Garbo.' Maria's friends, headed by Vergottis, were totally in favour of the project. In fact Vergottis was in touch with the German producers and together with Sander Gorlinsky, who was negotiating on Maria's behalf, he had been discussing terms and conditions with them. 'I went a couple of times to the island that summer,' Zeffirelli remembers, 'and could not believe the way Onassis manipulated her mind and unleashed her greed. At one moment she asked for twenty-five per cent of the gross plus about $250,000 for appearing in it.'

In August Maria interrupted her holiday to go to London to be at Vergottis's side following the death of his brother. Once again they talked of the project. Finally a compromise was reached and Maria, Gorlinsky, Vergottis and the German producers all met in Monte Carlo to complete the arrangements. Zeffirelli had agreed, Gobbi had agreed, the studio had been booked and at the Monte Carlo meeting the final details were ironed out. All that was needed was Maria's signature on the contract. She asked to take it with her to show it to Ari.

Two weeks later, Gorlinsky received a call at his office from Maria on the *Christina.* Could he, together with Onassis's lawyer, leave London immediately and come to Skorpios, where the *Christina* was anchored, to discuss the contract? A car rushed them to London airport where the Olympic Airways flight to Crete was held up until they arrived. In Crete, a private plane was waiting to fly them to Skorpios. Right from the start, their talks turned into legalistic wrangling. Quibble after quibble followed, until Onassis had torn the contract to pieces. When the producers arrived a couple of days later, the discussions became even more fraught. It was instantly obvious to all who was dominating them; so much so that when, at one point, Maria asked a question, Onassis cut her off: 'Shut up! Don't interfere, you know nothing about these things. You are nothing but a night-club singer.' 'I was hoping,' remembers Gorlinsky, 'that she would pick up the nearest bottle and throw it at him, but no, she just got up and walked out. She was totally under his thumb.'

'We are going to make the film on our own,' Onassis finally said to Gorlinsky. 'You find out how much they want to sell the rights for, and you become the producer.' When Beta Films eventually realized that in no circumstances would Onassis let Maria make the film with them, they agreed to sell their rights. Gorlinsky was despatched to Rome, with a suite booked at the Grand Hotel and the full resources of the Onassis offices at his disposal, to negotiate the hand-over and start on the film. Gorlinsky is now convinced that Onassis never intended to buy the film rights or indeed let Maria make the film. Apart from sabotaging the negotiations with Beta Films, he reinforced all Maria's own doubts and fears about launching into something new. He wanted a slave – and a new career in films is not conducive to slavery.

Two weeks after Gorlinsky had called his wife in London to ask her to make preparations to go to Rome for the film production, the whole thing had collapsed, and in October Maria announced publicly that she was withdrawing from *Tosca.* Vergottis telephoned her and implored her to reconsider. She was, he told her, making a big mistake, depriving both herself and the world of art of something very important. Maria, sounding like Onassis's mouthpiece, began talking about crooked producers who could not be trusted or relied on, and it was clear that nothing Vergottis could say was going to move her. In fact he felt that she had not even been listening. He lost his temper and began accusing her of having given up everything, including her judgement, for 'that man' who had now torpedoed her chance to make the film. It was Maria's turn to flare up. It is impossible to discover exactly what she said but it was abusive and hurtful, and one thing is certain – Vergottis never forgave her. It did not take her long to realize that she had gone too far. She sat down and wrote him a letter, explaining, asking him to understand. He did not reply, nor did he understand. A few months before they fell out, Maria had had dinner alone with Vergottis. He had tried to persuade her that it would be much more secure for her if, instead of owning twenty-five of the 100 shares in *Artemision II*, she were to invest the money as a loan to the company at 6.5 per cent interest. The ship had developed some technical problems and Vergottis had convinced himself, and was trying to convince Maria, that it was 'unlucky'; so he told her that it was too risky for her to own shares in it. Maria agreed with the loan arrangement on the understanding that she could at any point convert the loan into shares.

Meanwhile, Onassis had given her twenty-six per cent of his share, the other twenty-four per cent going to his nephew.

In November 1965, Maria asked for her loan to be converted to shares. Vergottis replied that there was no option giving her the right to ask for such conversion. Then Onassis, in one of his favourite roles as the traditional knight in shining armour, went into action. He demanded that Vergottis transfer twenty-five shares in the company owning the ship to Maria. Vergottis refused and when, soon afterwards, they met accidentally at Claridges, their meeting flared up almost instantly into an argument at the end of which Vergottis grabbed a bottle of whisky from the table and yelled at Onassis, 'Get out of here or I'll throw it at you!' His last word, shortly after that, was that if Maria and Onassis dared to go into the witness-box over the shares, they would be faced with a great deal of scandal both in court and in the press. Onassis flew into a colossal rage, branded his friend of thirty years a blackmailer and determined that, scandal or no scandal, they *would* go to court.

It was more than a year before the case got to court. When it did, Vergottis's counsel described how his client, after his telephone conversation with Maria over the *Tosca* film, 'there and then underwent a complete change of heart about her'. Whatever other feelings may have been there, part of his change of heart was undoubtedly his bitterness over Maria's total surrender to Onassis. His love for her and his devotion over the last six years had been a complex and inflammable mixture of paternal and other feelings. The realization, after the *Tosca* film row and her angry words, that he could not even be friends with her without their friendship being darkened by Onassis's shadow, lit the fuse. So by the beginning of 1966, from the small gallery of Maria's really intimate friends a very important one was missing.

Something very important was missing from Onassis's life as well. Since 1953 he had been the most powerful man in Monte Carlo. He called Monaco 'my headquarters of convenience', but there was much more emotion in his connection with it, and in the sense of power he derived from it, than the description implied. In 1964 Prince Rainier began the process of deposing him; by 1966 the State of Monaco had created 600,000 new shares in the company in which Onassis had the controlling interest and which in turn effectively controlled all Monaco's activities, and had also offered to buy any shares that the existing shareholders wanted to sell at the market rate. Onassis appealed and lost. He received a cheque for $10 million for his shares and, humiliated, left Monte Carlo, not to return until the month before he died. Monaco had been part of his glory. What was now to replace it?

For ten years he had believed Monaco was his for life. The *Christina* was anchored in the prime berth and the ostentatiously opulent Salle Empire, the dining-room of the Hôtel de Paris, had almost become an extension of his office. 'He was in heaven every time he came into the Salle Empire,' remembered one of his directors. 'It was like a diamond that belonged to him.' So when Rainier decided to assert his authority, the open confrontations and the secret intrigues that followed totally absorbed Onassis; much more was at stake than a few million dollars. Maria lived the ups and downs with him. He would talk to her about what had happened – or rather he would march up and down hurling sarcasms and abuse at Rainier and his court. He moved from raging to a mood of withdrawn melancholy with a rapidity that went on astonishing Maria even after she had become used to it. If it was not Rainier and Monte Carlo, there was always something else. Whether in Paris, on the *Christina* or on Skorpios, Maria, awed and expectant, awaited Aristo's next mood. Was he angry, or jovial, or wistful? As she knew very well by now, how he felt in himself determined how he behaved with her. Self-tortured and torturing, Aristo would slip from anguish to exhilaration, drawing her down or lifting her up with him.

It was in his moods of exhilaration that he would talk of marriage – and then the subject would be forgotten until the next time. At the beginning of April 1966, Maria announced her decision to renounce her American citizenship. 'After seven years,' she said, 'of struggling with divorce proceedings my lawyers discovered that by taking Greek nationality my marriage becomes simply non-existent throughout the world – except in Italy.' According to a Greek law passed in 1946, three years before Maria married Meneghini, no marriage of a Greek citizen was valid unless the wedding had taken place in a Greek Orthodox church. So, as Maria said with a certain glee, her marriage was effectively 'non-existent'. Not, however, according to Meneghini: 'As far as I am concerned Maria will always be *my* wife,' was his comment. But much more interesting to the press, the public and for that matter Maria was what the other man had to say. 'All along,' was Onassis's answer to *the* question, 'we have explained that we are very close, good friends. This new event changes nothing. Of course, I'm very happy that her seven years of struggle have ended so well. It is wonderful for her to be a Signorina again.' His statement would have been dripping with irony even without the sting in the tail, but then Onassis could never resist the opportunity for a verbal thrust.

This time Maria found it impossible to exercise her new-found yet already much-tried patience. The lid flew off and out poured anger and bitterness and a deep sense of injustice. Why? *Why?* And, more to the point, why in public – especially when he knew just how important dignity and keeping up appearances were to her? Perhaps *because* he knew how important they were. Whenever Maria exploded, and it was happening more and more, Onassis watched as though watching the temper tantrums of a child, but he was by no means unaffected himself. He may have been torturing her but he did not want to lose her. The extent to which *she* did not want to lose *him* was soon to be made patently and in a sense tragically clear.

Ever since she had fully realized her dream of success and achievement, and even before she met Onassis, Maria had one overwhelming desire: to have a child. Now, at the age of forty-three, she found herself pregnant. It seemed a miracle. 'I'm thirty-six,' she had said, at the beginning of her relationship with Onassis, 'and I want to live – I want a child, but I don't even know if I'm capable of giving birth to another being.' As the years went on Maria had tried to convince herself that perhaps she did not want a child all that much after all. It took the discovery that she was pregnant to make her see just how much she did want it, and just how much this had been a source of half-conscious but ever-present regret. All her instincts, everything in her that longed for life, wanted a child. Onassis did not. It was painful enough to have the man she adored reject, instead of celebrate, the child of their love, but he went further: he warned her that if she went ahead and kept the child it would be the end of their relationship. She was pitched into a torrent of doubt, fear, confusion. Her decision betrayed everything real and life-giving in her for the sake of a relationship that was increasingly tenuous and unreal. Her abortion, at the moment when she longed for a new source of energy and meaning, was her life's greatest might-have-been. *Poppea, Werther, Carmen* on stage, Verdi's *Requiem,* film versions of *Tosca* and *Traviata* with Zeffirelli and Karajan, these and many other repeatedly considered might-have-beens were nothing compared with the child that, had she dared give birth to it, could have pulled her out of the self-destructive inertia into which, as it was, her life gradually and unspectacularly slipped.

'One day when she was thirty-four,' recalled Meneghini, 'Maria confessed to me that, above everything, she wanted a child. She went on saying that again and again. But I told her that having a child would have put her career in jeopardy for at least a year. In fact a child would have destroyed the great diva that she had become.' So one of the two men in her life refused her a child because of her legend, and the other for the sake of a relationship that was about to end. Choosing to give in to Onassis's will was the turning-point. Her life's second great dream was slowly souring into nightmare. From now on their quarrels were only temporarily mended: they never really ceased. Maria's longing to be needed by Aristo was further from fulfilment than ever. Welcome everywhere, she was feeling indispensable nowhere.

At least the pleasures of being welcome and applauded everywhere were always available. On 31 May, when she arrived for the first night of the Met's visiting production of *Il Barbiere di Siviglia* in Paris, she was applauded as though she had just sung a marvellous Rosina herself. She acknowledged it with the style and aplomb that by now were second nature to her. The first time the audience had burst into spontaneous applause at the mere sight of her in the auditorium was a few days after her spectacular *Norma* in Chicago: 'Nothing like that had ever happened to me before,' remembered Maria. 'I must have seemed stupid, but I didn't know what it was all about. I was delayed getting there, and when I heard the clapping I thought the maestro must be entering the orchestra pit. When I realized they were applauding me I didn't know what to do.' Now she certainly knew what to do. In the American Ambassador's box, drinking champagne at the interval with Madame Pompidou and Jean-Louis Barrault, she looked poised, smiling, confident. On stage or in crowds this basically shy, uncomfortable woman glowed like an exotic being from some other land.

She was really at home in Paris and she had, for some time now, been wanting to buy an apartment and create her own home exactly as she wanted it. She wanted it to be 'their' home, but she had to accept that for the time being at least it was going to be hers alone. The second floor of 36 Avenue Georges-Mandel, overlooking what was to become *her* chestnut tree on the corner of the avenue, was designed and decorated not for Maria but for La Callas, by La Callas herself and Georges Grandpierre, the interior decorator who idolized her and identified with the grand style that she believed was proper for her. It was less a home than a tomb for a legend, in which Maria had turned the bedroom, and even more the bathroom, into a nest for herself. 'I always had the feeling,' said the Greek director Michael Cacoyannis, 'that Maria was living in someone else's perfectly well-run house.'

The Grand Salon with the Steinway, the Louis Quinze furniture, the jonquil-yellow lacquered commode and the grand Renaissance paintings; the Salon Rouge with all the chinoiserie – a pair of dogs, an elephant, a pagoda; the Venetian multi-coloured door separating the Grand Salon from the Rouge; the rare silk carpet in *petit point*; paintings by Bassano, Sebastiano del Piombo and

Fragonard; a Regency inlaid rosewood and violet-wood commode; the Louis Seize dining-room – all formed part of a grand, impersonal set for Callas's last performance. Except that there was no indication of what the person living on that set was doing or even what his or her interests were. All evidence that Maria was an opera singer – from a portrait of Malibran to all sorts of memorabilia from La Scala – was collected in the Blue Room and, of course, in the studio where Maria worked right to the end, even when there was no specific project to work on. An obsessive order pervaded the whole apartment. Clothes, gloves and handbags were documented as meticulously as her recordings, with a list giving the date each item had been bought and where, when and in whose company it had been worn.

In the bedroom she put the suite Meneghini gave her soon after they married, dominated by the eighteenth-century Italian double bed with its flower-painted and carved headpiece and an embroidered bedspread to match. But it was in the bathroom that Maria lived. It looked as though it had been produced by Zeffirelli in an extravagant mood; it was huge, in white and pink marble, with mirrors everywhere, covered in rugs and with thick, white curtains for the windows that gave on to the street. There was a settee and a large armchair, both covered in orange velvet, with a telephone and a record-player next to them. It was the most fully alive room at Georges-Mandel. Maria spent hours in her bath with its golden taps and hanging plants, surrounded by flowers. She would talk on the telephone, make plans, play records or, wearing one of her favourite multi-coloured caftans and reclining on her settee, receive friends. Her bathroom brought out the oriental courtesan in her, or rather it was the oriental courtesan who had created the bathroom.

Heading the supporting cast at 36 Avenue Georges-Mandel was Bruna. Two years older than Maria, brown-haired and always impeccably neat, she had been with her since before the Meneghini marriage broke up. There was something solemn about Bruna; she emanated a sense of having found in her work for Maria not only the job she wanted but also her destiny. She was Maria's maid, sister, mother, confidante, but at the same time she had an exquisite sense of her part in the play. Whenever there was anyone present, Bruna was almost deferential to her: *'Oui, Madame . . .', 'Que désirez-vous, Madame? . . .'* When they were alone they were friends talking away in Italian, often sitting at the oak table in the kitchen. Bruna was the outlet for Maria's immediate feelings and a source of earthy advice even on things she knew nothing about. It was to Bruna that Maria showed the script of *Medea* before she decided to go ahead with the film. And when she had a hernia operation shortly after she had moved to Georges-Mandel, it was Bruna who was at the hospital day and night. 'She didn't even want the nurse to touch me because she was ashamed,' said Maria later. 'Imagine that creatures like that should still exist! . . . ashamed to humiliate me to a nurse, cleaning me in private instead.' Bruna deeply loved Maria but she also loved and idealized the legend – and legends are not to be cleaned by a mere nurse in hospital.

With every year that passed, Bruna's most important job was to act as Maria's screen (*'Non, Madame n'est pas ici . . .', 'Non, Madame dort encore . . .'*), cancelling invitations Maria had accepted, protecting her, making possible her growing isolation in the middle of Paris. Consuelo, the cook, worked intermittently for Maria, and Ferruccio, the butler, was the other permanent member of the supporting cast. He looked as though he had stepped out of an Italian operetta, the perfect butler in uniform and white gloves with which he served dinner even if it was just Maria and a friend. Muffle the scream . . . the show must go on . . .

On 17 April 1967, while the creation of Georges-Mandel was under way, another show was about to begin in London. Maria, dressed defiantly in a scarlet dress and white turban and accompanied by Onassis, arrived at the law courts. They took their places side by side in the well of the court. A few minutes later the usher made the traditional announcement that warned those present that the judge was about to take his place on the bench: 'Be upstanding in court.' Mr Justice Roskill entered, bowed to the court, the lawyers returning the bow, and Sir Milner

Holland, counsel for Maria and Onassis, rose and began with words no less traditional: 'May it please your Lordship, I appear for the plaintiffs, Mr Aristotle Socrates Onassis and Madame Maria Kalogeropoulos, and my learned friend Mr Peter Bristow appears for the defendant Mr Panaghis Vergottis.' (Maria was claiming under her real name, but was referred to throughout the case as Madame Callas.) The case that was to occupy the front pages of the newspapers for the next week was about to begin.

Maria's broad smile as she arrived in court was betrayed by the condition of her legs, which, almost as much as her voice, were a barometer of her emotional state. They were swollen, with the veins protruding, and as the trial became more emotionally wrenching with each day that passed, the swelling and the discomfort increased.

'We are here,' Maria said at one point during her questioning by Vergottis's counsel, 'because of twenty-five shares for which I have paid, and not because of my relations with another man.' In fact the case became a painful retrospective of her eight years with Aristo, and in the cold, formal atmosphere of an English court, their answers, and especially Onassis's, seemed at times to be addressed to each other. It was as if they had unconsciously staged this whole performance not because of twenty-five shares, which as Onassis himself had said were hardly of any consequence in themselves, but to clarify, a little over a year before they parted, what was really happening in their relationship. And Peter Bristow obliged them by asking questions which seemed of little relevance to the case in front of the judge but of great relevance to the case at the back of Maria's and Aristo's minds.

COUNSEL: After you got to know Madame Callas, did you part from your wife and did Madame Callas part from her husband?

ONASSIS: Yes, sir. Nothing to do with our meeting. Just coincidence.

COUNSEL: Did you regard her as being in a position

equivalent to being your wife if she was free?

ONASSIS: No. If that was the case I have no problem of marrying her; neither has she any problem of marrying me.

COUNSEL: Do you feel obligations towards her other than those of mere friendship?

ONASSIS: None whatsoever.

Maria, of course, had hardly expected Onassis to use an English court as a platform from which to profess his undying love for her, but his answers, in their mixture of defiance, mendacity, hardheadedness and cruelty, clearly went far beyond an understandable reluctance to have his private life brought into what was supposed to be a purely financial dispute.

Meanwhile, Maria was desperately clinging to a legal technicality to protect in public the fiction that if only they *could* be married, they would be: 'You told us,' asked Peter Bristow in his cross-examination of her, 'that you are still married to your husband who is in Italy?' 'Under the Italian law I am very much still married to him,' was Maria's reply, at which point Peter Bristow reminded her – as if she could have forgotten – that Mr Onassis had said in his evidence that there was no problem about their marrying if they had wanted to. There was real desperation in Maria's attempt to uphold the illusion without contradicting Onassis, especially in view of her own public statement when she had taken on Greek nationality a year before that her marriage had in effect never existed. 'I may answer that immediately. If I go to America and have a divorce I can marry anyone. In Italy it would not be valid. Everywhere else it would be valid.' But Bristow, by this stage counsel for Truth rather than for Vergottis, was not going to allow her to escape. 'Do you regard yourself now as a single woman?' – a question which theoretically was open to only two possible answers: Yes or No. There was a long pause: 'In Italy, no. Elsewhere, yes.'

The question had referred to a state of mind. Maria had side-stepped it by repeating a statement of fact. What would have happened if she had suddenly succumbed to one of her uncontrollable impulses and had blurted out the truth: 'No, I do not regard myself as a single woman. Indeed for nearly eight years I have regarded myself as married to the man sitting beside me in the well of the court today, who not long ago informed you that he feels no obligation whatsoever towards me except that of mere friendship.' Would Onassis have dismissed her answer as a pleasantry, as he had done all those years ago when Maria had announced that they were getting married? What is certain is that the truth, whether spoken or only felt, remained unchanged. Maria did not give vent to her bitterness, but at one point Vergottis did so on her behalf. He talked about how Onassis asked him to transfer twenty-four of his shares to his nephew, but said nothing about what he wanted to do with the other twenty-six. Then he recalled how Maria had telephoned him in February 1965 complaining that Ari had promised *her* fifty shares. 'She said she had been with him for seven years or whatever it was then. She was furious about the whole thing.' The next day the three of them had lunch together. 'With a sly look,' Vergottis went on, 'he turned around and said: "I have given her twenty-six shares. Why don't you give her another twenty-five?" I could see she was upset. I patted her back and said: "I'll give you an option or the whole ship or anything in the world."'

It was the most telling vignette of the case: the three of them round the lunch table; Maria with that closed, hurt look of a powerless child that Onassis so often brought out in her; Onassis, slightly shamefaced at not only having denied Maria the domestic idyll she had been dreaming of but having even begrudged her the gift of the shares he had promised her; and Vergottis offering her his kingdom, or at least an option on it.

Onassis was in an expansive mood throughout the trial. The boy hero was going to show the world just how strong, brilliant and witty he was. When it was suggested by Peter Bristow that the money was a loan from Maria for the purchase of the ship, he replied dismissively that this was 'a myth of Aesop'. 'Why do we need Madame Callas's money? Maybe Mr Vergottis does, but I don't.' And when it was suggested that it was he who had turned

Maria against Vergottis, the wit was at the ready: 'Madame Callas is not a vehicle for me to drive. She has her own brakes and her own brains.'

The case took ten days, but as Mr Justice Roskill said in his summing-up, 'The final determination depends upon a simple question of personal credibility.... There is no escape – one would wish there were ... from the fact that, by one side or the other, perjury has been committed.' His verdict was that the perjury had been committed by Vergottis. He was ordered to transfer twenty-five shares in the company to Maria and pay all their legal costs, which had come to about £25,000. The case, the judge had said in his summing-up, 'had many of the elements of Sophoclean tragedy'; and once the dust had settled over the verbal pyrotechnics and the intrinsic fascination of the rich and the famous scratching each other's eyes out in public, these tragic elements could be clearly seen. Here was a seventy-eight-year-old sick man, with his doctor beside him throughout the trial, convinced that he was the victim of a conspiracy by two of the most important people in his life; here was a sixty-one-year-old man betraying in public both the woman who was, hard though he fought the realization, the great love of his life, and the man whom he had once called 'my closest friend'; and here was Maria, who longed more than anything for something real in her life, being drawn inexorably into the shadows of a performance even more artificial and implausible than the plot of some of the crudest and most garish operas she had sung in. For ten days, three people whose lives had once been woven intimately together had, themelves torn, been tearing at one another in public.

The final irony was still to come. Vergottis appealed and won the appeal, at the end of which a new trial was ordered. Onassis and Maria instantly appealed against this decision to the final court of appeal – the House of Lords. It was on 31 October 1968, eleven days after Jackie Kennedy had become Mrs Onassis, that the Law Lords decided against Vergottis. Maria and Onassis had won a joint victory at a time when Onassis was honeymooning with Jackie on Skorpios and Maria was deep in her anguish in Paris.

But that was still eighteen months away. Meanwhile Maria could hardly wait to get to Skorpios and abandon herself to the sea she adored. She was trying to convince herself that having some time with Aristo on the island she felt was their home would breathe new life into their relationship. In fact that summer of 1967, their last summer together, turned out to be the saddest and most fraught summer of an increasingly unhappy entanglement. Onassis had finally agreed to co-operate with Willi Frischauer over the writing of his biography. At first he had tried to bribe Frischauer by offering him $50,000 *not* to write it. When Frischauer refused – 'I am too old,' he told him, 'to accept money for not writing' – Onassis rather philosophically decided to co-operate: 'If I have to be raped,' he explained, 'I might as well lie back and enjoy it.' Frischauer was invited to Skorpios and very soon Onassis was enjoying the rape so much that he had hardly any time left for Maria. He was always late for meals, always absorbed in some aspect or other of his life, and often behaving as though Maria did not exist. Frischauer remembers her fussing and worrying 'like an irritated suburban housewife'. She was that, but she was also a woman who sensed that she was losing not only the man she loved but the centre of her life.

She returned to Paris full of apprehension; and her fears had plenty to feed on. Ari was spending less and less time with her, and one day she heard that Helen and George, Onassis's servants at his Avenue Foch apartment, had recently been ordered not to leave their quarters throughout an entire evening while he was entertaining a mystery guest; he would serve the food himself. Maria had always known that Onassis had never stopped having affairs on the side. She had accepted that, as she had so much else, as part of what Greek women were brought up to expect. But why all this sudden secrecy? She followed Maggie van Zuylen's advice; she carried on as if nothing was happening and asked no questions. And in some ways life went on as if nothing *was* happening. He went on calling her every day from wherever he was, and Maria, as always, would put everything aside to welcome him back. Lord Harewood remembers one evening, when they were talking at her home, suggesting that they go out to dinner. 'Oh no, I can't,' she replied unhesitatingly. 'He is coming on the morning flight from New York, and I must go to bed early and be fresh for when he arrives.'

At the beginning of November, as Ari and Maria were coming out of Régine's in Paris at two o'clock in the morning, they were approached by a reporter from *Oggi* magazine and asked the question they had been asked at least a thousand times in the last eight years: 'Is it true that you are about to get married?' 'You are late. We are already married. We married fifteen days ago,' came back Onassis, adding as an after-thought, 'It was a wonderful thing.' The reporter instantly filed his story mentioning as confirmation that they seemed unusually 'gay and light-hearted'. Some gremlin inside Onassis made him play this joke on the press just as the decision as to whom he actually wanted to marry was formulating in his mind.

Maria soon had the solution to the mystery of the guest at dinner in Avenue Foch. Ari and Jackie Kennedy had been seen dining together in New York: at El Morocco; at 21; at Dionysos; at Mykonos, together with Christina, Margot Fonteyn and Nureyev. By the beginning of 1968, Onassis had begun to be mentioned – though more in jest than in earnest – as a runner in the race for Jackie's hand along with such well-qualified favourites as the former British Ambassador to Washington Lord Harlech, or the glamorous Roswell Gilpatric, former Under-Secretary of Defense in the Kennedy Administration.

For a while Maria carried on with her policy of making no scenes. But the battle of emotions raging inside her – anger, fear, jealousy, pain – could not be contained for long. The explosion took place when Ari came back from New York with the announcement that Jackie would be coming on the *Christina* for a short cruise in the Caribbean. Maria had by then learned that he had not merely kept in touch with Jackie since that cruise in 1963, which she knew anyway, but that he had been having long, regular telephone conversations with her from all over the world. She remembered the time she and Ari were in New York and he had called Jackie at her Fifth Avenue apartment. 'Come over for a drink,' she had said. 'I'd love to, and I have Maria with me.' 'In that case, sorry, perhaps another time.' Then, Jackie's reaction was merely mysterious; now it took on sinister overtones. What were her intentions? Maria said some very bitter things, giving vent to all the emotions she had been holding back, but by the end she felt emptied rather than unburdened. There was no next step; there was no ultimatum she could issue; there was no future she could see except as part of his life. She had given her power over to him, and all she could now do was watch and wait.

And to watch him was to watch a man tipsy with the smell of fame and drunk at the prospect of more of it. If philotimia – the word that in ancient Greece came to mean an excessive thirst for prestige – had been a disease, then at this point in his life Onassis would have been described as a terminal case. He was a driven man and there was one goal: Jackie. On Jackie's part there was of course the need for security and the love of luxury, but, much more important, there was a zest for life that had been stifled by the mantle of near-sainthood that the American press had thrown over her. There is an incident that sums up just how powerful that instinct was in her. The day of her husband's funeral happened also to be her son's third birthday. Everyone had assumed that John-John's birthday party would be postponed. Jackie would not hear of it. For her it was a glorious coincidence that a day of grief and mourning could be crowned with a celebration of life, with noisemakers, paper hats, ice cream and toy trucks.

In May Jackie boarded the *Christina* for the Caribbean cruise; Maria stayed behind. The watching game was turning deadly serious; and the pain, killing. She knew that Jackie had been given the Ithaca suite, the suite reserved for special guests, the suite that was Churchill's, the suite she herself had stayed in. She knew, because she had lived it so many times, the routine on the *Christina,* the times for lunch and dinner, the ritual of cocktails on the deck at sunset; she knew the maids who would look after Jackie, the waiters who would wait on Jackie, the chef who would cook for Jackie. Johnny Meyer, Onassis's friend and publicity man, telegraphed him: 'Aren't you lonely without Maria and me?' Far from being lonely, he seemed elated. Jackie's pet-name for him was Telis (short for Aristotelis, the Greek form of his name), and 'Telis', singing and swimming with the ex-First Lady, was relishing the new depths of their intimacy.

In her private hell, Maria lived the cruise with them. It was at this time that she started finding it impossible to sleep without sleeping pills. And it was at this time that she longed more than anything for sleep to stop the torture of her mind. Nor was the torture the creation of a wild imagination. At the end of the cruise, back in New York, Jackie called Bobby Kennedy, the Kennedy closest to her, and told him that she was seriously considering marrying Onassis. He was, at the time, in the middle of his campaign for the presidential nomination, and he pleaded with her to do nothing until the campaign was over. Days later, on 6 June 1968, Bobby Kennedy was dead, shot by a mad gunman in Los Angeles, and Ari was on his way there to be near Jackie.

With the campaign tragically over, there were only two reasons left for continuing with the secrecy: Jackie wanted to consult Cardinal Cushing, who had married her to Jack Kennedy, over the Vatican's attitude to her marrying a divorced man, and Onassis wanted to ease the shock for Maria. Privately he had made his decision, and Jackie had made hers. Maria had become, together with the Vatican, one of the things that had to be tied up. But whether out of cowardice, fear of what she might do or an unconscious and very deep desire not to lose her, Onassis told Maria nothing. He went on seeing her at the same time as huge bouquets of flowers were greeting his bride-to-be every morning wherever she was, with just four letters on the card: TJWL.

After Robert Kennedy's funeral, Onassis and his daughter spent a weekend with Janet Auchincloss, Jackie's mother, at Hammersmith Farm in Newport. He returned to Paris and Maria; he went back, this time to Hyannis Port to spend time 'preparing' John-John and Caroline – swimming with them, going for long walks with them, telling them that although he would never replace their father, their mother needed someone to take care of her.

He returned to Maria; he went back to Hyannis Port, this time to meet the family matriarch. Rose Kennedy found him 'pleasant, interesting, and, to use a word of Greek origin, charismatic'. While at Hyannis Port, Ari invited Teddy Kennedy, now the effective head of the family, for a week's cruise in August 'to talk things over'. 'As I did not expect a dowry,' Onassis said later, 'there was nothing to worry about.' He returned to Maria who was by then on the *Christina* with Lawrence Kelly, who had flown in from Dallas to be with her. She had been the *Christina*'s hostess for the last nine years and nobody had told her, in so many words, that things had changed.

'Maria, now I want you to go back to Paris, and wait for me there.'

'Go to Paris in August? Are you mad?'

'You have to go.'

'August in Paris? Why? What do you mean?'

'I'm having company and you can't be aboard.'

'Who? And why can't I be aboard?'

She knew, of course, the answer to both questions, but she asked them as though, in the gap between asking the questions and receiving the answers, some miracle might happen. No miracle happened, and all that was left was fighting, swearing and finally announcing in desperation:

'Then, I'm leaving you.'

'I'll see you in September after the cruise.'

'No, you don't understand. I'm leaving you. You're never going to see me again – ever.'

Together with Lawrence Kelly, she left the *Christina* – never to return. From Paris she called Mary Mead. She was almost hysterical. 'Don't leave Dallas,' she said. 'I can't explain now, but Larry and I are coming over.' Mary Mead protested at the thought of summer in Dallas, and in the end, with Lawrence Kelly still at her side, Maria flew to New York and from there to Kansas City, where they stayed at the home of Kelly's best friend, David Sticklebar. All she knew was that she could not bear to stay in Europe; when she arrived in America, she realized that she could not bear to stay anywhere. There was nowhere she wanted to be and nothing she wanted to do. From Kansas City to Santa Fe, where the two wanderers were joined by Mary Mead and John Ardoin; from Santa Fe to Las Vegas, from Las Vagas to Los Angeles, where Maria was robbed at the Bel Air Hotel; from Los Angeles to San Francisco, to Cuernavaca, to Dallas and back to New York, staying mostly in hotels, watching westerns on television and talking, talking, talking. She talked about the Nazi occupation and walking miles to the mountain market for food, about bullets whistling by her in the streets, about hunger and misery and fear, and then she talked and talked about Aristo, memories of rejection and humiliation flashing through her consciousness with no sequence and no reason. With her two identities – the opera star and Aristo's woman – both in fragments, she went from hotel to hotel, having nothing and no one to go home to. Time and space had been abolished. All she knew, all she could identify with, was her pain. It seemed as though she would talk it out, let go of it; but no, she talked round it in circles, clinging to it, almost hoarding it – as if when the pain and the self-pity and the bitterness went, there would be nothing left at all.

In Cuernávaca, Mary Mead took a house, and they were joined by John Coveney, head of the classical division of EMI in America. It was also in Cuernavaca that Maria agreed for the first time since this traumatic trip had begun to go to a dinner party given by friends in the area. As the time for the dinner approached, she realized she could not face it. Mary Mead was not going to give in: 'The rest of us are going. Where would you like your dinner served – at the pool, your bedroom or the dining room?' When it came to that, Maria, unable to face staying alone, decided reluctantly to go. Mary Mead remembers what a revelation, in the state she was in, this Cuernavacan dinner turned out to be. 'She had lost all her self-respect and she was truly amazed to discover that people still loved her, still cared for her and admired her.'

But it took very little to tumble her back into a state of self-conscious insecurity, and it was very hard to stop being reminded of what she most wanted to forget. An August issue of *Newsweek* carried a picture of Teddy and Jackie leaving for the cruise on the *Christina,* 'en route to Greece'. In the middle of August, Doris Lilly, the *New*

York Post's gossip columnist, announced on the Merv Griffin Show that Jackie Kennedy would marry Aristotle Onassis. She was hissed and booed by the studio audience for disseminating misinformation that still smacked of sacrilege to the American public.

Early in September, Maria arrived in Dallas with two cracked ribs: she had slipped in her bathroom in Cuernavaca and fallen on the tiled floor. Suddenly the physical agony became a welcome distraction from the emotional agony. She started calling herself Maria Click because of the noise her ribs were making. John Ardoin, who was music critic of the *Dallas Morning News* and a great friend of Lawrence Kelly's, remembers her giggling like a schoolgirl the first day he collected her from the doctor's. 'I had to get a doctor,' she said, still giggling, 'who collects all my records and who blushed when he asked me to take off my dress.'

One afternoon, at John Ardoin's house, they began recording her thoughts on the sleep-walking scene from *Macbeth*. 'Let's talk some more, John,' she said when she had finished dissecting the scene note by note. 'Put another tape on. I need to talk.' The pain she was carrying in her had somehow to be exorcized before she could face Paris and what remained of her world. It was as if the shock of the break-up with Onassis had opened the sluices of all the bitterness and resentment that had been accumulating for years. She longed to make sense of it all, to understand and to be understood. When she decided, that afternoon in Dallas, to talk to John Ardoin, the man who had written the most comprehensive and most deeply understanding study of her singing, she knew that his respect and love for her were such that she could trust him completely. 'I know you will never misquote me, John,' she said. 'You understand me too well.' Nor did he betray her trust; the most intimate and painful details of their conversations he never published at all.*

These tapes are the most extraordinary document we have of Maria talking about herself. In the last years of her life she would spend hours speaking into a tape-recorder, but most of the time it was La Callas speaking in all her

*It was not until a year after her death that he made the full transcript available for this biography.

dignity and stature. In her conversations with John Ardoin, we can feel the legend creeping in every now and then, but most of the time it is Maria pouring her heart out in an English that has clearly suffered from nine years of speaking Greek with Ari. What we hear is a disjointed stream of consciousness welling up from a level deeper and more truthful than any from which she had yet spoken.

Not once in this flood of memories does she refer to Onassis by name. He is 'them' or 'they' or 'he' or an abstract presence hovering over everything she says: 'If for nine years you have been living a hidden life, and a humiliating life, it gets you, and you're not cured in two months.... When serious, strong people promise or guarantee relative happiness, then they have to live up to that. It's too easy to say, "Well you know ... I mean ... we did our best to be happy!" "Well, thank you very much ... for nine years." "Well, ain't that sweet?" as they say vulgarly. Where does it leave me? At least a friendship? Not even that. The way things have gone I can't be friends. How can he be my friend? Humiliating me that way. It's so easy to say, "No resentment." Sure, Christianity says – I've read it in books – "You must forgive, you must have no resentment." I don't have resentment, but I have hurt.'

Every word she spoke, every pause, is in fact steeped in both hurt *and* resentment. She felt that he had robbed her not only of her bourgeois respectability but, much more important, of her dream of a family that would bring meaning to her life: '... After nine years, not a child, not a family, not a friend! That's very little, you know. And you say, "God, why? Why should these things happen?" Also because I figure in my own stupid logic that if people have been privileged to reach great positions they should realize that their obligation is to be happy, somehow or other.... It takes very little to make me happy, but then when you're slapped down, it's not very pleasant, don't you think? Tomorrow you have a girl and you love her, and today she says she'll love you forever, and then tomorrow she treats you all of a sudden very badly. That's a big slap in the face. Now if that goes on every day up and down, you'll be a nervous wreck. Am I right? Would you still hope?... I would rather hope for the worst and have the best. Frankly, for nine years I thought I would have, and I found out.... How can a man be so dishonest? So, I don't know, so crazy. Poor man....'

All this outpouring was before the shock of the public announcement of Ari's wedding, which was still thirty-four days away. 'I don't like to lose. Who does? Frankly I'm terrified of going home. It's like the beginning of a performance...' She had hoped that Onassis would have led her closer to reality. Now that he had gone, she felt she had no option but to return to the performance – in life no less than on stage, and however terrifying the prospect of both. From Dallas, she made an announcement: 'Next season, I shall sing again at the Dallas Opera. Lawrence Kelly and Nicola Rescigno have been my friends for a very long time. It was with them that I made my debut in America. And it is with them that I would like to return to the stage.' She did not believe it; it was part of the performance. 'Anything to survive, my dear,' she told John Ardoin. 'At my stage of the game, anything to survive.' The announcement was part of the survival game; no date given, no opera, no cast, no director. More of an incantation than a statement of fact: next year, please God, make it possible that I may sing again, for there is nothing else left. 'Don't have any illusions, John. Happiness is not of my world.'

From Dallas, with Mary Mead and her fourteen-year-old daughter, Lainie, she flew to New York. Maria found in Lainie a much-needed outlet for her love and her attention, giving her advice on how to diet, how to discipline herself in her life and, above all, how never to give herself over completely to anyone. But Maria's despair, which even the fourteen-year-old had sensed, was a more powerful deterrent than any advice, especially as, while they were in New York, Onassis arrived and was everywhere reported escorting Mrs Kennedy about town. 'I can't bear watching her pain,' Lainie said to her mother. 'I hope I never, *never* care so much about anyone.'

Renata Tebaldi was opening at the time in *Adriana Lecouvreur.* Maria decided to go to the first night and, backstage afterwards, the two rivals fell into each other's arms. Maria had tears in her eyes. It was as if something had driven her to seek some confirmation that there was still harmony and reconciliation underneath all the bitterness and the hurt. And she found it backstage at the Met.

Back in Paris, she wrote to John Ardoin:

> Dear John
>
> Thank you so much for being such a warm affectionate friend – you really don't know what strength you give me – may God pay you all back for such love & respect towards me.
>
> I came back quite exhausted – too many emotions, I suppose – I am so fragile under this so called control.
>
> I do so want to be worthy of you all, & of course, myself.
>
> It is still a long life to live and I must be worthy of so much bestowed upon me.

And she signed it 'Yours affectionately, Maria Click'.

On 17 October 1968, at 3.30 in the afternoon, Nancy Tuckerman, Jackie's secretary, made an announcement to the press: 'Mrs Hugh D. Auchincloss has asked me to tell you that her daughter, Mrs John F. Kennedy, is planning to marry Aristotle Onassis some time next week. No place or date has been set for the moment.'

Maria was in Paris.

Three days later on 20 October, at 5.30 in the afternoon in the tiny chapel of Panayitsa (the Little Virgin) on Skorpios, where Maria loved to sit alone in the hot afternoons, a bearded Greek Orthodox Archimandrite, in gold brocade vestment, stepped forward to conduct a traditional Greek Orthodox wedding: 'The servant of God Aristotle is betrothed to the servant of God Jacqueline, in the name of the Father, the Son and the Holy Spirit . . .' Artemis, the bridegroom's sister, placed on the heads of the couple delicate wreaths with lemon blossom linked with a white ribbon, and changed them over three times while the priest was chanting. Gold wedding-bands were placed on their fingers and also passed between them three times. Alexander and Christina looked on grimly. Caroline and John-John watched dazzled. Patrol boats, reinforced by cruisers and helicopters from the Greek Navy, circled the island to keep reporters from getting closer than a thousand yards.

It was raining heavily as, a few hours later, round the wedding table on the *Christina,* Janet Auchincloss stood up and, dabbing her eyes, looked straight at her son-in-law: 'I know that my daughter is going to find peace and happiness with you.'

In Paris, Maria was arriving smiling at the film *première* of Feydeau's *A Flea in her Ear.* She was still smiling when in the early hours of the morning she left Les Ambassadeurs where she had spent the night celebrating the seventy-fifth anniversary of Maxim's. It was one of the most convincing, one of the greatest performances of her career. Only someone who had looked closely into her huge dark eyes could have seen the anguish that had dimmed their light.

Chapter Thirteen

'IF I could have a medicine that could give me strength, mental and physical, especially physical ... I'd be pleased with three years, three good years coming back to what I was. It's the beginning ... that's what I'm terrified of, the beginning....'

Since that last performance on the night of the wedding, Maria had existed in a mist, a dream, an intoxication, living and reliving the past in her mind – as though she could not only postpone but in some way avoid beginning again. The wheels of her mind would not slow down and only with sleeping-tablets and tranquillizers would they stop. At the deepest point of her despair, she found herself repeating, at first only half consciously and then with all her heart, 'God, give me what you want, but, above all, give me the strength to bear what you send me and to survive it.'

As soon as he read about the wedding, Francesco Chiarini, and old friend of Meneghini's who had remained a trusted friend of Maria's, rang her up from Brussels where he was on business. Maria asked him to come and see her in Paris. They talked of the past, of common friends, of what he was doing now, but there was something withdrawn, almost absent about her. Finally, she said: 'You know Francesco, you are a funny man. You've read what has happened to me, and yet you come and see me and not once do you mention it. Look at these.' She got up and fetched him a thick pile of letters and telegrams of condolence from other friends, including Prince Rainier and Princess Grace, and Visconti. From that point on, they talked of nothing else. Or rather he listened while she poured out some of the anger and the pain.

Ten days after the wedding, she wrote to John Ardoin in her own idiosyncratic English, again without once referring to Onassis by name.

> ... So many things have happened and sincerely I am reacting externally very well, I presume. But I am under severe pressure and am desperately trying to keep controlled. Of course I consider all this a liberation. But how little faith one is left with. One moment I am full of confidence and the next very little. I fight the last because it is not christian and noble and my feelings are essentially pure and all that goes with it.
>
> But, John, what a lonesome life I see for myself. No work I can do will be what I was used to and no man is to my expectations or standards – and that does not mean financial situation. Is it so much to ask of people to be loyal, honest, faithful and passionate? (always in the happy medium of course?)
>
> I am quite discouraged of being only sure of myself and *no one* else past, present & future. Am I such a strange creature? And why?
>
> Forgive this strange letter but I am in a strange moment.

When she looked ahead the only lifeboats she could see were work, new roles, new projects: a film of Puccini's life that Visconti wanted to make; Menotti's *The Consul*; Tennessee Williams's *Boom!*, turned into a film by Joseph Losey. She thought a lot about this last one but, in the end, playing the part of a star living among her diamonds and her memories on her Mediterranean island and being visited there by the Angel of Death seemed too close to the whirlpool she was trying to escape. Elizabeth Taylor took the part, and Maria went on discussing other options. One of them, a new production of *Traviata*, directed by Visconti, got beyond the discussion stage. They went as far as signing a contract with the Paris Opera, but very soon the prospect of a major new operatic production became too daunting. Too proud to cancel the contract, she demanded twenty to thirty days of rehearsals for the orchestra and chorus – a demand which she well knew the administration of L'Opéra would never meet. Making impossible and oscillating demands had increasingly become Maria's way of saying no.

And then, to everyone's surprise, she agreed to take part in Pasolini's film of *Medea* – not Cherubini's opera or Euripides's tragedy but the *myth* of Medea. 'When Franco Rossellini, *Medea*'s producer, and Pasolini proposed this one, I had no doubt. I immediately knew that this was the occasion I'd been waiting for, and I was determined not to let it slip by.'

It was an inspired choice. Had the film been a success, it could have led her not only to dry land but to a fresh start in her career and an opportunity both to translate the forces raging inside her into art, and to understand them better. Pasolini had sensed these forces and he hinted at them when he talked about why he wanted Maria for his Medea. 'Here is a woman in one sense the most modern of women, but there lives in her an ancient woman – strange, mysterious, magical, with terrible inner conflicts.' It was these forces and conflicts that fascinated him. He had once described himself as drunk on reality, and he could see the drama in Maria's life reflected in the drama of Medea. 'I'm aware of her professional abilities,' he said during the filming, 'but they are really of very little interest to me. It's from personal qualities in Callas that I realized I could make Medea.' Before they started shooting, he made some notes and showed them to Maria: 'Medea watches Jason, enchanted, lost in him. It is a true and complete love; in this moment it is Jason's virility that prevails. Medea has lost her dazed manner, like a disoriented animal. Suddenly she finds in love which humanizes her a substitute for her lost religious sense. In the sensual experience she finds the lost rapport, the sacred identification with reality. So the world, the future, her well-being, the meaning of things, all take shape again suddenly for her. It is with gratitude like one who feels reborn, that she lets Jason possess her, she in turn possessing in him the regeneration of life.'

Maria recognized the parallels, and through Medea she could relive her own story: the love that made her tap into the woman in her and in some sense humanized her;

the sensual experience of oneness; the new meaning; the new vitality like a rebirth. And in reliving her story through Medea's, she could exorcize some of her bitterness; she could see that it was not, after all, as it had seemed in the dark months that had passed, 'nine years of meaningless sacrifice'.

In the spring, Maria arrived in Rome to settle the details of her contract and discuss her costumes. Franco Rossellini met her at the airport. With him was Nadia Stancioff who had in the past done public relations for the Spoleto and the Venice Festivals and whom he had now asked to handle Maria's public relations. In her contract, though, Maria had stipulated a secretary, not a public relations officer, and indeed this is what Rossellini had told her she was getting. It did not take long for the misunderstanding to come to the surface. Once in her suite at the Grand Hotel, Maria took the cards from all the flowers that had been sent to welcome her and handed them to Nadia, asking her to type some thank you notes. 'And there are also all these bills to be paid,' she said handing them to her together with the cards. 'I'm not your secretary, Madame Callas,' Nadia said, and she went on to explain what she thought she had been hired for.

'Do you realize that you are talking yourself out of a job with Maria Callas?'

'I do, but I am a free spirit and I like to choose. Besides, I've heard some terrible things about you, and in any case, I don't like working with women.'

'You don't! Neither do I,' said Maria, completely won over by Nadia's directness. 'Well, you can stay for a few days and help me choose a secretary.' The next day, the parade of secretaries began: most of them froze at the typewriter at the prospect of working for the great Maria Callas. 'I'll do without a secretary,' Maria finally said. 'Nadia, you stay, you can help me with my lines, get rid of people and generally relieve me of things I don't want to do.'

That was the beginning of a real friendship between the two women: one dark and striking, the other tall and fair; Nadia, half-American and half-Bulgarian, complementing Maria's own Greek-American upbringing. Ironically, after ten days, Nadia, as well as being Maria's friend and barrier against intruders, was also doing everything a secretary would have done. One of the things that made Nadia reconsider 'the terrible things' she had heard about Maria was her attitude to Bruna and Ferruccio. She had brought them with her to Rome, and when she discovered that they had been put in two rooms in the attic, she became furious. She asked the manager to move them instantly to two of the hotel's best rooms. 'And if the production,' she added, 'does not pay the difference, then I will.'

As her friendship with Nadia grew, another fascinating and much more unlikely friendship was beginning for Maria: with Pasolini. Maria, who in her most petty bourgeois moments, had exploded against both Marxists and homosexuals, had found in Pasolini, a passionate Marxist and a notorious homosexual, not just a friend but, as she was to say after his death, a brother. He was a quiet, soft-spoken man with nothing flamboyantly Mediterranean about him. Unlike the average Italian he generally locked his hands together when he talked, and his hollow-cheeked, deeply-lined face showed little animation. Yet this unobtrusive-looking man had been, whether through his films, his views or his friendships with the criminal classes, the centre of colourful scandals which had, by turns, offended orthodox Marxists, orthodox Christians and the middle-of-the-road bourgeoisie.

At the beginning of June 1969 this Marxist mystic and Maria found themselves working together on *Medea* in a forgotten wild corner of Asia Minor. Goreme in Turkey, with its rocks carved into weird shapes, was exactly the place that Pasolini wanted – a place where it was at times hard to distinguish between myth and reality. From Goreme, they went to Aleppo in Syria, and then to Italy, to Pisa, to the lagoons and islands of Grado, to Tor Caldara and Tor Calbona near Rome. And wherever they were, out of rocks and deserts, blanched dunes and beaches, Pasolini recreated a strange, lost world of mystery and magic, a world where ritual, violence and the supernatural were part of everyday life. Even in the loneliest parts of Turkey, reporters, photographers and television cameras were following Maria to document her first, ambitious step into the world of film. Once, to get even closer to her, a journalist dressed up as a local peasant woman, and broke through the cordon surrounding Maria. Another time, protecting her face from the scorching Turkish sun with white muslin, Maria talked to the press about her Medea: 'She was a semi-goddess who put all her beliefs in a man. At the same time she is a woman with all the experiences of a woman, only bigger – bigger sacrifices, bigger hurts. She went through all these trying to survive. You can't put these things into words. . . . I began to look into the depths of the soul of Medea.'

There was in fact hardly any dialogue in *Medea* and Maria sings only once – a Greek lullaby to her son. During her last month in Paris she could hardly get up before midday; in Goreme she was up at dawn. She arrived on the set to be dressed and made up before anyone expected her, always carrying a little transistor tuned to some soap opera or other. Piero Tosi, who had designed her costumes, remembers how 'she'd follow every word with incredible concentration, participating in the action muttering "What's that? What did he say? Go! Go!" – all in Veronese dialect. She gets so involved with whatever she's doing, even if it's only some trivial broadcast.'

She was almost obsessively involved with Medea. In one scene, she was being taken in long-shot, and had to run frantically barefoot on a dry riverbed. She was wearing her heavy gown with huge ropes of pagan jewels, the sun was beating down and she was running, running until she fainted and collapsed on the mud. Pasolini and the entire crew ran towards her and as she came back to consciousness her first words were, 'Please forgive me! I'm so stupid. I shouldn't have done that. It's cost everyone so much time and money.' Maria, the professional, could not bear to be the one slowing things down. She was full of humility about her new adventure, constantly seeking advice, confirmation, reassurance. 'Tell me, is this gesture too grand? Too operatic? I know the rhythm of my own movements, but when the camera is moving as well. . . .'

Pasolini, fascinated by her face, kept wanting to shoot

her in close-up. It was the one thing that made Maria uncomfortable. She would beg him: 'Please shoot from far away, for me!' For the final moments of the film, she refused the stand-in who was available: 'Here,' remembers Piero Tosi, 'Maria reached the apex of her performance. Medea must build a great fire, and holding the bodies of her dead sons, perish in the flames while defying their faithless father. It was very dangerous, because she had to stand on a high wooden platform with flames soaring before her. It was a sacred ritual and Maria, blind as she was, had to hurl herself into the holocaust, or at least seem to do so for the camera's eye. Three times she acted out the scene, and during the last take she nearly fell right into the inferno. For Maria, it could have been done no other way.' When she was not filming, she was looking at the rushes again and again. Rossellini remembers getting bored going through the same rushes: 'I kept telling her, "Come on Maria, let's go and have dinner, or let's go to sleep." But she would not budge.'

'Didn't you find it exhausting to have to shoot the same scene many times?' they asked Maria at the end of July, when the shooting had moved to Italy. 'No, it's futility that exhausts me, not work. . . . There will be a great void when it's all over.' There *was* a void, but something had happened during these two months of living with Medea and Pasolini that nobody could take away from her. There was a deeper understanding of what the last nine years had meant and a deeper acceptance of the way they had ended. She had always called herself a fatalist, and often her fatalism implied resignation, a self-destructive giving up on life. But for the moment, the fatalism was of a different kind: an accepting trust that the patterns, large and small, of every aspect of her life, had some definite, however obscure, meaning. Her relationship with Pasolini, who had always, through both his poetry and his films, sought the meaning and the connections beneath the surface, encouraged this trust.

Their friendship seemed to deepen in the months after the shooting, when Pasolini was editing *Medea* and recording the folk songs and Greek Orthodox music for the background to the film. His editing, though, was hardly of service to Maria. His predilection for the gory and the monstrous meant that he made Maria, at times, look like Jimmy Durante. Nadia, who saw all the rushes with Pasolini, was appalled at the number of shots of sheer beauty that ended on the cutting-room floor. Maria went to Rome herself in December 1969 to look at the rushes, but, awed by Pasolini's intellect and trusting his artistic judgement, she said nothing. She was at the time feeling unusually full of optimism and goodwill. She rang Nadia when she arrived in Rome to arrange to see her: 'You can't come anywhere near me,' said Nadia, 'I am in bed with terrible flu.' Ten minutes later Maria was puffing up Nadia's stairs, with armfuls of the latest books and magazines. And when other friends arrived to visit the patient, Maria opened the door and, in high spirits, introduced herself as the maid. They looked rather puzzled, with that expression that says 'haven't we seen you somewhere before?', but no one called her bluff.

In the same mood of adventure, Maria left with Pasolini for Argentina to present *Medea* at the Festival of Mar del Plata. Then on 28 January 1970 she arrived, again accompanied by Pasolini, at L'Opéra for a first night of which she was doubly the star – on the screen and in the audience. The *première* of Pasolini's *Medea,* in the presence of Madame Pompidou, was one of the most dazzling galas of Maria's career. The *beau monde* was there in force. A box for four had been reserved by Aristotle Onassis, but on the day itself the reservation was cancelled; his wife was not going to be in Paris in time. Nonetheless, he was very much present in Maria's thoughts. She wanted a triumph that would erase the defeats of the past, a triumph that would convince him and the world – but him most importantly – that the past was done and that this was not merely a new beginning, but a new and glorious one. It was not a triumph; it was at best a *succès d'estime*. The gala audience applauded politely and went to dinner. It soon became clear that commercially the film was going to be a failure; its future lay in art cinemas and film clubs. Maria, who had reached millions through the élitist medium of opera, was going to reach only thousands through the popular medium of film.

In her present fragile state, anything less than a complete success would have been a failure for Maria. And psychologically this is precisely what *Medea* was. The hopes of the last few months had been dashed, and she was feeling let down, drained, like a magnet that had lost its charge. Whenever she tried to piece together the splinters of her broken life she found that the image of Aristo was still glued to them. The picture she presented to the world was very different. 'Everything is peaceful with me,' she wrote to her friend Dorle Soria. 'I'm working, practising and enjoying life. As for Daddy O, what is over is over, Sagittarians are like that....' Bravado was increasingly important as the fears it was silencing were becoming louder and more insistent: 'You mustn't go around making a spectacle of your weaknesses. You have to keep your dignity.'

In fact Onassis was back in her life – if, that is, he had ever left it. The day after his wedding, he left his bride honeymooning alone on Skorpios and flew to Athens for a meeting with the head of the Greek junta, George Papadopoulos, over 'Project Omega', a $400 million investment project that was to be carried out over ten years and be the biggest in Greek history. 'On that day,' said one of his associates, 'Onassis was the Sun King. He had everything.'

A few days later, he flew triumphantly to Athens to launch 'Omega' at a press conference. A few days after that, Jackie flew to New York and Onassis resumed his old life. It began with a phone call to Maria. *'Madame n'est pas içi,'* was Bruna's rehearsed reply. 'No, Madame has not told us when she will be back.' The phone call was followed by flowers, by more phone calls, by more flowers. And always: *'Non, madame n'est pas içi.'* It was a familiar game, and he was a master at it. He knew that with a marriage in between it was going to be much harder than before, but he also knew that it was only a matter of time and ingenuity before Maria opened her door and her life to him again. He was not short of either ingenuity or time and, as he longed to see her, he was prepared to take risks. He knew his prey well. He knew that Maria would do anything to protect her 'dignity', to avoid making a 'spectacle' of herself, so he chose the quickest route – whistling under Maria's window at 36 Avenue Georges-Mandel. When this failed, he started calling 'Maria, Maria'; and when *this* failed he threatened to drive his car straight through the front door.

Maggie van Zuylen had prepared the way. She had completely taken Maria's side and was furious with Onassis, but being the supreme realist that she was and knowing Maria's misery, she had started the long process of convincing her that nothing more could be lost by seeing him. Of course seeing him was by no means forgiving him, especially as she could hardly avoid being reminded of the existence of the new Mrs Onassis, of her first Christmas on the *Christina*, of her legendary shopping sprees, of Easter with Rose Kennedy, of Jackie's latest present from her husband, a set of earrings worth $300,000, or a diamond necklace and bracelet worth they did not know quite how much. All Onassis could hold against Maria was her first outburst when asked for a comment after his wedding: 'She did well, Jackie, to give a grandfather to her children. Ari is as beautiful as Croesus.' He reminded her of it at their first reunion, a quiet dinner at Maggie van Zuylen's home immediately after his first Christmas with Jackie. The first time Ari went to dinner at Georges-Mandel, Maria made sure they were not alone: Nadia Stancioff and Francesco Chiarini, an old friend from Milan, Hélène Rochas and the man in her life, Kim d'Astainville, were hastily invited. The house was filled with flowers and all was impeccably arranged for his arrival. Maria rang Chiarini to ask him to play host and sit opposite her at the head of the table; then she rang him again to tell him that she would, after all, ask Ari to sit there. 'You do what you want, Maria,' Chiarini said, 'but I don't think you are right. Ari is now a married man and it would be much more correct to put him on your right.' She did, but throughout the evening she continued to worry. 'She was behaving like a nervous teenager,' remembers Nadia, 'picking the dogs up, putting the dogs down, opening and closing the windows, arranging and rearranging the flowers. At one point, she started showing Onassis the albums of photographs from the shooting of

Medea, and prodding me to tell him stories from the filming: "Nadia, tell Aristo about what happened that morning in Goreme, or that afternoon in Aleppo, or that time in Grado", etc., etc. It was as if she wanted to show him that she could still do things, that life could go on without him.'

As he was once again becoming a regular feature of her life, forgiving him came more easily. What made it easier still was the disenchantment that very soon began to creep into Aristo's marriage. Jackie had, from the beginning, been his Narcissus pool; he could gaze at her and be flattered. But he was soon to discover that he could not sustain himself emotionally on that alone, nor on the surface affection that he and Jackie had for one another. At first Onassis was enjoying indulging the child-wife he had acquired, and protecting her from the Kennedys, the paparazzi, the world. 'Jackie is a little bird that needs its freedom as well as its security,' he said once, 'and she gets both from me. She can do exactly as she pleases – visit international fashion shows and travel and go out with friends to the theatre or any place. And I, of course, will do exactly as I please. I never question her and she never questions me.' Gradually, however, as Jackie spent an estimated $1.5 million in the first year of her marriage, removed his favourite allegorical friezes from the *Christina* and completely, extravagantly and by no means always to his taste, redecorated the Skorpios house, Onassis began to feel invaded and used. It is true that he had once said that 'if women didn't exist all the money in the world would have no meaning', but there was something compulsive, almost manic, about Jackie's spending. And the more he felt used by Jackie, the more he felt loved by Maria.

The turning-point came in February 1970, when all the letters that Jackie had written to her former escort, Roswell Gilpatric, fell into the hands of an autograph dealer and were published round the world before they could be returned to Gilpatric under the terms of a court order. There was one letter among them, written by Jackie from the *Christina* during her honeymoon, that raised a massive bruise on Ari's ego:

Dearest Ros

I would have told you before I left – but then everything happened so much more quickly than I'd planned. I saw somewhere what you had said and I was very touched – dear Ros – I hope you know all you were and are and will ever be to me –

With my love,
Jackie

The day after the publication of the collection of letters, Gilpatric's wife sued for divorce. Onassis was only affected by that one letter, but the blow to his Greek manhood was enormous and totally disproportionate to the actual content of the letter. There was such a deep fear in him of any real or potential social humiliation that a large part of his life – not least his marriage to Jackie – was lived in an attempt to 'show' the world, before the world had had a chance to 'show' him. Now the world that he had intended to dazzle and to some extent *had* dazzled with his marriage was quietly laughing behind his back: 'My God,' he was confessing to his intimates, 'what a fool I have made of myself.'

Jackie called to apologize and explain. He was a model of sophisticated, *homme du monde* understanding. Not long after that, he took his revenge. He spent four successive evenings with Maria and was seen leaving Georges-Mandel at one o'clock in the morning. On the evening of 21 May, Maria and he were photographed radiantly smiling at Maxim's. They were, it is true, chaperoned by Maggie, but it was too much for Jackie – which, of course, is precisely what it was intended to be. She called Ari from New York and warned him that she was leaving immediately for Paris. She was not met at the airport, but the same night, at the same restaurant, at the same table where Ari and Maria had dined with Maggie van Zuylen, Ari and Jackie dined alone. Neither of them seemed in a mood to enjoy the evening. There were long pauses and closed faces, but, after all, this was not a private dinner: Jackie was making a public statement to the world and to Maria.

Maria heard it all too clearly. She knew that Aristo had

opened his heart to her as to no one else. He had complained about Jackie, he had raged against Jackie, he had defied Jackie by appearing with Maria at Maxim's. But when Jackie instantly demanded a symbolic replay of his dinner with Maria, Aristo did what Jackie wanted. From Maxim's they went to Régine's where they stayed until 2.30 in the morning.

For Maria their four nights together crowned with their first public appearance since his wedding, and this at their favourite old haunt, had been much more than an exercise in nostalgia. He had made not just these five nights but the days in between hum with a joy she had almost forgotten. She could once again feel life flowing through her, and after nearly two years of being dignified, self-possessed, even cheerful, she could experience happiness, something she thought she had lost for ever. The joy was real, the life flowing through her was real, but on the basis of these few happy days she began to build her fantasies about the future. How extravagant they were we do not know. What we know is that the day after Ari's tête-à-tête dinner with Jackie at Maxim's, they were in ruins. Two days later, on Wednesday 25 May, Giulini and his wife went to dinner with Maria at Georges-Mandel. They found her worried, anxious and full of gnawing fears. 'Please stay for a while,' she said, when they were getting ready to leave. 'Don't leave me alone. Please stay. . . .' They did finally leave, both of them very perturbed about her emotional state. The next morning, Marcella Giulini called to find out how she was. She had been taken to the American Hospital.

At 8.50 that same morning, Edgar Schneider had announced on Radio Luxembourg: 'Maria Callas has attempted to commit suicide by taking an overdose of barbiturates. She has been urgently admitted to the American Hospital at Neuilly.' Maria had been taken there at seven o'clock in the morning. But had she tried to take her life? Or was she at the American Hospital, as the official story from Georges-Mandel had it, for her routine check-up, only earlier than usual?

Neither the official nor the sensational version was accurate. She was clearly not there at seven o'clock in the morning for a routine check-up, but neither had she attempted to commit suicide, at any rate with the conscious decision the assertion implied. In the previous three days, feeling once again betrayed, once again used, a rope in Onassis's tug-o'-war with his wife, an instrument in the service of his damaged pride, she began to feel life draining from her. A web of futility – the emotion she dreaded more than any other – had spun itself round her. It was the same pattern she had described to John Ardoin: 'My hopes are built to the skies and then banged down. Oh no. I've had enough of these ups and downs. I'd rather stay down all the time. . . .' She had, however temporarily, given up on life, and giving up on life is not such a long way from consciously taking it. She longed for sleep but it eluded her. The sinus trouble that had plagued her all her life had come back and at times she felt as though she could not even breathe. She took more sleeping-tablets to find sleep and more barbiturates to find peace. By the time the morning of 26 May dawned, she was so dazed that she was barely conscious.

By the middle of the afternoon she had left the American Hospital. But the news went on travelling. 'I've never received so many flowers without singing,' she said. The phone did not stop ringing. Reporters and well-wishers crowded outside Georges-Mandel. The news of her attempted suicide had struck a deep chord with the public, far beyond the fascination of the sensational. 'It's because of Onassis,' was the universal conclusion. And everybody who had ever been jilted, rejected, abandoned for someone else could identify with Maria in a way they would never have identified had she been just another of the rich and the famous unhappy with their lot.

Back at Georges-Mandel, Maria, whose will to live was still stronger than her will to die, was in a fighting mood: 'All this anxiety about me is very touching, but at the same time it's an invasion both of my private and my professional life.' After a few days, when the weekly paper *Noir et Blanc* repeated Edgar Schneider's claim, Maria asked her lawyer, Yves Cournot, to sue both *Noir et Lanc* and Radio Luxembourg. On 4 November she won the case and was awarded 20,000 francs in damages.

Meanwhile she had retreated back behind the armour of her legend. And she built the fortifications around her even higher than before. 'The less you give, the less you're hurt,' she said. 'Even if you meet something that's good you don't want it because you are so afraid. So even that is spoiled. You're not open-minded, you're not confident.' It seemed so logical: she had been hurt by people, by things outside herself; it must be because she was not sufficiently protected. Yet the more she cut herself off from life, the more frightening the chill creeping over her world became. 'It is very difficult to be friends with a star,' she said once. Frightened of being used, terrified of being hurt, she would hold back, always defensive, warding people off.

She was still trying to see the pattern that her life was to take. For the time being the pattern emerging was made up of ceremony and protocol: Maria, standing next to Jacques Baumel, the French Secretary of State, cutting the ribbon inaugurating the *Nocturnes du Faubourg Saint-Honoré* with the Republican Guard on horseback; Maria in Moscow, the official guest of Madame Furtseva, the Soviet Minister of Culture, judging the finals of the Tchaikovsky Competition; Maria at the opening night of the new season at La Scala, sitting resplendent next to Ghiringhelli in his box – still the unchallenged Queen of La Scala. At the beginning of the second interval, the audience suddenly broke into spontaneous applause punctuated by cries of *'Ritorna Maria'*. It was a passionate explosion for a woman whose every performance had had the hallmark of passion and who was now, visibly moved, acknowledging her public's gratitude for what she had given them and their longing to have her back.

In between ceremonial appearances she had, for the first time since Aristo's marriage, come back to Greece to stay with Perry Embiricos at Tragonisi, his private island in the Aegean. Tragonisi belonged to the Petalii group of islands on which various members of the Embiricos family were scattered. Maria had met Perry, who, like the rest of his family, was in shipping, through Onassis early on in their relationship. Now in his fifties, never married and a great music lover, Perry Embiricos spent a large part of the year on the island. It was kept in perfect order, with its beautiful main house, a ravishing garden and two cottages for his guests. Pasolini joined them for a few days, as did Constantine Gratsos and his wife, Anastasia. Gratsos had been a friend of Aristo's since the Argentinian days and his partner in the whaling business. He and Anastasia were the two people from Onassis's immediate entourage who stayed closest to Maria after the break-up. Maria had also invited Nadia Stancioff. 'I can't afford it right now,' Nadia had said, whereupon Maria sent her a ticket to Athens and was waiting for her at the airport so that they could fly by helicopter to Tragonisi. They spent hours lying on the beach, talking. 'She seemed obsessed by death at the time,' Nadia remembers. 'In an instinctive, almost primitive, way, she believed in reincarnation. "I wonder what I'll be when I come back," she said once. "I don't want to be buried," she told me at another time: "I want to be burned, I don't want to become a worm." Like many Greeks she was superstitious about preparing a will, as if writing things down brought bad luck.'

They all met together at meal-times, and after dinner they would play cards or listen to music; but most of Maria's day was spent in the water, swimming, fishing underwater and coming up with shells, strangely shaped stones, the odd piece of antiquity like an urn, and once even a small fish. She had a hard, peasant skin that tanned marvellously, and with her tan and her long hair pulled straight back, she looked confident, strong and free. She may have hated all sports, and even disliked walking, but she was a passionate swimmer. The sea was always a joy for Maria, bringing out the child in her, and with it all her optimism.

In that expansive mood, on her nameday, 15 August, she received a surprise visit. Onassis flew in by helicopter, kissed her on the lips under her big beach umbrella, put a pair of 100-year-old earrings on her ears, kissed Djedda, the poodle he had given her, was photographed doing all these things, and flew out again. All was once again forgiven. The Greek bearing kisses and gifts had wiped his record clean – until the next time. Maria was becoming more and more resigned to the fact that their relationship, however unsatisfying and even humiliating to her, still remained the most important thing in her life. So although many hopes had died, others still flickered, and there was in any case the precious knowledge, which time only confirmed, that she was his greatest friend. Whatever happened, she would be there; and whatever happened, and many things did, she was.

Talking about him in public, Maria would always come up with statements which, although true, were such a pale echo of the truth that they were nothing more than cautious evasions for public consumption. 'I have a great respect for Aristotle, and there is no reason for us not meeting here since Mr Embiricos is a mutual friend.' Or, with a touch more truth, 'He is my best friend. He is, he was, and he always will be. When two people have been together as we have, there are many things that tie you together. He knows he will always find cheerfulness, mutual friends and honesty when he sees me.' In private, Maria referred to her best friend's wife as 'the gold-digger', but in public, whenever asked about Jackie, she was always on her best behaviour. The tension and resentment can only be heard simmering in the pauses between words. 'The scandal comes about because I have never met his wife. It's not wished on the other side. Frankly, I don't understand why she doesn't come into my life. . . . No, I didn't know about the wedding, and frankly I don't think *he* knew about the wedding. You'll have to ask her.'

Maria saw 1971 in at a party in Paris given by André Oliver, Pierre Cardin's partner, but parties and night-clubs no longer held much attraction for her. Her days were acquiring a new pattern. In the morning she never got up, unless she absolutely had to, before midday. At night, she would do anything to postpone going to bed. Watching westerns on television was becoming her second favourite occupation; her first, which was almost an obsession, was listening to herself on the many pirate records and tapes her fans sent her from round the world. If she had friends in for supper, they would, more likely than not, be asked to listen to one of these unofficial recordings: perhaps it would be her Berlin *Lucia,* or on another night a concert in Dallas, or her Mexico *Aida*, or her *Tosca* from Rio de Janeiro. Maria, reclining on a couch with Pixie or Djedda in her lap, would listen intently, absorbed, almost in a trance, coming out of it only to offer a comment, self-contained, waiting for no reply, and then return to her own world until the tape was over. 'Didn't she sing well,' she would say sometimes, totally detached at Georges-Mandel from the Callas of Berlin, Dallas or Rio de Janeiro. At other times it rained reminiscences. But most of the time, Maria was listening on her own, the Callas triumphs trooping by in their old glory, the panorama of her life sweeping past her.

Maria's life was increasingly dominated by the past, a past transfigured by selective memory and imagination. She was living in that past and doing no more than existing in the bland present, and yet she would never, not even once, talk of retiring, let alone admit that she had. Would she dare sing again? The last major singing project she had seriously considered was a new recording of *Traviata*, which was due to take place in the second half of 1968. It is still known around EMI as the 'Great *Traviata* Fiasco'. It was to be recorded at the Hall of Santa Cecilia in Rome with Giulini conducting and Luciano Pavarotti as Alfredo. The negotiations were strewn with Maria's prevarications, but finally all was ready, the hall booked, the artists contracted. At that point, Peter Andry, head of the classical division of EMI, got a phone call from a distraught Maria saying that she could not possibly go on. It was immediately after her break-up with Onassis, and it was indeed true that she could not possibly go on, but it was nonetheless a great blow. 'It took until October 1970,' remembers Peter Andry, 'to clear up all the various claims from artists. When finally I brought myself to call her again it was "What's new?" and "What else?" as though nothing had happened.'

'What else?', 'What's new?', were Maria's favourite, automatic questions. She had no doubt that her legend could compete with and outdistance anything new. But could she? She had to find out, but cautiously, like an invalid taking his first uncertain steps after a long illness. In February 1971 a two-week master-class at the Curtis

Institute in Philadelphia seemed a safe beginning. On the way there, she stopped in New York for a question and answer session at the Juilliard School. The excitement that accompanied everything she did had attracted a star-studded audience to pack the Juilliard to see and hear her. Rudolf Bing and Göran Gentele, who was to replace him as General Manager of the Met, were in the audience listening to Maria expound on love, on drama, on directors, on becoming a singer, on her favourite roles and, above all, on resuming her career: 'I developed some bad vocal habits, so I retired to start again. Now I am ready. I've never stopped learning. Do you know what that means? It's a lifetime job. I'm planning to announce, and probably soon this year, my plans for singing again. I've never asked for anything. I've been asked. I know how to wait. And I'm always ready when the chance comes.' It all added up to the typical Callas response: a touch of earnestness, a touch of home-spun philosophizing and plenty of bravado.

While she was in New York, Maria saw a lot of Anastasia Gratsos. One afternoon when she was sitting with Anastasia in her hotel room talking, she decided on the spur of the moment to accompany her to her eye-doctor's appointment. 'And how long is it since you've had your eyes examined, Madame Callas?' asked the doctor. The answer was 'far too long', and the result of the examination which followed was that Maria discovered that she was suffering from incipient glaucoma which, if not arrested, could have led to blindness. Every two hours from that day on she had to put drops in her eyes. She bought a beautiful little Louis Quinze alarm that she hung round her neck, which was set to go off at two-hourly intervals. Wherever she was, sometimes in the middle of a conversation, Maria would excuse herself and go and put in her drops or, if she was with friends, she would put them in there and then.

Armed with her drops, Maria left New York for Philadelphia. She arrived to find eighteen students none of them remotely ready for the advanced work which interested her. She made them sing one by one, made some suggestions about vocal technique and returned to New

York. The Philadelphia experiment had to be decreed a failure, and the American press wanted to know what would follow. In her suite at the Regency, in black trousers, and a frilly white blouse, Maria received more journalists. As always, she began by introducing them to the poodles: 'Djedda is the brown one and Pixie the white.' Ari had given them to her, and she had named Djedda after the Saudi Arabian town where Ari was doing business at the time. When Maria hugged the little dogs, there was no doubt of her love for them; but when there was work to be done she would send them out of the room like a severe mother with her distracting children. 'Shoot,' she smiled to the journalists, opening her big, dark eyes in mock terror. 'Have you given up the operatic stage?' came the question everyone wanted answered. She bridled. 'Not at all! I study constantly and I would be delighted to return to New York in a new role in a new production – something in the order of *Anna Bolena*. Everybody wants me to sing *Tosca* but I'm bored with *Tosca.*' It was seven years since she had appeared in a new production and on the final night the curtain did not rise on the last act. That memory still haunted her, but rarely in public and almost as rarely in private did she strip off some of the veils of her celebrity to give others a glimpse of her private agony.

Now, as she felt her energies ebbing away, she needed even more the vitality that she always got from being the focus of attention. It was as if when she was watched, observed, admired, she became more alert inside herself; and this alertness in turn became vitality. Back in Paris from New York she accepted the Honorary Presidency of the Gala of the Artists' Union. Michael Cacoyannis remembers her on the opening night of the Gala, which was a spectacular circus night with everything from acrobatics to lion-taming. 'She beamed with pleasure. She needed confirmation that she existed and the limelight provided it.'

On this occasion, however, she had also enjoyed the time before the Gala. She loved circuses as she loved Disneyland, but as a child she was never taken to them. She now had an opportunity not only to enjoy the circus but also to indulge a child's fantasy by commanding the acts she wanted on the bill. The organization had given her a code name, Germaine, so as to keep the identity of the President of the Gala a surprise, and Germaine's wishes were to be obeyed: 'Germaine wants . . .', 'Germaine prefers . . .', 'Germaine adores . . .', or 'No serpent numbers, Germaine hates snakes. . . .' Maria herself called no one by his name. It was *'Mon ange'*, or *'Mon grand diable'*. 'We could talk to her about anything,' remembers Dominique Perrin, who organized the Gala, 'except Onassis. This always caused her pain.'

It was in 1971 that the shadows began to lengthen across the bright surface of Onassis's life. The man who had fulfilled his dream of being one of the most conspicuous people on the planet, as well as his dreams of power and wealth, was beginning to discover that he was not omnipotent and could not control everything and everybody. On 19 July, his 'pet', Christina, got married in Las Vegas to Joseph Bolker, a forty-eight-year-old real estate dealer with four daughters from a previous marriage. Onassis heard the news of his daughter's wedding on Skorpios while celebrating Jackie's forty-second birthday. He raged for hours, cut Christina off from her trust and for the next six months subjected them, according to Joseph Bolker, 'to extraordinary pressures', until finally the following February they started divorce proceedings. Meanwhile Onassis had received a much greater shock – and about this he could do nothing. On 22 October his first wife, now divorced from the Marquess of Blandford, was secretly married in Paris to his lifelong rival, Stavros Niarchos. It was eighteen months after her sister Eugenia, who was married to Niarchos, had died on their private island from a combination of physical injuries and a large quantity of barbiturates. After three expert examinations of the body, the investigating magistrate instituted proceedings against Niarchos and called for his arrest. The Piraeus high court decided against charging him, but the gossip and the rumours went on raging, and were still rife when, just over a year after the case had been officially closed, Tina married the man over whom a grim question-mark continued to hang.

Onassis's shock was shared by his children, whose mistrust of Niarchos – a mistrust with which they had both been brought up – had deepened even further since their aunt's death. For quite a long time after Tina's marriage to Niarchos, Ari refused even to acknowledge her existence. It was not so much a question of hurt pride; his primeval sense of decency, his very world, with its precious few fixed points, had been turned upside down.

But the greatest blow was even closer to home: it was the realization, which he could no longer hide from himself, that his own marriage had been a calamitous mistake. 'Cold-hearted and shallow' is how he was describing Jackie, who had only two years earlier been 'like a diamond, cool and sharp at the edges, fiery and hot beneath the surface'. He craved love, but had to settle instead for flattery and attention, for being talked about and stared at. While Jackie was finding this Greek drama with its ragings and explosions impossible to cope with, Maria lived through them with him. It was to Maria that he ran for the love that, now that he had everything else, he was beginning to see was the only thing he really wanted. He would fly over to see her or, more often, he would talk with her for hours on the phone.

Throughout this time Maria was in New York, preparing for the master-classes she had agreed to give at the Juilliard, starting in October. From the Plaza, where she was staying, she wrote to François Valéry, one of her closest friends in Paris: 'My very dear François – Imagine I'm writing to you! How are you? I'm busy – well – and studying – I already started yesterday! Believe it or not. . . . I wish you would drop me a line every now and then because I will not be back until mid-November. This month is my studying, then my classes start. All my love, Maria.' She was 'studying' with Alberta Masiello in a room at the Juilliard, and studying is the right word. She was feeling and behaving like a hesitant beginner excited at the slightest sign of progress. 'Did you hear?' she would exclaim to Masiello, 'I sang a whole phrase . . .' or 'Did you hear? I sang two phrases today.'

Tito Gobbi remembers seeing her in New York at that time and taking her to dinner with his wife and daughter

Cecilia: 'After dinner we took her back to the Plaza, where she was staying and just before going into the lift, she turned to me and said: "Oh Tito, I am so lonely, I am so alone here, I don't even have my little dog, why don't you buy me an ice-cream at the corner?" We went round the block, and bought our ice-creams in the street – just a way of postponing the moment she would once again be left alone.' Soon after that Maria, unable to bear the loneliness any longer, sent for Bruna to come to New York with the two little dogs.

The master-classes at the Juilliard began on 11 October. They were classes with a difference, taking place on the stage of the Juilliard theatre with a gala crowd in the audience which, over the two six-week sessions, included Franco Zeffirelli, Placido Domingo, Tito Gobbi, Gina Bachauer and Grace Bumbry among many other notables.

No applause is allowed, but there is, nonetheless, a loud burst of it when Maria walks in from the wings. She waves her hand for silence: this is a class, not a performance. 'Are we all settled?' There are pictures of her at the Juilliard with her long, auburn hair falling in thick waves over her shoulders, her horn-rimmed glasses more on than off (after all Ari is unlikely to be watching), involved, smiling, at ease. The emphasis of the teacher, like the emphasis of the performer, is on reaching the emotional heart of the music, communicating its drama. She listens absorbed, sometimes beating time with her ballpoint. Sometimes only her ever-expressive eyes show whether she approves or disapproves; sometimes with a regal wave of the hand she stops them.

To the young tenor singing a duet from *Butterfly:* 'Do you know what you are saying to her?' 'Yeah, I'm telling her "At last you're mine."' 'Then *sing* it that way,' she snaps back.

To the soprano who has just gone through Gilda's 'Caro nome': 'Gilda is a passionate girl, you know; you must convey to the audience all her palpitating emotion before you even begin to sing. The very act of breathing is an emotion.'

To a tenor slightly lacking in intensity: 'Come on now, Mario. More passion. You are a Neapolitan, you have no excuse.' But when he makes to embrace the soprano, she instantly interrupts: 'No gestures! With the *voice*!'

To a Korean baritone singing the prologue from *Pagliacci*: 'You have a big voice there; let it out . . . I don't care if you crack on the top note, but hit it hard. Caruso cracked many times.' And not just Caruso. But only once did Maria allow her pupils and the audience into her own private agony. A young soprano had just finished singing Aida's 'O patria mia', and had made a bit of a mess of it. She turned to Maria to explain: 'There are three or four notes I just can't manage.' 'Likewise,' was Maria's reply, and the self-mocking smile did not stop the shivers from running down everyone's spine.

When she was asked once what was the greatest key to performing music well, Maria had replied: 'You must make love to it.' Yet when a student soprano at the Juilliard neglected the trills in a Verdi aria, Maria stopped her: 'Where are those trills?' 'Do I have to do them?' pleaded the girl. 'Could you imagine a violinist or pianist,' she snapped, 'even a beginner in this conservatory, refusing or unable to perform those written ornaments? He would be thrown out; considered incompetent. With singers, it is no different – whatever they might think.' This combination of technical mastery and musical passion was what made Maria unique. But could this secret be communicated? For that matter were the Juilliard master-classes the opportunity for music's retired High Priestess to pass on her wisdom and her secrets to the younger generation? Or were they a safe way for the greatest dramatic singer in the world to try out her strength in public, illustrating her teaching by singing but without running the risk of being judged? There is no doubt that, although Maria became totally involved with her pupils, she did see the master-classes mainly as an attempt to break through her terror of singing in public by doing so as an extension of teaching on stage. And there is no doubt that most of the notables in the audience, from former colleagues to the new General Manager of the Met, were there not so much to hear Maria's advice on interpretation as to hear Maria demonstrate her advice. 'Suddenly,' wrote Richard Roud, 'during the *Butterfly* duet, one heard a ghostly third voice – Callas singing along with the soprano. Then, like something out of the past, that magnificent voice welled up. Like the curate's egg, however, it is magnificent only in parts. A phrase of five or six notes comes out with all the black velvet splendour of the old days: then without warning it goes. Like some ancient tapestry there are patches where the colours are still bright, where the gold threads still gleam, but there are others where it is so threadbare that you can see right down to the warp and woof.'

Despite all the caveats, Maria did get from the Juilliard master-classes the simple confirmation that she could once again face the public without the paralysing panic of the last years of her career. But she could not have enough reassurance; she wanted another opinion. Michael Cacoyannis happened to be in New York producing *Bohème,* so she arranged to sing just for him one afternoon at the Juilliard theatre, which she had booked in great secrecy. 'She asked me to sit somewhere where she couldn't see me,' recalled Cacoyannis. 'She was nervous and apologetic. "I've just come back from the dentist," she explained. "So I'm not in very good voice. . . ."'

It is a haunting scene. The great Callas, nervous as at her first audition, singing in an empty auditorium for one man, a friend who she knew cared for her, but whom nevertheless she wanted hidden somewhere in the dark, so that she could not even feel him there even though, blind as she was, she would in any case not have seen him; and yet eagerly, anxiously, waiting for his opinion, for reassurance. 'You can do it, Maria,' he said.

There were not many left who believed that she could. She asked Peter Menin, the head of the Juilliard School, whether he thought she could do it. 'It was an honest question, and it deserved an honest answer,' he remembers, 'so I said no. The room she had been working in with Masiello was acoustically very good, a room that flattered the voice. This and the response she got during the master-classes had encouraged her too much. But demonstrating a phrase beautifully is not the same as carrying off a whole evening.'

In March 1972, the master-classes were drawing to a

close, and the future lay barren ahead of her. George Moore, President of the Metropolitan Opera board, had unexpectedly offered her the job of Artistic Director at the Met. She was sufficiently interested to spend a lunch-hour at the Oak Room at the Plaza discussing with Schuyler Chapin, then Manager of the Met, the dreadful state of opera houses. But no more.

It was around this time that di Stefano came back into her life. The last time they had sung together was on 22 December 1957, the last night of *Un Ballo in Maschera* at La Scala. 'Maria, let's come back together,' he said now, and he said it again and again. Maria never answered 'no' straight away, even when she had no intention of ever saying 'yes', but in this case she had a much greater investment in the discussions. For a start Maria dreaded the emptiness stretching ahead once the master-classes were over. Even more important, in terms of reliving her old triumphs, di Stefano was infinitely better than a hundred pirate recordings. He was like a walking embodiment of her glorious years. All the old animosities, fights and walkouts melted in the warmth of reliving their past together. Di Stefano's tenor voice was one of the best of the century, but the animal intensity with which he sang had very quickly used up his voice. 'What is so exciting about him,' someone had said in di Stefano's heyday, 'is that he is dying as he is singing.' By the time he met Maria again his career had rather ingloriously petered out. It was a curious match, grounded in weakness: di Stefano, musically dead for years, feeding off Maria's legend and Maria, consumed with fears, feeding off his raw Italian bluster which at first she took for strength. Deeply lonely, Maria let herself drift into a relationship that gave her some joy but mostly caused her great pain. Di Stefano was married, and, according to Maria's strict moral code, one does not have affairs with married men. What made it even harder was that di Stefano's wife – another Maria, as it happened – was someone she knew and liked. As always for Maria, when action and belief diverged, guilt closed the gap. She remained, right to the end, extremely secretive about their relationship, and only to her godfather did she write openly and freely.

Their match was rooted in the past, but di Stefano was determined that it would at least have a professional future. The first attempt was a recording made in London at the end of 1972 with Antonio de Almeida conducting. The greatest secrecy shrouded all the arrangements. Until the last moment the London Symphony Orchestra did not even know who the soloists would be. Verdi and Donizetti duets were recorded and re-recorded. There were many problems, one of them being that di Stefano seemed unable to sing except at full volume. But they were all determined to perform the miracle, and slowly, patiently, resurrect two of the century's greatest voices.

On 4 December, a few days after the recording sessions had begun, Maria heard the news of her father's death in Athens. He was eighty-six years old, and by then nearly blind. After his marriage he had returned to live in Greece, and had become even more remote from Maria's life. So she felt all the more strongly that many things were unresolved; and now he was dead. She felt a warmth for him she had not often experienced in the last few years, and this intensified her grief. She remembered once, when she was a child, walking with him in New York. She wanted an ice-cream but would not ask for it. She stopped in front of the ice-cream vendor and pulled her father's jacket, but she would not ask. And when, then and later, she longed for his attention and tenderness she still did not ask. Nor did he. So there they both were, meeting mainly on her first nights, but drifting apart, by then both of them finding it hard either to give tenderness or to receive it. And the rift his remarriage had caused seemed now so harsh and unnecessary.

His death had another effect, in many ways much more painful. It opened the doors to the greatest of all the remaining items on the agenda of her life – her relationship with her mother. 'I would never make up with my mother, and I have very good reasons,' she had said a year earlier. 'She did many wrong things to me, and blood is just not that strong a tie. I don't feel I have to act and say "mother darling". I just can't fake.' It was by no means so clear-cut. Her resentment was one side of the equation; her guilt was the other. When the buzz of the world had subsided, the guilt recollected in solitude became too intense, too uncomfortable to be ignored. She still could not bear, as she said, to 'make up' with her mother, but she needed to do something to exorcize the guilt, so she began sending her money. Evangelia saved all the pink receipt slips from the bank as though they were love letters. And in a sense they were; or, if not love letters, they were at any rate the first evidence of a thawing in their relationship.

Maria's conflicts with her family came up in one of her most pained, incoherent and contradictory outbursts to John Ardoin, beginning with a reference to a recent telephone conversation with her sister. 'But when you have a family and that family kicks you like mad. . . . And then on top of it she says of mamma's growing, pappa's growing older you know. Now what would you feel like? I could strangle that girl, girl – a woman of over fifty. You tell me that they're growing older. Well of course they're older, so am I, everybody's growing older. So what do we have? Four homes isolated, mine and three of theirs. Miserably alone. At least I have accomplished something that is true. But why should I have accomplished something alone, and why should I now be alone at home when we all should be, all four of us, one helping the other. . . . Not the least thought. A revolution happened in Paris. Do you think my parents called or my sister? Not one. My friends called, admirers who don't even know me, from London, from Italy. My ex-maid, my ex-cook called me. That makes you think, you know . . .'. And seven years later, in August 1975, she came back to the same bitter theme, and even some of the same bitter words, in a letter to her godfather.

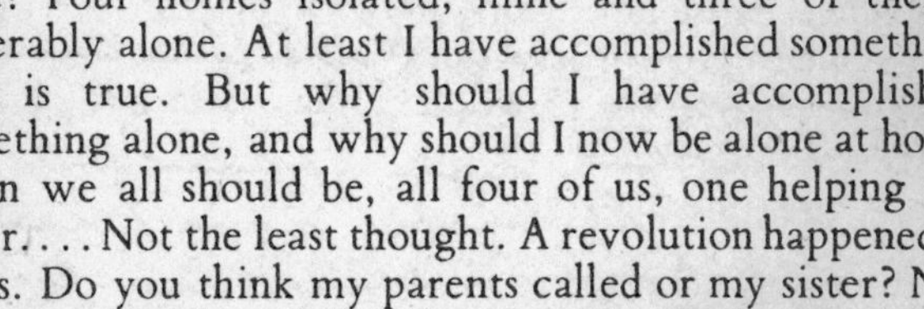
is for my mother and
sister; - have seen my sister
buy and furnish a lovely
home on her own and beg
for a part-time maid to
me, I cannot understand -

I also give my sister some money every month and I know she does not need them. She's had Embiricos's inheritance then why beg for $300. I understand their saying they cannot live on the money I send them but they live very well, I hear. Also my sister wrote she has heart trouble and cannot work (clean her house, that's all she does and has ever done) It's the cheapness of their souls I cannot stand! They never say — Maria — how are you? Do you need anything? Are you sick? Everybody cares about me but they never gave a damn about me — It's not new but I still cannot get use to it. Only when they need money do they write.

"Never mind if you see me complaining but it's a pity we are not a united family — We all would of been less lonely.

There is not one word from Maria on the subject of her mother and her family spoken from any standpoint other than that of the victim. Her unconscious longing to end the division with her family became much more intense and conscious when there was no longer any hope of having a family of her own. And yet she did nothing, and indeed thwarted all attempts to bring them together. The longing was real, but the fear was no less real; nor is the paradox so hard to understand. If Maria had been reconciled with her mother, she would have had, for the first time, to stop blaming her for eveything in her life, and this would have started the process of ending one of her most persistent and self-destructive patterns. There were very many things for which she could blame her mother, just as there was a lot of truth in her complaints about Meneghini, the Rome Opera House management, Ghiringhelli and Rudolf Bing. But her sense of having been victimized and her underlying self-pity became a poison running through her life and corroding everything long after the events themselves or the actual harm done. 'God, I'm still feeling the result of Rome,' she said in 1968, exactly ten years after her Rome walk-out. 'I could not go on with the performance, I could not be killed that way. It would be stupidity. If I had my vocal possibilities, if I hadn't been sick, I would have stood there. I've done that thousands of times at the Scala, everywhere. I'm famous for having defended myself well. The tigress, they call me. But do I need to be crucified? I didn't have my voice. It was slipping all the time, with an aggressive public. And so forth and so on, and this and that, and my mother and now him. I've got to sit back and take it and try not to say anything, for whatever I do say will be to my disadvantage. Whatever I say, it will be undignified for me, not for them. Who cares? So I don't have even one friend. Why?'

This outburst, which puts Maria in the centre of a hostile world out to do her harm, to betray her, to 'crucify' her, sums up the way she perceived reality. 'Only my dogs will not betray me,' she said in the last few months of her life. By the end, these convictions had become a veil which would not allow her to experience or even see anything that contradicted them. What she looked for she discovered, what she expected she brought to pass; yet towards the end, the same woman who had against all odds made herself everything that she had become, was seeing life as something that hapened to her, and herself as at the mercy of others, as the victims of their hostility, their incompetence, their dishonesty. And this in turn increased her pain, her anger and, above all, her fear.

Yet she did have glimpses of how, contrary to what she believed, she had in herself the key to change all this and to find the peace that was eluding her. 'All these things have become reflexes. . . . I look at myself and I say, "Well, Maria, you had better start working on your subconscious now, to clean out the bad thoughts or the bad reflexes that have been created."' But this would have meant daring to delve into the depths of her consciousness where she had all these years been storing hurts, bitterness, anger and resentment; having truly confronted them and understood them, she could, for the first time, have been free of them – and free of her mother, free of her ex-husband, free of all the assorted enemies she went on carrying on her back right to the end. But she did not dare set out on the journey she had outlined for herself. She was becoming more desperate, more isolated, more bitter with each year. The recording, in the middle of which she had received the news of her father's death, turned out to be a failure. Despite the most skilful editing, she decided that it could not be released.

It was her last foray into a recording studio, but she needed to work. 'Work, work, work, that's everything,' she said at the time. 'The important thing for me is to work. There is of course love too. But if I believe in love, I believe also in my art, and art demands discipline.' The mantle of the Vestal Virgin that she had worn willingly, singlemindedly, even passionately for over twenty years, she was now clutching to herself, assuming an old role that she did not want, because she was afraid to fall back on herself.

The woman who as a young girl had crossed the Atlantic alone with $100 in her pocket, ready to brave everything to build her career, was now scared to take any step without di Stefano to lean on. The Teatro Regio in Turin, which had just been completed and was described by enthusiasts as 'the most beautiful theatre in Europe', was to open its doors on 10 April 1973. They wanted a spectacular opening, so they asked the most spectacular person in the world of opera. As they knew that she would not agree to sing, they invited her to make her debut in a new career by directing *I Vespri Siciliani,* with which they were planning to open the first season. Yes, said Maria, but only if di Stefano can be my co-director. The Turin management agreed – after all, having Maria as an opera director was a spectacular coup, di Stefano or no di Stefano – and Maria began work.

Two months before she started rehearsing she was to be the witness to a deep misery she could do nothing to ease. On 22 January 1973, Alexander Onassis took off from Athens in his father's Piaggio for a test run to check on a personal pilot before assigning him to the plane. Seconds later, the Piaggio banked sharply, causing the plane to cartwheel for 460 feet and crash. Alexander was recognized only by the monogram on his bloodstained handkerchief. His right temple had been reduced to pulp and his brain was irreparably damaged. Onassis's son had been the most important person in his life, not because of their relationship, which was by no means a wholly happy one, but because the son represented the future – the only intimation of immortality for a man totally caught up in the world. By the time Onassis and Jackie arrived from New York, Alexander was being kept alive by a life-support system in an oyygen tent. A few hours later all hope had gone. Onassis asked them to wait until Christina had arrived from Brazil and then 'to torture him no more'. In his first shocking paroxysm of grief, he refused to have Alexander buried. Nobody quite knew what he wanted instead. In between spells of catatonic pain and outbursts of rage and blasphemy, he wanted the body 'deep-frozen'. Then he wanted him buried inside the chapel on Skorpios – a privilege reserved for saints. Finally he agreed to have him buried by the side of the chapel and have the grave covered by an annex later.

After the funeral Maria provided his only hold on life. She had herself been deeply shaken by Alexander's death. Six months earlier, when the man who had succeeded Rudolf Bing at the Met had died in a car crash in Italy, she had written to Dorle Soria: 'I was horrified by the death of Gentele.... We think we are here forever, and we plan ahead, but you never know.' When Maggie van Zuylen had died the year before, Maria had been afraid to surrender to her grief, with its inescapable reminder of her own mortality. Now, as she began to understand the depth of Ari's sense of loss, she was too shaken to resist any longer the full power of her fear of death, and she could think of nothing else. But it was his pain that hurt her most. When he first came to see her after the funeral, she was appalled by the sight of the man who walked in, and after a few minutes with him she was even more frightened. He was not the man she knew, but he was still the man she loved. It was as if a lifetime's guilt had crystallized around Alexander's death. If he had only changed the Piaggio for a helicopter, Alexander would be alive; if only he had not asked to have the new pilot tested, his son would still be with him. . . . Maria could see that his grief and rage, unchecked and turned against himself, were destroying him. At such a time his conviction that behind the crash was a conspiracy by his enemies, baseless though it was, at least directed some of the poisonous rage away from himself and towards the imaginary but hated villains. He offered half a million dollars to any informant and half a million to a charity of his choice. 'He had built himself,' recalled one of his aides, 'a whole edifice of suspicion and paranoia; the number of suspects and supposed motives was almost limitless.' He seemed determined to spend everything he owned and the rest of his life to find out who had killed his son; that someone had, he was in no doubt.

For Maria, seeing him like this – he suddenly looked old and wrinkled, all vigour spent – and listening to his manic outpourings had the shock effect of revealing that the man she had for years idealized was not, after all, the omnipotent hero of her imagination. Suddenly the world seemed a more barren and dangerous place. At no point, though, did she yield to the temptation of being drawn into his web of despair and paranoia; the life in her and her love for him rose to the challenge. It was her existence and, even when he was not with her, the knowledge of her existence and her love that helped pull him through, at least for a time. Yet a vital string had snapped and the signs were everywhere. His business losses during 1973 were enormous. On paper his worth dropped from nearly a billion dollars to half that amount. He was spending less and less time with Jackie and told her bluntly that he was no longer interested in indulging her luxurious frivolities.

While Maria's great love was dwindling into a caricature of his former dynamic self, she became engrossed in work as a measure of self-preservation. But everything went wrong in Turin. 'Maria knew nothing,' said Zeffirelli, 'of moving a chorus or creating a stage-picture. As always she went by instinct, but here, something else was needed. She was also very badly served by others. She needed a stage designer who would have taken all the production worries out of her hands so she could concentrate on the acting of the singers.' The designs and costumes of Aligi Sassu were in fact heavy, even ugly, and to compound the problems the conductor, Vittorio Gui, fell ill shortly before the performance and had to be replaced by his assistant. The first night was the big operatic event of the year. The publicity surrounding Maria's new debut was enormous and expectations stood dangerously high. In the reviews the following day, one could hear the sound of the thud: 'The well-intentioned lady did little more than turn the lights on and off.' 'Where is the thrilling, tempestuous personality of the singer of the century hiding? Certainly not in this direction . . .'

Her collaboration with di Stefano had so far produced one failure in the recording studio and one in the opera house. This would have been a good time to say goodbye, but she had nothing else, or at least that is what she told herself. On 20 May, they left together for Japan, where they did a master-class for the winners of the *Madama Butterfly* competition. Luckily, it is not as easy to fail in a master-class.

One dream remained: a come-back singing together. John Tooley, who had succeeded David Webster, had suggested a concert just for her at Covent Garden with a full orchestra. Di Stefano wanted a series of recitals round the world with only piano accompaniment. He insisted, encouraged, reassured and insisted again. Finally Maria agreed. Gorlinsky began to book: London, Hamburg, Berlin, Madrid, Paris, Amsterdam. . . . As the bookings piled up, Maria grew scared and, when Gorlinsky announced that he would be presenting Renata Tebaldi and Franco Corelli at the Albert Hall, she found a reason to call off the tour. 'How can you do this before our tour?' she complained. But di Stefano was insistent, di Stefano was persuasive – she was, after all, his only lifeboat – and at last Maria signed the contract. There was one fee for both of them and one contract, in Maria's name: she was agreeing under its terms to supply di Stefano.

Maria's world tour, the come-back she and everybody else had prophesied, speculated about, gossiped over, was to be launched at the Royal Festival Hall in London. Ivor Newton, now in his eighties, was to be the accompanist, but as the insurance company would not insure the concerts without the presence of a younger accompanist, he asked Robert Sutherland to come on the tour as his number two. They both began practising with Maria at Georges-Mandel. 'She could not decide what she wanted to sing,' remembered Ivor Newton, 'and kept changing the programme. "Don't worry about it being too short," she would tell me. "Applause will take up most of the time."' But the more the news about the excitement generated round the world was passed on to her by no less excited friends, the more scared she became. And the more she heard about the thousands clamouring for tickets in London, in Madrid, in Düsseldorf, in Amsterdam, some of them the new generation that had never heard her before, the more she panicked. Each day she would alternate a thousand times between flight and advance. She wrote to her godfather on 1 September:

> I am preparing for my concert tour and I'm scared stiff but I hope that I will be calm and well by my first one on the 22nd of this month, because the expectation is great and of course I am not what I was at 35 years – let's hope for the best.
>
> I send you all my love and please love me as I think I deserve.

All my thoughts are with you.
Your god-child
Maria

It was the first in a series of tender, loving letters written to her godfather during and about the tour, as though at this time of trial she needed even more than before to express her love and draw strength from his.

Her health, as always, was suffering under the pressure; this time it was her eyes. As the day of the concert approached, the pain in them became so bad that she had to stop every few minutes to put drops in. In the middle of September Maria, di Stefano and Robert Sutherland left Paris for Milan. They spent their days practising in di Stefano's studio, but Maria was feeling weak, apprehensive and unable to cope. The Festival Hall concert on 22 September was cancelled. Would she or would she not go on with the tour? Without di Stefano to bolster her up, to urge her on and to play on her professionalism and her pride, there is little doubt that she would *not* have gone on. But di Stefano was there, and on 25 October at the Congress Centrum in Hamburg, Maria was once again, after eight years of silence, singing in public. It was instantly clear to everyone who cared for her that the tour was going to be the greatest artistic disaster of her career. It was not the wobble, or the sharp changes of register, or her inability to sustain long phrases, or even the obvious care with which she was husbanding what remained of her vocal resources, holding back on both volume and intensity; it was the way in which her preoccupation with vocal survival had robbed her – and us – of that rare expressiveness, that unique ability to go to the heart of the music and through both the blazing power and the fragile beauty of her voice, to stir, disturb or caress us. 'Like a monochrome reproduction of an oil painting,' was William Mann's summing up of the effect a few months later.

From Hamburg they left for Berlin. Robert Sutherland, who was turning the pages for Ivor Newton, had already discovered that mouthing the words for di Stefano to hear and giving him his musical entries was even more important for the concert. 'The page turner sang along,' wrote a reviewer in Berlin. It was also becoming embarrassingly obvious that Ivor Newton, great accompanist though he had been in his prime, was simply too old for the strain of a major recital tour. He began having dizzy spells in the street and fantasizing about his death: 'If I have a heart attack while Maria is singing a high note,' he said to Robert Sutherland, 'you are to push me off my stool and take over as though nothing had happened.' While Ivor Newton was dreaming of a glorious death in the middle of accompanying the great Callas, Maria was frightened that if they had told him that they did not want him to continue on the tour it might really have killed him. So Ivor Newton stayed on.

From Hamburg to Berlin, to Düsseldorf, to Munich, to Frankfurt, to Mannheim, to Madrid, to London, to Paris, to Amsterdam, to Milan, to Stuttgart, the world watched the drama of a tragic decision unfold. It was as if Maria had decided to destroy Callas in public, choosing to make her come-back with a partner who should have stopped singing years earlier, with an eighty-year-old semi-retired accompanist, in a repertoire which her voice could no longer handle and, most important, without the support and the excitement of a full orchestra, which she needed now more than ever. It was as if she had dared the audience to hear her and then go on believing in the legend that had brought them to the concert halls. And they did go on believing.

Once, when Maria had been ill for one of the *Tosca* rehearsals at Covent Garden, John Copley took over her exits and entrances so that the rehearsal could go on. 'Mario, Mario,' cried Mr Copley from the wings – Tosca's first words before she makes her entrance. 'What a voice!' exclaimed a lady reporter who was covering the rehearsal and had somehow missed the news that the great Callas would not be there.

It was only the ghost of the great Callas on tour. Yet it was an unbroken succession of ovations, an hour-long programme stretched to over two by the applause. In London, at the end of the performance, the audience thronged to the stage to shake hands with Maria, to throw her flowers, their eyes moist or glazed with emotion. Yet the tour both in Europe and round America – where Robert Sutherland finally replaced Ivor Newton – had, as John Ardoin put it and as many critics implied, 'tarnished the artistry of her greatest years'. For Callas, the perfectionist, the *primadonna assoluta* of the twentieth century, it was a tragic ending to a glorious career, For Maria, growing increasingly isolated and fighting the desperation threatening to engulf her it was, despite the terror of each performance, a much needed confirmation that she was loved. 'Why do they love you?' she had asked herself. 'Not because I sang a beautiful aria or note, there must be more to it than that.' And the tour convinced her that there was. 'She has long commanded,' wrote Richard Dyer after her concert in Boston, 'our attention, our gratitude, our awe. Now in her struggle and in her exhaustion she asks and earns, at cost to herself and to us, what she had never before seemed to need, our love.'

Her second concert in London was on 2 December 1973, Maria's fiftieth birthday. In the middle of the prolonged applause at the end of the concert, Ivor Newton returned to his stool and di Stefano started to sing 'Happy Birthday'. The audience went wild, and it was love, not just admiration or enthusiasm, that filled the auditorium. Afterwards Maria told Ivor Newton, 'I thought you were trying to force me to do an encore. . . . I could have killed you. . . . Then I forgave you everything.'

The tour had fed her with love and had, for a while, banished the sense of futility that had filled the last few years. She had, at first, tried to convince herself that it was all going as well as it could. She wrote to her godfather from Frankfurt:

> Tonight I'm singing my fifth concert – God willing. I'm quite happy, dear Leo. People love me – of course they know I am not as I was 15 years ago, but they are extremely happy so why should I complain . . .
>
> Well working does me good anyway.
>
> I love you – keep well – *my very special person* –
>
> Your Maria

But as the tour went on, and even without the critics' comments which made her feel as though she was being pecked by the hard, strong beaks of a flock of nightmare birds, she knew that, as an artist, she had failed. 'Don't tell me anything,' she said to Peter Diamand when he went to see her backstage at the Festival Hall. *'I know.* Go to Pippo. Tell him something, anything to pep him up. Do it for me . . .' She knew, but in a television interview with David Holmes she tried hard to fight the knowledge. Its five minutes twenty seconds provided one of the most painful scenes ever shown on television. You can hear in her voice, you can see in her eyes, the anguish she is pushing back. Yet what really catches at the heart is the almost surreal contrast between the truth we see and the words she speaks. 'During the concerts I will improve even more the whole status of the voice. . . . In a year's time I'm sure that I'll be much better than what I am . . . what I actually am now, because I have not worked certain muscles for eight long years. . . . Every evening is an improvement . . .'

So she said, but by the time she got to New York in February 1974, the tour seemed endless, without purpose or achievement. The fears had increased and the despair had deepened. Dario and Dorle Soria went to see her at the Stanhope where she was staying. 'The television was on,' remembers Dorle Soria. 'We offered to switch it off. "No, I never turn it off," she said sharply. "Do you?"'

The night before her concert she went on taking one sleeping-tablet after another, without counting, hardly knowing what she was doing. The following day she could not get out of bed, let alone sing. Dr Louis Parrish arrived at her hotel to try to reduce, according to the official announcement, 'the acute inflammation of Miss Callas's upper respiratory tract'. In the State medical directory, Dr Parrish was listed as limiting his practice to psychiatry, but as the executive director of Carnegie Hall put it, 'Well, if it's psychosomatic, she's still sick.' An hour before the concert was due to start, the large, fashionable New York crowd milling around in the lobby was told by Dario Soria that the performance would now be held on 5 March. A man tried to rip down a five-foot-high poster advertising the concert; another shouted, 'She's done it to me once, she won't do it again.' Police on horseback were trying to clear the traffic-jam as chauffeur-driven cars kept pulling up to deposit their passengers for the concert and then speeding off when they heard the news, with the passengers still inside.

Maria had asked Robert Sutherland to go to Carnegie Hall to observe the reactions. An excited fan summed them up: 'It may be a cancellation, but this is the biggest event of the season.' The isolated outbursts of anger did not affect the general feeling of resignation and compassion. The audience knew, or at least sensed, that a human drama was being played out behind the cancellation that had nothing to do with tantrums and whims.

It is very doubtful whether di Stefano, the man who was supposed to be her source of strength at this time of trial, ever understood her. He was himself under tremendous strain during the tour, over his daughter whom he adored and who was, in her early twenties, slowly dying of cancer. As the tour went on, his quarrels with Maria were becoming more and more violent. At first he had a way of saying things, sometimes absurd things, that made her laugh, giggle and feel like a young girl. Now the periods of rows and unpleasantness in between these good times were becoming longer and longer.

From New York they flew to Boston where they had a concert planned for 27 February. On the day itself, they had a fight, at the end of which di Stefano stormed out. Maria called Sol Hurok in New York: 'Ask Vasso,' she said, 'if she's still in New York.' Vasso Devetzi, a concert pianist, herself Greek and a close friend of Maria's, was at the Regency with her suitcase packed ready to leave for Paris when the order was issued: 'You are going to Boston. I'm sending you the press lady to help you get ready. A helicopter is waiting to take you there.' In Boston, Maria was furious: 'Imagine him leaving me alone . . . ,' she kept telling Robert Sutherland. 'And in Kennedy country!' That day the only rehearsal they had was while she was having her hair done. Robert was playing the piano in one room and Maria was singing in the other while the hairdresser was putting her hair up in a chignon. When Vasso arrived, Maria still was not too sure what she was going to sing. She never knew until the last moment what she was going to sing out of the large selection included in the programme. Vasso Devetzi played Handel, Schumann and Chopin. After di Stefano's roaring and crooning in falsetto, it must have come as a relief.

'Mr di Stefano is indisposed,' had been the announcement. By the time they returned to New York for the postponed concert, he had stopped being 'indisposed' and on 5 March, they were ready to face together their select audience at Carnegie Hall. A few hours before they were due to leave their hotel, Maria heard of Sol Hurok's sudden death. He had organized her American tours since the 1950s, but the effect of the shock went far beyond the unexpected death of an old friend. His death on the afternoon of her concert was for Maria, in her present highly susceptible state, an omen of ill luck. She was overcome by an irrational but overwhelming feeling that from now on anything she undertook would be a failure. She was finally persuaded to go on with the concert that night to avoid a second cancellation for the same audience, but she was in a distraught state.

For anyone who cared for her or even for anyone who knew where the next note was meant to be, it was sheer agony to watch her struggling through with her voice in ruins and to wonder just how far off target she would be. Before the concert began, she had made a speech dedicating it to Sol Hurok's memory and apologizing for her overwrought emotional state. At the end of the concert she nearly had a complete breakdown on the stage. She suddenly launched into a long, bitter and largely incoherent attack on the way opera houses, and especially the Met, were being run. Once again she saw herself as the victim of managements which would not give her adequate rehearsal time and proper artistic conditions in which to work. It was rambling, painful and, with practically the entire Met establishment there, intensely embarrassing; it was impossible to miss the agony under the aggression. The audience froze as the mask fell away. No one knew how long she would go on for, or indeed whether she would ever stop. Suddenly, very revealingly, she changed tack. Singing at the Met, she said, with the support of the orchestra, chorus and scenery, was a game compared to what she had done tonight. It was partly self-justification but, even more, a bitter judgement on herself; she could no longer refuse to see how hopeless was the way she had chosen to come back to the stage after eight years.

She did finally stop. There had only been one interjection: '*You* are Opera,' someone had shouted from the balcony in the middle of her attack on opera managements. Otherwise there was hushed, anxious, astonished silence. It was like a parody of the great moments when she had dared to step out of character and use the words and the music to make a personal point against Ghiringhelli, against a hissing audience, against her enemies at large. These moments had magnificence; her speech at Carnegie Hall was a desperate act by a broken, exhausted woman, not so much daring as driven to humiliate herself in public. Almost catatonic within concentric rings of fear and despair, she had cried across the barrier for help, but the cry had been disguised as an attack, and even those who heard and understood hardly knew how to respond. As she stepped out of the stage door at the end, hundreds of people were waiting, applauding. Holding in her arms the roses Sol Hurok had sent her for the concert, she began to weep. Suddenly she threw one of her roses to the public; then another; then the whole bunch In the scramble to get one of the Callas flowers, a way was opened, big enough for Maria to walk across to her car.

Di Stefano was increasingly uncomprehending and the strain between them at times made it seem unlikely that they would complete the tour together. Four days after New York, in Detroit, Pippo was 'indisposed' again and three days later, in Dallas, he was 'indisposed' once more. Finding pianists to fill the gap had become an important side activity of the tour organizers: Ralph Votepek stepped in in Detroit and Earl Wild in Dallas. By the time they got to the West Coast, there was cause for real alarm. Maria rang Gorlinsky: 'I'm finished. I'm through. It's impossible to work with this man. I'm leaving. I'm going home.' She had, it is true, been 'through' before, but this time she seemed in earnest, and no amount of coaxing and cajoling would make her change her mind. So Gorlinsky had to turn up the temperature. 'Okay, Maria, let's cancel the whole tour. It doesn't matter to me, I'm insured. But it's going to cost *you* a million dollars, because Pippo is bound to sue you for breach of contract.' Maria finally agreed not to storm off but to talk it over with di Stefano. She did, and they decided that they would go on that night, but that their first concert on the West Coast would be positively their last concert together. '*Caro* Pippo' rose to the solemn occasion. 'If we're not going to sing together any more,' he said, 'let's have some fun.' So, when it came to the *Carmen* duet, instead of singing, '*Carmen, je t'aime, je t'adore . . . ne me quitte pas*', he sang 'Goodbye Maria, it's been nice knowing you.' To which she sang back: '*Cher* Pippo, go to the devil.' According to Maria, the audience never caught on. After that, of course, they could not possibly part, at least not yet.

The last stop was Montreal, where they were joined by di Stefano's wife. From the start she had accepted with equanimity her husband's relationship with Maria. Ironically it was the same kind of equanimity with which Maria accepted di Stefano's casual affairs during the tour. 'I can't compete with twenty-one-year-olds,' she told Robert Sutherland. And she certainly did not want to compete with his wife; her presence made Maria increasingly nervous and insecure. One night when both Pippo and Robert Sutherland were in her suite, she asked Robert to take her hair down. Throughout the tour this had been di Stefano's privilege. Now he sat staring at them in heavy silence for the duration of the ritual.

Maria summed up their relationship a few months later in a letter to her godfather: 'Pippo, of course, is in love and I also up to a certain point. Maybe three years of habit – and nothing else as temptation. Men – real men, are difficult to find. Imagine the kind of man to be my companion.' Aristo was still the only 'real' man, or at least the only man she really loved.

In the autumn of 1974, she left with di Stefano for the Far East and the last leg of their tour. They gave nine concerts: in Seoul, Fukuoka, Tokyo, Osaka, Hiroshima and Sapporo. And so it came about that, on 11 November 1974, Sapporo, a city with a population of just over a million near the head of Ishikari Bay in northern Japan, was the last place on earth to hear Maria Callas sing live on stage. At the beginning of the tour Maria's hernia recurred, causing internal bleeding and terrible pain. She returned to Paris in a state of total collapse. For the first few days, even her memory seemed to have gone. Her doctor called a neurologist to see her; through his pills, and rest-cure she began to gain some peace and strength, and her memory started to come back.

Maria was still in Japan when, in October 1974, Tina was found dead in the Hôtel de Chanaleilles in Paris. Onassis was so shaken that he could not even bear to attend his ex-wife's funeral. As for Christina, she instantly demanded an autopsy to find out the cause of her mother's death, and even when it was confirmed that Tina had died from an oedema of the lung, she remained full of suspicion, bitterness and outrage at Niarchos. Christina, who had herself skirted death a few weeks earlier with an overdose of sleeping pills, needed desperately to make some sense, however irrational, of all the tragic, sudden deaths; first her aunt, then her brother, now her mother. She became convinced that if her father had not married Jackie they would somehow have been averted. Jackie was, for Christina, the ill omen that had spread disaster in their family, and she started openly bemoaning the fact that she had herself helped drive her father away from Maria.

While Maria's career was petering out in the unlikely surroundings of the Ishikari River, Onassis was starting on the final lap of his own life. Since Alexander's death he had been having trouble keeping his eyes open for long and talking without slurring his words. At first he put it down to physical and emotional exhaustion and refused to find out more about it; but it was only a question of time before he had to enter a New York hospital. His condition was diagnosed as *myasthenia gravis,* a defect in the body's chemistry which makes impossible the routine transmission of impulses through a faulty connection of nerves and muscles. He could only keep his eyes open by taping the drooping eyelids to his eyebrows, and he had to have a regular series of painful injections, which was the only way to minimize the effects. The disease was incurable, though the doctors assured him it was not fatal. The body had turned against itself, and Onassis had turned viciously against the woman whom he now irrationally considered as the source of his accumulating woes. He saw his marriage to Jackie as the moment when his sun had begun to set: marrying her was his life's supreme act of betrayal. The first faulty connection had not been between his nerves and his muscles, but between his heart and his actions. His heart had pointed him towards love, towards Maria; his actions had taken him towards more of all the things he already had – more fame, more power, more glory. Committing himself to Maria would have been a step towards reality, but he had clung to images.

'He had climbed to the top of a tree,' said Constantine Gratsos, 'and there was nothing there.' His life had been dominated by the belief that once he reached the top of the tree he would find fulfilment; so he had to convince himself that there was a higher branch that he had missed, such as marrying the world's most famous woman. When he discovered that this had been one more empty acquisition, he turned against his wife as if it was she who had forced the illusion on him. It was in this mood of dejection and bitterness that he had received the thunderbolt of Alexander's death. 'I don't think he ever knew what he wanted,' said Gratsos. 'The difference was that in his last years he knew he would never get it.' He began to feel that somehow it was Jackie who had cheated him of that mysterious 'it' that he could not even put a name to, and he began, by no means altogether consciously, to take revenge on her. His first concern was to reduce to the legal minimum, and if possible below it, Jackie's share in his estate. Having done this in his last will and testament and fearing that she might challenge it, he added a codicil: 'I command my executors and the rest of my heirs that they deny her such a right through all legal means, costs and expenses charged on my inheritance.'

It was not enough. He decided to divorce her but only after he had made it as humiliating as possible for her. He hired a private detective to follow her with the specific brief of producing evidence of adultery. Then he invited Jack Anderson, the celebrated Washington columnist, to lunch. He began with deliberately controlled complaints about her on the lines of: 'What does she do with all those clothes? All I ever see her wearing is blue jeans.' The hard facts were to follow later at Onassis's office after he had himself discreetly withdrawn, and his primed aides took Anderson on a thorough sightseeing tour of all the piles of ledgers, memos and letters documenting Jackie's frenzied extravagance.

At the same time, Onassis, telling Jackie nothing, asked Roy Cohn, who in the 'fifties had been one of McCarthy's investigators, to represent him in divorce proceedings. By then he had moved out of Jackie's apartment and was staying in his suite at the Pierre. He had considered divorcing her as early as 1972 but now any remaining doubt had evaporated, and all that was left was the driving desire to hit her as hard as possible. While Onassis was drawing up a master-plan of all the steps to be taken before the announcement of divorce proceedings, Maria was singing in Japan. In the dim picture of lost happiness by which Onassis was haunted, Maria was the only clearly defined figure. She had not been strong enough to pull him out before the current began to draw him down, but in some part of himself he knew that she could have been. As for Maria, being interviewed a few months earlier during her American tour by Barbara Walters of the *Today* programme, she described Onassis in public, for the first time in fifteen years, as 'the great love of my life'.

Was there still time? Sick and broken though Onassis was, the life in him said 'yes'. But it was a very faint 'yes' from a very exhausted man; and the events that followed submerged it. In December 1974, his aides finally revealed to him the disastrous state of Olympic Airways; they had not dared to tell him before that the airline was no longer capable of generating enough money to keep its planes in the air. Olympic Airways may not have been a very big part of the Onassis empire, but emotionally, being his main link with Greece, it was the most important. He stepped in and, in a parody of his former business style, tried, through all-night meetings and endless, compulsive wrestling with the Greek Government, to save the crown of his business kingdom. His moves were all mistimed and miscalculated – the panic moves of a desperate man. He lost every round of the negotiations, and on 15 January 1975, he had no option but to sign the document handing Olympic Airways over to the Greek Government. 'Emotionally and for his sense of grandeur,' said Professor Georgakis, who had been Olympic's Managing Director, 'it was the final blow. For once he was not begged to remain.'

A few weeks later he collapsed in Athens. The French liver specialist, Dr Caroli, advised flying him to Paris for an immediate gall-bladder operation; the American heart specialist, Dr Rosenfeld, recommended flying him to New York for intensive treatment to strengthen him before any operation was contemplated. Onassis chose Paris. The one thing he made sure he took with him for what turned out to be his last journey was the red cashmere blanket Maria had bought him from Hermes for his birthday earlier in the year. He had the operation on 10 February; he never recovered complete consciousness. For the next five weeks in Room 217 of the Eisenhower Wing, he was kept alive by a respirator and fed intravenously. In the room next door, the mother of Vasso Devetzi was being treated for cancer. Vasso was there every day talking to the same nurses, seeing who was going in and out of Room 217, always getting the latest news of his progress and reporting to Maria. It was the kind of coincidence that convinced Maria that there are no coincidences.

Maria felt as though she was tied to the same machine that was keeping Aristo alive. Vasso was coming back with the news: they have replaced all his blood; Jackie came to the hospital today for half an hour; they have given him a massive infusion of antibiotics; Christina has not left his bedside all night; he has been put in an oxygen tent.

Maria could not bear it any longer. She felt that he was as much part of her as her own breath, and yet she had no right to be at his side. And the doctor had said that he could survive in his present condition for weeks, even months. She decided to leave Paris, to leave Europe. She rented a house in Palm Beach and at one o'clock on Monday 10 March, together with Bruna, Ferruccio and Consuelo, she flew out of Paris. On Saturday, at 12 Golf View Road, Palm Beach, she received the last report from the American Hospital. Aristo was dead.

Chapter Fourteen

WHILE Jackie was flying back to Paris; while in the hospital chapel Archbishop Meletos was praying over the body lying on an open bier with a Greek Orthodox icon on the chest; while the *Christina*'s flag was lowered to half mast; while the funeral party was landing on Skorpios; while Jackie, Christina, his three sisters, Teddy Kennedy, John-John and Caroline were kissing the icon placed on the coffin lid; while the coffin was being lowered into the concrete vault – Maria was lying semi-conscious in her rented home in Palm Beach.

His death had struck her an almost mortal blow. Existing in a world that did not contain him seemed pointless. The past had vanished and, in her deep suffering, there was no future. Through the interminable days that followed, her only real action was reaching for one of the many bottles on her bedside table for more tranquillizers, more sleeping-tablets, more forgetfulness.

There was still life in her though, the numbness began to fade, and the spirit to stir. Soon she was getting up and wandering about the house, watching television, swimming, lying in the sun. Her godfather went to stay with her; so did her friend John Coveney. 'One morning at breakfast,' he remembered, 'a parcel arrived full of letters and telegrams forwarded to Maria from Georges-Mandel. She started opening them and passing them on to me. They were all letters and telegrams of condolence. At one moment she stopped: "All of a sudden I am a widow," she said.' One of the letters brought her news of Visconti's death. After a massive stroke three years earlier and a year in a wheelchair, Luchino had died two days after Aristo, on 17 March.

Late in April, Maria returned to Paris. 'What else?' she kept asking the few people who called or came to see her. 'What else?' She knew that there was, there had to be, something else, but she did not dare look. She sat solitary for hours wondering how it had all happened. 'I have too much pride,' she had said once, 'to ask for pity.' Time moved on sluggishly while Maria, from the old photographs and the old recordings, the years of headlong gallop and the beginning of old age, sought to reassemble a self. She began thinking a lot about buying the house in Palm Beach. Having another base away from Georges-Mandel, in the sun and a few thousand miles from Paris, might give her the chance of a fresh start, a break with the past and all its memories. Twice she decided to buy it, and twice she changed her mind. Any big decision, and sometimes smaller ones, seemed very hard to make.

She had promised at the end of her tour in Japan to return there with di Stefano to sing Tosca. Without any longer knowing why, as if something in her had years ago been set in motion and would not stop, she began practising again. 'I'm working hard,' she wrote to Leo at the end of June, 'because this year I either have to be *much* better or nothing.' A month later she wrote again. 'I have come to a big decision. I'm stopping singing. I'm fed up with the whole business! . . . After my last tour I came back so sick that I'm terrified now that the months are coming to that date. My nerves can't stand the strain any more.' Her return to Japan was cancelled, and di Stefano persuaded Montserrat Caballé to take Maria's place in *Tosca*. 'I'm still with Pippo,' she had written to Leo in June. 'I cannot find anyone else better. Richer maybe, but poorer in feelings, and all that goes against the grain. I only wish we had fallen in love when he was famous – and had a fabulous voice – because he has many human qualities.' The death of his daughter at this time brought them temporarily closer together. She had been young, beautiful and intelligent; and Maria, who had watched with concern and admiration her fight to survive and had drawn strength from her will to live, had grown to love her.

While di Stefano was singing in Japan, Maria went to

Ibiza to spend part of the summer with Evelynne Archer, the sister of Anastasia Gratsos. By the time she got back to Paris, she knew that her relationship with Pippo could not last much longer. At the end of August, in a touchingly honest letter to her godfather, she explained how she felt:

> As for P. I still care for him but of course not as I did – but how does one say it to him. After the death of his daughter he lives for this love of ours. I am hoping that destiny will take care of things so as the hurt and shock will not be hard on him. He is not the type to fall in love with another woman. I would hope for that but I doubt.
>
> Maybe I might meet someone and that would be the ideal solution. This way I would not care whether he gets hurt or not. (Terrible of me, isn't it?)

Leo wrote answering her letter point by point. He carefully annotated every single letter from Maria and even underlined the key sentences, responding with detailed practical advice, like the most loving and caring lonely hearts columnist. 'The only thing to do is to get busy,' he wrote back on this occasion. 'You must go out more. Don't be interested in the age of people. Look at the older generation. There are plenty of people who would love to invite you. . . . You are free and you should accept such invitations.'

She did begin to accept a few invitations. Frederick, who did her hair, would arrive at Georges-Mandel to prepare her for the evening: 'I would be putting her hair up and then many times, as I was getting near to finishing, the anger would begin mounting inside her. "Why go? Why go anyway? Take it down Frederick. I'm not going."' Frederick would take the chignon down; Bruna would telephone to explain that 'Madame is indisposed'; and Maria would get into bed and watch television until late into the night. She wrote to Leo to explain:

> I received your very dear letter and smiled I admit – I too would *love* to find a wonderful companion –

like you were for Sally – but my dear Leo, such men are impossible to find...

In my condition he has to be *intelligent*, well-off, someone I can lean on with devotion and faith. He has to be *honest*, generous and not try to change me, like our dead friend.

Where are such men? I know that if I don't go out frequently I cannot meet them – but I go out and I find superficial, presumptuous men that are not interested in all the lovely things that make our life livable. I don't think they exist today but I would *love* to find such a man. That would be the solution to my psychological problems.

With the exception of her letters to her godfather, her lifelong reluctance to express any emotion on paper had become almost absolute. Even when Lawrence Kelly, who was, after all, one of the few people she ever became intimate with, was dying of cancer in Kansas City, she could not face writing to him. Mary Mead rang her up first to urge her and then to implore her to write to him: 'I can't, Mary. I really can't,' Maria kept replying. 'Let me talk to him on the phone.' 'But Maria, you don't understand, he can't talk. He doesn't have more than a few days to live.' But she did not write.

She was feeling terribly alone. Sometimes in the middle of the night, longing for some warming contact, she would call a friend. 'What's new?' she would ask; 'What else?' They would chat for a few minutes, and she would hang up, but sleep still would not come. 'I'm used to working at night,' she said. 'I'm used to thinking. It's my job, my chemistry.... At night you gets lots of funny ideas, pessimistic ideas, and I'd like to shake them off. Can you go for a walk, really walk your feet off, get really tired, do something? A woman can't do it. I'd be picked up by the police. I'm beginning to think I should get a big dog and have him around.... Can you take a train, go some place when you get desperate? What does a woman do?'

She was feeling trapped, but would not see that she was mistaking convention for necessity and clinging in her desperation to the very beliefs about what a woman can or cannot do and what a legend should and should not do that were keeping her imprisoned. Yet she did want to understand. In her need to make sense of what had happened, she even talked of writing her autobiography. Sometimes lying in bed, but more often in the blue room, she started putting fragments of thought on tape. Most of the time it is Callas speaking but there is a fascinating moment when Maria takes over only to have the microphone snatched from her by Callas seconds later: 'I would like to be Maria, but there is La Callas who demands that I carry myself with her dignity. I'd like to think that the two are really one, because Callas too was once Maria and I have put all of myself at all times into my music. All that I have been has always been authentic. I have worked with all possible honesty, and Maria too. If anyone really wants to understand me, he will find me entirely in my work. ... Perhaps, after all, we can't separate Callas, the star, from Maria – the two are in harmony.'

But they were not. Maria was suffocating under the weight of La Callas. Even in those few sentences, at one moment we hear Maria speaking, complaining of the demands made on her by Callas, and the next, Callas taking over, trying to convince an imaginary audience that her art was her whole life. The tapes are in French throughout, which may be significant; it was easier to retreat into self-deception in a language that was not the one most natural to her. '*Cher public*,' she says at another moment on these tapes, '*je vous demande de me voir comme une musicienne qui a consacré sa vie à la musique* [Dear public, I ask you to see me as a musician who has consecrated her life to music]. Do not believe all the lies they have told you. I suppose it's my fate that they say all sorts of things about me. The only thing that counts is that the public is impartial, that they know that I have totally devoted my life to my art.' The High Priestess was addressing the faithful, denying her humanity – denying Maria, who carried in her not only the needs and weaknesses that Callas despised, but also the seed of a mystery and a fulfilment of which her art could only be a part. 'I wish I had more religious fanaticism,' she said once, the very intensity of her longing for a thread into a higher reality reflected in her unexpected use of 'fanaticism'. She longed for honesty, for authenticity, but at this point in her life she was mired in disillusionment, focusing on all the falseness she could see around her. John Tooley, who right to the end would go to see her whenever he was in Paris, remembers her falling increasingly into this bitter mood: 'Whenever we talked about any new singers, conductors or directors, she would attack them all, convinced that there was nothing good around any longer. If I was on my way to see an opera, she would always say, "What do you want to go there for? Why don't you stay here with me?" Her loneliness was sometimes unbearable.' She had even stopped asking 'What else?' and 'What's new?' Alan Sievewright went to see her to ask her to narrate *The Soldier's Tale* for a recording that he was producing. 'I'm not very keen on Stravinsky,' she said. 'I don't really like modern music.' And when Alan pointed out that, written in 1914, *The Soldier's Tale* was hardly modern, she confessed: 'I don't really even approve of Puccini. Mine is the nineteenth century.' When she was in such moods, her opinions often seemed arbitrary, as if she were determined to isolate herself from those around her.

Towards the end of 1975, she wrote to her godfather:

> ... I don't know what to do. I know I have to work but what. Maybe start practising again and recording *on my own.* I might love singing again – but I have to sing alone – and with orchestra. The offers are a lot – but I have to look into myself deeply – and know what I want.

'To sing alone and with orchestra ...', '*on my own*'. It is clear from this letter that she had, by now, stopped trying to hide from herself the disastrous misjudgement of the last tour, singing without orchestra and with someone she had to carry both professionally and often emotionally. It is equally clear that she no longer knew what she wanted, and, therefore, she no longer knew what to do. In the same letter she agonizes once again about di Stefano; she asks her godfather for advice but as she already knew how strongly opposed he was to the relationship, it is more as if she is asking him for the strength to break off what she herself called 'an unhappy love affair'.

> Di Stefano is deeply in love with me - But I'm cooling off because - well - who knows - only I want him to realize it little by little - His daughter's death gave him a terrible blow. He already knows that I'm not the same with him - but - patience - If we had fallen in love 15 years ago - when he gained a great fortune - and sang like a God - things could go well but he bitterly says that I am rather well off - he has nothing but love to offer me - because neither I or he would want him to divorce. So it's become an unhappy love affair - He is detached with me for the reason of the death of his daughter - (I think) maybe not - But I have all these personal problems to solve - plus find some-

thing interesting to do as soon as I'm well.

I like to hear from you and your advice – and of course your news –

All my love

Maria –

29-10-75

It was in this mood of uncertainty and dejection that she received, in November 1975, the news of Pasolini's murder. His body had been found on a beach road near Rome, where the boy he had picked up had clubbed him and then run over him in Pasolini's own car. It was yet another shock at a time when she felt she could take no more. 'I've only known one Pasolini,' she said shortly after his death, 'so sensitive, full of concern. He was passionate about politics, which I never was, but we never tried to force our views on each other. His ideas on art, on life, were so powerful and original that you could not remain unmoved by them. If there was another Pasolini, I never knew him.'

She began shutting herself off more and more from everybody. All the people in her life knew by now that any arrangement they made with Maria was more likely than not to be cancelled at the last moment. 'She would call,' remembers Gaby van Zuylen, married to Maggie's son, 'and say, "Gaby, shall we meet tomorrow to go shopping?" Then she would call back, "Shall we go to the movies instead?" The next day, she would call again and cancel altogether. You had to be endlessly available.' And most people were not; many stopped calling altogether.

Two or three persevered. François Valéry, the French Ambassador to UNESCO, was one of them. He was a bachelor, charming, cultivated, and with a great love and knowledge of music. The first time he had set eyes on her off-stage was in a restaurant in the Bois de Boulogne. He called the waiter and asked him to take to her table a plate on which he had put a personal cheque with '*un million d'admirations*'. Then they had met again at Maggie's. Callas felt very good with him – an ambassador, civilized, dignified-looking, meeting all the worldly standards that mattered to her. But their relationship included Maria as well as Callas. 'She could totally relax with me. She asked me many intimate questions, and she talked freely herself. Almost provocatively, she wanted to stress how normal, how female she was – she talked about not feeling too good when she had her periods, about what they did to her hair at the hairdresser's, and she talked a lot, when they were still together, about how much she enjoyed sex with Ari. "He really did love me," she said once after his death. "You can't lie in bed."'

Towards the end, François Valéry was her main escort, but the pattern persisted:

'Will you take me to the cinema, François?'

'Of course, Maria.'

The following day: 'No, I can't make it tonight, my hairdresser is coming. No, not tomorrow; tomorrow I'm practising. Wednesday?'

Wednesday dawned: 'François, can we change tonight? I'm not feeling too good today.' But François Valéry would call again and in the end they would meet. What she loved doing most was going to the movies, sometimes seeing one after another. One night they went to see the latest de Sica film and then a thriller; she had an ice-cream during the first film, an ice-cream during the second and two Toblerones in between. Not surprisingly, when François Valéry asked where she wanted to go to dinner, she answered that she was not at all hungry. 'Shall we go home instead?' she said. They went, and sat in her bedroom talking. 'It's one o'clock in the morning,' she suddenly said smiling, 'and here we are in my bedroom alone . . . very compromising.' 'I felt she wanted me to stay. For the first time in my life I was embarrassed. I wanted to kiss her and at the same time, like a boy on his first date, I didn't know how to go about it. In the end I told her what I felt: "You scare men, Maria. They respect you too much." She was really angry, and yet it was true.'

And Maria knew that it was true. 'There are not very many men who can be near me,' she had said once. 'It's a sort of handicap to be famous. Also I have a very active mind, a strong personality, and I might frighten real men away.' It was not her mind or her personality that were daunting so much as the famous Callas aura she could assume at will. 'We would be sitting talking,' remembers Vasso Devetzi, 'and suddenly the telephone would ring, and in front of my very eyes, her voice, her whole demeanour, would change. She had instantly switched to Callas; as soon as she hung up, I was back with Maria again. It was automatic.'

It was so automatic that it had become a straitjacket in which Maria was finding it increasingly difficult to breathe. Yet she went on desperately believing that Callas was her only protection; caught up in this illusion, she never discovered her real strength. In the summer of 1976, this obsessive concern with protecting her image, so that the image could in turn protect her, became almost farcical. Maria, desperately needing a holiday, had gone with Vasso Devetzi to Halkidiki in the north of Greece. After eight days there, swimming, sun-bathing, teaching Vasso to swim and sun-bathing some more, Maria, for the first time since Aristo's death, was beginning to feel life flowing through her again. 'The difference between the ancient Greeks and me,' she had said, 'is that I don't cry about tragedies until they happen. And if they happen, again I don't cry; I cope with them.' And she *was* coping.

Then on the eighth day they went to dinner at Ouranoupolis. Somebody recognized her, and the next day reporters and photographers swarmed into the little village where they were staying. For the next four days, Maria stayed locked in her room, with the shutters closed in the suffocating August heat, terrified that if she stepped out she would be photographed in her bathing-suit or her beach-robe. Even Vasso did not dare go swimming in case they photographed her and stuck Maria's head on top. So, to protect the flawless unreality of the image, Maria stayed cooped up in her room, getting more and more depressed, and eating chocolates and 'vanilla', a Greek sweet that she loved, to make her forget the sea waiting outside.

Callas had once again, almost literally this time, imprisoned Maria, and the holiday that should have been a much-needed restoration became a further torment. The fragile equilibrium she had reached during these eight carefree days was once again disturbed. Anxious and dejected, she returned to Paris. Old friends seeing her again were shocked by the changes that had come upon her in the last months. She looked stooped and the lines round her eyes seemed full of tension. Since Ari's death, she had, for the first time in over twenty years, stopped watching what she ate. 'I've gained weight,' she wrote to Leo, 'and I've lost my will-power to diet – isn't it terrible?'

Nineteen seventy-six had brought few excitements, few surprises, but before it was out, the di Stefano chapter was finally closed. 'The relation I had is definitely finished,' she wrote to her godfather in October. 'All I have to do is ask for my few belongings in his home at San Remo – but I don't even want to do that. So I leave things as they are.' Before Christmas she wrote again as if to convince him – or was it to convince herself? '. . . Also the other thing that bothered you (P.) is no longer in my life. Thank God. . . . Are you going on a holiday for Xmas? I'm staying here. I'm comfortable at home.' Comfortable she was, but there were days when even her favourite room, her bright bathroom, darkened. The tiger lilies growing round the bathtub twisted into a sinister little jungle, and the white curtains in the window overlooking the street made ominous shadows. She was adrift, waiting for the lightning to strike. 'I am over fifty,' she said to Vasso, 'I am free, I have all the money I want to enjoy myself. And what do I do? I work.' She did go on working, without joy, without aim, simply to fill the gnawing emptiness.

And yet there were moments, sometimes when she was practising, sometimes when she was listening to her old recordings, or even sometimes when she was playing with her little dogs, teaching them to sing, when she would vibrate again with the joy of music. It happened when

Leonard Bernstein brought Sylvia Sass to Georges-Mandel. Bernstein and the young Hungarian soprano, whom critics had been hailing as the new Callas, had come just for an hour and had kept the hired chauffeur-driven car waiting outside. Ferruccio, the perfect butler, showed them in. At first Maria was on her best Callas behaviour. 'So you are the new Maria Callas,' were her opening words, heavy with irony. She put Sylvia in the Blue Room while she sat in the drawing-room imperiously issuing orders. 'Sing this, that, the other.' Finally, in the middle of Violetta's first aria, she even started talking to Bernstein while Sylvia was singing and then sang the aria herself, instructing Sylvia to repeat it exactly. That was too much for Sylvia, who finally asserted herself. 'I admire you tremendously,' she said, 'for me you are almost a goddess, but I am not a copy of Callas and I never will be. In a few days I'm singing *Traviata* in Hamburg and it would be better for my confidence and my voice if I went.' It was what Maria needed to drop the façade of the aloof legend. She was instantly transformed into a young woman fired by another young woman's enthusiasm for her art – and all the love that was inside her, bursting for an outlet, apart from Djedda and Pixie, was poured out towards Sylvia. They stayed together for four hours, long after Bernstein had left in a taxi for his rehearsal, and until the chauffeur waiting outside had broken the spell by coming up to announce that he had to leave for another job. This time Maria dispensed with Ferruccio, took Sylvia to the door and waited, waving to her, until she had disappeared. 'I won't forget the strength and the tenderness in her eyes as she was looking at me from the door,' remembers Sylvia Sass. 'What she gave me that evening will be with me for my whole life. Even now, when I am singing or thinking about my singing, something she said, a sentence, a few words, come back to me. I somehow knew looking at her standing at the door that I would never see her again.'

Montserrat Caballé, one of the leading contenders for Maria's vacant throne, had also called when she was having difficulties with *Norma*. 'I have trouble with the trio that ends the first act,' she confessed.

'I can't do this at the end of a telephone,' Maria snapped.

Caballé went to Paris to see her, but Maria's role was not really that of the oracle. She was a performer, not a teacher; and in any case the magic that was hers was not transferable.

There was one last attempt at a come-back. Charles Vanne, a friend who was running the *Théâtre des Champs Elysées*, offered her the theatre to practise in to get the feel of singing on a stage again. One day, a reporter from *France Dimanche* sneaked in while she was singing, took some photographs and wrote a devastating article about the collapse of her voice. Her inner resolve, that had been mastered with such difficulty, was blown away. She was in agony. Once again, for the last time, she sued. And once again she won – this time, after her death.

She was shrivelled, shrunken, isolated. Yet even in her isolation the world was very much with her. And even though she had stopped searching through the dead past looking for meaning, the past was still with her, still haunting her with the ghosts of its bitter resentments and its tortured guilts. 'I have nothing,' she told John Tooley at the beginning of 1977, soon after her fifty-third birthday. 'What am I going to do?' After the *France Dimanche* article, the dream of a real come-back was dissolved; but, even dissolved, the dream continued to sustain her. 'Why isn't anyone writing an opera about Mary Magdalene?' she would ask. She had suddenly become fascinated by her and started reading and rereading the passage in the Bible in which she washed Christ's feet. But nobody was writing an opera about Mary Magdalene.

She had somehow to flee the anguish in her heart – if not any longer into work, at least into talking about work. John Tooley suggested *Cavalleria Rusticana* with Placido Domingo; then he suggested a new major production of *Tosca*. Together with Zeffirelli they discussed first *L'Incoronazione di Poppea*, then *The Merry Widow*. Maria balked at the idea of an operetta. 'Too undignified,' she would say. 'Let's do *Traviata*', 'Let's do *Traviata* with Giulini.' And she went on saying it until a few months before she died: 'Let's do *Traviata*, Franco.'

'If she had accepted some compromises in the first act,' said Zeffirelli a year after her death, 'she could have been singing it yesterday.' Perhaps she could, but the will to launch into a new adventure, a new trial, was not there. It would be rekindled every now and then, flicker uncertainly and then die, until the next time when someone would manage to make the fire burn up for a while. In between, curling up in front of the television to watch someone else's adventure in the Wild West was so much more inviting. She was drowning in a pool of lethargy and memory, but the instinct to expand and grow was so intense in her that when she stifled it, it began to choke her.

In February 1977, she wrote to Leo:

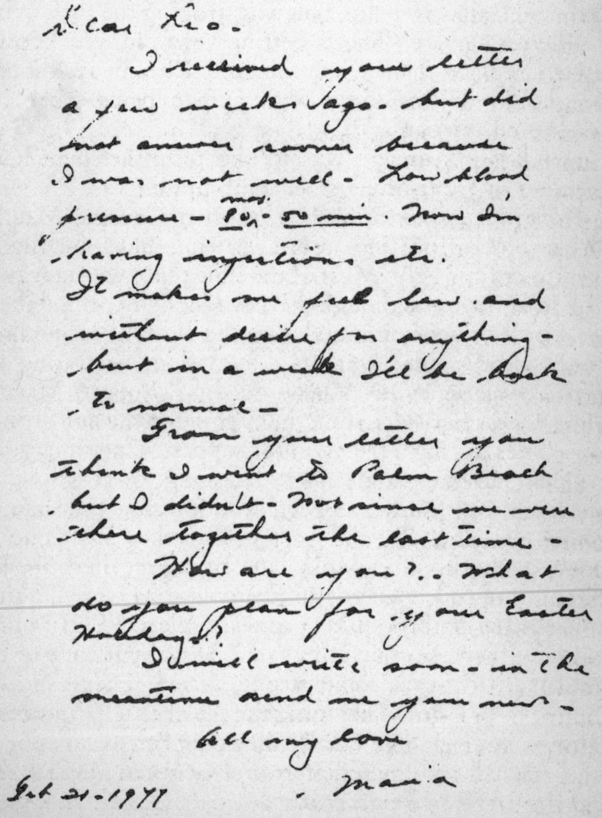

Dear Leo.

I received your letter a few weeks ago. but did not answer sooner because I was not well - Low blood pressure - 90 max. - 50 min. Now I'm having injections etc.

It makes me feel low. and without desire for anything - but in a week I'll be back to normal -

From your letter you think I went to Palm Beach but I didn't - Not since we were there together the last time -

How are you?.. What do you plan for your Easter Holidays?

I will write soon - in the meantime send me your news -

All my love

Maria

Feb 21 - 1977

It was the shortest letter she had ever written to him, as if even this had now become an effort; it was also the last. She complained about her low blood pressure: 'It makes me feel low and without desire for anything – but in a week I'll be back to normal.' But she never was. The decline was now inexorable.

In the spring of 1977, she asked Vasso to prepare a will, leaving everything to Bruna and Ferruccio. She never signed it.

In July, Alan Sievewright went to see her again about doing a special discussion evening with her at Covent Garden on her roles, her life and her career. 'Everything they want to know about me is there in the music,' she said. '. . . Callas is dead.' She was stroking the little white poodle on her lap: 'She is getting very old, you know. I always replace them when they die. I've always thought we should do the same with human beings, but I've discovered we can't.'

Her last pilgrimage was to Skorpios; she spent hours kneeling in front of Aristo's tomb praying.

Back in Paris, in the hushed luxury of Georges-Mandel, Maria was suffocating, too despairing and too resigned even to cry for help. Most of the time there was a faraway look in her eyes, as though there was nobody behind them; but a part of her continued with the old routine: walking Pixie and Djedda, watching television, practising the Verdi *Requiem* with Vasso, reading Robert Massie's *Nicholas and Alexandra*, sometimes going to the hairdresser, sometimes having a friend in for supper, sometimes going to the movies, sometimes laughing or arguing or gossiping. But Maria had been dead for some time and, on 16 September 1977, the part of her that had gone on existing gave up. She awoke late, Bruna recalled. She had breakfast in bed, then got up and took a few faltering steps towards the bathroom. There was a piercing pain in her left side; then the sound of a fall. She was put back to bed and made to drink some strong coffee. They rang her doctor; he was out. They rang the American Hospital; the number was engaged. Finally they rang Ferruccio's doctor who started out immediately for Georges-Mandel. She was dead before he arrived.

Epilogue

EVANGELIA was going out for the evening. Waiting for her friends to collect her, in a red dress and a string of pearls, she was half-watching television and half-listening for the buzzer to ring when the news was flashed on the screen: Maria Callas is dead.

Driving from Yorkshire to London, Edith Gorlinsky stopped at a pillar-box in a country lane to post the card she had written to Maria. Back in her car, she switched the radio on just as the news-reader was announcing that earlier that day Maria Callas had died in Paris of a heart attack.

The immigration official at Paris Airport looked closely at Peter Diamand's passport: 'So you are the Artistic Director of the Edinburgh Festival. Did you know Maria Callas?'

'Yes. Why?'

'She is dead,' he replied with that special eagerness of someone who is first with the news.

'It's not possible,' snapped Peter Diamand. He rang Peter de Jong, the head of EMI in France; he was not there. He went on ringing one friend of Maria's after another to reassure himself that it was not possible, that she was not dead. No one was in. He waited until three o'clock in the morning and then went to the Arc de Triomphe, where he knew he could get the first edition of the morning newspapers. He did not have to look far. There it was on the front page: *La prima donna du siècle: La cantatrice Maria Callas est morte hier à 13h 30 des suites d'un accident cardiaque.*

In Athens, Vasso Devetzi was preparing for her concert that night at Herodes Atticus, when Bruna called her from Paris: '*Madame est morte.*' A few hours later, with faltering voice, she broke the news to the Athenian public from the stage of the ancient theatre.

Victoria de los Angeles was rung by the French Press Agency at her home in Barcelona. It was a very bad connection and for the first couple of minutes she could not understand what they wanted. Finally she heard: 'What is your reaction to the death of Maria Callas?' All the French journalist could hear at the other end was uncontrollable sobbing.

John Ardoin was in San Francisco to hear Renata Scotto in *Adriana Lecouvreur*. He was having lunch with the pianist Ivan Davis and some other friends, when one of them who had been idly looking at a newspaper suddenly stopped and pointed out to John a small, last-minute item on the front page: 'Maria Callas is dead at 53.' 'That was all I read. I pushed away from the table and got up to leave the restaurant. I had no idea where I was going or why. All I knew was that I had to get out. I only realized what I was doing after Ivan, who had also known Maria, stopped me and brought me back to the table.'

Laid out on her bed in a grey gown with a cross and a rose resting on her bosom, her eyes serenely closed, her lips slightly parted and her long auburn hair framing her white face, she looked beautiful and seemed to be at peace. 'Her hair was so rich, so full of life,' remembers Peter Andry, who together with a few other friends visited Georges-Mandel on the day of the funeral. 'I shuddered at the thought that in a few hours it would all be ashes. I felt a strong urge to touch her, to cut a lock to preserve it for ever. . . . I wish I had.'

Long before the funeral service was due to begin at 4.30 in the afternoon of 20 September, there was a large crowd outside the Greek Orthodox Church on Rue Georges-Bizet. By 4.30 there was expectant silence outside and chaos inside. Her sister, Peter Andry, Vasso Devetzi, John Coveney, Peter de Jong, Sander and Edith Gorlinsky, Franco Rossellini, Bruna, Ferruccio and Consuelo, made up the official party, but it was the photographers and the television crews that seemed to be in charge: pushing and shoving to get better pictures of the congregation, rearranging the flowers to get a better view of the ribbons on the wreaths (from the President of the French Republic, from the President of Greece, from Covent Garden, from La Scala ...), adding to the buzz, the charge, the anticipation. Suddenly the priests started chanting; for the first few minutes it was not at all clear whether they were trying their voices or whether the service had already begun. The buzz, which had continued through the chanting, became even more excited when Princess Grace and Caroline arrived late, and the voices of the priests had to do battle with the clicking of the cameras and the noise of the television crews. It was as if everybody was expecting something to happen: for Onassis to be resurrected, her mother to descend on the altar and launch into a speech, Maria herself to rise from her coffin and demand another rehearsal before the service could proceed. The ceremony had started almost unnoticed amid the buzz and it ended in the same vague and haphazard manner. Even the coffin was pushed from the centre of the church in the frantic attempt to get a better shot of Princess Grace leaving.

At the same time in Rome, in the little Greek Orthodox church off Via Veneto, a mass was being said for Maria. The congregation of fourteen included Nadia Stancioff who had organized it, Giulietta Simionato, Piero Tosi and a man in an old grey raincoat whom nobody knew but who had been crying throughout the service, his grief deeply etched in each line of his face.

Back at Rue Georges-Bizet, the air was full of flowers and tension as the coffin was carried out. When it appeared at the door of the church, the hundreds of people outside, many of them with eyes moist or tears streaming down their faces, broke into sudden applause and cries of 'Bravo Callas', 'Bravo Maria'. It was the last spontaneous, heart-felt goodbye, the first deeply moving moment of this absurdly impersonal afternoon.

'What happens now?' asked Princess Grace of Peter Diamand.

'I don't know.'

As the congregation forlornly began to disperse, the cortège, followed by the two official cars, started towards the cemetery of Père Lachaise. Only Bruna, unable to cope with more social mourning, had left the party for the emptiness of Georges-Mandel, there to grieve alone.

In an enormous, high-ceilinged, freezing hall like a concrete Valhalla, they waited. Forty-five long minutes passed until at last someone appeared to lead them through long corridors to a cellar; there, two men in blue overalls were waiting with a trolley between them, and on the trolley a casket not much bigger than a cigar box, containing the earthly remains of Maria Callas. From the cellar the procession of the sister, the butler, the cook, the agent, the friend and the representatives of the music and film industries moved on along more seemingly endless corridors to where the boxes were stacked row upon row. The procession stopped. Maria Callas: 1923–1977: Number 16258.

The tributes had been pouring in for days: 'The greatest musical performer of our time,' said Lord Harewood in London; 'We will not see her like again,' Rudolf Bing announced from New York; 'Goddesses do not die,' declared Rolf Lieberman, the director of L'Opéra, in Paris. Round the world, radio and television programmes were honouring her, and concerts, galas and discussion evenings on her art were dedicated to her memory.

On 16 September 1978, the first anniversary of her death, a marble plaque with gold lettering went up outside 36 Georges-Mandel:

Ice est décédée
Maria Callas
Le 16 Septembre 1977

Meanwhile the ex-husband and the mother had taken up their positions: the battle for Maria's fortune, estimated at $12 million plus future record royalties, had begun. Meneghini unearthed a will made by Maria in 1954 leaving everything to him. As she had left no other will to supersede this one, he claimed that he was the sole beneficiary of her last testament, and a month after the funeral, on his application, the Georges-Mandel apartment was sealed by legal order. At the same time in Paris her sister was lodging a counter-claim on behalf of the family. It was the last link in the chain of Maria's legal entanglements, although this time, it is true, she was responsible only by omission. Her failure to leave a will expressing her real wishes had led to an irony even greater than all the ironies and paradoxes of a life full of them: the two people for whom she had nothing but bitter words, and to whom she would have least liked to leave anything at all, were both now posing as the sole rightful heir.

Mercifully they both quickly realized that if they fought it out in court, the slenderness of their emotional claim to Maria's fortune would have been made embarrassingly clear. An agreement was reached, the case was settled out of court, and the estate was divided between the two octogenarians. 'I don't want the money for myself but to make her known all over the world,' announced Meneghini, blatantly oblivious to the absurdity of wanting to make well known one of the most celebrated people on earth. The mother, more sensibly, refrained from announcing to the world how she proposed to dispose of the millions that suddenly belonged to her, although she assured me in Athens that she would give some of it away to provide dowries for a couple of poor Greek girls. Bruna and Ferruccio were taken care of before the estate was split, and once Georges-Mandel was sold, Bruna left Paris for her village in Italy and Ferruccio to work for Christina Onassis.

On 14 June 1978, in a large, crowded room at the Georges V in Paris, the contents of Georges-Mandel were put up for auction. While the room was being prepared for the sale, it seems a tall pair of doors opening on to a hallway suddenly flew open with such force that a commode was overturned, the porcelain on it broken, and a painting dashed to the floor; yet it was one of those still, Parisian summer days with no breeze at all. And even more unaccountably, as the bidding began one of the first lots, a mirrored tray, was being held up for inspection when there was a crack like a rifle-shot, and the glass split and fell to the ground. After an initial gasp of awe, the people in the room were frozen in silence, as if they half expected Maria herself to make a dramatic and furious entrance.

In the front row, a robust, white-haired man was bidding furiously. 'I came here to save my memories,' Meneghini announced to the press. And he did buy back many of them, from a jade pendant he had given Maria to the eighteenth-century marital bed on which she had died. An admirer who could not afford Maria's Steinway bought the piano stool, while those who could not afford any of the paintings, carpets, pieces of furniture or *objects d'art*, returned a few days later to bid for the washing machine, one of the three vacuum cleaners, or at least a saucepan that 'belonged, you know, to Maria Callas'.

On the day after the first Christmas following Maria's death, somebody had tried to forge a particularly morbid link with her by stealing her ashes from Père Lachaise. It was a short-lived link; hours later they were discovered in a remote part of the cemetery, but not before Evangelia had accused her ex-son-in-law of stealing her daughter's ashes.

'Even now that she is dead, Meneghini wants to hold on to my child,' she told the Greek press, 'but Maria's ashes belong to her homeland.'

In the spring of 1979, the ashes were taken to Greece, with full honours, and ceremonially scattered in the Aegean.

'How shall we bury you when it's over?' they asked Socrates just before he died.

'Any way you like, if you can catch me.'

Maria's ashes were lost in the sea she loved. She lives on, like every great spirit, uncaught for ever.

Source Notes

Before I undertook my own research I read the existing books on Maria Callas and, while I was writing the manuscript, I took the opportunity to read new books as they appeared. I would like here to express my thanks to the following:

John Ardoin and Gerald Fitzgerald, *Callas* (London: Thames & Hudson, 1974)

Evangelia Callas, *My Daughter, Maria Callas* (New York: Fleet Publishing Corporation, 1960)

Camilla Cederna, *Chi è Maria Callas?* (Milano: Longanesi & Co, 1968

Stelios Galatopoulos, *Callas: La Divina* (Elmsford, New York: London House and Maxwell, 1970)

Eugenio Gara, *Die Grossen Interpreten: Maria Callas* (Frankfurt/Main: Wilhelm Limpert-Verlag, 1959)

Denis Goise, *Maria Callas, la diva, scandale* (Paris: Editions Guy Authier, 1978)

George Jellinek, *Callas, Portrait of a Prima Donna* (London: Anthony Gibbs & Phillips, 1961)

Jacques Lorcey, *Maria Callas* (Paris: Collection Têtes d'Affiche, 1977)

Pierre-Jean Remy, *Maria Callas, A Tribute* (London: Macdonald & Jane's, 1978)

Serge Segalini, *Images d'une voix* (Paris: Editions Francis Van de Welde, 1979)

Giovanna Tortora and Paolo Barbieri, *Per Maria Callas* (Bologna: Edizioni Recitar Cantando, 1979)

Henry Wisneski, *Maria Callas, The Art Behind the Legend* (New York: Doubleday, 1975)

John Ardoin's *The Callas Legacy* (London: Duckworth, 1977) proved invaluable. It is not only the definitive book on Maria Callas as an artist but also a remarkable labour of dedication, scholarship and understanding.

CHAPTER 1. Most of this chapter is based on my talks with Maria's mother, Evangelia Kalogeropoulos, in Athens and with Maria's godfather, Dr Lantzounis, in New York. My talks with Nadia Stancioff, Mary Mead and Anastasia Gratsos to whom Maria had talked at length about her childhood filled in many of the gaps.

CHAPTER 2. My account of Maria's life in Athens before the war is based on my talks with her mother and on Maria's interview with *Oggi* (10 January 1957), on her interview with Kenneth Harris (*Observer*, 8 and 15 February 1970) and on the transcripts of her televised conversations with Lord Harewood broadcast by the BBC on 15 December 1967 and 23 January 1968. For the first steps of her career I drew on these sources as well as on the Greek newspapers of the period.

CHAPTER 3. Apart from my talks with Maria's mother, Evangelia, and with Nadia Stancioff and Mary Mead, an important source for this chapter was Efi Zaccaria, whose husband, the bass Nicola Zaccaria, was singing at the time with the Athens Opera; Efi Zaccaria's reminiscences of Maria during that period were an important first-hand account of the war years. For the historical background I relied on C. M. Woodhouse's *Modern Greece* (London: Faber, 1968), on David Holden's *Greece Without Columns* (London: Faber, 1972) and on Lord Moran's *Churchill, The Struggle for Survival 1940/65* (London: Constable, 1966). After the Germans occupied Athens in the spring of 1941 the German newspapers began to carry occasional reviews of operatic and concert performances in Greece; *Deutsche Nachricten* was the newspaper I consulted, especially when other sources gave conflicting dates for Maria's performances.

CHAPTER 4. With Maria back in New York, Dr Lantzounis became once again an important source not only for his factual information, but also for his awareness of Maria's feelings and state of mind at the time. John Ardoin, who had talked with Maria at length about her early struggles in New York, filled many of the gaps.

CHAPTER 5. Maria's televised interview with Lord Harewood provided much of the information on her working technique, her relationship with Serafin and her attitude to the different roles she sang during her first years in Italy. I also drew on Serafin's article, 'A Triptych of Singers' (*Opera Annual*, London:

John Calder, 1962), on Roland Mancini's 'Tullio Serafin' (*Opéra*, 1 March 1968) and on Jan Maguire's 'Callas, Serafin, and the art of bel canto' (*Saturday Review*, 30 March 1968). Other important sources were her interview with *Il Gazzettino* (22 July 1947) and accounts of her first performances in *Il Gazzettino* (1 August 1947), *Il Secolo XIX* (12 May 1948), *Il Messaggero* (4 July 1948) and in *La Stampa* (18 September 1948). Maria's letters to her mother and her godfather described her feelings during the Verona period and, together with Zeffirelli's reminiscences of Verona, they helped me evoke the world she encountered as she began her career alone in a new country.

In considering Maria's critical and historical position in the operatic tradition, I had the help of, among others, John Ardoin, Peter Diamand, Lord Harewood and Harold Rosenthal. Among the books I consulted the most useful were Robert Rushmore's *The Singing Voice* (London: Hamish Hamilton, 1971), J.B. Steane's *The Grand Tradition* (London: Duckworth, 1974), Harold Rosenthal's *Great Singers of Today* (London: Calder and Boyars, 1966) and Olivier Merlin's *Le Bel Canto* (Paris: René Julliard, 1961). Among articles evaluating Maia's contribution to the world of music I found particularly valuable Edward Downes's 'Bel Canto in 1956' (*Opera Annual*, London: John Calder, 1956), Teodoro Celli's 'A Song from Another Century' (*Opera Annual*, London: John Calder, 1959) and Robert Skidelsky's 'Fact and Fiction about Callas' (*Spectator*, 1 October 1977).

CHAPTER 6. From this chapter onwards the reports and reviews of Maria's performances begin to proliferate. Too numerous to cite individually, collectively they are an important indication of the growing excitement surrounding Maria's career.

It is at this point in her life that Maria and her mother part forever; their last days together in Mexico are etched in Evangelia's memory, and she is the main source of the personal details of Maria's Mexican visit. John Ardoin's detailed and vivid account in *The Callas Legacy* of Maria's performances in Mexico was especially useful.

From 1950 onwards, Maria wrote regularly and with increasing intimacy to her godfather; her letters reflect her real state of mind behind the headlines and interviews in the popular press. For my account of Maria's Veronese lifestyle, her first home and her role as Signora Meneghini, I have drawn on Zeffirelli's recollections as well as on Maria's letters.

From this chapter on I begin to draw on the reporting of Maria's performances in *Opera* Magazine. Harold Rosenthal provided clarification and detail during our talks, and Lord Harewood's tribute to Maria at the Queen Elizabeth Hall in London on 10 April 1978, and his insights during our conversations proved invaluable.

Victor Seroff's *Renata Tebaldi* (New York: Appleton-Century-Crofts, 1961), Spike Hughes's 'Italian Opera House Traditions' (*Opera Annual*, London: John Calder, 1957) and my talks with Peter Diamand provided considerable information about La Scala during the period Maria first sang there, as well as about her relationship with Ghiringhelli. Stendhal's *Life of Rossini* (London: Calder and Boyars, 1965) still provides the most colourful account of Italian attitudes towards foreign performers; attitudes may differ today but they had changed very little between the time Stendhal was writing and the time Maria made her first appearance at La Scala. Gian Carlo Menotti's account of Ghiringhelli's hostility to Maria appeared in a ninety-minute documentary on Maria's career produced by Peter Weinberg for the Educational Broadcasting Corporation in America, and broadcast on 2 December 1978.

Sander Gorlinsky provided information on the circumstances of the signing of Maria's first contract with Covent Garden, as well as on Meneghini's procrastinating tactics and his relationship with Maria.

CHAPTER 7. For accounts of Maria's performances I have drawn, in this and in subsequent chapters, on the *Corriere della Sera, Musica e Dischi, Musical America, Opera, Music and Musicians, High Fidelity* and *Opera News*. The beginning of Maria's long connection with EMI is colourfully described by Walter Legge in an article which appeared in *Opera News* in November 1977. For the atmosphere prevailing at Covent Garden during Maria's first appearance and for her relationship with David Webster I have drawn on Montague Haltrecht's biography of Webster, *The Quiet Showman* (London: Collins, 1975) and on Harold Rosenthal's *Two Centuries of Opera at Covent Garden* (London: Putnam, 1958). In her interview with Peter Dragadze (*Daily Mirror*, 16 October 1977) Maria talked about her reaction to the first cutting remarks on her size and her subsequent decision to lose weight. I also drew on her interview with Derek Prouse (*Sunday Times*, 19 March 1961) to whom she recounted her frustration at having to sing *Medea* without the gaunt lines she felt the part demanded, and on my talks with Christian Bischini.

For Maria's collaboration with Margherita Wallmann I have drawn on Wallmann's *Les Balcons du Ciel* (Paris: Robert Laffont, 1976). Maria's own words in her comprehensive interview with

Derek Prouse describe her attitude to *Medea*. For her feelings about Lucia I have drawn on her broadcast interview with Edward Downes (WQXR, 30 December 1967).

The tapes of John Van Eyssen's conversations with Francesco Chiarini, a good friend of Maria's at the time, and with Carla Nanni Moncenigo, whose mother was at the Fenice in Venice when Maria first sang there, were an important source for this chapter. For Maria's debut in Chicago I have relied a great deal on Claudia Cassidy's reports in the *Chicago Tribune*, her interview with Maria (*Chicago Tribune*, 21 November 1954) and her article in *Opera News* (November 1977) after Maria's death.

CHAPTER 8. For the beginning of Maria's collaboration with Visconti I have relied on interviews with Zeffirelli and Alexis Minotis, on Monica Stirling's biography of Visconti, *A Screen of Time* (New York: Harcourt Brace Jovanovich, 1979) and on my talks with Jon Vickers, Efi Zaccaria and John Ardoin, on Dorle Soria's and Walter Legge's articles in *Opera News* (November 1977) and on Carla Nanni Moncenigo's reminscences. My quotations from Maria herself come from the above-mentioned interviews with Derek Prouse, Claudia Cassidy and Lord Harewood.

CHAPTER 9. Giulio Gatti-Casazza's memoirs, *Memories of the Opera* (London: John Calder, 1977), provided some useful background material on the Met. Rudolf Bing's memoirs, *5000 Nights at the Opera* (New York: Doubleday, 1972), George London's article, 'Prima Donnas I have Sung Against' (*Opera Annual*, London: John Calder, 1959), Dorle Soria's article in *Opera News* (November 1977) and Francis Robinson's reminiscences, were important sources for Maria's debut at the Met. My talks with Dario Soria and with Katy Katsoyanni, who had been a great friend of Dimitri Mitropoulos, provided much additional detail and Maria's letters to her godfather as well as my conversations with him give a sense of Maria's feelings at the time.

Elsa Maxwell's autobiography, *R.S.V.P.* (Boston: Little, Brown and Co, 1954), as well as the reminiscences of Rosemarie Marcie Rivere, Mary Mead and Franco Zeffirelli helped me build the portrait of this notorious gossip columnist and socialite and understand more fully the part she played in Maria's life. Michel Glotz, Dario Soria, Peter Diamand and, of course, Maria's godfather, provided much of the detail behind the front-page events of this chapter. The quotations from Maria come from her already cited interviews with Derek Prouse, Lord Harewood and Kenneth Harris.

CHAPTER 10. My talks with Lord Harewood, Alexis Minotis, Mary Mead and Jon Vickers provided the basis for the early section of this chapter. Maria herself talked about the events that led to her dismissal from the Met in the *Dallas Morning News* (8 November 1958), in *Newsweek* (9 April 1959) and, at greater length, in *Life* magazine (20 April 1959). Of the many accounts of Maria's concert appearance in *Il Pirata* at Carnegie Hall, I found Winthrop Sargeant's report in *The New Yorker* (7 February 1959) especially helpful.

For the reaction to Maria's first appearance at the Paris Opera I have drawn on Olivier Merlin's article 'La Callas, Monstre Sacré' (*Le Monde*, 18 December 1958), and on interviews with Maria in *Arts* (10 December 1958) and in *Le Figaro* (17 December 1958). Maria's official comments on marriage and Meneghini derive from an interview she gave to John Cruesemann for the *Daily Express*. For an account of her feelings during the break-up of her marriage, I have relied on my talks with Edith Gorlinsky, Nadia Stancioff, Mary Mead and Anastasia Gratsos, with whom Maria discussed, especially later in her life, these difficult months. The interview that Biki gave to *Paris Match* a few days after Maria's death, and Maria's interview with Peter Dragadze for *Life* magazine further clarified her own and others' reactions at the time.

CHAPTER 11. For this chapter I have drawn on my talks with many of Onassis's intimates and especially Constantine and Anastasia Gratsos, Harry Kapetanakis, who was director of Olympic Airways in Paris, and Costa Haritakis, a regular companion in Onassis's nightlife. Of the numerous books written about Onassis, the ones I found most helpful were *Aristotle Onassis* by Nicholas Fraser, Philip Jacobson, Mark Ottaway and Lewis Chester (London: Weidenfeld & Nicolson, 1977) and *Onassis, An Extravagant Life* by Frank Brady (New Jersey: Prentice-Hall, 1977).

Maria talked about her desire for a child and a new life in an interview with Marlyse Shaeffer (*France Soir*, 13 February 1960). Her discussion of her work at this time comes from the interview with Derek Prouse.

Teddy and Gaby van Zuylen, Sander and Edith Gorlinsky, Princess Grace and François Valéry provided me with details of various aspects of Maria's life during these early years of her relationship with Onassis. As always, her letters to Dr

Lantzounis were the most important evidence of her feelings at that time. These letters, together with the many long letters Dr Lantzounis sent to Maria outlining in detail the financial and other arrangements he was making for her mother, were the main documents of this phase of Maria's relationship with Evangelia. Dr Lantzounis also gave me access to all the letters and documents from doctors, solicitors, and the Welfare Department regarding Evangelia's eventful life in New York during this time.

CHAPTER 12. Franco Zeffirelli and Tito Gobbi provided me with a great deal of background material for Maria's performances in *Tosca*. I also drew on Tito Gobbi's memoirs, *Tito Gobbi: My Life* (London: Macdonald & Jane's, 1979) and Montague Haltrecht's biography of David Webster which I have already mentioned. For Maria's Tosca in New York I found particularly helpful the following articles: Alan Rich's in the *New York Herald Tribune* (20 and 21 March 1965), Harold Schonberg's in *The New York Times* (21 March 1975) and Paul Hume's in the *Washington Post* (4 April 1965). I have also drawn on reports in *The New Yorker* (March 1965), in *Time* magazine (26 March 1965) and in *Saturday Review* (3 April 1965). Rudolf Bing, Nicola Rescigno, John Ardoin, John Coveney and Peter Andry provided valuable information about Maria's attitude to her work as her career drew to a close, and Nicola Rescigno provided me also with much additional detail on Maria's forays into the recording studios at this time.

Neville Cardus's open letter to Maria appeared in the *Guardian* on 30 January 1964. On the possibility of a new career for Maria as a mezzo, I found particularly helpful Olivier Merlin's article 'Callas Perdue et Retrouvée' (*Le Monde*, 7 June 1963) and an article by Herbert Weinstock, 'Woman of the Week' (*Opera News*, 20 March 1965).

Franco Zeffirelli and Sander Gorlinsky were the main sources of information on the doomed attempt to film *Tosca* with Maria. Edith Gorlinsky and Anastasia Gratsos talked to me about Maria's abortion, and Nadia Stancioff about Maria's pain at recollecting it years later.

Georges Grandpierre, who decorated Maria's home in Avenue Georges-Mandel, described in detail each room in the apartment. Marie-Hélène Rothschild's taped conversations with John van Eyssen, as well as my talks with Gaby van Zuylen and François Valéry, enriched my account of Maria's life in Paris at the time. The quotations about Maria's feelings for Bruna came from her taped conversations with John Ardoin.

For the proceedings of the case against Vergottis I have used the court reports in the *Daily Telegraph* and the *Evening Standard*.

Mary Mead was my main source for the final days of Maria's relationship with Onassis, and Mary Mead, John Ardoin and John Coveney described in detail the two fugitive months that followed. My account of Maria's emotional state at the time is based on her letters to her godfather, to John Ardoin and to Anastasia Gratsos, and on the transcripts of her taped talks with John Ardoin. The rest of the direct quotations from Maria in this chapter come from the interviews with Derek Prouse, Claudia Cassidy and David Holmes as well as from the transcripts of her one-hour interview with Micheline Bauzet for French radio (*France Musique*, 8, 9, 10 February 1965).

CHAPTER 13. The opening quotation in this chapter comes from the tapes of Maria's talks with John Ardoin. Her letters to her godfather and to John Ardoin, and Francesco Chiarini's reminiscences were the keys to Maria's state of mind at this time. My talks with Franco Rossellini, and especially with Nadia Stancioff, provided the background material on the filming of *Medea*. Gaby van Zuylen and Nadia Stancioff described Maria's first meeting with Onassis after his marriage, while Anastasia Gratsos and Peter Diamand were very helpful in establishing the facts behind Edgar Schneider's assertion that Maria had attempted suicide.

For my account of the months before and during the Juilliard master-classes, I have drawn on my talks with Anastasia Gratsos, Tito Gobbi and Dr Lantzounis, as well as on John van Eyssen's taped interviews with Peter Menin and Alberta Maziello. Also, I spoke often with John Ardoin, who has written the definitive, as yet unpublished, book on the master-classes. Among the many articles written on the Juilliard master-classes, the ones I found most helpful were: Alan Blyth's 'The Untransferable Callas Magic' (*The Times*, 16 November 1971), Francis Rizzo's 'The Callas Class' (*Opera News*, 15 April 1972) and Richard Roud's report in the *Guardian* (8 April 1972).

The remainder of this chapter is based on my talks with Michael Cacoyannis, François Valéry, Robert Sutherland, Ivor Newton, Sander Gorlinsky, Alex Gregory, Mary Mead, John Tooley, Peter Diamand and Vasso Devetzi. For my account of Maria's outburst at the end of her Carnegie Hall concert I have relied on Dorle Soria's article in *High Fidelity/Musical America* (January 1978) and on my talks with Alex Gregory, Mary Mead and various others who were present that night. For the details of George Moore's offer to Maria of the position of Artistic Director at the Met, I have drawn on Schuyler Chapin's memoirs, *Musical Chairs, A Life in the Arts* (New York: Putnam, 1977).

Maria's letters to her godfather were, once again, invaluable. I have relied on them not only for direct quotations but, most importantly, to portray Maria's turmoil during these years. Other quotations from Maria in this chapter come from her talks with John Ardoin and from the following articles: Jack Buckley's 'An Ancient Woman' (*Opera News*, 13 December 1969), Angela Cuccio's 'Callas on Callas' (*Women's Wear Daily*, 23 November 1970), Judy Klemesrud's 'Maria Callas Speaks Her Mind on Fashions and Friendship' (*The New York Times*, 30 November 1970) and Mary Blume's 'The Callas Connection' (*International Herald Tribune*, 3 and 4 February 1979); also from reports in *Newsweek* (15 February 1971), the *Sunday Telegraph* (1 October 1972) and the *Daily News* (8 February 1974), and from Maria's televised interviews with David Holmes (BBC, 29 November 1973), with Mike Wallace (CBS, 3 February 1974) and with Barbara Walters (NBC, 15 April 1974).

CHAPTER 14. Shortly before Maria's death her letters to her godfather became even more intimate. The letters, as well as my talks with her godfather, are the most important source for the last few years of her life. Extracts from the tapes on which Maria reflected on her life were featured in the Musée Carnavalet exhibition in the spring of 1979. These extracts, as well as her interviews with Mike Wallace and Barbara Walters, provided more direct quotations from Maria. Frederick, her hairdresser, John Tooley, Alan Sievewright, François Valéry, Gaby van Zuylen, Charles Vanne, Vasso Devetzi and Sylvia Sass supplied much detail on Maria's life as it was drawing to a close.

EPILOGUE. The epilogue is based on my talks with Maria's mother and with Edith Gorlinsky, Peter Diamand, Vasso Devetzi, Xavier Vivanco, John Ardoin, Peter Andry, John Coveney, Peter de Jong, Sander Gorlinsky, Franco Rossellini, Princess Grace and Nadia Stancioff. I have also drawn on the following reports in the Greek press: *Ta Nea* (26 October 1977), *I Apoyeumatini* (25 October, 7 November 1977, 24 and 26 May 1978) and *I Vrathini* (29 December 1977).

Acknowledgements

I was in Los Angeles when George Weidenfeld called me from London a few days after Maria Callas's death to ask if I would be interested in writing her biography. It is hard to believe it now that she has become part of my life, but I would never have thought of writing this book had George not suggested it. For the suggestion and the encouragement that followed I am deeply grateful to him. The first few months of research were the hardest, and the help of Jeannie Chandris over this period was invaluable. Just down from Oxford, she threw herself into the job of research assistant with enthusiasm and dedication. She conducted the first exploratory interviews; she spent hours in newspaper libraries cataloguing everything she could find on Maria; and, like the most accomplished sleuth, she put together a directory with addresses and telephone numbers of hundreds of people round the world whose lives had touched on Maria's. For all the work she did and for her unending support and humour I am deeply grateful to Jeannie.

The book, of course, could not have been undertaken at all without the help and co-operation of the many people who had at various points in her life been close to Maria. Their names appear in the Source Notes, and I would like here to express my profound thanks to them.

The first draft was read by John Ardoin, to whom I owe a special debt of thanks, not only for his suggestions and corrections, but for all his generous help and guidance throughout the writing and re-writing. This book also owes a great deal to Maria's godfather, Dr Lantzounis. Through our talks, through his extensive comments on the first draft, and especially through all Maria's letters and the many documents and photographs he made available to me, he provided some of the most intimate material on Maria's life.

The second draft of the book was read by Peter Diamand, Anastasia Gratsos, Lord Harewood, Harold Rosenthal, Michael Scott, Sir John Tooley and Gaby and Teddy van Zuylen. I am very grateful to them all for the comments they made and the changes they suggested. I am also indebted to John van Eyssen, who read the manuscript and made available to me the tapes of his interviews with many of Maria's friends and colleagues recorded during the months when he was collecting material for the film on Maria's life that he planned to produce with Zeffirelli.

Different sections of the book were also read by Sander Gorlinsky, Robert Sutherland, Nadia Stancioff and Sylvia Sass, who amplified what I had already written about the periods or incidents in Maria's life in which they were closely involved. My profound thanks to them as well as to Alan Sievewright, who gave me access to his substantial collection of Callas material; to Peter Andry, who allowed me to see Maria's correspondence with EMI; and to Mary Mead for sharing memories and ideas throughout the writing of the book.

Michael Sissons, my agent, gave me invaluable advice, both when I started working on the book and after he had read the first draft. For everything he, Victoria Pryor and Pat Kavanagh did for the book I will always be grateful. My deep thanks also go to my two editors, Alex MacCormick in London and Fred Hills in New York, who guided me through the book's successive drafts; to Chris Warwick and Miranda Ferguson; to Faith Perkins for the picture research, and to Genevieve Andrews for the index.

This is my third book and the one which through the long months of research, writing and re-writing put the most strain on my friends' love and understanding. Jane Brewster read, and often re-read, every draft of the book, spotted mistakes, made suggestions, found books and press cuttings, and worked with me through her pregnancy and even on the morning of the day she was admitted to hospital to give birth to Lily. To her and to Lily, for so patiently waiting until the book was ready for the printers before demanding to be born, go my deepest, loving thanks. Helena Mathepoulos, right from the beginning, steered both people and new material my way; Iain Johnstone and Peter Ferguson arranged for me to see the BBC videotapes on Maria; Howard Grossman in New York was always willing to do whatever needed to be done on the other side of the Atlantic, whether finding an out-of-print book, checking records at City Hall or re-checking facts with people I had interviewed. Elizabeth Baekeland, Richard Blackford, Dimitri Coromilas, Barbara Comerford, Halina Szpiro and Warwick Wynschenk checked drafts at various stages when time was short and all help was needed. I am grateful to them all, as well as to Gwen

Margrie, who typed the first draft, and to Angela Sen, who typed and re-typed whole chapters and passages she must now know by heart. A substantial part of the book was written in Spain at the home of Fleur Cowles and Tom Meyer. I want to thank them both for their hospitality and for their understanding when I would disappear for long hours under what will forever be known as the Maria Callas tree.

My father provided from the beginning the Greek connection, sending me cuttings from the Greek press and staying in touch with Maria's family and friends in Athens; from my mother I received not only constant support but many invaluable insights through our talks about Maria long into the night; and my sister Agapi was a continuous source of encouragement and enthusiasm.

The book is dedicated to Bernard Levin. Without his unfailing support and understanding, and without all the long hours he spent reading, criticizing and improving, I wonder sometimes whether there would be a book at all. The dedication is only a small token of my loving gratitude.

Index

In this index, the name Maria Callas is abbreviated to M. Opera houses and theatres are listed under the town or city in which they are located.

NON-FICTION

GENERAL

☐ **Truly Murderous**	John Dunning	95p
☐ **Shocktrauma**	Jon Franklin & Alan Doelp	£1.25
☐ **The War Machine**	James Avery Joyce	£1.50
☐ **The Fugu Plan**	Tokayer & Swartz	£1.75

BIOGRAPHY/AUTOBIOGRAPHY

☐ **Go-Boy**	Roger Caron	£1.25
☐ **The Queen Mother Herself**	Helen Cathcart	£1.25
☐ **Clues to the Unknown**	Robert Cracknell	£1.50
☐ **George Stephenson**	Hunter Davies	£1.50
☐ **The Borgias**	Harry Edgington	£1.50
☐ **The Admiral's Daughter**	Victoria Fyodorova	£1.50
☐ **Rachman**	Shirley Green	£1.50
☐ **50 Years with Mountbatten**	Charles Smith	£1.25
☐ **Kiss**	John Swenson	95p

HEALTH/SELF-HELP

☐ **The Hamlyn Family First Aid Book**	Dr Robert Andrew	£1.50
☐ **Girl!**	Brandenburger & Curry	£1.25
☐ **The Good Health Guide for Women**	Cooke & Dworkin	£2.95
☐ **The Babysitter Book**	Curry & Cunningham	£1.25
☐ **Pulling Your Own Strings**	Dr Wayne W. Dyer	95p
☐ **The Pick of Woman's Own Diets**	Jo Foley	95p
☐ **Woman X Two**	Mary Kenny	£1.10
☐ **Cystitis: A Complete Self-help Guide**	Angela Kilmartin	£1.00
☐ **Fit for Life**	Donald Norfolk	£1.35
☐ **The Stress Factor**	Donald Norfolk	£1.25
☐ **Fat is a Feminist Issue**	Susie Orbach	95p
☐ **Living With Your New Baby**	Rakowitz & Rubin	£1.50
☐ **Related to Sex**	Claire Rayner	£1.25
☐ **The Working Woman's Body Book**	Rowen with Winkler	95p
☐ **Natural Sex**	Mary Shivanandan	£1.25
☐ **Woman's Own Birth Control**	Dr Michael Smith	£1.25
☐ **Overcoming Depression**	Dr Andrew Stanway	£1.50

POCKET HEALTH GUIDES

☐ **Migraine**	Dr Finlay Campbell	65p
☐ **Pre-menstrual Tension**	June Clark	65p
☐ **Back Pain**	Dr Paul Dudley	65p
☐ **Allergies**	Robert Eagle	65p
☐ **Arthritis & Rheumatism**	Dr Luke Fernandes	65p
☐ **Skin Troubles**	Deanna Wilson	65p

TRAVEL

☐ **Guide to the Channel Islands**	Anderson & Swinglehurst	90p
☐ **The Complete Traveller**	Joan Bakewell	£1.95
☐ **Time Out London Shopping Guide**	Lindsey Bareham	£1.50
☐ **A Walk Around the Lakes**	Hunter Davies	£1.50
☐ **England by Bus**	Elizabeth Gundrey	£1.25
☐ **Britain at Your Feet**	Wickers & Pedersen	£1.75

HUMOUR

☐ **Ireland Strikes Back!**	Seamus B. Gorrah	85p
☐ **Pun Fun**	Paul Jennings	95p
☐ **1001 Logical Laws**	John Peers	95p
☐ **The Devil's Bedside Book**	Leonard Rossiter	85p

REFERENCE

☐ The Sunday Times Guide to Movies on Television	Angela & Elkan Allan	£1.50
☐ The Cheiro Book of Fate and Fortune		£1.50
☐ Hunter Davies's Book of British Lists		£1.25
☐ What's Wrong With Your Pet?	Hugo Kerr	95p
☐ Caring for Cats and Kittens	John Montgomery	95p
☐ The Drinker's Companion	Derek Nimmo	£1.25
☐ The Complete Book of Cleaning	Barty Phillips	£1.50
☐ The Oscar Movies from A-Z	Roy Pickard	£1.25
☐ Collecting For Profit	Sam Richards	£1.25
☐ Questions of Motoring Law	John Spencer	£1.25
☐ Questions of Law	Bill Thomas	£1.25
☐ It's A Fact 1, 2, 3, 4		85p

GAMES AND PASTIMES

☐ The Hamlyn Book of Brainteasers and Mindbenders	Ben Hamilton	85p
☐ The Hamlyn Book of Crosswords 2		60p
☐ The Hamlyn Book of Crosswords 3		60p
☐ The Hamlyn Book of Wordways 1		75p
☐ The Hamlyn Family Quiz Book		85p

WAR

☐ World War 3	Edited by Shelford Bidwell	£1.50
☐ The Black Angels	Rupert Butler	£1.35
☐ Gestapo	Rupert Butler	£1.50
☐ Hand of Steel	Rupert Butler	£1.35
☐ The Flight of the Mew Gull	Alex Henshaw	£1.75
☐ Sigh for a Merlin	Alex Henshaw	£1.50
☐ Hitler's Secret Life	Glenn B. Infield	£1.25
☐ Wing Leader	'Johnnie' Johnson	£1.25

GARDENING/HOBBIES

☐ 'Jock' Davidson's House Plant Book		£1.25
☐ A Vegetable Plot for Two — or More	D. B. Clay Jones	£1.00
☐ Salads the Year Round	Joy Larkcom	£1.25
☐ Sunday Telegraph Patio Gardening	Robert Pearson	£1.00
☐ Greenhouse Gardening	Sue Phillips	£1.25

COOKERY

☐ A-Z of Health Foods	Carol Bowen	£1.50
☐ The Giant Sandwich Book	Carol Bowen	£1.50
☐ Vegetarian Cookbook	Dave Dutton	£1.50
☐ Know Your Onions	Kate Hastrop	95p
☐ Indian Cooking	Attia Hosain and Sita Pasricha	£1.50
☐ Home Preserving and Bottling	Gladys Mann	80p
☐ Home Baked Breads & Cakes	Mary Norwak	75p
☐ Easy Icing	Marguerite Patten	85p
☐ Wine Making At Home	Francis Pinnegar	80p
☐ Cooking for Christmas	Shona Crawford Poole	£1.25
☐ Mixer and Blender Cookbook	Myra Street	80p
☐ Pasta Cookbook	Myra Street	75p
☐ Diabetic Cookbook	Elisabeth Russell Taylor	£1.50
☐ The Hamlyn Pressure Cookbook	Jane Todd	85p